CU00846964

Insight

Insight
Jamie Magee

Insight: Book One of the "Insight" Series

This is a work of fiction. All of the characters and events portrayed in this book are fictional, and any resemblance to any real people or event is purely coincidental.

Copyright © 2010 by Jamie Magee

All rights reserved, including the right to reproduce this book or portions thereof in any form. No part of this book may be reproduced in any form or by any means without the express consent of the publisher and author, except where permitted by law.

ISBN-13:978-1467937368
ISBN-10: 1467937363

Cover art rights owned by Jamie Magee
Cover art design by Marek Purzycki
First printed copy, November 2011
Created in the United States of America

For Amanda, Chancey, and Jessie –
your enthusiasm was my inspiration.

“It is not in the stars to hold our destiny but in ourselves.” William Shakespeare

Contents

Chapter One

I was terrified; the summer air blew through my open window as I tossed and turned in bed, lost in a dark dream. I was having one of the bad dreams where I could not feel the ones around me; they had no emotion, or even a mood. The same dream had haunted me since childhood, and the heavy weight on my chest was almost unbearable, leaving me with shortness of breath. On top of that, the adrenaline rushing through my body gave way to hair-raising chills.

Being unacknowledged by the people in this place had become normal. They seemed lost in their own personal hell; lines gave definition to their faces, and the world around them was gray. In order to lift the weight from my chest and wake from this horrible hell, I would have to find the one who had called me here, the one I could feel - whom my touch could help.

I made my way through the gloomy street, pushing through others as they walked by in a solemn state. I reached out with all my senses, and could I hear the sound of arguing growing louder; that had to be my way out, and the weight on my chest grew stronger - telling me I was right. Fear began to race through me, though, so I tried calming myself by remembering that they could not see me, that I was a ghost to them.

Small windows lined the tall gray cement walls; darkness lingered behind most, while lights illuminated others. There was no grass, trees, or sign of birds or any other life beyond the hopeless people all dressed in long black cloaks. Everything was so controlled and uniform; the absence of color, music, and laughter was almost as scary as the emptiness in their eyes.

As I walked closer, fear overtook me upon the realization of what I'd I anticipated: the one who had called me was close. The weight was reaching a degree of unbearable pain, and my emotions were nearing anger. *Why did it have to hurt?* I tried to push away the invisible force that was torturing me, but my efforts were in vain - just as they always have been.

The arguing was coming from one of the small windows on the first level. A man was yelling as a woman cried out, not being heard. On the front steps, I saw a little boy; he looked to be five or six, and he maintained a blank stare into the darkness with purest of blue eyes. His hair was long and messy, and the clothes he was wearing were tattered and dirty. I felt so sorry for him; I wanted to take him from there, but that was nothing short of impossible. Putting my anger and fear aside, I sat down next to him and placed my hand on his small back. I thought of how happy he could be if he were only given some sense of being loved. How great he would feel if he could be the center of some lucky parents' world. The little boy dropped his eyes as he felt me; oddly, his emotion shifted to regret and sorrow. Not understanding, I focused on peace, and his emotion slowly gave into mine, bringing a sense of peace into his little body. I hoped that I would have been able to bring him happiness, but my time there was coming to an end. Silence came, and the little boy disappeared, as the people on the street did. The wind whistled through the barren cold walls, and I could only hear my heartbeat.

I stood, bracing myself for what I knew would happen. A tall dark figure emerged from the shadows, his contemptuous laugh echoing through the darkness. He has been in every nightmare I've ever had, taunting me, trying to force me to succumb to him. His face is always hidden by the darkness, and the dragon tattooed on the inside of his arm told me he was the same one. This figure was once a child, but now, both young adults, we played the game that brought only him pleasure. He crept closer to me, laughing under his breath. He then reached for me, and I knew from my previous nightmares that a burning white light was about to push right through me. I crossed my hands in front of my face, blocking the surge of light.

When the light did not come, I slowly lowered my hands. The figure was standing just in front of me; I still could not see his face, but I could feel his eyes searching over me. He grasped my wrist, where I have a tattoo of an Ankh, a beautiful cross that opens at the top with a loop. My instinct was to pull away, but I could not make my mind and body agree. With his touch, I felt a hypnotizing, warm sensation that eased through my wrist, up my arm, and circled through my body, taking the weight off my chest. His thumb traced over the cross, and I sensed him smirk.

"This is true…I will find you now," he said in a deep, controlled voice. He pressed his thumb in the center of the loop, and the warm sensation turned into a blazing burn. I screamed through the pain, finally waking.

My screams brought my father into my room; he's always the first person to respond when I wake in the night. I have never told my parents the details of the nightmares. Since before I can remember, I've always felt the emotions of the people around me as if they were my own. If I told him how scared I really was, I would have to feel his fear - as well as my own - so putting the event behind me seemed much simpler.

"Willow, wake up," my father said; he's always had a calm feeling to him.

I opened my eyes and sat up quickly, finding myself safely in my own room - right where I belonged. I then grabbed my wrist, still feeling the pain.

"You haven't had one of those dreams in a while," my father said, turning on the lamp.

The last one I'd had came on the eve of my eighteenth birthday in November; it was now mid-August, and we all hoped I'd simply grown out of them. It seemed, though, the odd characteristics that I developed during my childhood would never really leave me.

"I don't understand; the new moon was two days ago," my father said, almost to himself.

When I was a child, I had nightmares with each new moon. So, I'd fallen asleep that night without a fear in the world, thinking I'd successfully passed through another month without having to face that figure; it seems, though, that he will always be connected to me.

"I'm alright, Dad. Really."

My father was full of fear. I looked at him; his hazel eyes had turned to a shade of brown as they always do when he's concerned about something, and he shook his head slowly, not agreeing with me.

"Let me see your wrist," he said quietly.

My father is Dr. Jason Haywood, and he always seems to always know if I'm hurting more than I let on. I've never been able to fake myself well - or sick, for that matter.

When I got the tattoo of the Ankh, my mother, Grace, was furious, and she grounded me for the first time in my life. My father, though, simply asked why I'd chosen that one; I never really had an answer. The symbol stood for eternal life, which was something I'd always found fascinating. My friends were picking out butterflies and flowers, but the Ankh seemed more fitting for me.

I slowly uncovered my wrist, expecting to see a burn; instead, inside the loop at the top of the Ankh was a small star. I felt my father's shock, fear, and disbelief, and my eyes widened as I tried to understand. I then got up and pushed past my father.

"Where are you going?" he asked, standing to follow me.

"I just want to wash my face, Dad. I'm fine; go back to bed," I said over my shoulder, trying to block his emotions.

The bathroom was next to my room. I closed the door behind me, rushed to the sink, and began trying to scrub away the star. I couldn't believe it; I didn't understand what I'd done to deserve this. *Why do I have to be so different*?

Feeling the emotions of the ones around me isn't the only aspect of my gift; while I'm awake, I can also see images of the people who are not here. They all need my help and are seeking someone to comfort them, so I touch them and somehow give them the emotion they're craving. With each touch, I'm taken to wherever they may be, and when I release them, I'm pulled back into my reality.

I've never understood why they could not see me, where I went, or how I even managed to do what I did, and every day I'm haunted by these questions. When the nightmares stopped a few months back, the images seemed to fade as well. Since helping the images is the only thing that makes sense about what I can do, I channeled my aggression through painting, trying to capture the emotions I'd changed; this gave me the desire to help again.

Recently, though, I put my brush down, and haven't so much as doodled on a napkin since. My mother believes I have a creative block; she's an artist, too, and sees my painting as a rare talent. In a couple weeks, she is sending me to a school of art in New York… the thought of having a nightmare so far from home is terrifying in and of itself.

My wrist was red and raw; the star was still there. I splashed water on my face, then stared into the mirror, trying to look past my emerald green eyes; I wanted to see the answers somewhere inside of me.

I could feel my parents downstairs; they were filled with a sense of urgency and panic. I took a deep breath, wishing that I could change the emotions of the ones around me. If I could, I would go down there and move them back to the peace and excitement that belonged to them.

I dried my face off and put lotion on my tattoo, trying to ease the burn. I then turned off the light and opened the door, just wanting to go to my room and hide. I could hear my parents whispering at the bottom of the stairs, and I looked over the banister to see my father fully dressed. He was trying to calm my mother down – but he was having little success. He grabbed his keys and kissed her before opening the front door to leave.

My own confusion outweighed the stunned emotion my mother was feeling as she stared at the closed door.

"Mom?" I said slowly, walking to the stairs.

My voice startled her, and she jumped and looked up at me. With a fake smile filling her face, she tried to find the familiar excitement that her emotion usually carried. She reached back and pulled down her long dark hair, trying to hide the red blemish that always surfaces on her chest when she's hiding something.

"Where is Dad going?" I asked.

She looked down, then back up at me - trying to find words that would not be completely untruthful.

"Um, he…well, you see, he had go meet someone. At the…at the hospital," she said, pulling her robe closed.

"It's, like, two in the morning," I protested, halting halfway down the stairs.

My mother's eyes fell to my tattoo, and I felt a surge of fear as she saw the new addition. Not feeling like trying to explain it, I casually moved my arm behind my back.

"Honey, you know how good a doctor he is. They just need him; it's nothing really," she said, trying to convince herself.

My father is an amazing doctor. He never really prescribes medicine or has to run painful tests to find a cure; he just seems to know what's wrong and how to heal it. People come from every state just to see him. So, I almost believed her for a moment – that is, until I felt a dread rise inside her.

I was about to get angry when I heard my baby sister, Libby's, bedroom door open at the other end of the hall. Only six, Libby is a lot like my mother; they both live with a constant child-like excitement rushing through them. Squinting her dark eyes in the light of the hall, Libby pushed her long, dark, tangled hair out of her face.

"Is it time to get up?" she asked me.

Seeing her way out of having to answer any more of my questions, my mother climbed the stairs quickly.

"No, baby girl, Daddy just had to go help someone," she answered.

I felt Libby's confusion; even she knew that that was odd. My mother reached Libby and took her hand.

"Come on, sweetie, I'll lay with you," my mother said to Libby, guiding her into her room.

Libby looked back at me, and I shrugged my shoulders, letting her know that I didn't understand either.

I stood awestruck for a moment before going back to my room. Leaving the light on, I then climbed under my covers, and immediately my mind went back to the words that the figure had said: "I will find you now." The details of the nightmares, the images, and feeling people around me are traits that I've always kept to myself out of fear that my family will think that I'm insane if I tell them.

As a child, I only had nightmares during a new moon, but every single night I dreamt of another place. There, I always found the same person...I cannot recall a single day of my life that I have not seen him.

This beautiful person has always mesmerized me with his intense blue eyes, which give way to perfect lips highlighted by beautiful dimples that come to life when he smiles at me. His shoulders are broad, and his tall frame is lean and muscular.

I took in a deep breath and closed my eyes, holding his image in my mind, hoping this time that I'd find him instead of the unexpected horror that I'd already faced that night.

I slowly opened my eyes to a bright sunlit field. Relief swept through me as I started to search for the one who gave me peace.

It felt like I belonged there, like it belonged to me, and there was only one flaw: silence; I had never heard the voice of the one I love. Everything looked so pure. The grass, trees, and flowers smelled so sweet, the birds and butterflies drifted silently through the air, a small creek led into a larger waterway that fell into a beautiful gentle waterfall. Here, I was sure that I would find him - and I wished every day for this dream to come to life.

He was there, watching the water, waiting patiently for me to come. Feeling me approach, he turned and smiled at me as he brushed his dark, wavy hair out of his eyes. A smile filled my face, and I felt the air leave my lungs as I took him in, a life force.

Each time my nightmare would come before our meeting, he could see it in my face, and his concern and anger for whoever had hurt me was clear. Stepping closer to me, he read my eyes again, and the smile in his eyes faded. I looked down, almost ashamed that I was so weak. He held out his arms, and I fell into his embrace. I wanted to stay here, to hear him… all the insane things that happened to me would be worth it if only he were real.

The sound of lawnmowers woke me before I had a chance to say goodbye to my blue-eyed boy. I looked down to see the star still resting inside my Ankh and shook my head in disbelief. Knowing that I couldn't lie still for another moment, I pulled myself up. On my bedside table, there was a note from my mother.

> *Libby is playing with Abby today. Abby's grandmother is taking them to a movie this afternoon. Can you meet them at the theater at four? Meet me at the gallery, we'll get dinner.*
> *Love Mom*

My mother, Grace, owns an art gallery at the corner of Main Street. She has a big showing this week, and most of the paintings are mine; she assumes that if see I the reaction of the public, I will be inspired to paint again.

Now that the nightmares had returned, I was almost sure that I'd see an image today…it would feel good to paint again.

I had just finished getting dressed and was wondering what I was going to do with myself when I heard a knock on the front door. From the top of the stairs, I could see my friend, Dane, through the glass window that surrounded the door.

I have known Dane my entire life, and I will never see him as anything more than a friend. He's a little older than me, tall, with an athletic build. His eyes have always held seriousness beyond his years. In truth, we both felt out of place in this modest life in which we were raised.

Walking down the steps, I took in his calm demeanor - which felt refreshing after last night. I opened the door and met him with a smile, but his smile faded when he saw me.

"Rough night?" he asked, almost teasing.

I rolled my eyes and waved him in. He followed me to the patio that lined the back of the house, where I sat down on the swing that faced the yard. Dane sat down beside me and stretched his long arm out behind me.

"You OK Willow?" he asked, looking down at me. I nodded, staring into the distance.

"Did the nightmares come back?" he asked.

I looked up at him, not shocked that he had guessed so quickly; it was no secret among any of my friends that I was a violent sleeper.

"Do you want to talk about it?" Dane asked, dropping his arm from the back of the swing to around my shoulders.

I didn't mind it. Dane wasn't like the other guys in town; I never once felt uncomfortable by his emotions.

"No, I'd rather just forget," I said, almost to myself. I could feel his frustration as he tried to think of a way to help me.

"Was it a new moon last night?" Dane asked.

I shook my head no. I felt Dane's confusion; even he knew that it was odd for me to have a nightmare on any night other than the new moon. My friends would always stay at my house during those times, as if they could protect me from the bad dreams. Dane had told me to just stay awake. I considered the thought, but when I realized that meant I wouldn't see my blue-eyed boy - I chose sleep.

“I wonder why this one was different,” Dane muttered. I shrugged my shoulders. I felt as though I’d let my family and friends down; they’d been more relieved than I was when I had gone so long without a nightmare.

I stood slowly, hearing Dane sigh before he stood to follow me wherever I chose to go. A gust of summer air brushed through the trees, causing one of the branches to scrape against the roof of the patio. Feeling a sudden quick fear shoot through Dane before he had a chance to process what the noise was, I smiled at his reaction.

“Maybe you just have nightmares because of this house,” Dane said, blushing a little.

My house is over a hundred years old, and it has always been in my family. It is the most historic and admired home in the town of Franklin – but for some strange reason, Dane has never been completely comfortable here.

I felt a gentle pull on me, the way I always did when an image would emerge, looking for my help. In the center of my yard, a young woman appeared, and a sinking feeling quickly absorbed me. I blinked to make sure I was not imagining anything. She was on her knees, wearing a long black coat, holding a letter in her hands, she was crying breathlessly.

I stepped off the patio and walked slowly in her direction with Dane following right behind me. It would not be the first time he had watched me help an image; in fact I was sure I had lost count of how many times he had actually come. He never asked any questions or even spoke about it; each time, he would just act as if nothing had happened.

My eyes searched over the woman, trying to understand if the sorrow I felt coming from her was grief or loneliness. After a moment, I knelt in front of her, reached out with my hands, and touched her shoulder.

With my touch the gentle pull grew into a force that moved me forward. A tingling sensation absorbed me, and the air around me shifted to freezing. It was dark, and snow fell softly through the air. The woman never raised her eyes to meet mine - the images never do. I tried to remember an emotion of absolute bliss, the way I always felt in my good dreams. I could then feel her emotion shifting to the same bliss. Her tears began to dry, and a small smile came to the corners of her lips. I let go, slowly taking in her details. The same force that pulled me in pushed me away, and I took in the tingle as it passed again.

I was back in my yard in the small town of Franklin on a warm summer day. I felt Dane standing behind me, his emotions calm. When we were kids, I could feel how scary this was to him; now, it's as common to him as a simple conversation.

I took a deep breath before I turned and walked back to the patio. Dane followed me as I sat back down in the swing he passed me and went into the house. I looked blankly at the door, trying to figure out what he was doing. He returned abruptly with a sketch book and stick of charcoal, then walked over and handed them to me before taking a seat.

I leaned back in the swing, pulling my legs to me to balance the pad. My hand then flew across the page as I outlined the woman. I realized how observant Dane really was; he understood the significance of my art. He stared at the image with pride filling him.

When it was done, he smiled and shook his head. "Well, the rebellion thing didn't work - maybe we should play up the nightmares," he teased.

He and my closest friend, Olivia, tried to help me come up with excuses for not going away to school. The school was my mother's dream - not mine - and in truth, if it were up to me, I would never leave Franklin. I knew everyone here. Their emotions were familiar, and I knew how to block them if need be. The thought of being in a huge city filled with millions of emotions was exhausting, and I seriously contemplated Dane's words before we both broke into laughter.

"What time is it?" I asked

He looked at his watch. "Three thirty," he said, a little shocked by how quickly time had passed.

“I have to walk down and get Libby for Mom,” I said, standing and folding the sketch pad closed.

“I’ll walk with you; I have to work tonight,” Dane said, stretching before he stood.

His mother, Gina, owned a small Diner in town named Gina’s, and Dane seemed slated to run it one day – but that was a fate he would never choose for himself.

My house sat just one block from Main Street, the heart of town. I slipped on my sandals and walked side by side with Dane down the sidewalk. Almost everyone we passed waved hello and followed with a ‘Tell your dad I said hello.’

Dane just shook his head.“Your dad should, like, run for President; he would so win, “he said, nodding as someone else said ‘Say hello to your dad’ to me again.

“You’re probably right,” I muttered, suddenly remembering him leaving last night and the way my mother was acting; I was still eager to find out what had gotten into them.

My friend, Olivia, is working at the theater for the summer; her passions are movies and books, so it’s a fitting job for her. Olivia is one of those people that I enjoy being around because words are not always needed. We are the two girls who sit on the sidelines, watching others in our class. Because Olivia is small and has the same olive skin and long dark hair as I do, teachers often would mistake one of us for the other. Our eyes are comparable, too, but I’ve always thought that mine were stranger than hers. When she saw me and Dane coming, a smile filled her bored face.

“What have you guys been up to today?” Olivia asked.

“Sketching,” Dane answered, raising his eyebrows.

Olivia’s smile fell.

“Man, I really thought that one may have worked,” Olivia said, almost to herself. She was sincerely trying to help me stay here.

“Wait,” Dane said, raising his hands to make his words have more of an effect. “I have good news: the nightmares are back,” he said in a sarcastic, comical tone.

Olivia's eyes widened. "Really?" she asked, looking at me.

I nodded, a little embarrassed.

"Do you guys have any good news for me?" she asked.

"Afraid not," Dane said quickly. "Hey I gotta go. If your lights are on when I get done tonight, I'll stop by," he said to me. I nodded and watched him go.

"I don't think I will ever figure the two of you out," Olivia said.

I turned quickly to give her a dirty look. I was always teased about not dating Dane – or anyone, for that matter.

"Just kidding," Olivia said, smiling and raising her hands defensively. I knew she was, and I brushed it off.

The doors to the theater opened, and I could see Libby coming up the aisle with her friend and her grandmother.

"Hey, let's do something tomorrow," Olivia said, knowing that I'd soon turn my attention to Libby. I nodded again and walked to meet Libby. When she saw me, she ran in my direction, full of excitement.

"Oh, that was the best movie ever! The princess had green eyes like you!" Libby said in a rushed, excited tone.

"Are you sure? I thought only witches had green eyes?" I teased.

Not finding it very amusing, her wide smile lessened. I waved goodbye to Olivia, and Libby told her friend goodbye. She must have known I was supposed to take her to mom's gallery because she turned in that direction as we left the theater and all but pulled me down the sidewalk.

"Willow, why are you walking so slow? I want to see mom. Which pieces of yours are in the show?"

Libby never had just one question.

"It's just nice out; I want to enjoy it."

"What pictures of yours are in the show?" she asked again. She knew I was avoiding the answer.

"I don't know; Mom didn't ask me."

Libby started going on about which ones were her favorite, and I listened half- heartedly as I scanned the crowd, looking for another image; the woman wearing a black coat had left me with a craving to help someone else.

People were rushing in and out of the doors of the gallery when we arrived. We didn't see Mom at first, but Libby spotted her as the people scurried around us.

"There she is."

My mother, dressed in the unique style that reflected her artistic ability, was wearing one of my father's pin-striped shirts. She had fashioned it into a dress with a wide belt, black tights, and several long gold and silver necklaces. Both of her wrists were full of silver and gold bracelets, and by next week every teenager and trendy mother would have on the same outfit, her energy filled all those that she came across.

I waved at her to let her know we were there. Libby then took my hand and said, "Let's find yours."

It was not hard; one of the first ones in the presentation was mine. It was of a little boy in a field, surrounded by wild flowers; I had painted it almost a year ago. The emotion was happy in this painting. He was so sweet, but when I first saw him he was filled with sorrow, he had lost something. I only tried to give him patience. Just as I was to leave him, I saw what he had lost come back to him. It was his best friend, a yellow lab. It made me smile to remember him.

"Who did you draw?" Libby asked.

"It was just someone I thought of," I said with caution.

"There are my two angels," I heard my mother say.

Libby was in her arms before I could turn to her voice.

"Did you like your movie?" she asked Libby

The energy that those two put off was unbelievable. Libby nodded and went into a full recount of the movie, and my mother's eyes met mine as Libby spoke. Wanting to avoid her stare, I began to walk down the hall in the gallery and look at all the paintings. The emotion of the art work - not just mine - was powerful, and the most amazing part was feeling the emotions of the people who gazed at them. If they understand the painting, they feel it - and it always makes me smile.

My mother caught up with me." How did your day go? Did you sleep in?" she asked, trying to catch my eyes.

"Yeah, I'm good," I said, not looking at her.

"We're going to meet your Dad at Antoine's for dinner," she said with a bit of relief.

"Speaking of sleep, I bet he is tired. Since he had to work last night," I said, now looking at her, letting my eyes tell her that I had not forgotten their odd behavior last night.

A surge of suspense rushed through her, and she stood speechless before turning and trying to look busy, talking to the lighting crew. *When I get home tonight,* I thought, *I'm just going to have to just demand a solid answer from them.*

Antoine's was busy, which wasn't surprising, as nice as it is. Dad managed to get us a table out on the street. He seemed lost in his thoughts, which was odd because he is usually very attentive to us. I melted into my seat, keeping my eyes down and tracing my forbidden tattoo, as well as the new addition now there: a small star…it's now a part of me.

I listened as Mom and Dad went over their days with each other. They were interrupted often as people would pass by and stop and talk to them. I listened and added in a laugh or "yes" or "no" when the questions would come my way. My eyes were on the people all around us; I had not given up my search for another image.

I was more worried that it would be another six months before another image would come. I could feel my father watching me, following my gaze. When he exchanged glances with my mother, I could feel his concern. *What is it with him lately?*

As dinner ended, I felt a familiar pull on me, so I quickly searched the crowd for anyone out of place. Across the street, I saw three girls walking toward the direction of our home. They looked wet and were huddled closely together, trying to calm each other. I looked at my mother and saw her sketching something on a napkin.

"Mom, do you care if I go by the art store before I come home?" I asked, needing an excuse for the detour that I was planning.

"That's fine with me. I'm surprised you haven't made any plans for tonight. Hannah and Jessica stopped by the shop today, looking for you."

Jessica and Hannah were friends of mine and big fans of my mother. My father seemed to grow a little tense; I felt his emotion shift to concern, and he spoke before I had the chance to respond.

"What could you possibly need at the store? Between you and your mother, you could open a store on your own." His voice seemed uneasy as he spoke.

My mother hesitated, then looked across to my father. I could feel her optimism; she did not seem to be as cautious as my father was trying to be.

"I just want to see if they have anything new. I think Monica is working anyway," I responded, a bit defensive.

My mother reached out and put her hand on my father's hand. Bringing his attention to her big brown eyes, she spoke softly, almost imploring him to listen to her.

"Jason, let her go."

He started to say something, but she put her fingers to his lips, and with their eyes locked, she seemed to reassure him. Taking advantage of the distraction she had given me, I stood quickly.

"I won't be out late," I promised. "Hey, Libby, give me a hug."

"Can I go with you?" Libby asked, dancing in her seat. It was obvious she just didn't want to sit there anymore.

"Young lady, it's close to your bed time. Give you sister some space," Mom said, putting her sketch in her purse.

As I walked passed them, I did not look at my father. I then shouted, "Love you guys," over my shoulder as I walked toward the art store.

Unfortunately, the images were walking in the opposite direction of the art store, toward where my parents were sure to be walking shortly. The art store was just a few spaces down from the restaurant, so I went in quickly, trying to give them time to leave. My friend, Monica, was sitting behind the counter, reading a magazine.

"Hey, Willow," Monica said

"Hey," I said, staring out the store front.

Monica is a good person, honest with her emotions.

"What are you looking for?"

"Nothing, really; I was just getting some space between me and my parents."

"Willow Haywood, why on earth would you ever want to do that?" she asked sarcastically. "Wait - don't tell me you're sneaking off to meet one of your many admirers…who's the lucky guy? Dane? Josh, maybe?"

I grimaced as she said the names, which only made her laugh.

"Hey, go to the lake with me tomorrow. Hannah and Jessica are going," Monica said, walking toward me and trying to see what I was looking at outside the store.

"Yeah, I guess. I'll see if Olivia wants to go to," I said, still staring impatiently out the window.

"Guess what? There's a new guy in town. Chase has been showing him around today. He is drop dead gorgeous, tall, and muscular - but not too muscular, like Josh. He has the most amazing eyes; they just pull you in when he talks to you."

Monica's dramatic description made me laugh. She had always been a bit boy crazy, not a good trait to have in a small town; there are not a lot of them to go around.

"Who is he?" I asked

"His name is Drake. Chase met him this morning; he's renting out the studio at Chase's house - and he's going to the lake tomorrow, too," she continued.

"Monica -"

"I'll pick you up at noon," Monica asserted.

I let out a deep sigh. "Fine. Look, I gotta go. I'll see you tomorrow."

"Love – ya," Monica yelled as I walked out.

Waving goodbye and walking back onto the street, I looked back toward Antoine's; my family had left, and the streets were clearing out. I could see Mom and Libby almost a block ahead of me, and, wondering where my father went, my eyes searched for the group of three.

My house was only a block away now, and just as I was thinking of turning back - I felt the pull again…I saw them a few feet in front of me. The images were very quiet; three girls, young. I wasn't sure what was wrong. Their faces held an expression to which I'd rarely been called, and there was utter silence all around them. My stomach dropped, and I felt a little sick; I always felt this way just before I got in trouble. If I had any sense, I would see this as a sign to turn around and go home – but my curiosity won over my anxiety, and I stepped closer.

The night air seemed to chill as a breeze swept through the trees, and I could feel emotions all around me. Beyond my images was one full of anguish. I looked back, and all I could see were the people in the distant lights of the streets. Not sure where the anguish was coming from, I ignored it and decided to help the images.

Breathing in, I looked at the girls and reached out for the one closest to me. Instantly, the pull and the tingling sensation absorbed me once again, and I smiled as I relished in the feeling. The night became darker, and I felt the cold rain. The girls trembled as they walked. Their exhaustion was apparent in the manner in which they carried themselves; they were finding their way back.

I let Libby's face flash through my memory, and with it the warmth and energy that came off her. I then placed my other hand on the girl to the far right. Noticing that the two girls on the outside were clearly stronger, I took my right hand and placed it on the girl in the middle. I watched as determination crossed her face. I could see a house with all the lights on inside, and the girls could see it, too. I let go, and a force pulled me back. I then stood still, trying to hold on to the tingling sensation I felt.

"Un – hum…"

Hearing someone clear their throat, I turned slowly – and right behind me was my father.

"Hey, Dad," I said nervously.

"Willow, do you want to tell me something?" he asked.

My stomach turned…did he see me disappear - or did he see me reappear?

"About…?" I answered shyly.

My father closed his eyes and raised his head to the night sky; he was really upset, more so now than he had been at dinner.

"Do you realize how far you went that time?" he asked, lowering his head and looking carefully at me.

"What?" the wind was knocked from me.

"Do you even know what you are doing?"

"Do *you*?" I retorted.

My father cleared his throat again and hesitated as an older couple walked by. "Willow, we need to talk. I need to explain something to you."

I swallowed hard, not sure that I wanted to know what he thought he knew.

Chapter Two

My father put his arm around my shoulder, and we walked in the direction of our house. His mood was shifting; I could feel his relief.

"Willow…you are a gifted child - and I'm not talking about painting," he began.

We both stared forward as we walked. My body was tense; I'd rehearsed over and over again exactly how I would tell my parents about my gift, and now the shock of their knowing was overwhelming to me.

"The gifts you have come, in part, from me," he said in his familiar peaceful tone.

I looked slowly up at him and noticed that he was smiling down at me.

"Which ones?" I asked

"Well, I cannot feel other's emotions, if that is what you are asking," he said quietly as he smiled slightly.

His blunt answer made my stomach drop; I had no idea that he or they knew what I could do.

We made it back to our home. My father then led me around the side of the house through the back gate, where he knocked on the kitchen window to get my mother's attention. I could feel her excitement and her anticipation, and I really didn't know what to expect from the upcoming conversation.

She made her way out with three glasses of tea and set them around the table. She then ran back inside and returned with her phone, a notepad, and a pen. I kept my eyes down, waiting for her to settle. When she did, Dad continued.

"Would you like to know what I can do?" my father asked. As he settled in next to my mother, I nodded. He continued, "Well, I can see what is wrong inside the body."

"Anything?" I asked.

He nodded and smiled.

"Well, that explains a lot; you are a really good doctor," I said, not meaning to sound sarcastic. My mother smiled proudly at my father.

"Do you have a weird gift Mom?" I asked.

"Oh, sweetie, I am from this dimension," she said innocently.

My father closed his eyes.

"What?!" I said louder than I intended. I felt sick to my stomach and thought they had officially lost their mind.

"Um, dear…we really have not gotten that far yet," my father commented.

My mother's eyes widened, and she looked down - avoiding my stare - as her anxiety built. I sat forward in my seat, my mouth and eyes wide open.

"What are you trying to say that I'm part - alien? Seriously, you guys better not be messing with me," I finally managed to say.

Dad leaned forward and put his hand on my knee.

"No, no, Willow. Listen, you are not an alien; you are definitely from earth - just a different part of it."

I furrowed my eyebrows together, questioning his every word.

"Listen, when you do what you did tonight, you are using a string - and those strings connect other dimensions…I'm from a different one," my father said.

"String – what are you talking about, another dimension?"

My father cleared his throat."The string is like a hallway that leads to other doors, and behind those doors are dimensions much different from this one. Honestly, I do not completely understand the way you have taught yourself, but you do pass through the string."

"Look, those people I help are normal; they don't look any different than we do," I argued, refusing to play a part in the reality he was painting for me.

"We are all people, we all look normal; these dimensions are only different because of the choices made as a whole," my father said, engaging my blank stare.

"I don't get it…why are you telling me this now? What is the deal?" I said, failing to find reason in his words. Dad looked at Mom, then back to me. I could sense his concern.

"It is time to go home," he said quietly.

"This is home; this town is perfect, safe, and beautiful," I argued, looking back and forth between them.

"And my dimension would make this world humble in its beauty," he said in a whisper, his eyes gazing in deep reflection.

"Then why are we here? Why have you had us live a lie? Why have you not told me that I'm not crazy for all these things that I can do?!" I almost yelled, standing, and beginning to pace the patio.

Dad shifted in his seat and looked at Mom; he smiled, encouraging him to go on. My father then stood and put his hands on my shoulders, forcing me to look at him. His hazel eyes had shifted to a light green, which matched the calm I felt coming from him now.

He smiled slightly and said, "My dimension, Chara, has a trait: we all leave to find our soul mates. We are driven by a feeling deep inside."

I tilted my head and furrowed my eyebrows. My father smiled wider as he let his hands fall from my shoulders; I could sense relief coming from him. It was like he was opening a flood gate that has been closed too long.

"I left at twenty to find your mother. When she decided that she would rather live in my dimension, I went to find another traveler to help me lead her home but the storms inside the string had somehow closed my passage. I found other passages over time, but by then you were born, and I thought it would be safer to stay here for now."

"Storms," I repeated, still not understanding what a "string" was.

"Yes, not like rain and thunder, though. You see, the string is made of energy; it flows, sometimes too aggressively. We always lead a new person home with the help of a seasoned traveler. If our dimension is not in your blood, all you will see is darkness; it can be very frightening," my father said, looking back at mother and trying to warn her of what she would have to face.

"So, is the storm over now?" I asked, still not understanding his vague explanation.

He looked back at me slowly. "Not really; we just think it is time," he said as I felt dread come over him.

"If you couldn't get Mom there, then how are you going to get us all there now?" I asked.

"I went to meet a friend of mine, Ashten, last night. He is on his way home to get his family, and they will help us all get there."

Shifting my eyes between my mother and father, I wondered if my nightmare had trigged this sudden urge for him to be honest with me.

"So what's your plan - for us to just vanish? I have friends here. I have a life here…we all do." I argued.

"Willow, just trust me," my father, said desperate for me to be more agreeable.

"What are you not telling me? You didn't just wake up this morning and say, ' – Gee, I think I'm going to tell Willow that we are from another dimension – ha ha, she will love that,' did you?"

My mother stood and put herself between me and my father.

"Honestly, we have been thinking about it for a while. Libby is already six; we want her to grow up there," Mom said, trying to defend my father.

"Why didn't you want me to grow up there?" I asked sarcastically.

I had never been jealous of my baby sister; I could just feel that they weren't telling me everything - and honestly, it had to be big. They are not afraid of telling me I'm from another dimension, so what could be so bad in comparison?

"It was just different then," my father said under his breath.

I raised my eyebrows, encouraging him to go on.

"Listen, bad people are everywhere, and we were told that someone very dark was in the string…they…they…we just didn't want to travel through there with you being so young," my father said in a frustrated tone as a sea of deep emotions swarmed through him.

"So, the bad guy is gone now…?" I said shortly.

"Not, exactly, but Ashten has very strong boys, and they will make sure we all weather the storms and make it home safely," my father answered.

My mother wrapped her arm around my shoulder."Willow, tomorrow we are going to tie up some loose ends, then the next day we are going to go home where we belong," she said with a sense of finality.

"Are we never going to come back?"

"We will come back to visit, but we belong there," Dad said.

"What am I supposed to tell my friends? I have known them my whole life - you want me just to disappear, like they mean nothing to me?" I argued.

As I spoke, both of them were shaking their heads "no."

"Look, I've called all of their parents tonight, and I told them you were accepted to a school in Paris. They are happy for you," my mother said.

"This is a good thing, Willow. We should have gone home long ago," Dad said.

The phone rang, and my mother reached to answer it. When the other person on the line spoke I watched her pick up a pen and draw a line through a name; she had composed a list of people to say goodbye to, which made this all very real.

Too stunned and angry to ask any more questions, I rolled my eyes, then turned and walked in the house.

"Sweet dreams tonight, OK," Dad called after me.

On the walk up the stairs to my room, I was in a complete daze. If I did not see images, or have strange dreams, I would consider having my parents' sanity checked.

I had never felt more alone in my whole life. I was close to my parents, and I never could have imagined that they would have keep something like this from me. I pulled myself into a ball on my bed and rocked myself back and forth, refusing to cry. Flashing back over my childhood, I tried to remember if there had been any hidden clues I'd missed.

I heard something hit my window. Knowing it was Dane, I let out a deep breath, then wiped my eyes quickly making sure there weren't any tears - and walked to the window. I quietly opened it and climbed out onto the rooftop. Having done it more times than I could remember, I grabbed the branch of a large oak tree by my window and made my way down, feeling Dane's anxiety as he braced himself to catch me if I fell. Once on the ground, we walked quietly to the edge of the yard, where we sat on a small bench. I could feel Dane's emotion growing heavier, and I wondered if my mother had already called his.

"You know you were supposed to use the nightmares to keep you from going to New York - not send yourself to another continent," Dane whispered.

"I don't think we're going to find an excuse to keep me here," I said, covering my face with my hands.

"You know you're eighteen - you could just tell them no," Dane said, feeling defeated.

"Yep, and you could tell your mother that you don't want to have anything to do with that Diner," I rebutted.

He nodded, then we both laughed quietly. Neither of us had any intention of not following our parents' wishes. It wasn't that we were afraid; it's just that we had no idea what we were supposed to be doing - until that moment came - we would follow.

"What am I going to do without you, Willow?" Dane asked.

"I don't know; maybe if you're not hanging around me so much, you might find a girlfriend," I said, trying to lighten the mood.

Dane looked at me crossly, showing me that he wasn't amused.

"What? - I know Monica still has a crush on you," I said, trying not to laugh out loud.

"Monica likes everybody," Dane said, rolling his eyes.

"Hey!" I said in her defense - even though it was true.

"I didn't mean it in a mean way; she's not what I'm looking for," Dane said as he leaned forward.

"You'll find her," I said, rubbing his back.

"I'm going to tell you something weird, Willow."

I held my breath; I wasn't sure how much more "weird" I could take that night. "I've never seen you as more than a friend," he said, looking at me.

I nodded and let my breath out. I felt the same way about him; he was like a brother to me.

"But I get this feeling that if I stay close to you, I will find what I'm looking for," Dane finished.

We sat in silence for a while, staring at the night sky. I wondered if he were right, that if we stayed close to one another we would find our place.

"Dane, will you do me a favor?" I asked. He looked at me, surprised that I had to ask, then he nodded.

"Will you watch out for Olivia while I am gone?" I asked.

Dane nodded, understanding why I was so concerned. Olivia had lost her parents when she was only ten, and she now lived with her cousin Hannah. Those two could not be more different; in fact, I think I'm the only one that understands Olivia - and that's only because I can still feel her grief and loneliness.

"You're coming to the lake tomorrow, right?" I asked

"I have to work most of the day, but I'll meet you guys out there at night," he said regretfully.

"Night?" I asked. I thought we were just going to get some sun and go home.

"Yeah, they're supposed to build a bonfire. I think a lot of them are camping out; it's supposed to be a big farewell thing for you," Dane said.

"You know I love you guys, but I am not sleeping out there," I said, elbowing him.

"Ahh come on…you're not scared - are you?" Dane teased.

Just then, the back porch light kicked on, and my father opened the door. I felt a little anxiety rise inside of Dane; he respected my father as much as anyone else in town. My father looked in our direction, and a surge of confusion came from him. Dane then stood and held my hand as he walked me to the patio. He hugged me, then politely nodded to my father before he left.

I kept my eyes down and passed by my father. I made it halfway up the stairs before he said anything.

"Willow."

I stopped mid- stride, then turned to look at him standing at the bottom of the stairs. I could not understand what he was so confused about.

"You can feel the way I feel about your mother and the way she feels about me, right?" he asked.

I nodded.

"Do you feel that way about Dane?" he asked.

"Yeah right - not even close, Dad," I answered as I started to climb the stairs again.

"Are you sure? If you did, that would change everything," he said, climbing the stairs after me.

I froze and looked down. It would be so easy to lie right now and say that I did - but would they let me stay here, where I knew it was safe?

"How?" I asked

"I told you that our dimension believes you are supposed to be with your soul mate. If you feel that way about Dane, then he is your soul mate, and we were wrong about you," he explained.

I sat down on the step where I was standing. The emotion between my parents is beautiful; it's a love that's unconditional, timeless, and I knew without a doubt that I felt that way about the blue-eyed boy I'd dreamed of. I would even say that I loved him more, but then I realized that my father had let something slip.

"Who was wrong about me? What am I?" I asked.

My father sighed, realizing he had misspoken. He climbed the few steps between us and sat down next to me.

"I'm going to tell you a story," he said.

I felt a sense of trepidation come over him. I turned on the step, facing him - wanting to know everything.

"Every dimension has different beliefs, rulers, and ways of living. There is one dimension, Esteroius, which is very dark. This entire dimension is ruled by the Blakeshire court. The ruler of that court is a man named Donalt, who has ruled that dimension for longer than anyone can remember. He has a very large palace, where the priest and their family live, and they make up the court," he said, looking at me to make sure I was following him.

I nodded, telling him to go on.

"When I was young, I traveled. I was one of the ones that helped others find their way back and we had taken people to that dimension before." His eyes drifted to distant memories. "It always felt like a rescue mission rather than a love story."

He paused and looked over at me, and I could sense grief coming from him.

Clearing his throat and looking forward again, he continued. "We had never once brought home someone who lived in the court, but one day a good friend of mine, Justus, came to me and told me it was his time to find his soul mate. He wanted my help, so I went with him – but I was shocked when he led me into Esteroius."

My father's eyes turned green as he smiled, remembering his friend.

"Justus walked right to the gate of the palace, as if he didn't have a fear in the universe. There, on the inside walking by, was a young, beautiful girl. Justus looked at me and said 'That's her…'"

He paused, and I felt his emotion turn to sorrow.

"Long story short, she came home with Justus. Her name was Adonia, and her father was Alamos, Donalt's highest and most trusted priest."

My father stopped and stared down at his wedding band. I could feel his sorrow growing, so I put my hand on his. He sighed, then continued

"Now, shortly after this, I left to find your mother, so what I know was told to me by Ashten Chambers. It seems that every time Adonia would go home to see her father, they would ask her and Justus questions about our blood lines: how we traveled, where we went…Justus became convinced that Donalt and Alamos were plotting to take on other dimensions, so he forbade Adonia from going home again…but she missed her father, so she convinced another traveler, Livingston, to take her home. When she got there, the court held her captive. Livingston rushed home to tell Justus, and Justus, Livingston, and Beth, Livingston's soul mate, then went to bring Adonia home."

My father's grief intensified, so I knew it ended badly. He sighed and looked down, then continued, "When it was over, Livingston carried Justus's body home…no one really knows what happened to Adonia or Beth. Ashten said that it's been very difficult for Livingston since that day."

My father hesitated as he thought back. I could feel his regret; it was if he were carrying a burden that was more than he could handle.

"A few years later, a little boy was seen alone in the strings. Livingston warned the people in Chara that this child was being controlled by Donalt and his priest, Alamos. I assume the little boy was Justus'; I don't know any other way he'd be able to travel the strings."

My father looked to his side at me, and his eyes searched over my face carefully. I sensed his remorsefulness.

"Livingston told Ashten that the child was looking for a girl that was born in the eleventh month and could feel the souls of others."

With those last words, I held my breath; I was born in November, and I guess you could say that I could feel the souls of others. As his eyes continued to search over my face, it was easy to see that he was looking at his little girl - not the young woman that I'd become.

"Over time, Ashten managed to learn how to navigate through the storms, and he found me and your mother just after your sixth birthday…we knew that you could feel emotions. We were living in one of the largest dimensions in the smallest town, hundreds of miles from any real doorway. We thought if we stayed here, you'd never be found by anyone from Esteroius," my father finished.

I let his story replay in my mind as I tried to understand why I was connected to that little boy. I was beginning to think that my nightmares were connected to him. My mind replayed the last nightmare that I'd had: the memory of the suffocating pain on my chest and the burn that made itself known across my face.

"Willow, are you OK?" he asked.

"I just don't understand…why was some kid in another dimension looking for me?" I asked.

"You are a direct descendant of the first recorded people in our dimension, and Livingston believes they are trying to control a prophecy first made millions of years ago."

"What prophecy?" I asked, wanting to know what they were protecting me from.

"Its foolishness; don't worry about it," My father said quietly. I could feel him struggling with a mix of emotions.

"Then why are you worried about it?" I asked.

He sighed deeply before answering me. "You have to understand, they did not only predict your birth month - they predicted the day, hour, and minute."

I continued to stare forward. My stomach was turning; the thought that I'd have to face that figure one day was terrifying. I didn't understand what I had done to deserve this.

"Willow, the stars can be read a million different ways - they do not state our lives. I wanted to shield you from this, for you to live a normal life."

I looked at him like he was crazy. Did he really think I had a normal life?

"Do you have any idea how hard it was for me to grow up not knowing any of this? I mean, you could have at least told me I wasn't crazy. Do you know how hard it is for me to be in a large room with everyone's emotions hitting me like a ton of bricks? Try and imagine puberty with my friends; that was exhausting. Not to mention the fact that people would appear out of nowhere, needing my help. Do you know I was convinced they were ghosts until I was like eleven? "

"I never realized that you were struggling," he said as a surge of regret came over him.

I nodded and closed my eyes for a moment; I knew it didn't matter how angry I was - it wouldn't change the past. So, I let my anger go, sighed, and slowly opened my eyes.

"My nightmare is the reason you're telling me this, isn't it?" I asked, looking down at my tattoo with the star inside the loop of the Ankh.

My father reached over and gently grasped my wrist, looking intently at the star as he spoke.

"It was predicted that on the *Blue Moon* of your eighteenth birth year, all those who seek you will find you."

"All?" I questioned.

My father nodded as he gently moved his finger across the star.

"I assumed that prediction meant that your gift would be magnified and that you would be able to help more people. When

I saw this mark, I realized that the prediction meant that the child would finally find you."

"What do you mean, 'Blue Moon?'" I asked

He gently let go of my wrist and looked me in the eye.

"A Blue Moon is the second full moon in a month. It's not very common." He then sighed and looked down, and I sensed his anxiety growing. "We only have eleven days remaining until the *Blue Moon* will rise, and I want you safe in Chara when that night comes," he said, looking back at me.

"When did you plan to tell me all of this? What if I did not have that nightmare?" I asked.

"When you were twenty, when it would be time for you to find your soul mate," he answered, feeling relived that he could talk openly with me.

"Who decided that twenty was the magic number?" I asked, realizing that meant another two years before I would find my blue-eyed boy - if he were real.

"No one did; that's just when we get this urge. It's undeniable…it's all you think about," he said, leaning back and smiling.

"How do you know where to go? People can't find each other in *one* dimension - much less several." I said

He stretched his legs out on the steps and looked at me.

"Travelers can see several passages, but the others who don't travel on a daily basis can only see one, and the passage they see leads them to their soul mates. Once in the passage, they follow a feeling - the other person is usually looking for them as well. It really is a beautiful thing to witness."

"So how does a traveler know if they can see more than one passage?" I asked

"For travelers, their passage is always brighter in their eyes, like a beacon," he answered, winking at me.

"So when I go into the string, I will see a beacon leading me to my soul mate?" I asked, seeking clarification.

My father's smile lessened a little. "The 'beacon' will shine when it's supposed to," he said as his eyes searched over my face. I could feel anticipation wrapped in dread coming from him.

"OK, then tell me what the string looks like to begin with."

He raised his eyebrows and tilted his head, and I could feel pride coming from him.

"Well, it's like standing in the center of a bright light; you feel surrounded by it. As you walk, you see hazes of different colors - they are the doorways to other dimensions."

"Is it big? I mean, how do you know where to go?" I asked

His eyes danced over my face as his smile widened. "There are three traits that define a 'traveler,'" he said. "Seeing the passages is only one. Another is that travelers have the ability to feel their way home. Everyone has their own way of using that feeling to navigate. For me, I would picture my dimension in my mind, then visualize the paths to where I needed to go."

I looked at him like he was crazy. That didn't make any sense; I knew where my house was, but that didn't mean I'd always be able to find my way home.

"You'll see," he said, laughing at my expression.

"What is the third trait?" I asked, hungry to know everything.

"It's the ability to understand every language."

"All of them?" I asked, astonished.

He nodded. "That one is very important. You see, travelers do more than just pass through the string; we also learn about all the cultures and help the person who is searching to abide by them."

"What do you mean?"

He laughed at the eagerness in my voice. "If you take someone to a dimension, they have to understand what is customary for the time that they live there. We teach them everything they need to know, then get them settled."

"Settled? You don't just leave when they find someone?" I asked.

"It just depends. In some dimensions, a fast courtship is customary. In others, it could last years. When I knew I was coming to this dimension, Infante, I planned to stay for at least a year - and if your mother had not wanted to leave, I would have stayed here for the rest of my life."

"So you would have left everything and everyone you loved?" I asked

"When you find your soul mate, you find the person that completes you. They are everything and everyone you love." He paused, "I am eager for you to meet your grandparents, though." he said, raising his eyebrows.

My mouth dropped open; I didn't know I had any living grandparents. My mother's parents had died before I was born, and my father had told me that his parents were in a beautiful place - I had taken that as Heaven, not another dimension.

"Why have I not met them before?" I asked.

"My mother, Rose, feared that if she came to Infante, your hiding spot would be revealed. She and my father, Karsten, just wanted you safe."

I looked down, suddenly realizing that my family had made a lot of sacrifices on my account. My father looked down at my tattoo, then back at me.

"You have never told me what your nightmares involve," he said softly.

I traced the star with my finger, remembering the dark figure and the sensation of his touch before it burned me."I help someone, then I see a dark figure."

"Every time?" he asked. I nodded.

"Is that figure the only one you dream of?" he asked. I looked up at him, feeling his concern beginning to build.

"I dream good dreams every night," I answered evasively

My father's emotion moved to relief, then he looked down, avoiding my eyes.

"Are you sure you can get Libby to Chara safely?" I asked. "I don't want her in danger because of me."

My father nodded, and I felt his confidence build.

"Ashten said that they'd discovered new passages the storms have made. They are trying to find a way home without passing the Esteroius dimension." I took in his confidence and let it calm me. Feeling a sense of relief, I knew that I'd now be able to ask for help with my gift. I'd even be able to explore it more.

"Do you want to ask me anything else?" he said.

"So, Chara is only different because of the culture? Do I need to learn anything before I go there?"

He smiled widely at me and beamed with pride. "Different cultures have come together as soul mates, leaving a perfect blend of harmony in their wake," he said, smiling. "We have a simple faith. Life itself is a gift from God, and love is the most powerful thing in the universe."

"It sounds too perfect," I mumbled, trying to see it in my mind.

"You will be happy there - I promise," my father said quietly. He looked so tired. "Tomorrow, just have fun with your friends; it may be a few months before I feel safe enough for you to come visit," he said as he walked back down the stairs.

He looked back up at me and smiled. I smiled back, then stood to climb the stairs, trying not to think about leaving my friends. Right now, I just needed to make sure that my family got to Chara safely.

Chapter Three

This dream is different; it's not the sweet place that I always go to, or even that dreadful nightmare. I'm standing next to a large white windmill in the middle of a field. In the distance, I can see a beautiful home, and there are beautiful flowers of every color throughout the field. I kneel down to get a closer look and see that the petals on the flowers are all different; some look like roses, others look like daisies…it's as if they coexist - but have no knowledge of one another.

Next to me, I find a flower more unique than the others. The petals are deep blue with emerald green tracing through the center, and the colors are separate - yet one. I stare in awe as I look across at the other flowers and they begin to sway with a breeze that brushes through the field.

I stand slowly, wanting to explore, when all at once I feel a pull from behind me – the same way I feel when I touch one of my images. I feel a rush of love and excitement absorb me, then I look over my shoulder - and there behind me, my blue-eyed boy stands. As I look in his eyes, I can feel his disbelief. He steps closer to me and reaches his arms out, then I lose my focus and wake without warning.

I laid in my bed, trying to find my way back to my dream, but my effort was hopeless; the daylight peered through my open drapes. I sat up and grabbed my sketch pad out of the tote bag beside my bed, then turned to a clean sheet and began to sketch as quickly as I could; I was afraid my memory would leave me before I could call back the details. I sketched the beautiful field and the unique flowers, highlighting the most unique flower - the blue and green one - by making it larger than the others. I made a mental note to add the color later, hoping that I'd be able to find blue and green paint that would do justice to the colors in my dream.

My mind drifted to my blue-eyed boy. I wanted him to have a name, to hear his voice. Most of all, I wanted to find him. I decided to sketch his perfect face, and I almost felt normal as I gazed into the sketch that was coming to life. I did not want to wait two years to find him.

I could hear my sister and mother giggling in the bathroom next to my room, so I placed my sketch book in my tote bag and pulled my robe on as I walked to the bathroom.

"What's so funny this early in the morning?" I asked.

"Look at this bathing suit I found for Libby," Mom answered.

It was bright yellow with a big smiley face on the front and a sad face on the back.

"It makes sense: happy to see you come, sad to see ya go," I said, teasing Libby.

"I thought it was perfect when I saw it," my mother said, looking me over and sizing up my night of sleep.

"I get to go swimming today, Willow!" Libby said, excited.

"You do? Where?" I asked.

"I'm going over to Abby's grandmother's house again."

"So, I assume you're still going to the lake with everyone today?" Mom asked.

I nodded, remembering that this would be the last day I would be with them for a while.

"I told everyone that I talked to that we were just taking a trip to Paris to see the school and look for a place; they think we'll be back in a few weeks," my mother explained

I looked down at Libby, trying to judge her response to my mom's words.

"Libby is very excited about our trip," Mom said. As she finished pulling her hair back into a pony tail, Libby smiled up at me, then left the bathroom and went to her room to get her sandals.

"Willow, I promise...we did not keep this from you to be spiteful; we have always had your best interests in mind."

I didn't show any expression on my face; the whole thing had left me confused and exhausted. Libby charged back into the bathroom, dancing in place while waiting for my mother.

"Come here, munchkin, give me a hug. I love you. Have lots of fun today," I said, looking down at Libby.

Libby wrapped her arms around my waist. "Miss you," she whispered.

Mom kissed me goodbye, then I turned and went back into my room and closed the door behind me. All I wanted to do was go back to sleep, but I knew I'd have to find a way to wear myself down in order for that to happen. I went to my closet and pulled out a few luggage bags, then rushed around my room, going through all of my stuff and deciding what could stay for now. No matter how much I tried, I couldn't stop thinking about those blue eyes.

Monica called, saying she would be there around eleven instead of noon; we were going to pick up Hannah, Jessica, and Olivia. After packing my bags, I dressed for the lake, covering my burgundy bikini with a black sun dress. I was sure to get a dirty look from Monica when she picked me up - she hated it when I wore dark colors.

My father's study is by the front door, and I could feel him in there as I climbed down the stairs; he felt nervous. At first, I didn't realize he was on the phone, but as I landed on the bottom step I heard him say, "I agree, we will take those precautions. I will head out first thing in the morning."

I walked to his study, wondering what had upset him. When he saw me, he said, "OK, Ashten, I have to go; Willow is on her way out for the day…yeah…no…OK… tomorrow."

Dad hung up the phone and smiled at me; he was nervous and trying to hide it.

"What's going on?"

"Nothing…um, we're just going to alter our story a little bit."

"Why?"

"It's nothing …I'm going to leave in the morning and tell everyone that I'm going to Washington to help an old colleague…then we'll tell them that you guys are going to wait for me in New York."

"Why? Where are we leaving from anyway?"

"We're going to leave from Montana…look, Willow, we're about to disappear…we kind of need to confuse our path so no one will worry…just don't be very conversational about what we're doing…just let them assume.

I grinned from ear to ear. I have never been very conversational; I liked being mysterious.

"Yeah…that shouldn't be too hard for you," he commented.

Hearing Monica honk her horn outside, I pulled my big, dark sunglasses over my eyes and smiled at my dad.

"Let the mystery begin," I said. When he hugged me goodbye, he seemed to ease up on his mood, but he was still nervous.

Monica was shaking her head at me as I climbed into her car. She loved to wear vibrant colors, and today she was wearing a bright yellow dress and make up…she must really like this new guy, Drake.

"Ya, know we're going to the lake - not a funeral," she commented.

"Would you like me to stay here?"

"Yeah, right, this is your last day here; you're not sulking alone. I knew you were good, but Paris – geeze, I bet you never come back from there."

I was glad I was wearing my sunglasses; they had never seen me cry, and I didn't want them to start now. I would miss Monica. I would miss all of them.

We picked up Hannah and Olivia first. Olivia climbed in the back seat with a huge book in her hand. I smiled at her. Monica and Hannah looked at each other and rolled their eyes. Secretly, Olivia and I loved to drive them crazy by being unconventional.

We picked up Jessica next. I could feel how sad she was as she walked toward the car. I stepped out to hug her, and she was taken back for a moment; I wasn't really a hugger.

"Can we please cry later? We're burning daylight here," Monica yelled through the window.

The lake was only thirty minutes from Jessica's house. Once we were on the highway, Monica turned down the radio and said, "OK, ladies, I really think this new guy is the one." Everyone laughed out loud.

"Stop! I'm serious - wait until you meet him. He, like, has a magnetic force of his own," Monica continued.

I could feel that she was serious, but there was no way Olivia, Hannah, or Jessica would be convinced she was sincere.

Monica pulled up in front of one the trucks that lined the shore line, and I could see Josh and Chase unloading their jet skies. Everyone but Olivia and I rushed to claim a spot on one of the tailgates. I leaned on the side of the car and watched all my friends, trying to burn the memory of their faces and emotions inside me. Olivia leaned up against the car beside me and opened her book to a marked page.

"Good book?" I mocked

"It's better than those three," she said, shaking her head. "It's going to be a blast when you're gone."

"What do you want me to do, stuff you in my suitcase?" I said, halfway considering asking my father if that were a possibility.

Just then, a rather large, very nice red Jeep pulled up to where the other trucks were parked. Chase jumped on the bed of his truck, waving the Jeep in.

"That must be the new guy. Looks like he has money - as well as being attractive," Olivia commented.

I did not answer her, simply because I was perplexed. I could not feel a single thing coming from the Jeep. It was a void, like it was driving itself. I could feel the excitement coming from my friends as they waited for him to park and get out. I squinted my eyes to get a closer look.

I drew a short breath; as he stepped out of his jeep and sunlight hit his face, he was extremely attractive, tall, and lean built. His dark brown hair was swooshed back out of his face, and his eyes were coal black. His best feature was his dominant profile.

Drake walked over to Josh and Chase, and Monica peeked through the cab of the truck where she was to gauge my expression. I quickly changed it from perplexed to boredom. She then smiled and turned forward, stretching out and posing as Drake got closer to her. Through my dark glasses, I followed Drake as he walked, checking with my senses each person that he passed; with him, it was empty.

"What do you suppose he did to his arm?" Olivia asked.

I had not noticed the brace on his right arm; it was very white against his tan skin. He was wearing a black sleeveless shirt and white swim trunks. "Come on, let's go watch Monica make a fool of herself," Olivia murmured.

"No, I want to stay here."

"What's wrong?"

"Nothing, I just…I don't know." My stomach was tying itself in knots; I had never felt so uneasy around anyone.

"OK…I can look mysterious, too," Olivia said as she pulled down her sunglasses, opening her book again.

Chase and Josh were very different from Dane; they were teenage boys who were only interested in one thing. I had managed to dodge Chase's annoying emotions throughout high school. When Dane was around, Chase behaved, but when he wasn't Chase took every opportunity to annoy me, so I would have to suffer until Dane got there.

Chase stood on his tailgate, looked me up and down, and yelled in my direction, "Willow, baby, would you like to join us sometime today?"

I was glad I couldn't read minds; his was sure to make me sick to my stomach. Olivia rolled her eyes and threw her book through the open window of the car; she knew she'd have to play Dane's part until he got there.

"So, have you talked to Dane since they told you that you were leaving?" Olivia asked.

"Yeah, he'll be alright - and so will you," I said, still staring at Drake, trying to figure out why he was blank.

"Come on, one day you might miss being annoyed by Chase," Olivia said, pulling my arm toward the others.

I could feel how excited Chase was; he whispered something to Drake as I walked closer. Drake just stared at me as if the others had disappeared, and I felt my heart beating through my chest. The gift that had brought me so much grief was instantly missed around this Drake guy; I felt blind.

"Baby, this is Drake," Chase said as he put his arm around me.

I pulled my sunglasses on top of my head so Chase would get the full effect of my glare. I heard the girls giggle; Chase let his arm drop and looked at Drake.

"I told you she was feisty, didn't I?" Chase said to Drake.

Drake walked over to me, and I questioned his every step. He stopped inches from me and stared into my eyes. Monica was right; he was magnetic - though I didn't find it appealing the same way she did.

"The good doctor's daughter; we meet at last," he said smoothly, still staring at me.

"Seems you aren't having any trouble making friends here," I said blankly.

He didn't say anything; he just stared at me with his dark eyes, pulling me in, and smiling confidently.

"Now, that's a new approach…I don't think any of us have ever tried staring her down," Chase said sarcastically.

Everyone laughed out loud. I took advantage of the distraction and broke eye contact, then slid by him onto the tailgate next to Monica and Jessica.

Josh called Drake and Chase out to the jet skis; Drake looked back at me as he walked away, smiling cunningly.

"When do you leave again?" Monica asked, teasing me.

I rolled my eyes and pulled my sunglasses down.

Monica hopped down and walked over to where Drake was. I could feel how flirtatious she was; it seemed that she wasn't joking, that she really liked this guy. Monica managed to talk Drake into taking her out on the jet ski, and I felt a relief as I watched them in the distance, but this guy had really werided me out; the further away from me he was the better.

I leaned back next to Jessica, who was lost in a magazine article. "Hey...when did you get that done?" she asked. Out of the corner of her eye, she had spotted my star inside my Ankh.

"The other day. It's no big deal; I went alone," I said, avoiding details.

Jessica was hurt; she was the one who'd convinced me to get a tattoo in the first place. She saw it as a breakthrough in our friendship. The last thing I wanted to think about, though, was how it got there; instead I lay down and drifted into a peaceful afternoon nap as the sun warmed my face.

Dreaming always came quickly to me. I opened my eyes in the field again. This time, I was closer to the beautiful home that I'd seen in the distance last night. I say home because it felt like my home, only I had never been there before. The home was a rustic red brick with white porches that wrapped around both levels of the house. There were beautiful plants hanging on the wide porch, just as beautiful as the ones in the field. I could feel a warm breeze flow through my hair, and I smelled the sweet flowers.

When I reached the porch, I followed it around to see where it led, and as I went to turn around the side of the house, I was stopped. Just inches in front of me, he was there - again. As I looked into his eyes, I lost all feeling; they were so blue, so mesmerizing. He was smiling down at me, staring, questioning why I was there, then he slowly moved closer to me, searching every part of my face. Next, he focused on my smile, and hesitating slightly - he leaned closer and gently touched his perfect lips to mine. Though the heat of his body was absent, I felt myself melt from the inside out. My head spun wildly, and I reached my arms around him though we had seen each other every night, this was our first kiss - and it seemed so overdue. I wanted him to be more real, and my only hope was that I would stay asleep there in the dream with him. That hope was lost, though, when I heard someone say my name, waking me.

Dazed from our kiss, I pulled myself up, and pushed my sunglasses to my head.

"Willow, I said what's your sign? I want to read your horoscope," Jessica asked, shaking the magazine she'd been reading. I didn't answer; her words were lost in the background. I deeply considered going home and trying to fall asleep again.

"Fine, then I'll just look," she said.

"Scorpio," I heard a smooth deep voice say. I looked to the void from where it had come, and I saw Drake. He was right - but how did he guess that?

"Is that right?" Jessica asked, still trying to find my birthday in one of the signs.

I didn't answer her; I was staring at Drake.

"How did you know that?" I asked him coldly.

He smiled at me and walked to where I was sitting. He hesitated in front of me, then reached for my face, cradling it in his hand and tracing the base of my eyes with his thumb. His touch moved me, literally; I felt my skin hum under his. My stomach dropped…I had felt that way before - it was just before that evil person had burned me in my dream. I held in the breath that wanted to escape.

"Only a Scorpio could have those eyes," Drake said, just loud enough for those closest to me to hear.

I felt Monica's jealously rise, as well as the shock coming from the others. I looked at his arm, expecting to see a tattoo of a dragon, but I only found the cast that Olivia had spotted earlier. I looked back into his eyes, and he winked at me, turned, and walked toward the lake. Chase followed him, astonished.

"OK so that was weird," Jessica said, closing the magazine and losing interest in looking up anyone's horoscope.

I sat stunned, trying to remember a single time that I'd seen the figure's face in my nightmare. I had always imagined it as a gruesome devilish person, not tall, handsome, and human. Then I realized that I'd never felt the emotion of the figure either. If this were the guy in my nightmares, would that not make him the kid that was looking for me? I shook my head silently, arguing with myself. If that were him, he would not hang out at a lake; he would have, like, tried to kidnap me or something.

I sighed deeply and hoped my imagination was running away with me. I then looked out to the water's edge and saw Drake smiling seductively at me. Monica saw the exchange and stepped in front of me, blocking my view.

"Let's get the coolers out; they're going to start the fire soon," she said.

I managed to avoid Drake for the last two hours, though I could feel his eyes follow me as I helped Jessica and Hannah pack the coolers back up. I sat down on the opposite side of the fire from him. Every once in a while, I would glance in his direction - only to find him staring at me through the flames. They seemed to accent his perfect features, and I didn't see how he could be this evil person that my father had feared…he just looked too perfect.

"So, are you ready for Paris?" Josh asked me, settling next to Jessica, who was beside me.

I shrugged my shoulders, not wanting the attention.

"Paris…" Drake said, leaning forward and taking the opening in the conversation. "That's a big step. Are you sure you're ready?" he continued, winking at me with a seductive smile on his face.

"I've been 'ready' for this for a while now," I responded in a chilly tone.

"I doubt that, love…Paris…Paris is a whole other world. All the rules are different," Drake said, brushing his dark brown hair out of his face and leaning back again, trying to pull me across the fire with a stare that would halt anyone. It was as if we were having a coded conversation all our own; Olivia looked back and forth between me and Drake, knowing that she was missing something.

Josh threw a football at Drake."Come on, man, let's play," Josh said.

Drake stood slowly, smiling at me through the flames. A lump settled in my throat. I wanted to go home, so I decided that as soon as Dane came, I would get him to take me.

I listened half-heartedly as Hannah and Jessica reminisced over the stupid things that we'd done in our childhood. I went to take a drink of my water, only to find it empty. I then reached behind me and found the cooler empty, too.

"I think there's some water in the cooler I put in the trunk," Monica said.

I nodded and stood, my legs a little wobbly from having fallen asleep. I hadn't realized how warm the fire was until I stepped out into the darkness around it and found the night air cooler than usual. Trying to focus my eyes, I made my way to Monica's car. Once I arrived, I had to open the car door to pop the trunk. When I raised up and closed the door, Drake was there; it was like he had appeared out of the darkness.

"Going somewhere?" he asked smoothly, stepping forward and smiling adoringly.

I felt my heartbeat rise in my ears as I tried not to be pulled in by his eyes.

"Just getting some water; go play your game," I remarked.

He laughed under his breath, reached his hand out, and ran his fingers under my eye. The warm sensation knocked the wind out of me; the feeling was beyond comprehension.

"I don't want to play games…I want you," he said, cradling my face.

The more he touched me, the more the sensation rushed through me; it was so hypnotizing, I closed my eyes. I felt his arm go around my waist, then he pulled me closer, and everything started spinning slowly as he leaned his forehead to mine.

"Now, let me see your eyes…I went so long without them," he whispered.

I tried to focus on the reality in front of me. No matter how good everything felt, he was bad – and I knew in the back of my mind that his touch could turn to fire. I slowly opened my eyes.

"Our time has come; you belong to me," he said in a whisper, staring inside of me.

I felt a fire rise in my heart. Nothing had ever felt more wrong in my life. I pushed him back as headlights flashed across us.

"Don't make this hard," Drake said, laughing carelessly.

I felt Dane; those were his headlights. He had seen Drake's arms around me - and me pushing him off.

"What's going on here?" Dane shouted as he slammed his truck door closed with more fury than I'd ever felt from him before. The others heard him and started making their way to Monica's car.

"Ahhh…does he think he's your little boyfriend?" Drake said, looking harshly at Dane.

"Yeah – he does," Dane said fiercely.

Drake laughed out loud and wrapped his arm around me, and I felt the warmth of his touch paralyze me. Dane then charged forward and pushed Drake back, freeing me. Drake caught his balance and stepped forward to charge Dane, but Dane was already stepping forward to charge Drake again. Josh and Chase jumped in the middle of them, Josh holding Dane back while Chase stood in front of Drake.

"Look man!" Josh screamed at Dane, trying to get him to look at him. "I know you're upset about Willow leaving, but that doesn't mean you need to take it out on strangers," he said, using all his force to hold Dane back.

"Dane! – Dane!" I yelled. "Take me home – Dane, do you hear me?"

Dane finally stopped pushing against Josh and held his hands up to show that he was done. Josh let go, and Dane reached for me. I ran to his side, and he wrapped his arm around me and briskly walked me to his truck. He then opened the driver side door and helped me in. Olivia ran and jumped in the passenger side.

When Dane turned his lights on and turned to leave, I locked eyes with Drake; he looked unshaken by the whole event.

"Did he hurt you?" Dane asked, still furious. I shook my head 'no,' still stunned.

"I'm staying at your house tonight," Olivia announced, holding on as Dane peeled onto the highway.

"Was that the new guy that's staying at Chase's?" Dane asked.

"Yeah, Drake," I said

"I'm glad I got here when I did," Dane said through his teeth.

"What did I miss?" Olivia asked, confused.

"Nothing…he just tried to make a move, no big deal," I said, dreading telling my father that Drake was there.

"I don't know where that guy is from, but he needs to learn his boundaries," Dane said, turning up the radio.

When we got to my house, Dane walked quickly inside. Once there, he climbed the front steps two at a time.

"Where are you going?" I called after him.

"To make sure your windows are locked," he said over his shoulder.

My father stepped out of his study and looked up at Dane, then down at me.

"I'm going to go call my Aunt," Olivia said, following Dane.

"What's going on?" my father asked, confused.

"Is that kid's name 'Drake?'" I asked.

The fear that spiked in my father told me that it was. He pulled me into his study and closed the door.

"Did you see him?" he asked me, panicked.

"Yeah, he's been at the lake with me all day," I answered, trying not to lose my calm.

"Did he try anything?" Dad asked.

"He had just gotten me alone when Dane showed up…he's not what I imagined," I said, looking confused.

"Don't underestimate him, Willow," my father said sternly.

"What are we supposed to do now?" I asked

"I'm going to see if I can move our flights up," he answered, still panicking.

He went to his phone and started dialing. I paced back and forth, more scared and confused than I'd ever been; Drake had made everything a reality. Dane knocked on the study door, and when I opened it I saw he was finally calm, he must have felt that I was safe now.

"Did you tell him?" Dane whispered. I nodded.

We listened as my father went back and forth with an operator, then he hung up the phone, questioning himself.

"Dane, can you stay here until tomorrow morning?" my father asked.

Dane nodded, a little surprised by the question.

"I've managed to move my flight to an hour from now, but I can't get theirs any earlier than 9 a.m. I just don't want to leave them alone if Willow is shaken up."

"That's fine. I'll call my mom," Dane said, walking to the phone.

I motioned for my dad to come into the hallway, and he moved quickly.

"Dad what's the deal? Why are we still flying all over the place? Let's just go."

"First of all, we have to leave a believable paper trail for the people here. Second of all, we can't pass through the string now. When Ashten called, he said the others were separated from him in the storm," my father said.

"Are they hurt? Lost?" I asked.

"No, they know what they're doing. Ashten is sure they'll be here soon. He said Drake only uses the large passages; that is why he didn't try anything…he has a different plan to get you to come with him," my father answered.

"Like what?" I asked

"I don't know, but we're not going to stay around here and allow him to do it. Do you think Dane can keep you safe?" he asked.

I looked back and saw Dane hanging up the phone.

"He did a good job tonight," I said, still not believing that Dane was capable of being so angry.

My father nodded, "OK, I'm going to tell your mother; make sure you're packed and ready," he said, feeling surer of himself.

I hugged him and climbed the stairs, but not before looking back at him, afraid that I might lose someone in all of this. About the time I reached the top of the stairs, I felt my mother's emotion shift to panic - and I knew my father had told her what was going on. In my room, Dane pushed my bed to the wall with the window on it, then he stretched out on it with heavy eyelids. Olivia was pulling out the futon couch, which was big enough for the both of us.

I went to my closet and pulled out the bags that I'd been packing to make sure I had everything.

"Do you need help?" Olivia whispered, trying not wake Dane, who had drifted to sleep.

"No, I think I have everything. I'm going to take a quick shower," I answered.

She nodded, opened her book, and stretched out.

As I stood under the scalding water in the shower, I replayed the past few days; if I'd known what Drake had looked like, I don't think those nightmares would have been nearly as bad. I regretted not just asking him what he wanted with me, then I laughed at myself as I realized that I was considering having a sane conversation with someone so dark.

Then it hit me: if Drake were real, then the blue-eyed boy was, too. My eyes raced back and forth as I tried to think of a way to find him; I was afraid my father would make me wait another two years - or at least until after we'd solved this Drake issue. I turned off the water, a little excited about going to sleep. The memory of our first kiss brought heat to my already hot face. I dressed quickly, packing my stuff as I went. There was a soft tap on the door, and I felt my mother on the other side. I pulled the door open and let her in.

"Are you alright?" she asked, looking me over. I nodded.

"I have Libby all packed up," she said, leaning against the counter.

"You're ready, aren't you?" I said, smiling and feeling her excitement.

"I've just daydreamed about this for so long," she said, looking me over.

"I guess it's my fault you had to stay here…" I said under my breath.

"No, no, it's no one's fault," she said, then paused, remembering that I'd seen Drake. "What was he like? I mean, is he, like, this evil-looking man?" she asked, filling with curiosity.

I shook my head no. "Actually, he is very good looking," I answered.

My mother hesitated again, searching for words. "What did he feel like?" she finally asked.

I froze for a second; I was not used to being open with anyone about feeling emotions."I couldn't feel him," I said, remembering what I could feel: his touch.

"I don't understand," she said, standing up.

"He was just a void… he's the first person I've ever met like that," I said as I grabbed my bag, not wanting to talk about it.

She sensed it and nodded. "I'll see you in the morning," she said in a whisper when I opened the door.

Olivia had fallen asleep with her book open across her chest, and Dane was in a deep sleep. I tiptoed into my room, put all my things together, then set them in the hall. When I sat my tote on the top of the pile, my sketch book fell out; laying on top and staring at me was the sketch that I' d made of the blue-eyed boy. I stared down at it for a moment before picking it up…I just wanted to talk to him. I tore a page from the back of the book and pulled a pen out, then I walked back in my room and sat on the edge of the futon bed. With shaking hands, I wrote, *I need you – help me find you.*

I lay down and stared at the note that I'd written. My plan was to focus on him and the words and hope that I could somehow take it with me. I didn't let any bad thoughts race through my mind, only him as my eyes felt heavier and heavier.

Feeling sunlight on my face, I opened my eyes and saw the house in front of me. I felt adrenaline rush through me as I realized I would see him. I looked down in my hand and saw that my note was there. I then ran to the porch and circled it, but he wasn't there. I went through the house, not focusing on any details. Searching every room, I found the place empty. My heart felt heavy as each moment passed; I did not know how much longer I could stay asleep. I went back outside and searched the fields, trying to see if I could feel him – and in the distance, I was sure I did. I walked through the field toward a small hill top. He was getting closer, so I started sprinting in his direction. All at once, I saw him coming over the hill. He was surprised to see me. I crashed into his chest and hugged him, then slid my hand down into his and handed him my note. He started to pull it open, then I heard a loud crash and jumped to my feet.

Olivia had knocked over my bedside lamp while she was folding up some blankets.

"Sorry," she said in a loud whisper, "I didn't mean to scare you."

I looked down to see my hand empty; the note wasn't there. Did it work? Was that real? I looked and saw Dane still sound asleep on the bed.

"Your mom came in here; you have to leave in an hour," Olivia said, pushing the bed into a couch. I could feel how sad she was. I shook my head and tried to come to my senses, then I grabbed a change of clothes and went to the bathroom to dress quickly. I convinced myself he'd read it and that the next time I slept he would tell me where he was. Then I would make my dad take me to him - and if he refused, I would find another traveler, they couldn't be that hard to convince.

I heard the front door open and felt Jessica, Hannah, and Monica climbing the stairs. I met them in the hall. They were so sad and full of dread. I led them into my room. I didn't have much time, and I wanted to make sure I wasn't leaving anything behind. When they saw Dane asleep on my bed, I felt embarrassment come from everyone but Monica; she found it funny.

"So I guess you were serious when you told Drake she was your girlfriend?" Monica said loudly, falling onto the bed next to him.

Dane sat up quickly and surveyed the room, replaying the last words he'd heard. He then rolled his eyes, slid by Monica off the bed, stretched, and smiled at me.

"I need a quick shower," he said to me as he left the room. A stunned feeling came over everyone but Olivia.

"So, are you guys serious?" Jessica asked, awestruck, not believing she'd missed something.

Olivia belted out into laughter; she knew how absurd that comment was.

"I bet they are," Monica said in a teasing manner. "This whole time, Willow's been playing the innocent one - and then the day she leaves, the truth comes out."

As I listened to her, I shook my head and scanned the room for anything else I may want to take with me.

"Hey, Drake said to tell you he was sorry," Monica said in a more serious tone.

I looked at her quickly. "For…?" I asked.

"He said he must have scared you, but he was only trying to carry the cooler to the fire for you," Monica said, believing every word she said. I rolled my eyes.

"He's not that bad of a guy. He invited us all to go to Florida with him. He has this huge boat, and he said we could go out on the ocean," she continued.

"Tell me you aren't seriously considering going off with some guy you just met?" I said harshly.

My words shamed Monica, and she looked down as the room grew silent.

"We're all leaving for school in a few weeks, it would be nice to go to the beach first," Hannah said, defending Monica.

"Promise me you won't go anywhere with Drake," I said, feeling a growing sense of dread within me.

Hannah looked at Monica."We can still go to the beach, but Willow's right: we don't need to go off with a guy we just met."

Monica looked down, trying not to show how annoyed she was with us. Hannah looked back at me and smiled.

"We got you something," Jessica said, breaking the tension. She handed me a black bag with burgundy tissue paper. I was sure she was the one who'd wrapped it; if it were up to Monica, it would have been hot pink. I sat next to Olivia on my bed and pulled the ribbons on the bag.

"We've all been working on it since graduation. We were going to give it to you last night, but you left so fast," Jessica said, proud of herself.

Inside was a large photo album, and on the front of it was an abstract painting of the five of us that Jessica had done. The photos started when we were all in diapers, and they went all the way through graduation night. The album was full of birthdays and summers; everything we had ever shared. I smiled as the flashbacks flew through my memory.

"I could not have asked for a better gift; this means the world to me... I will cherish it forever."

"Just don't forget us when you're famous – deal?" Jessica said. I nodded, then stood, pulled all of them together, and hugged them.

When Dane was through in the shower, he loaded my mother's car with our luggage and drove us to the airport. He even went in with us, not leaving until we reached the security gates. My mother and Libby walked on, giving us a chance to say goodbye. I stared forward at the gate, then back at Dane; I was so scared.

"You can't be afraid of the next step, Willow; we all have to grow," Dane said.

I looked up at him and smirked. "That's pretty deep," I teased.

"Maybe one day, I will listen to my own advice," Dane said, laughing at himself.

"You will," I promised.

Holding back my tears, I reached up and hugged him. I didn't understand why growing had to hurt so badly. After I let go of him, I kept my eyes down, and I could feel his sorrow; it was tearing me apart…I never saw my life without Dane in it. I walked away, waving behind me.

Chapter Four

The flight was close to two hours long, so I decided to try and fall asleep; after all, I wanted to know if the blue--eyed boy had read my note. As my eyes fell shut, I rehearsed the speech I was going to give my father about finding him.

I didn't find my way to that beautiful world or to the horrible nightmare; instead all I saw was a blue moon, which was full and filled the entire sky. I gazed at its detail and felt the energy that came from it. Slowly, it started to rise. In the gleam of blue light, I saw Drake to my right, and to my left I saw the man I was searching for. The dream was surreal - then all of sudden, the landing gear hit the ground, and I awoke quickly.

Libby had fallen asleep, too, so I carried her through the airport and cradled her as my mother rented us a car. My mother drove through the last hours of daylight, then I took over at nightfall. As I drove, I searched the sky, looking for the moon and wondering what the dream could have meant.

My mother took over again at daybreak; since she had been to Ashten's home before and knew the way, she would need to drive when we got closer. I gladly closed my eyes, hoping I'd find my direction from the one I was about to seek.

The weight that I always felt on my chest was immediate. My sense of emotion was taken from me again, and this time the people around me could see me; they stared in my direction. The room I was in was more beautiful than any other room I had visited in these nightmares. The ceilings were high, and the walls were decorated with beautiful paintings; for some reason, though, I could not focus on the images that they reflected. There was no furniture in this room. The floor was a red velvet carpet, and doors that stretched from the floor to the ceiling were centered on every wall. One of them led outside, into sunlight. Women were lining the walls, dressed in royal colors for a formal occasion; others made adjustments to what I was wearing. They had dressed me in a gown, much like a wedding dress, with lace and flowers woven into the design.

The wooden doors in front of me opened, and I could feel someone. Whoever it was was not afraid like the ones I always felt here; instead, they were happy. My heart beat grew louder as I gasped for breath under the pressure on my chest; I wanted badly to wake, to help whoever needed me and leave. Through the doorway, I could hear whispering.

A beautiful woman of age with mesmerizing green eyes glided over to me. Her hair was placed perfectly on her head, and jewels decorated her neck. When she reached me, the ones around me scurried away. She took my hand, and as her skin touched mine, the room vanished and I was surrounded by a white glow. In this moment, the weight on my chest was released. The woman smiled at me, as the relief was apparent on my face. I could feel her intensely now. She was compassionate, and it was as if she loved me.

"You know you have been quite difficult to find, my dear," she said in a motherly tone.

"Who are you?" I asked softly.

She circled me, smiling proudly, her green eyes sparkling.

"I'm Perodine…you have known me from your first heartbeat."

"What do you want?" I asked, nervously, looking around.

"My dear, I want you. I have waited well over four million years to see you this way."

"What? Why?" I asked, trying to understand.

Perodine had stopped in front of me and was beaming with excitement.

"You are very gifted, my dear, and I have loved very few..." she tilted her head, placed her hands on my shoulders, and captured my gaze. "I have loved you...you must listen to me: your heart is the power - the one who sees must have it."

"Why do you take my gift? Why do you bring me pain?" I asked, shaking my head and looking for clarity.

"It has never been my intention to bring you pain. I have protected you, given you the power."

"I don't understand," I said, trembling.

"I cannot undo what was once said - when the Blue Moon rises, you will choose again."

"Choose what?" I asked, panicked.

Perodine went to speak, and as she did, I could feel pain through her. With her eyes closed, and she breathed in and said in a hushed voice, "Our time now is over."

The room flashed back, and the others in the room gasped. The pain on my chest intensified, and I gasped for breath, trying to focus on the room. Perodine was taken away by men in long black robes; she glanced over her shoulder at me, and it was as if she could feel my pain.

I could feel someone's warm breath on my neck, then a mesmerizing hum swarmed every part of my body as their lips touched my skin. I turned and saw Drake, who then smiled and wrapped his arm around me, paralyzing any response I could have tried to make.

"They are waiting," Drake said, smiling adoringly.

The glass doors opened, the roar of a crowd erupted, and I walked unwittingly with Drake to the balcony. The sky was a beautiful blue, and the sunlight warmed my face. The crowd grew louder as they saw us standing side by side, and looking down I saw a sea of color surrounding the people who cheered below.

My eyes peered up at Drake, watching his coal black eyes smile at me. He was pulling me in, trapping my gaze, and my willpower was losing a battle that any other girl would have lost the first time that she saw him. Then, above the crowd, I heard the sweetest voice.

"Willow..."

I turned to look back in the room and saw Libby standing there. I could not feel her, but I could see the fear in her eyes. Not hesitating, I ran to where she was, but she vanished before my eyes, the roar of the crowd grew silent, and the sky turned gray.

"You're mine," Drake said unsympathetically.

I turned back to where he was and raised my arms to block a light I was sure would come. As I moved my hand, I saw that my wrist was bare and that the Ankh was gone. I fell to my knees, gasping as I tried to understand why it was gone. Drake smiled down at me, enjoying my agony. As chants echoed against the walls, I closed my eyes and found the image of the one who always made me feel safe: my blue eyes. The room shook, and the paintings crashed to the floor. The noise shocked my body, causing me to wake with a scream. My mother was so frightened, she veered off the road.

"Willow - what? Are you OK?" she was yelling at me.

I felt my eyes focus as I looked down at my wrist: the tattoo of the Ankh and one lonely star was still there. I was safe - at least for now.

"Just a bad dream; I'm fine."

"We got you some breakfast – well, lunch. You were sleeping so soundly that I didn't want to wake you...I wish that I had now."

"How far are we?" I asked, looking at the secluded highway.

"Only an hour. Are you sure you're OK."

"Yeah, Mom; just a dream," I shuddered as it flashed into my memory.

As I calmed down, my eyes raced over the dream. This was bigger than me, and I knew then that I was going to make my father let me find the blue--eyed boy. I didn't care how old I was,

I didn't want to choose anything on my own. I sat back slowly and turned my head to see Libby sleeping soundly in her seat. I watched her chest slowly rise and fall, assuring myself that she wasn't having a nightmare. Looking at her, I knew that she was a part of this, too - and I had to protect her.

My mother turned off onto a small road, where a beautiful mountain played the role of a breathtaking background. We then turned off onto a less traveled path. Without warning, a beautiful massive log home nestled next to a breathtaking river came into view. I could feel the excitement and relief coming from the two people on the porch of the cabin. As we got closer, I could see my father standing next to an attractive man whom I assumed was Ashten. He was smiling and patting my father on the back; strangely, he looked familiar to me. I woke Libby up as we stopped. My mother was already in my father's arms, and Libby and I followed her lead. When we got to the porch, my father introduced Libby and me to his lifelong friend, Ashten Chambers.

"Jason, your girls are beautiful. You're a lucky man," Ashten said, looking curiously in my eyes, then to my father.

I could feel an overwhelming anxiety and anticipation coming from them. My father told us that the others should be there soon. He then escorted us into the beautiful cabin.

The entire front room, from floor to ceiling, was made of a glossy wood. The ceiling was angled into an A- frame with wide beams that stretched across the room. All the furniture seemed to complement the mountain setting, and the smell of pine lingered in the air. I unloaded my tote on the counter and picked up Libby's bag to carry it upstairs.

Libby and I found our rooms. The cabin had six bedrooms, so Libby got her own room, which made her happy. I brushed her hair and listened to her tell me of all the fun she was going to have in her new home. My mother had told her that we would have to travel very far before we could reach our new house and that all her new friends would be there. I decided to take a hot shower; all the traveling had given me jet lag, but the last thing I wanted to do was close my eyes again. When I got back to my room and started to dress, I could not find my brush anywhere. Libby then walked in and handed it to me - and I stood stunned, holding it… Libby did not often go out of her way to help me out since she was used to us taking care of her.

"I couldn't find your sandals," she said sadly.

"Why were you looking for them?" I asked.

She looked at me as if I'd lost my mind, "cause you told me you needed your brush and asked if I had your sandals."

"When did I say that?" I asked, shaking my head to make sure I wasn't going crazy.

I could feel frustration coming from her. "Just now. Mom wants you to come downstairs," she said, crossing her little arms.

My mother topped the stairs, looked in my direction and said, "Willow, can you please come downstairs?"

Wide-eyed, I looked from my mother back to Libby - convinced I was now delusional.

"Mom, did you send Libby to tell me that?" I asked slowly.

Now she was looking at me as if I were crazy. Slowly, she shook her head no. I walked over to Libby, knelt down in front of her, and said, "Libby how did you know about the brush and Mom?"

I was making her angry. "You told me to get your brush. I heard Mom ask you to come downstairs."

I felt the shock come from my mother, but it couldn't compare to mine. It was like watching Libby take her first steps all over again. She had found her insight, but I knew she didn't understand it; she didn't even realize what she was doing.

"Hey, I'm sorry. I just forgot. I'm pretty tired from our trip; forgive me please," I said, straightening her shirt.

Libby hugged me tightly and said, "I guess it's OK that you're acting weird… just don't give me your coodies."

My mother turned on her heels and went downstairs in shock - and I followed quickly behind her. Ashten and my father were sitting on the couches in the center of the room, and their conversation halted when my father saw the look on my mother's face. She walked over to my dad and said in a low tone, “I think Libby has a gift, Jason.”

A surge of fear and denial came over my father and Ashten.

“What is it?” Ashten asked quickly.

My mother looked in my direction; I guess she thought it would sound more believable coming from me.

“It’s like she has a window in front of her; she can see what’s coming. Just now, she brought me my brush just as I began to look for it, and she told me Mom wanted me before Mom came upstairs. She doesn’t even know that she’s doing it,” I said.

My father looked warily back at Ashten, then forced a smile as he looked at the concern on my mother’s face.

“We just need to watch her. We can’t confuse her; the insight is just now showing itself. It could grow stronger or leave her all together if we provoke her to use it.” he said

I saw Ashten nod in agreement. I knew that they were right; I had to find my own way of understanding what I did. I think if I had known what it actually was, I would have feared it; instead, I grew to depend on it.

“Willow, I told your father that you had another nightmare,” my mother said, changing the subject. “Could you please tell us what it was about?”

I felt my stomach turn. “It was nothing,” I said, looking away.

“Was it the same as the other nightmares?” my father asked

I shook my head no. I hesitated, wanting to take on the emotion of it on my own, but then I felt his genuine concern. I began in a hushed tone, “I dreamed I was in a huge home, like a palace. Libby was there, and so was Drake. There was a large crowd that cheered as we stood side by side. It was just a product of the last few days; nothing to worry about.”

I could feel the fear coming from the three of them, just as I thought I would…if they only knew the rest.

“That will never happen. You’re going home to Chara, where you will always be safe,” my father said as he sat forward.

His words were soothing and gave my mother peace, but I could still feel the unrest coming from Ashten; it was like he knew something more. He kept his eyes low, avoiding mine, and guarding his emotions.

My mother shook off the conversation, then went to the kitchen and started unloading bags of food. My father looked at Ashten, then leaned back. The room grew tense. Gathering all my nerve, I looked at my dad.

"I need you to do something for me," I said in a shaky voice.

He looked up at me, afraid of my request.

"On the way home, I want you to help me find my soul mate," I said, feeling surer of myself.

I saw my mother freeze as she heard my words, and I felt a guilty sense of relief come over Ashten and my father.

"Willow, you're only eighteen," my father said in a tender tone. "I think you're just a little overwhelmed by what you've learned about Chara."

"Dad, it shouldn't matter how old I am; I need him," I said, growing angry.

My father shook his head in disbelief.

"Willow, you haven't even seen the string yet. What if the beacon is not there?" he asked

"He will tell me where to go. I dreamed of him…look, I can show you what he looks like," I said, walking to the counter to get the sketch out of my tote.

Ashten and my dad followed me over and watched as I turned the pages. I smiled when I flipped to the page he was on, then turned it so they could see. Shock hit Ashten, and he ran his fingers through his hair, turned away, and started pacing.

"Ashten, calm down," My father said, wide-eyed.

My mother circled the counter, took the sketch from me, and stared at it.

"Jason, I cannot do this," Ashten said through his teeth. He then walked briskly back to the couch, sat down, and leaned forward stiffly. "Do you have any idea how angry he's going to be?" he continued as dread filled him.

My eyes raced back between them, trying to understand what I'd triggered.

"This is just one part, Ashten," my father said, running his hands through his hair.

"Part of what?" I intervened.

Ashten stood and walked over to me.

"I want you to understand where I'm coming from," he said, trying to be polite.

My father stepped protectively in front of me.

"Jason," Ashten said, raising his hand to let my father know he meant no harm. "I've made mistakes," he continued looking at me. "I've overlooked a truth that lived before me, but my only intention was to protect my family."

"Protect your family," I repeated, then I realized why Ashten looked familiar to me: he had deep blue eyes, soft dimples, and was built just like the one in my dreams.

"He's...he's your son. What are you protecting him from - me?" I asked as my cheeks filled with heat. I was so angry, I couldn't feel the emotions of the room. My head began to spin, and I felt sick to my stomach, betrayed.

"Not from you," Ashten said, realizing I didn't understand.

My father stepped in front of me and put his hands on my shoulders. "Willow, I need you to calm down – you'll faint if you don't," he said, trying to catch my eyes.

I gently pulled his hands off me. I was in a daze, trying to understand how close the dream really was.

"Tell me his name," I said, focusing on Ashten again.

"Landen...Landen Chambers," he answered, looking away.

"Willow, sit down; we need to talk about this," my father said, reaching for my arm.

I stepped back, dodging his touch. I then raised my hands and started to say something, but I was too angry. I took two steps back, then walked to the door; I wanted to be alone. I opened and slammed it behind me as hard as I could – and no one dared follow me.

The daylight was leaving, and the stars could be seen above the light blue sky. There was a river that ran behind the cabin, and I walked down to it in a daze. Once there, I followed its path until I reached a mound of large rocks. I then climbed up on them and listened to the aggressive river that rushed by.

I had come to the point in my life where everything I knew had changed: my nightmares had returned, I was told I was from another dimension, Drake had found me - and...Landen was real. I replayed my last dreams, the one of the Blue Moon with Landen and Drake beneath it, and then the one where Perodine had told me I would have to choose. If that were all that I had to choose, then I'd made this bigger than it really was. I couldn't understand how that could be so important.

Looking back at the cabin, I could see Libby sitting on a bed in the upstairs bedroom, coloring quietly. Her innocence touched my soul. She now had insight, a gift. I had seen her vanish in my nightmare. I was angry that my family was being pulled into the curse that was chasing me.

I was going to make sure that she made it home safely, and I hoped she wouldn't struggle the way I had. I wouldn't wish a single nightmare on her - or anyone, for that matter. As my eyes glassed over, I pulled my knees up to my chest and fought the urge to cry. My thoughts then flashed through all that I'd seen, and the voices of my memories overlapped, screaming at me...everything inside of me felt like it was falling apart.

I felt a gentle pull on me - the way I always felt when I helped one of my images - so I quickly looked up, thinking someone needed me. I stood slowly, stared into the darkness next to the river, and reached out with my sense of emotion. I felt a blanket of peaceful love with a sense of urgency, and the night air in front of me began to move; it looked like a wave gently swaying with a current. A thin light began to emerge, then Landen stepped through the wave. I felt the air leave my lungs and adrenaline rush through every part of my body.

"Landen..." I said in disbelief.

In the darkness, I could see his beautiful blue eyes widen, and I felt the disbelief coming from us both. We stepped quickly to one another... he reached for my face and pulled me to his lips, then he slowly put his arms around my waist and pulled me closer. I slid my hands up his chest and wrapped my arms around his shoulders.

We slowly parted, keeping our faces close, staring into one another's eyes.

"I found you," he said with the lips of an angel.

I smiled. He ran his thumb across the bottom of my eye, then he kissed my lips softly again before whispering, "I love you."

I smiled and lay my head on his chest.

"I love you," I said.

I felt him slowly turn and look at the cabin, then down at me. He raised my chin so I would have to look at him.

"Willow?" he said with disbelieving eyes. I nodded.

Anger came over him as he looked back at the cabin.

"What's wrong?" I asked, panicked, thinking I had done something wrong.

"You were here the whole time, and he kept me from here," Landen said.

I nodded, feeling his frustration.

"How did you come to me before?" he asked as confusion came over him.

"What do you mean? I dreamt - just like I always do," I said, confused.

Landen shook his head no. "I was not asleep…I thought it was real," he said, furrowing his eyebrows.

"How is that possible?" I whispered breathlessly as my heart began to race.

He looked down, then back up at me. "I do not know; I've never known anyone who has dreamed of the same place and person so vividly - every night," he said, searching my eyes.

"Neither have I," I said, trying to catch my breath.

"You have always been real to me," he said, pulling me closer to him.

"Have we always had one another?" I asked, feeling the sensation of relief sweep over me.

Landen smiled and kissed my forehead before he said, "Knowing that gives me some peace."

As we held each other tightly, I felt relief overcome him, and I finally realized that the one thing that I'd searched my whole life for had always belonged to me. I felt foolish for wasting so much of my life in worry. As the reality began to sink in, Landen looked at the cabin, then down at me. He then smiled and a tucked a loose lock of my hair behind my ear.

"I've been following my beacon for the last few days, but it kept moving."

"We were traveling here to meet your father," I said quietly, feeling all of my anguish melt away; I knew now that I was safe in his arms.

"What happened?" he asked as concern came over him.

"There's this guy, Drake, who wants me to come to his dimension with him," I said in a rush.

"Drake Blakeshire?" Landen asked, anger immediately overtaking him.

I nodded as his eyes widened, and I felt his urgency. He put his arm around me and started to walk in the direction of the wave from which he'd come. I looked over my shoulder to the cabin, where I could still see Libby; I wasn't going to leave her here.

"Wait…Libby, my sister…I can't leave her," I said, stopping.

Landen followed my eyes to the window where she was sitting. His anger fell, and compassion filled him.

"Let's get her, then we'll go," he said assertively.

"Our parents won't let us take her without them," I warned.

He smiled a shy smile as he said, "I finally found the missing part of me, so my father is not going to make decisions for me anymore." The love he felt for me rose inside him. "I should have listened to my soul," he said, pulling me closer.

We walked slowly to the cabin, neither of us knowing what reaction we'd receive. I focused on the emotions coming from the cabin; they were of regret, sorrow, and anticipation. I knew that they never meant to hurt us; Ashten meant it when he said that all he wanted to do was 'protect' his family, and I was a part of that family. I stopped Landen.

"Being angry didn't get me very far, and I can feel them; they're sorry for what they did. They had to have had their reasons, and we need to listen if we want to know them," I said, staring up at him.

He nodded, pulled me closer, and kissed the top of my head.

Chapter Five

Ashten was slowly pacing the living room floor, and my parents were leaning against the bar that separated the kitchen and the living room. My mother gasped when her eyes met mine, then they moved slowly to Landen's. I felt her overwhelming happiness, and without a word, she walked over to us and embraced us both. Landen shyly hugged her back, refusing to lose his hold on me. Standing behind my mother, my father reached his hand out to shake Landen's hand. His relief to see Landen at my side was more than obvious in his eyes; it was as if his watch over me had ended.

"I'm proud to meet you, son, I couldn't ask for a better person then you to love my daughter. Your father is an honorable man, and I'm sure that you are as well."

Ashten had stopped pacing and was staring at Landen with a deep sense of pride and sorrow emanating from him. He looked in his son's eyes and mouthed the words, "I'm sorry."

Landen nodded; I felt his respect for his father outweigh his anger. I tightened my grip on Landen, letting him know that he was doing the right thing by remaining calm. He looked down at me and smiled slightly.

"I have found her now – that's all that matters. We need to leave now," he said, looking back at his father.

Ashten stepped forward, cautiously. "Son, we have to take them all. Libby may have been the only one in the dream, but you know just as well as I do that he'll stop at nothing to get what he wants," he said, staring at the dread in Landen's eyes.

"What is he talking about? What dream?" I heard Landen say.

"I had a nightmare; Drake was there…Libby disappeared."

As he pulled me closer, I felt Landen's sense of urgency grow; he realized why I wanted Libby to go with me. Landen looked back to his father and said, "I will lead them both."

Ashten looked at my father; both of their expressions matched the confusion coming from them.

"Landen," my father said softly, "were you just speaking to Willow?"

Landen nodded; now the confusion was coming from me and him.

"Did she answer you?"

"Dad, of course I did…what's wrong with you guys?" I said.

"Are they always like this?" I heard Landen say.

My mother seemed to have figured out what was going on; meanwhile I was getting angry at the three of them.

"Landen, Willow, you're not using words," my father said in a tender tone.

My breath left me and my heart pounded in my ears as I tried to comprehend what they were saying. I felt Landen's emotions swarming out of control, blending with the awe, fear, and respect coming from our parents. There was no way that that was possible; I couldn't read minds - and I didn't want anyone to be able to read mine…it was private. I listened closely to see if I could hear Landen's thoughts, but I heard nothing. I closed my eyes. *"Landen, can you hear me?"*

"I can."

I looked up at him.

"Do you hear everything, or can you only hear me when I'm talking to you?"

"I guess when you're talking to me," he thought. As his eyes raced over my face, the connection, the love that we felt, seemed to overcome the initial shock.

"Do you think this is bad? I mean, is this common in Chara?"

Landen shook his head slowly no, then looked cautiously at his father.

"What is this, Dad? How are we doing it?" I asked, stumbling over my words.

My father looked at Ashten, and I could tell that he was searching for words to my questions.

"Alright, we all need to just have a seat and talk this through."

We all followed my father to the kitchen table. Landen and I sat side by side. He held my hand under the table, his piercing blue eyes judging his father's every move.

My father looked at my mother, trying to size up her take on what she was seeing, then he nodded in Ashten's direction for him to begin. Ashten sighed as he gathered his words, first looking at Landen, then settling his eyes on me.

"The first people to our world, the woman Aliyanna and the man Guardian, could speak without words, and they shared each other's dreams," Ashten said. Landen shook his head slowly from side to side, and his eyes drifted down to me, letting me know that he knew this story; his disbelief told me so. Ashten went on. "They were both born in Esteroius. Aliyanna held a power that could move the universe, and the priests in Esteroius tried to gain control of it. When they failed, they pushed a force of energy at Aliyanna and Guardian, who was trying to protect Aliyanna. The force of energy used against them pushed them into the string, and once there they found their way to a different dimension: Chara. When their children grew up, Aliyanna and Guardian taught them the paths in the string so they could find the ones that they were meant to be with. Couple by couple, our world was born, and everyone has to leave to find the one that they're meant to be with."

"What does that have to do with us?" I argued.

"There has never been another couple with the same insights, and you both are children of our dimension," Ashten answered.

"So…is this bad or good?" I asked.

Ashten and my father exchanged weary looks; it was obvious they were keeping something from me. The room grew silent, and the tension between Landen and his father intensified within seconds.

Suddenly, Landen stood up. "Your silence gives me reason to leave now," he said, gently pulling me to his side.

Ashten stood and said, "Landen, it took you two days to get here - do you want to put that little girl upstairs through that? We need to wait for the storms to grow calm, or at least for Livingston and Marc to arrive."

"You know Livingston? Who is Marc?" I asked, using our new gift.

"Livingston is my uncle, and Marc is his son," Landen answered in the same manner.

Landen looked into my eyes, then to the stairs that led to were Libby was playing; through his emotions, I felt him weigh each consequence. He then sighed and calmly sat back down, and the room filled with relief. I sat down slowly next to Landen, trying to place all the names and faces with the story my father had told me.

The tension in the room was broken when Libby appeared at the top of the stairs.

"Is it time for dinner? I'm hungry," she asked as she walked down the stairs, smiling at Landen. It was like she knew him and loved him already.

"Yes, dear. We were just deciding what we're going to have," my mother answered "Let's all have some dinner and get some rest. I'm sure everything will be clearer in the morning." She seemed to have brought our conversation to a peaceful end.

My father and Ashten excused themselves to the back porch - I'm sure to discuss Landen and me in private. Libby walked over to Landen's side and slid her small body under his arm. They stared at each other, and the emotion between them seemed familiar to me; like I'd felt love between them, the love only a family could have. Libby reached her tiny hand to Landen's face, and when he smiled at her, she giggled; it was a joy like I'd never seen from her before.

"I like the name 'Landen'; do you like the name 'Libby?'"

"I feel like I know her. How does she know my name?"

"It's her insight. She started using it today; it's like she has a window in front of her. She doesn't know that she has it yet."

He shook his head in disbelief. *"It has to be more than insight,"* he thought quietly.

"I do. It's one of my favorites," he said, humoring her.

"Willow is your princess?" Libby said, looking back and forth between us.

"Yes, she is," Landen agreed.

"I told you princesses have green eyes," Libby said, crossing her arms, proud of her prediction. She then looked at Landen and said, "Daddy wants to talk to you." Landen looked down at his watch, and we waited as the seconds ticked by. Two minutes and fifteen seconds later, my father opened the door.

"Landen, can you come out here please?" my father said.

Landen reluctantly stood, kissed the top of my head, and walked to the door, peering at me through the glass as he closed it. As their conversation began outside, I knew they weren't saying anything upsetting because calm came over the cabin.

When dinner was ready, the men came back in, the calm still with them. For Libby's sake, the conversation had no stories of other dimensions; instead, we listened to stories of my father and Ashten's childhood. I felt closer to my father; I'd never realized how little I knew of him before my mother came into his life.

As we cleaned the kitchen after dinner, I could feel how happy my mother was for me. She would look at me, then to Landen, who was playing a card game with Libby; little did she know, he was timing her responses. Ashten walked into the kitchen, followed by my father.

"I think we all need our rest. It's been a long day, and a longer one awaits us. I'm going to sleep in the living room in case anyone makes it through tonight - I don't want any false alarms," Ashten said to us.

My father walked over to his medicine bag, pulled out a white tube, and handed it to me.

"This is for the burn on his shoulder; it will get infected if he doesn't treat it," he said, looking over at Landen.

"You're hurt?"

"It's nothing," he thought.

I raised my eyebrows, doubting his words, but he just gave me a playful grin.

"Good night," my mother said over her shoulder as she carried Libby up the stairs.

I left Landen in the living room; I could tell that he wanted to talk to his father. I stopped in Libby's room to kiss her goodnight. She was already sleeping; it had been a really long day. I didn't realize how hard the trip had been on her.... it made me realize how fragile she really was.

I changed quickly into my pajamas:some simple cotton shorts and a white T-shirt. I then noticed my sketch book lying across my bed with Landen's portrait facing up; my mother must have brought it up there. I pulled out the photo album the girls had given to me, wanting so badly to share it with them. I then scooted to the center of the bed, turned to the sketch of flowers, and placed it next to a picture of the five of us; I realized that our lives were now like the flower: all original, beautiful, and living side by side – yet unaware of one another.

Feeling Landen coming up the stairs, I looked to the hallway and saw him stop at Libby's room. As he looked in and watched her sleep, I could feel his confusion and turmoil; I wondered what he was thinking. He then looked down and sighed before walking to my room.

"Are you OK?" I thought when he got closer.

He smiled at me, walked over to the bed, and slid by my side. *"What happened? Why is Drake looking for you?"* he thought.

I looked down at my wrist to the star that rested in the loop of the Ankh. Landen followed my eyes, then looked back up at me, panicked and angry.

"I didn't see his face when I dreamed, but I'm more than sure that Drake did this." I felt relieved that I could finally talk to Landen.

His anger rose so high, I could see the heat behind his dimples - and I knew then not to tell him that Drake had been in all my nightmares.

"How did he do it?" he thought.

"He just touched me," I thought, remembering the pain of the burn.

"You told your dad, and he decided to run home," he guessed.

"He saw the star, then left. I never told him what happened."

"That was four nights ago, right?" Landen thought, sitting forward a little.

I nodded. *"Why?"* I asked, seeing that was important.

"Four days ago, Livingston came crashing into my father's house and pulled him away. They left, and only my father came back. He told us he'd found Jason and needed help brining his daughters home," Landen thought.

"They found my dad a long time ago, when I was six. My dad said they knew Drake was searching for me and had decided to stay there until I was older," I corrected.

"This doesn't make any sense," Landen thought, running his hands through his hair.

"Did you know about Drake? – his parents, Adonia and Justus?" I asked.

Landen nodded, stiffening his jaw. *"I've seen Drake. Marc and his brother, Chrispin, lost their mother that day. That's all we talk about...when we are alone,"* he thought, looking down.

His thoughts grew silent. I folded the album closed, set it on the side table, and reached for the sketch pad .When I picked it up, Landen slowly touched my arm and reached for the pad, pulling it closer and looking at the details of the flowers.

"How do you remember them so clearly?" he thought softly.

"It's easy to recall them," I thought, feeling a little embarrassed. I reached my finger to the pad and traced the outline of the blue and green flowers, each with different petals.

"I think they represent you and me," I thought, shyly looking up at him.

I saw him smile and felt his hand as he placed it on mine, tracing the petals.

"Where were we? Whose house was that?" I thought.

"Ours," he said softly.

I smiled back at him. He leaned closer to kiss me, and as he pulled forward I felt him tense at the pain coming from his shoulder.

"Can I see?" I asked.

He squinted his eyes, feeling embarrassed. *"Really, it's nothing,"* he thought, trying to smile.

I knew it was something; I could see the pain in his eyes. *"I need to put the medicine on it anyway."*

Landen gave me a wary look, then unbuttoned his black shirt; underneath, his white shirt had a huge hole in the shoulder. He pulled it over his head, and I gasped at the sight of it.

"I told you it's nothing," he thought, trying to downplay it.

He was wrong; the burn started at the top of his shoulder and curved around his shoulder blade. *"How did you do this?"* I reached for the medicine my father had given me and rubbed it across the wound.

"It's just the storm. I wasn't paying attention - I was being careless." He breathed out in relief as I gently rubbed the cream over the wound, then he lay on his side, allowing the medicine to dry.

"What did they want with you outside?" I asked.

Landen smiled up at me through his thick eyelashes, which outlined the pools of blue - my window to his soul. *"Your father told me that he'd never shown you how to travel, that you didn't travel the way the rest of us do."* He thought with a mischievous grin on his face.

I loved it when he smiled and his dimples came to life.

"How do I do it differently?" I asked, shaking my head and bringing myself back to reality.

"Well, the rest of us travel through the strings, like the one you saw me come from; your dad said that you use people, that you see them through emotions." He tilted his head, finding it somewhat amusing.

I made a face; it bothered me, being different…I'd always been different, but I thought that after all this, after finding Landen I'd be normal.

"How weird am I?" I asked, holding my eyes low.

"It's not weird." He pulled my chin up, still smiling, so I'd have to look him in the eye.

"It has to do with your insight; the insight of emotion is not a common one. In fact, it's unique that you, your father, and sister all have a gift."

"But, they're all different."

"You still all have one," he argued.

"Do you have one?" I asked.

"I do." he said, reaching down to the quilt at the end of the bed, pulling it over him, and settling in to sleep.

"Are you going to tell me?" I protested.

He was enjoying keeping me in suspense. He leaned forward and kissed me again, sending my head into a numbing spin - trying to distract me, I'm sure. He was crazy if he thought he was going to sleep without telling me.

"What is it?" I thought as loud as I could.

He reluctantly stopped kissing me and stared closely into my eyes with a small smile.

"Well, it's not as interesting as all of yours. I can determine truth or intent, but it's flawed; people can change their intent in an instant."

"How does it work?" I wondered.

Landen lay back down, still staring at me.

"I feel it; I can feel if they believe what they're saying. The intent is harder to explain. I don't see it or hear it, but I know what they intend to do."

"Do they think it came from your dad? Does he have insight?"

"No. That's why your family is rare; there is usually one gift every other generation."

I suddenly realized that I didn't know anything about his mother, or whether or not he had any brothers or sisters. *"Where is the rest of your family? Are they in Chara?"* I asked, watching him grin as he tucked a piece of my hair behind my ear so he could see my face more clearly.

"My mother, Aubrey, and my sister, Clarissa, took a cab from an airport in New York to a hotel and have been shopping, using you mother's credit cards. My brother, Brady, is in Washington, using your father's credit cards."

"Why?"

"They're just trying to leave a paper trail for your world. Because you lived there so long, they needed to fade you away,"

I slowly shook my head in disbelief; I wasn't sure how I felt about fading away from all the people I loved there.

"It was just a precaution," Landen thought, seeing the effect that his words had on me.

I nodded understanding. *"What did you talk to your father about?"* I asked.

"It wasn't really a talk. I asked if he knew you were the one I dreamed of when he asked me to come here, and I asked why Drake wanted you."

"What did he say?" I asked, looking for any answer.

"He was silent." Landen paused, then looked up at me *"He understands my insight. He knows if he doesn't answer, I won't be able tell if he's telling the truth"* he thought, growing angry again.

"What is his intent?" I asked

"All I can see is that he wants us safe at home," Landen thought.

"None of this makes any sense to me," I thought, leaning back.

Landen pulled himself up on one arm and looked over me, taking in every part of me in. *"Everything has its reason; it may not be clear to us tonight, but one day it will be. You and I have proved beyond any doubt that our beliefs are not false. We are meant to be with someone, the one. I found you. No one can keep us apart now, and our love will now be the story told to define how sacred love is."*

I leaned up and kissed his lips. "*I do love you,"* I thought softly.

"And I do love you."

I replayed his words in my thoughts as if they were beautiful music.

"Are you sure your family is OK with running around this dimension for us?"

"My sister loves Infante, especially New York; she's always thought that she'd find the one she's looking for there. She told me she was ready to look the day my father came home, asking us to come here."

"Infante...is that what this dimension is called?" I asked.

Landen nodded *"It means' young,'"* he thought.

"How is it young?"

"Travelers consider it young because the cultures are still divided and war still occurs here."

"What does Chara mean?"

Landen smiled, and I felt a love come through him. *"'Joy',' happiness,'"* he answered

"So, Chara has no war or different cultures?"

"There has never been a war in Chara, and because everyone leaves to find someone, our culture is blended. Everyone has characteristics from several dimensions."

I smiled, thinking of how beautiful the people in Chara must be. I wanted to know everything about Landen's family.

"Has Brady found his soul mate?" I thought

He smiled at me; I could tell that he had a great admiration for his brother just by the way he said his name.

"Yes, her name is Felicity. She's at home. Their first child will be here soon."

A baby…I remembered when Libby had come home; she was my doll that came to life.

"How old are they, Brady and Clarissa?"

"Clarissa is twenty and Brady is twenty--five. That's why my father didn't believe me when I told him about you; apparently, you don't get the urge to search until you're in your early twenties – and he thought I was too young." Landen thought, rolling his eyes.

I laughed quietly, knowing how absurd it was to put a timeline on love.

"Thought…?" I pointed out.

"It's more than clear that you and I are both older than our given ages." Landen thought.

I smiled at the thought of having an old soul; my parents had accused me of it more than once. I settled in next to Landen. Struggling to keep my eyes open, I studied every feature on his face, assuring myself he was still real.

"How come we need so many travelers to get us home?"

"I think my father and I can do it. You and your dad can travel, and Libby is close enough she wouldn't need a lot of help, so that only leaves your mother. We're really just waiting on the storms to settle."

"What causes the storms?"

"It's a disruption in the energy near the strings. They say the storms have only happened in the last two generations; one theory is that all the technology is disrupting the natural energy around us."

"Are they dangerous?" I asked. I couldn't imagine little Libby in a vast storm.

"They're more confusing than dangerous…it's like being out in open water - then all of a sudden a mass of wave's turns you and you lose your direction."

"How did you get hurt?"

"I thought there was a passage where there wasn't one, and I pushed through with my shoulder; I was just in a hurry to get here."

We lay in absolute silence, studying each other, lost in our own thoughts. I felt my eyes close against my will, and without hesitation, Landen was there at my side as we stood at the doorway to our home. He smiled down at me, then wistfully picked me up and carried me across the threshold, kissing me gently as he sat me down inside. I walked through our home with him at my side. All the rooms seemed so vast; the windows reached from the floor to the ceiling, letting in the sunlight. We walked up the wide staircase into a large room, our room. A gentle breeze flowed through the long white curtains, framing the wide double doors; the sun glided over them, making them seem as if they were satin. We then passed through the open doors and stared into a field of beautiful flowers, the sun dancing across them. I truly did feel like I was home – and home was at his side.

Chapter Six

The sunlight peered through the open window, warming my face. Before I opened my eyes, I smiled peacefully. When I reached for Landen, though, I didn't find him. Libby's small frame was under my hands, and I opened my eyes to see her tiny sleeping head on my pillow. I hesitated, searching my memory, then I rose quickly, thinking it was all a dream. Suddenly, a sinking feeling hit my stomach, and I reached out with all my senses finally finding the one that defined me: Landen. I could feel the love coming from him, and a sense of relief swept through me, realizing that he was only downstairs. There were four people down there with him, but what stood out was his love, a sense of excitement, peace, and anxiety to come from the others.

Their emotions giving me no alarm, I lay back down and traced Libby's small features as she slept at my side. I couldn't recall when she'd come in there. Hoping that she hadn't had a nightmare, I shuttered as I remembered mine once again. Whatever the case, Libby seemed calm enough now, so I decided to get ready for whatever the day held for me. When I returned to my room, Libby was sitting up in my bed. A smile filled my face;

her hair was nothing less than a savage nest, though she did look well rested.

"Good morning, sleepy head," I said.

She smiled a sleepy smile at me.

"When did you come in here?" I asked

She looked around the room, seeming shocked to find herself there.

"I don't remember."

"Were you sleep-walking?" I asked, teasing her. Libby hadn't been a bed jumper since she was really little. Back then, she would rotate through the night between her bed, mine, and then Mom and Dad's

"Are you hungry?"

She nodded.

"Then let's get you dressed; I think we have company downstairs."

I was brushing out her hair, a difficult task when she looked at me. "I like Livingston; he's nice just like the others," she said, looking back in my direction.

I suddenly realized she was doing it again - because I hadn't even met him. I'd assumed that he was the one downstairs, but she already knew him. I wondered how difficult this would be, for her to live life constantly ahead of everyone else. I could only pray that she would find a way to embrace her gift, as I had mine… at least she wouldn't have to hide her insight.

When we walked downstairs, we heard laughter coming from the kitchen; the emotion of joy was illuminating the room.

"Ah, there they are," my father said proudly.

They were all at the table: Ashten, Landen, and a man I assumed was Livingston, all dressed in black.

"Good morning," Landen thought, smiling at me as he got up from his chair and walked toward me with my favorite playful grin. Kissing me softly, he sent a tingle through my soul. I blushed; he was still real…everything was still real.

"You left me," I thought teasingly.

He shook his head, showing a playful pout. "*Never,*" he thought.

I could see that everyone was watching our wordless communication with a sense of admiration.

Livingston raised his eyebrows as a grin spread across his face. He was slightly older than my Dad and Ashten, and he had dark brown hair with a hint of silver tracing through it. He also shared their same trait of dimples and deep blue eyes.

"Willow, Libby, this is Livingston," my father said proudly.

I could only imagine how great it must be for him to be reunited with his lost friends.

"Have a seat, girls; I have your breakfast ready," Mom said warmly.

Everyone else had already eaten, making me wondered how much of the day Libby and I had spent sleeping. Libby asked if she could have her breakfast in front of the TV; normally, that would have gotten an instant no, but sensing the direction of the conversation, my mother agreed.

"So, Willow," Livingston began when Libby was successfully distracted. "They tell me you can sense emotions. Do you mind me asking: are they simple emotions, or enhanced ones?"

I'd never thought of defining what I did. Emotions always seemed to be a good way to sum it up for me, but Livingston caused me to reflect on what I felt when people were around me.

"Umm, I'm not sure…I mean, some things I feel are more like a mood, as well as an emotion."

"Fascinating…so how would you describe me?"

His tone was complacent, and he didn't hold any real expression in his face; one might say he was calm.

I smiled at him, "Nervous," I said, sure of myself.

Livingston shifted uneasily in his seat and looked cautiously at my father and Ashten. Landen noticed the exchange and looked at Livingston, judging his every move.

"Fascinating," Livingston finally said.

I tried to explain it more clearly. "The people that I' m around the most, I can sum up in one word. I could tell you that my dad is almost always peaceful, and my mother and Libby have an energetic emotion constantly coming from them. I can feel the calm coming from Ashten and Landen. At the same time, I could tell you if they felt sad, scared, or even prideful."

"That does seem like more than just emotion, and it complements Landen's insight," Livingston said.

I smiled at Landen, losing myself in his blue eyes; for a moment, I forgot I was in the middle of a serious conversation.

"So, explain to us from your point of view how you travel," Livingston asked.

"I don't know…I mean, I see people who look like they need help, I feel a gentle pull, I touch them, and then I'm there. But after seeing what Landen did yesterday with the string, I don't think I'm all the way there. You see, they don't see me, and when I let go, I'm home again."

My father was smiling at me, a strong sense of pride coming from him. He tried to help me explain it more clearly. "I've followed Willow before; it's like she makes a path where one doesn't exist. I was able to see the way back. If she were taught how we travel, she'd be able to see it, too."

"How far does she go?" asked Livingston.

"Mostly she stays here, but she's gone as far as Olecence before. More recently, she's gone further than I'd care for," he said, winking at me.

I wondered how many dimensions there really were; so far, I knew of four.

"Wait, what do you mean I 'stay here…? You can jump around in one dimension?" I asked.

The room erupted into laughter. It must have been a funny question to those in the room who could travel - the normal way, but my mother and I seemed to think it was a valid question.

"I'm going to show you the strings. Today, you'll see that Livingston is just in awe of you …they're only laughing because you have no idea of the power you hold."

I smiled, but I was blushing.

"Willow, I don't mean to upset you, but your mother told me something that I find just as fascinating: she said you couldn't feel anything coming from Drake…you told her he was a void," Livingston said, leaning forward in his seat.

Landen gave me a curious look, beaming with relief.

"No, there was nothing there. I think that's why I felt so uncomfortable around him; I knew it wasn't me because I could still feel everyone else."

Landen reached his arm around me. With that statement, I knew that I'd made everyone a little nervous.

"Willow," my father said in his trademark peaceful tone. "Have you ever felt anything close to…evil?"

Livingston closed his eyes, sighing softly, and I could feel remorse coming from him. My eyes grew wide, and my mouth opened. I had to admit, I hadn't – I'd felt anger, but evil was not a word I could ever find to describe anyone I'd ever met; I felt blessed that that would be my one exception. I shook my head slowly no.

"That's good. I don't want you to ever have to," my dad said, quickly feeling relieved.

"Are you ready? I think we both need air." Landen thought, looking at me.

"Is it safe?" I asked, feeling nervous.

"We're going to stay close. I'm going to show you my way, and then you're going to show me yours."

"I bet my way is cooler," I said slyly.

I was sure it wasn't, but I wanted to make him laugh, and it worked: he laughed out loud, and once again they all stared at us in wonder.

"I want to go, too, Willow," Libby said as she walked into the kitchen. Everyone looked at her with bemusement.

"Well, Jason, Ashten," Livingston said, sighing and looking at Libby. "I would have to say that you two have a very talented bunch on your hands."

Like my father and Ashten, Livingston, was holding something back from me and Landen - and Landen saw it, too; he gave his father a daring look as we left the cabin. As we walked along the river's path, he tried to prepare me for what I would see in the string.

"Have you ever swum in open water?" Landen asked.

I'd lived in a landlocked state my whole life; the few times that we had vacationed at the beach, I never went in any further than my knees.

"Not exactly...do I need to be a good swimmer or something?" I asked, unable to hide how nervous I really was.

He laughed at himself and searched for a different analogy. When he couldn't find one, he began again, "When you're in the string, it's like swimming in natural water; you're going to feel something like a gentle current. It's easy to walk through, but I don't want it to scare you." He looked down at me, and I could tell he was judging my response. "Everything but the passages is going to be white," he finished. When we finally reached the place where I'd found him. I breathed in deeply, feeling my anxiety and his excitement. "Can you see the string?" he asked.

I could, but I still couldn't figure out why they called it a string; it looked like a ripple in the air, and you could see everything behind it... it reminded me of a glare coming off a scalding hot road in the summer's sun. I nodded, he took my hand, and we stepped into the ripple, the string.

It was so beautiful. Everything was a glowing light, and there was no depth or height. I could feel solid ground beneath me, though the ground shared the same white glow. I felt the gentle current. It didn't scare me; it was very relaxing. The air wasn't cold or warm - it was perfect. I could hear a mesmerizing humming sound. I let a childlike smile cross my face, then Landen took my hand, and we began to walk. As we moved, the scenery never changed.

"How do you know where you're going? Do you visualize it, like my father?"

Landen stopped, looked down at me, and smiled. The string had highlighted his eyes. It was like a light was shining through from behind; I'd never seen anything so beautiful.

"I follow intent, and I can feel it through the string. When it changes, I know I'm either entering another part of the dimension that I'm near or approaching a different one. Can you feel emotions from here?" he asked as his eyes searched over my face.

I was so distracted by the beauty of the string that I hadn't noticed. I could feel Landen's love as the most powerful emotion around me, but in the background I could feel others; they were common emotions: worry, happiness, and sadness. I nodded.

"I think that when you learn the cultures of the dimensions, you'll be able to use your insight of emotion to help you navigate."

"How do Clarissa and Brady navigate?"

"Brady has a lot of Aquarius in his birth chart, and he can hear music through the string. He says that every dimension has its own rhythm. Clarissa is dominant in Taurus, and she's known for her voice. She says that she listens to the tones of the voices through the string."

My eyes widened; I was beginning to see that that they relied heavily on the Zodiac in the dimension of Chara.

"What's a birth chart?"

"It's just a map of the heavens at the exact moment that you were born. When the planets align a certain way, they can highlight a dominant trait."

"Does the dimension Esterouis study the Zodiac like Chara does?"

Landen nodded; I could feel that he had great disdain for that dimension.

"Chara looks to the heavens to find a positive way to impact the world around us; Esterouis looks to the heavens to find a way to control others."

"Drake knows I'm a Scorpio," I thought, remembering that my father had said the people in Esterouis had predicted my birth.

"I have a feeling that Drake knows more about what's going on with this Blue Moon than you and I do," Landen thought, I felt his anger rise. He wrapped his arm around me, and we began to stroll through the string.

All at once, I could see a purple haze on the right side of the string. "It's turning purple!" I shouted.

My tone scaring him, he jumped at the sound of my voice, and I realized that talking to him without words would serve as a beneficial tool in the string. Laughing at my excitement, Landen pulled me closer.

"OK, purple is good; this is a natural path."

"Do you know where it leads?" I asked.

"I do," he thought, amused. He wasn't going to tell me, and I was learning that those two words were code to see if I could figure it out. We walked for a least fifteen more minutes before we reached the purple haze. The color resembled a summer sunset; it was so breathtaking, I felt like I was standing on a rainbow.

"When you come to a passage, always step through it with caution - you don't ever know for certain what you'll step into," Landen cautioned.

A wary look coming across my face, my curiosity peaked as to where it would lead. As he took the first step into the haze, Landen pulled me close, and a tingle teased my skin as the haze surrounded me. I then felt a burst of humidity in the air and heard a loud roaring noise. Fearing that we had somehow found our way into some horrible danger, I focused my eyes as the haze fell behind us - and they couldn't believe what they were seeing: a vast waterfall; it was the most amazing thing I had ever seen.

"Where are we - Niagara Falls?" I asked, humbled.

He smiled widely at me. *"This is Victory Falls,"* he answered.

"Where is Victory Falls?"

"Zimbabwe," he thought, smiling at me.

I knew that the shock on my face was apparent, I couldn't fathom how we'd gotten there…I tried desperately to recall anything from geography class - but I was sure I didn't know for certain where Zimbabwe was.

"It's so beautiful... so big..." I thought.

"It's over a mile wide and very old."

"How old?"

"One hundred and fifty million years. It's a powerful natural source of energy, and that's why it was so easy for you to see. We passed several other passages before we reached this one," he thought, studying my face for signs of understanding.

I could see that I had so much to learn, and I knew; I didn't ever want to be alone in the strings; I was sure to be lost.

"Are they all this beautiful?"

"Everything that you see will amaze you - even if you've been there before. Each place has its own story to tell... if you listen, you can hear it, and feel it".

Landen was right; I could feel this place. I could feel that all those who knew it loved it and respected it, and the waterfall itself knew it was powerful…it was a life force all its own.

"Can you see your way back?" he asked.

I looked behind us, but there wasn't a purple haze or a wave in the air.

"No," I thought in a worried tone.

He didn't seem surprised by my answer. He stood behind me, wrapped his arms around me, and held me tightly.

"Close your eyes and remember the way you came...remember the feeling you had as you passed through... find the energy."

I did as he said, replaying the feeling that I had as I walked through the haze.

"Now open your eyes," he thought.

When I did, the wave was there again.

"I can see it!"

"OK, you lead the way," he thought.

I walked slowly through the wave. The roar of the waterfall was gone, and the air was perfectly still again. Only the haze remained behind us.

"How come it wasn't there at first?" I asked, looking back at the haze.

"It was there - you just were never taught to see it. The strings are all over every dimension you've walked by more than you could ever know. Our eyes can see them; you just have to learn to call on what you were born with."

I looked around the string, and to my right I could see an array of colors that seemed to stretch out for miles in every direction; they looked like they were blocking our path.

"I can see more colors - is this a wall?"

"This is where the string divides. Focus on the hazes, and you'll see that the more dominant hazes are framing different paths."

I studied what I thought was a wall in front of me, and as I stared, I could see that the darker hazes outlined three passages. The colors of the three passages were so bright, they spilled out of their paths and joined the others. It looked like every color that existed was blended perfectly together; they flowed on the gentle current I was feeling. The glow of the white passages reflected on the hazes, looking like diamonds…I was humbled by the beauty before me.

"Three paths" I thought softly as I stared in awe.

Landen smiled; I could feel the excitement rise inside of him. *"The storms create these paths, and more passages are created with each aggressive flow of energy. When our parents where young, storms were rare; they only really occurred once a year. Around the time we were born, they were so fierce that only the most experienced travelers were able to navigate through them,"* he explained.

"My father said his passage to my mother closed. Is that normal?"

Landen shook his head no. I could feel his mystification. *"In our entire history ,it's only happened to your father. My grandfather, August, told me that everyone searched endlessly for the gifted healer."*

"That's a little scary," I thought.

Landen nodded. *"I just wish they would have brought you home when they did find you,"* he thought.

We began to walk. I wasn't sure, but I thought we were going back the way we had just come. I searched the glow all around us, looking at all the hazes that had been absent to me before.

There were little speckles along the sides of the walls of the string. They were all different colors; some small as dust, others as large as a doorway. We stopped before one of the large yellow doorways.

"I told you that purple was a natural path...why do you think the color to this one is different?" Landen asked.

It was like being in a classroom; he was making me think, teaching me.

"Well, yellow and purple are both calm colors...could be natural... just not as strong?"

Landen held his arm out, indicating that he wanted me to lead the way. My steps were cautious; he may have known where it led, but I didn't. For all I knew, I could have been in Australia, and a big scary snake would be at my feet when the yellow haze left me.

When the haze passed, the same tingle as the last was there; the feeling was growing more familiar to me. As the haze faded, we stood on a rocky cliff overlooking a beautiful, deserted white beach, the water was so clear. Suddenly, I heard a loud noise, and I turned to see water crashing through a hole in the rocks. As I stood in absolute astonishment, I could feel the energy leaving as the water fell.

"Do you want to stay here for awhile?" he asked, laughing at my reaction.

I did, but I was hungry for more. Feeling proud of myself, I pulled Landen back into the string. Feeling the pride coming from him, I knew I had done well.

"You're quick; it took me almost ten times before I could find the string alone."

"I'm sure you were only a little boy; it's not the same for me," I assured him.

All of the sudden, my smile faded; I could feel someone in the string with us - I was certain of it. They had an emotion of excitement. In the string, emotions were intensified, and this person's emotion was, too.... they were as strong as a room full of people.

"Landen, someone else is here... I can feel them."

Landen was already looking past me, and his eyes suddenly grew brighter; whatever he had felt made him happy.

"Landen, is that you?" a deep voice said.

Out of the bright light, an image came forth. Dressed in all black was, a young, attractive man. He was tall like Landen with wavy brown hair, and his eyes were so dark - but they had the same glow behind them as Landen's did.

"It's Marc."

"Marc, where have you been?" Landen asked, excited to see him.

Taking stock of the fact that Landen was not alone, Marc looked at me as if he couldn't believe his eyes.

"I don't believe it - you found her!" Marc's voice rang with excitement. "I'm so glad Landen found you," he said, smiling at me. I could feel his excitement rise. "Do you want me to help you get home before I go and help Jason's family?" he said, looking back at Landen.

"This is Willow, Jason's daughter," Landen said pulling me closer to him.

Marc's eyes widened, and I could feel his bewilderment. "That isn't possible...that would mean you're both from Chara," he said, looking back and forth between us.

"Willow and I must be the exception in the history of Chara. Listen, Dad found Jason a long time ago; he only wanted to come home now because Drake Blakeshire is looking for Willow."

"Willow is the Scorpio? Why would he be looking for her? It's more than clear that the two of you belong to one another," Marc argued, growing confused.

"Everyone is silent when I ask questions...they're hiding something from us," Landen said, his anger rising.

"That must be why Ashten and Dad asked us to find a path that avoided Esterouis," Marc said, looking back and forth in the string.

"Did you find one?" Landen asked

"Yeah, the one you told me to check. A storm is beginning to stir that way, and we need to wait at least a day before we pass through it. Where are the others?" Marc asked.

"Back in the cabin, I was showing Willow how we travel."

"Well, I guess I don't have to come up with an excuse for showing up without you. Are sure you don't want to just go home? We can make it if we're really careful," Marc said in growing concern.

"We're going to wait; we want to make sure Libby, Willow's baby sister, gets to Chara safely," Landen said, looking down at me.

Marc nodded. "I'm going to let you finish up your lessons; I'm beat," he said as he began to move past us. "Stay clear of the gray paths," he warned as he disappeared in the glow.

"Is gray bad?" I thought. Landen smiled down at me. *"No, they're just man made, so it's hard to judge what you're stepping into. Infante is known for having the most."*

"Were you going to come and help my family? Is that what Marc meant when he said at least he wouldn't have to come up with an excuse for showing up without you?"

Landen shook his head no as he smiled at me. *"We were leaving the day I saw you and you gave me that note. I told Marc and Brady I was going to find you, and I didn't care if my father wanted me to or not. They both agreed with me. Marc said he would find an excuse for me not showing up at the cabin."*

Landen and I made our way through the string, stopping at every color that caught my eye. In one morning, I had traveled from Montana to Zimbabwe then to the beaches of Key West. We gazed at the northern lights and stood at the peak of Mt Everest. As I looked at the Grand Canyon, I knew that I was blessed to have seen so many wonders that others could only dream of.

"OK, so maybe your way is cooler," I said, turning into him and now looking at my own personal natural wonder.

"Not too bad for a first date," he thought. I loved his character; he had a way of making everything seem so natural.

"How do you know so much about my world – but have only found me now?"

Landen sighed deeply, and I felt him grow angry at a memory he had with in him. *"I was not allowed this far from my home – specifically to Infante - by my father. Marc and Brady would take me there from time to time, though. I always felt pulled here - but I could never see my beacon. My time was short; I didn't want to disrespect my father's wishes…I regret that now."*

"Did he tell you why?"

"He was always silent when I asked…it doesn't matter anymore." He smiled and looked down at me, and I felt his excitement rise. "*It's your turn. Where do we need to go to help you get started?"*

I didn't think I'd every traveled outside of Franklin; it was easy to see someone out of place in your own hometown.

"I just need people."

"Jason said that I wouldn't be able to see the people you could see. " he thought

"Really?" I thought, surprised.

Landen shrugged his shoulders, not really understanding it either.

Chapter Seven

We found our way to a quaint little town that was a lot like Franklin. The buildings all dated back to the 1800's, and shops and restaurants lined the streets. We settled in at little café, which was set in front of a square park that centered the town. People were pushing strollers, walking their dogs, and lounging on the benches. On the other side of the park was a beautiful church. Flowers decorated the steps, and I could only assume that a wedding was in process. I found myself wondering more about the beliefs in the place where I would spend the rest of my life.

"Landen, are there churches in Chara?"

My thoughts caught him off guard, and he looked at me with questioning eyes. *"Are you asking me if there are churches, or if we believe in a higher power?"*

"Well, would you not need a church to worship a higher power?"

"Would you?"

I was starting to realize that my perception of faith had been altered by my dimension. Landen was right: if there were a higher power, as I believed, would he keep an attendance record at a man made institution? As I studied the beautiful church across the way, I could feel Landen smiling at me as he watched me take in my new revelation.

"Willow, that's a beautiful place, and I'm sure when you're in the church you can feel a sense of power - but is it the same as what you felt this morning? Do you see yourself closer to

God there? Did you feel Him as you stood gazing at that powerful waterfall or at the peak of the mountain?"

Landen was right. Everywhere we had gone had a majestic feeling, a story to tell me; I felt God as I stood there. All of the sudden, the bells on the church began to chime, the doors opened, and people made their way to line the streets.

"*So if there are no churches, does that mean that there are no weddings?"* I thought before I could stop myself. I felt heat rising in my cheeks.

Landen raised his eyebrows, tilted his head, and gave me my favorite grin.

"*Do you want a wedding?"* he asked sincerely.

I blushed profusely, feeling foolish, and I couldn't say or think a single thought. Landen moved his chair closer to mine, wrapped his arm around me. We watched the couples make their way out.

"Do you think he sees her as I see you?" Landen asked, looking at the groom, then back to me.

I could feel the bride and groom from where I sat; there was a love between them, but it wasn't as powerful as the emotion that Landen and I shared.

"In Chara, we do celebrate when couples find one another. Friends and family welcome home the ones who were searching and their soul mates." Landen paused and looked deep into my eyes before continuing. "*We believe that we are each other's gift from God. We thank the heavens every moment for the love we feel. In Chara, we do not swear before God to honor and cherish*

one another; that's a promise we make when we say 'I love you.' You and I are more committed to one another than they could ever be. This is forever - this life and the next."

I could feel Landen's love; it was the most powerful emotion around me - the strongest one I'd ever felt in my life. He pulled my face closer to his and said, "I love you, Willow. I always have, and I always will."

"I love you, too."

Ready to show Landen my way of travel, I began searching the people around us; everyone seemed to be in place. Focusing my sense of emotion, I searched for one that would be unique to the setting. Not finding anyone in the park in front of us, I searched the streets as people walked by. I wasn't sure, but I thought I felt a gentle pull on me. I spotted a young man pacing back and forth; he looked as if he were rehearsing a speech, playing the words across his lips. He was a young man, and I would describe the emotion he was feeling as anxiety. I watched him as he stopped his pacing and took a step forward, then halt and start pacing again. I was almost sure he was an image. He was stepping forward to a tree – but a tree would definitely not need a rehearsed speech.

"Landen, do you see that young man over by the Dogwood tree?"

Landen followed my eyes and shook his head no. "*What do you see?*" he asked.

"Well, he's nervous; he's pacing and rehearsing words to himself."

"What's his emotion?"

"Anxiety," I thought.

"Are you sure he's an image?" Landen asked as he continued searching the people on the streets.

"If I get closer to him and feel a pull on me, then I'll know for sure," I thought as I stood.

Landen stood with me. *"What do you mean, 'pull?'"* he asked.

"The images pull me to them, then after I help them, they push me back to where I began," I said, taking his hand.

We began to walk closer to the young man. As we did, he stopped his pacing again, then stood in place and pulled a little box out of his pocket. I knew then what he was nervous about, and I started to walk faster; I could tell he was losing his nerve.

"OK, you hold onto me. I'll let go of him when it's over," I instructed Landen.

Landen held my hand tightly. The memory that I was going to use would be so powerful, this young man would have enough courage to last him for a lifetime. As I reached for his arm, the day shifted to evening, and the air had a gentle breeze. He was standing outside of a quaint apartment building. I let the memory of seeing Landen outside my dreams for the first time come to me. The tension then left the young man, he breathed in, and ran forward. I lost my touch.

Landen and I were back. I don't think I've ever felt as happy for one of my images before.

I smiled up at Landen.*"Well, how was that?"* I thought, proud of myself.

Landen looked around to see if any had seen us come or go. Finding no one paying attention to us, he thought, *"I think you have me beat."*

"What? There's no way - there was no wave or beautiful light."

"Yes, there was; you just didn't see it," he thought, smiling.

What did he mean by that?

"You just crossed the string and made your own light. The pull you feel is the energy of the string," he continued. *"Look at where he was, remember the way you felt... do you see it?"*

I could see; it was a wave, where one did not exist before. I took Landen's hand and stepped through, not knowing if we'd be with the young man or back in the string. When I heard the hum and felt the current, though, I knew we were in the string.

"Look, do you see the green in the wall?" Landen asked.

I looked to the right and could see a light green haze, the same size as me. Landen walked to the left side of the string and pointed out the twin image on the other side of the string. As I realized what he was saying, a smile came across my face.

Without warning, the hum of the string grew louder. The current was moving faster, and I felt my breath leave me. Landen pulled me down to the ground and wrapped his arms around me tight; the energy filling the string was so powerful, it vibrated every part of me. Just when I thought I couldn't stand another moment, everything was still again. I rose in a daze, and a numbing feeling came over me. The walls of the string had changed, and my green haze was no longer there; we had moved.

"*Did I do that?*" I asked, afraid of what his answer might be.

"It was just a storm; they're unpredictable."

"*Do you know where we are?*" I asked.

Landen looked at the walls of the string. Once he found his place, a smile came across his face. "*Well, we're back - a little faster than I would have preferred,*" he said, smiling at me.

There was a light blue haze, and as we stepped through it the river that ran along the cabin was in front of us.

As we walked toward the cabin, I felt all the emotions that I loved - the ones that only a family could give you. Libby was running down the river path as fast as she could, excitement coming from her; she is so precious. When she reached us, she leaped into Landen's arms and reached across to pull me to them.

"You guys left me all day," she said in a playful voice. "Did you take Willow to your castle?" she asked Landen. He lifted her above his head, making her to scream with laughter.

"Did you?" she said through her giggles.

"No, not yet - but I will very soon. When I do, you get to come, too. How does that sound?"

"I get to live with you?" Libby assumed.

Landen was starting to learn that nothing got past Libby.

"Well, you get to live very close with your mom and dad."

"How close?" she pressured.

"Close enough that you can run there in less than a minute," Landen said, setting her down. Libby seemed to be satisfied with his answer, and I was, too; I needed Libby close to me.

At the cabin, dinner was on the table. Marc had made it there safely, and the cabin was filled with a sense of joy. The stories of all the places travelers had seen sent my imagination running wild. I watched my father's eyes dance as he laughed at the stories being told of his childhood. My eyes always found their way to Libby, as she'd insisted on sitting in Landen's lap for dinner; he didn't seem to mind. I wondered what she'd filled her day with or if she'd picked up on her insight. Libby seemed not to be surprised by anything anyone was saying, but she was careful to answer when she was required.

When Libby finished her dinner, she slid off Landen's lap and went into the living room. Once there, she stretched out on the floor and began to color across one of my sketch pads. Landen and I stared at her as the others continued to reminisce.

"I wonder if she has a gift of art, too," Landen thought, smiling at me.

"If she does, she'll humble my talent," I thought.

"Willow, we want to talk to you about something," my mother said.

I looked away from Libby to my mother, letting her know she had my full attention. Ashten and my father sat up in their seats and leaned forward. Livingston got up from his seat and poured himself a cup of coffee. Marc, who was sitting on the other side of Landen, turned his attention to my mother.

"Maybe they're going to tell us what they've been hiding," I thought.

Landen shook his head no and smiled. *"They want to know what culture you want to follow to celebrate our union,"* he thought.

I looked at Landen quickly.

"That's Grace's intent right now," Landen thought.

I smiled at him, then looked at my mother. She was looking back in forth between Landen and me, like she was waiting for us to complete our silent conversation.

"In the culture of Chara, you and Landen are already as one. That culture is new to you. If you want to adhere to the culture you were raised in, we can go to a chapel tomorrow." she said.

I looked at my mother with a confused gaze. I'd never been the girl that daydreamed of a wedding day; in fact, I'd always told my mother that I wanted to elope, the way she and my father did.

"Um..." I said, looking to Landen for help.

He just smiled back at me. I knew he'd be content with whatever I chose to do.

"Well, today Landen explained the beliefs in Chara to me, and, honestly, they make more sense to me than the ones here," I said, looking back and forth between my parents. "But, I mean, if it would make the two of you feel more comfortable, we could go to a chapel."

I felt pride coming from Livingston and Ashten and a deep love coming from my parents. My mother smiled widely, reached across the table, and touched my hand.

"There is not a belief that Chara has that I do not admire. I've always adored that the union of a man and woman is between them; it doesn't matter what their family or friends think or want. I'm sure you can feel how happy I am that you feel the same way," she said. I smiled at my mother and leaned into Landen.

"Man, I would have really liked to have seen Landen in a tux," Marc said, elbowing Landen in the side.

Landen looked at Marc and shook his head, then looked down at me as if we were all alone.

"Are you sure you don't want to go to a chapel?" Landen thought.

"I love you. I always have, and believe me - I thank God with every breath that you're real. I don't need a chapel," I thought, breaking out into a wide smile.

I would wager that I was happier at that moment than any blushing bride. Landen tilted his head and gazed into my eyes.

"I love you."

My father stretched his arm around my mother as they stared happily at us.

Ashten smiled and leaned back in his seat."I can't wait for Aubrey to see the two of you together," he said to us.

I blushed as I remembered how many people that I still had to meet, realizing that I already loved them all.

"Landen, do you agree that we should wait another day before we travel home?" Livingston asked as he sat back down at the table.

Landen looked across the room at Libby, who was still coloring.

"I don't want to take any risks. We should wait for the storm that's turning to pass," Landen said.

I could feel eagerness inside Livingston. If it were up to him, we'd already be on our way.

"I'm going to get Libby ready for bed," I said, standing.

Everyone else stood and started to clear away the table from dinner. I took Libby upstairs, and we took turns in the shower. After she was ready for bed, I read her a story. I noticed that she was losing the excitement that I loved about her; it was as if she'd aged over the past few days.

"Libby, is there anything you want to talk about or ask me?" I whispered to her.

Her eyes found mine, and she searched my face; I could feel her running through different emotions: anxiety, a little fear, then returning to the common thread of excitement.

"I think I'm different," she said in a quiet voice.

"You are different. Everyone is, and that's what makes us all so special."

"Willow, I think that I am…I have…I can," she was struggling to find the words, I felt her emotions rush, and I squeezed her tight.

"I know. Don't worry about it. It'll all make more sense as you get older. Don't rush it; you'll find your way," I said, playing with her long brown hair. I felt a calm come over her.

After she drifted off to sleep, I left her room. As I passed through the hallway to my room, I heard the discussion downstairs in full debate. I could still feel Livingston's eagerness. I could also feel Landen's frustration, and it was obvious we weren't going to get any answers that night. I climbed on my bed with my sketch pad in my hand, then turned to a blank page and stared, trying to decide what to draw first; it was hard because my day had been so amazing. I felt my mother, and when I looked up she was leaning in the doorway. She smiled at me warmly; she had her energy and excitement with her again.

"Can I come in?" she asked. I scooted over on the bed, making room for her to sit beside me.

"I can only imagine what sketches will come out of the day that you've had," she said. I smiled as it rushed through my mind. Mom saw the photo album on the table and grabbed it, smiling as she looked at the pictures. She then started turning the pages, watching my friends and I grow up over the years.

"Do you miss them?" she asked. I nodded.

"Can you imagine what they'd say about you finding Landen?" she said, smiling. "What did you think of the string?"

"It was amazing…indescribable. It would change…the feelings, the colors…it all changed," I answered in a rush.

"I wish I could see it," she said, feeling envious.

I suddenly realized how scary only feeling it would be.

"So, Landen and you…" she said, shifting her emotion. I felt myself blush.

"Is everyone still shocked about us?" I asked, sitting up a little straighter.

"Not shocked. It's just amazing; I still cannot believe that you don't have to use any words to communicate…did it scare you?"

"We didn't even realize it."

"Is it everything? I mean, can you hear his thoughts now?" she asked.

"We only hear each other when we speak to one another. I'm not sure if he could hear me now or not."

"What about the dreams - are they the same place?"

"I think so. The last few have been at this beautiful home in our new world."

"I bet it's the one he built," she said, smiling wider.

Landen building a home…I tried to picture it: his hands not callused, his skin not browned from the sun.

"They all help. The family starts the house when the children are around the age of ten. It's not something that happens overnight, though. Your father said his was nearly finished when he left; he had spent ten years on it," she explained.

The way I felt about the home was intensified; it would always represent Landen to me.

"You know the houses are run off natural energy; the whole dimension is run off the power of sun, wind, and water," she said.

This world was becoming a utopia to me. It was as if the world that I'd I lived in had the same choices, but failed to take the right path. It's not as if we were not intelligent enough; I'd heard many people speak out about the environment. If my memory served me right, I think a lot of wars were started over energy…to think of all the lives that could have been saved. I wonder if those people had ever found their soul mate, if any of their children were born…the new clarity that I was getting was something I wished everyone could see.

"Ashten went to see Aubrey today; you know it's hard to be away from your soul mate for a long time. Clarissa found hers as well," my mother said.

I felt bad for Ashten and Aubrey being separated; it had to be hard. The thought of not having Landen close to me did not sit well.

"Did he say what she thought about Landen and me?"

"Aubrey and I are a lot alike; she can't wait to meet you, and she's very proud of her son," she winked at me.

I drifted off to sleep while my mother was still in the room. At first, I slept without any dreams. Slowly, though, my home came into view. I walked into the house, stopping to smell the flowers on the front steps. Once inside the house, I made my way through the rooms I'd seen the night before. I made plans to create paintings and place them, highlighting my first time in the string and the wonders of the world where my childhood was spent. I traced my fingers through the designs in the framework that bordered the center of the walls.

I was in a large room. The couches and chairs all had beautiful patterns on them, and I ran my fingers across each one; you could feel the handmade stitching.

In the center of the wall was a vast fireplace framed by a beautiful mantel, and along it were pieces of what looked to be crystal. The shapes were all amazing, but one caught my eye: a willow tree. It was six inches high, and the branches and leaves each broke out into their own crystals. The sunlight peering through brought out an array of colors. Stepping closer, I could see a little knob on the base of the tree. I gently picked up the delicate tree and twisted the knob; I felt it wind up like a music box, and I could only imagine what song would come from it, I set it down just as gently, then stepped back to listen.

As the music began to play, I felt Landen's hands on my shoulders. He kissed my neck softly, and I turned slowly into him and smiled up at him. He then took my hand, and we danced to the lullaby coming from the little music box. It played on and on, and we danced through our dream in our home built with his hands in a world that had made all this right.

As we woke the next morning side-by-side, I felt rested, peaceful. For a moment, the conflicts that we faced had no meaning; we would find our way home.

"Did you have a good discussion downstairs last night?" I asked.

He looked intently into my eyes and carefully thought his words through before he spoke. "All we came up with were more questions. It doesn't make sense why the string doesn't burn you when you pass through. Your dad said that was always his biggest fear; he could always see the green haze around you, but it didn't ever hurt you - inside or out. We can't figure out why you can't change the emotions of the ones that are in your presence, or why the emotions that call you are so simple. It's amazing that you can see them through an entire string."

"Do you know why they can't see me or feel me?" I asked.

"You never completely leave the string; you stay in the haze just on the edge," he concluded.

That seemed to make sense; it just bothered me that I'd never seen the haze before.

"Livingston thinks that if you focused your energy, you'd be able to affect the ones in your presence. If you could, you'd be able to give courage or a sense of empowerment to those who need it. He knows that there are good people in all the worlds - even in Esteroius," Landen, said, looking away. I could feel that he was uneasy with his thoughts.

"You don't like his ideas, do you?"

"He believes what he's saying, but they're guarding their intentions, not thinking about anything but the moment they're in."

"What do you think it is?"

"I don't know, but I don't think it's anything we should look forward to hearing," Landen said, tightening his jaw.

"The way we feel is a choice, and I hope Livingston doesn't think I'll be able to change those who aren't willing."

"That's exactly what our fathers and I said."

"So when do we leave? What's the plan?"

"That storm we were in was just a little one. Marc looked in the string last night, and it got worse after we left. It should completely pass by late tonight. We're going to leave early tomorrow so Libby won't have to travel through the night. Today, we're going to go to one of the towns here and practice what you do so we can better define it; you can't help anyone until you can control it."

It wasn't anyone's intention, but I felt like a science experiment; it made me uneasy. Showing Landen was one thing, but I already felt embarrassed, thinking of the others watching me and critiquing what I was doing. I rolled on my back and stared at the arched wood above us, wishing I could just tell them to save myself from embarrassment.

Libby ran into the room and dove onto the bed, making a place for herself between us. She was already dressed in a bright yellow swimsuit and sundress.

"I wish you guys would go swimming with me instead of a silly hiking trip," she said, a big pout on her face.

Questioning her words, I looked at Landen but, he was just as lost. I just assumed it was another story my mother had told her to keep the peace.

"We'll miss you, and I promise to come back soon," I said to her.

Libby laughed out loud when I started to tickle her – then all at once she went rigid, and her eyes were somewhere else, looking past the room. I sat up quickly, feeling the fear coming from her, then I shook her lightly and called her name. Landen stood up and lifted her to a sitting position. Her fear impacted us both, and we were reaching the point of panic. Then, all at once it was gone, and she resumed her normal excitement. Landen and I sighed deeply, and Libby looked at us as if we'd lost our minds.

"Did her emotion change, too?" Landen thought.

"It did. She had fear, but only for an instant; now she's fine .What do you think she saw?"

"I don't know. I just hope whatever it was passes just as quickly."

I couldn't have agreed more; she was too young to see something that would cause her that much fear. A sickening feeling came over me, accompanied by an intense sense of dread.

Landen and I got ready for our day. When we went downstairs, I was surprised to see that only my mom and dad were there.

"Where is everyone?"

"Marc and Livingston went to check the progress of the storm. Dad went to see my mother."

A sense of relief came over me; I wouldn't have to be anyone's science experiment after all. When I looked at Landen, he was grinning.

"You didn't think I'd let them make you uncomfortable, now did you?"

It seemed my father had taken on the cooking duties for the morning. He was fixing his famous omelets, and the smell filled the cabin. I heard my stomach growl as I breathed in.

"I hope you guys are hungry. There's more than enough." my father said as we sat at the table.

My mother was sketching the Mountain View that served as the background to the cabin that we'd called home for the past few days. Everyone seemed at peace, even Libby.

"Are you going with me and Landen today, Dad?" I asked my father.

He was surprised and flattered by my question. "I think I'm going to stay here with your mom and Libby," he said, sitting down.

I was sure he had his reasons. Secretly, though, I really just wanted to see the way his hazel eyes would look in the string, I imagined they'd be green - the way they were when he was happy.

"So I heard you had a good day traveling yesterday, that it came quickly to you," he said.

I looked at Landen, and he grinned back at me. I wasn't sure I liked being the topic of conversation.

"I promise I didn't tell them everything; they don't even know where we went," Landen thought. He was learning to read me as easily as I read him.

"So where did you two go anyway?" my father asked.

Landen raised his eyebrows and tilted his head as he took a big bite of his omelet. I was reading him now, and he was saying loud and clear, *'I told you so.'*

"Well, a lot of places. We started at Victory Falls," I answered.

We had my mother's attention now; she'd put her sketch down and was looking at me, a surge of energy coming from her.

"Zimbabwe?" she asked

There was no holding back the laughter from my father, Landen, and me. My mother sat back in her chair and tried to imagine how. I knew how hard it must be for her; the shock that. I felt was still clear in my memory. After I told my mother of the rest of our travels, she was excited for me. I wished I could show her…maybe one day either my father or I could take her.

Landen and I took the rental car and drove to the closest town. It was a tourist town, and we hoped it would be easy to find someone who was unhappy when they were vacationing.

"Landen, do you think I could really help people close to me, like Livingston does?" I thought as we strolled across the sidewalk that lined the town.

"I think there's a reason for your gift. I don't want you to rush it; it'll happen when it's supposed to," he answered.

I wasn't sure if he didn't want me to rush it because he was afraid of how I'd use it, or if he thought it would go away - the same way they said Libby's would if we provoked it.

"Do you really think I can, though?"

"*I know you're special,"* he said giving me my favorite playful grin. *"Did you like your tree last night?"*

It had been dancing through my thoughts all morning, and I wanted to ask him if everything were really that perfect in our home. I smiled.

"*Is it really there?"* I thought. His eyes told me it was.

"Where did you get it from?"

"Your grandmother, Rose, gave it to me almost two years ago. She told me when she saw it, all she could think about was me. I thought it was strange then. Looking back, I think she was trying to give me an advantage."

I could not wait to meet Rose; I already felt connected to her. Out of the corner of my eye, I saw someone: it was Monica's mother, Sharon - and she was hysterical. I felt a panic rush through me; something was wrong. Why would she be in Montana? Then I felt a pull come across me, and a sinking feeling fell through my stomach as my eyes raced over her. I knew without a doubt Sharon was an image.

"What's wrong, Willow? Willow?" Landen said, trying to follow my gaze.

"Sharon is an image," I thought with a shaking voice.

"*Who is Sharon?"* he asked, growing more concerned about me.

"Sharon lives in Franklin. I'm friends with her daughter, Monica."

"*Are you sure she's an image? What does she look like?"* He'd followed my stare and was searching for her.

"*She has on a black dress. Long blonde hair. She's crying, screaming."* I knew he couldn't see her; there was no way not to feel sympathy for her.

"I have to help her, Landen."

Landen's gift of intent was working; he knew that's what I was planning to do, and he was ready to argue his point of view.

"It could be a trap; she's in Franklin...if Drake is anywhere near her, he'll see you."

"Landen, I have to help her... something has to be really wrong – what if he's hurting them?" I felt a sick feeling rise and settle in my throat.

It would be my fault, and I wouldn't be able to live with myself.

"*What if you just call and see?"* He knew he was fighting a battle that I wasn't going to let him win.

"Landen, I have to help her," I thought in a pleading tone. "*You'll be there; and you can pull me back into the sting if he's there. I'll even let you take me all the way home if he tries anything."* I felt confident in my words, I knew the others would get Libby and my mother to me, or that Landen could even go back for them if need be.

Landen covered his face in his hands, and I could feel the turmoil stirring inside him. I felt his pain; he knew I was going to go, and I knew he was trying to think of ways to stop me. He knew if he tried by force, I'd just find another way.

"OK, let's just compromise. You can't stay, no matter what you see; if it's bad, we'll get the others - and we'll all help," he thought.

I could handle that compromise. I didn't want to put myself in danger; I just wanted to help her.

We walked to where Sharon was. She wasn't screaming anymore, and she looked like she was calming down. Landen held my hand as we passed through the crowd.

"Willow, don't say anything to her. You have to keep your concentration; you can't do anything differently than you normally do. I don't know what could happen if you do."

I was having doubts, what if I had put Landen in danger? I argued with myself, I had to help.

When we reached Sharon, Landen stood behind me and wrapped his arms tightly around my waist. His anxiety was growing stronger by the second; putting him through this was torture. Taking in a deep breath, we reached for Sharon, and the string pulled us through with a rush of energy. We were in the police station. Sharon was not alone, other parents were there – in fact all the parents of my friends were in the room with her. Using all my strength, bringing her a feeling of safety was all I could do. Her tears stopped, but she didn't smile. I knew I was only giving her temporary peace. Deciding that was the most that we could do, we let go.

Stopping in the string, I could still feel Landen's arms around me; his anxiety was replaced by sorrow. When I turned to face him, his face held the same emotion. He pulled me closer to him. He saw more than I did, and he knew what was wrong, why they were so upset.

"What happened?" I asked.

I knew my thoughts were as pleading as my face. Landen hesitated, just like he always did when he didn't want to tell me something.

"Landen."

He breathed in. "*There are six missing,"* I heard his words, but I couldn't process them at first.

"He took them," I thought, remembering how Monica had wanted to go with Drake to the beach to go out on his boat.

"I don't know how...he'd have had to take them one by one; Esteroius is two dimensions from here."

He was rocking me back and forth, trying to clam me down, and the humming and gentle current of the string was helping him. All at once, Landen stopped. His whole body went stiff, and I could feel anger coursing through him. Then, I heard who was making him angry.

"Well, well...what do we have here?" It was Drake's deep, charismatic voice.

Landen moved, shielding me with his body.

"Have you hand - delivered my queen to me?" Drake said, laughing.

My adrenaline rushed to my defense. I was infuriated with Drake; he had now crossed the line. Landen's anger rose to meet mine.

"You know, I'd expected to have to deal with her father, or maybe her little boyfriend, Dane - but you, my friend," Drake paused while looking Landen up and down, "you seem to be a more worthy opponent." He began to circle us. "...mmm ...yes... a degree of chivalry always makes a good story." Drake tilted his head, smiling arrogantly and winking at me. "It will be a good one to tell our son, when I tell him how I won you - and every dimension."

As he stopped in front of us, his eyes moved from me to Landen. They were locked in a dead stare, and both of them had jaws locked. The rage I felt in the string them was so powerful, it took my breath away.

"She's not leaving with you," Landen growled through his teeth.

"You would think that a man of Chara would want the color to return to Esteroius," Drake said, crossing his arms across his chest.

"You don't need Willow to release those people; it's you and your beloved Donalt that hold them captive," Landen said in a harsh tone full of disgust for Drake.

"Willow's destiny is threaded through mine," Drake said, glancing at the tattoo of the dragon on his arm, then to my Ankh.

I lunged at him, pushing him into the wall of the string.I could hear the singe of his clothes as he quickly stepped forward. His rage intensified, and every muscle in my body hardened, trying to block out the sheer force of the emotions coursing through the string. He didn't scream in pain; instead, a proud grin filled his face, and he chuckled under his breath.

"Where are they?" I screamed at him as Landen pulled me behind him and blocked Drake, who was stepping toward us.

Drake looked at Landen with an arrogant sneer. "She's always belonged to me…I've been with her more nights than you could ever imagine," Drake said, clearly enticed by my outburst. "Willow, are you going to make this easy or hard on yourself?" he said glaring Landen.

Before I could answer or manage to pull a thought forward, a rush of energy with an unbearable force plowed through my back, knocking me into Landen. The flow intensified, and Landen pushed into Drake, then turned and pulled me close to him. We were both watching the sides of the string; the hazes were rushing by so fast, there was no way to be sure where the passages were. The hum suddenly rose to a roar, and I felt every part of my body vibrate.

"Let me go first; it won't burn me," I thought, feeling my confidence build. I pulled Landen's arm and stepped through the moving wall into an open field.

"Do you know where we are?" I asked, shaking. I looked back at him. The string had burned his arm, and there was a large hole in sleeve of his shirt. "You're hurt again!" I gasped.

Landen looked down at his arm, then around to find our place. My body was so weak from the storm, it started to tremble.

"It's alright; it'll be all alright - I promise," Landen said as he picked me up and held me as tight as he could. Over his shoulder, I saw Libby, and I blinked a few times, thinking the stress had caused me to hallucinate .She seemed frantic - then I felt a pull reach for me.

"Libby!" I gasped. "It's Libby – she's scared!" I screamed.

We ran the twenty-yard distance between her and us.

"Landen, hold on to me!" I yelled, reaching for his hand as I reached for Libby.

When my hand touched her, I screamed her name. When she looked at me all the fear left her face. Everyone was there with her, and Landen shouted toward Ashten.

"Drake is in the string! Willow's friends are in danger!"

Without hesitation, Ashten, Marc, Livingston, and my father stepped through the passage I'd made. Landen was still holding my hand.

"Stay here. I love you. Stay here"

He let go, and my passage was gone.

" LANDEN!" I screamed.

He had vanished.

Chapter Eight

My mother was kneeling in front of me. She was speaking, but I couldn't hear her. A pain was creeping through every part of my body; everything hurt, and I felt like I was being torn apart. I desperately tried to see my passage so I could follow Landen, but it was gone. I was still holding tight to Libby, and she was holding just as tight to me.

"Willow, what happened?" My mother's words finally reached me. When I didn't respond, she ran to the phone. When the other person answered, she said "They're in the string - all of them. Willow made a passage in the center of the cabin, but she won't tell me what happened…is that safe...are you sure?"

There was a pause.

"OK, OK, OK," she then hung up the phone and was back at my side again.

"Willow, I need you to calm down; you're scaring me. They know what they're doing. He can't hurt them - I promise."

I knew I was scaring her, but I couldn't calm down. As the seconds passed by, the pain intensified. I was worried about the people Drake had taken. All my friends flashed before my eyes, and pain was taking over every one of muscles; it was so hot, it turned cold - sending trembles through me. I needed Landen…I needed to feel his emotion.

The cabin door opened, and there stood a beautiful woman, the same age as my mother. She had a small frame, long dark hair, and eyes that were a beautiful pale green. Sympathy filled her face. She ran to where my mother was holding me in the center on the cabin floor, still kneeling where Landen left me - telling me to stay there.

"Did you see them on your way here?" my mother asked.

The woman shook her head no.

"Is it safe for Clarissa to be in there?" my mother asked. I had not registered who this woman was; she had to be Landen's mom.

"She's fine. Her soul mate can see in the string; it s like he was born to travel through them. She went back for him. Brady will be here any minute."

Looking into her eyes, I was overcome with grief … Landen would always have to fight to protect me.

"I'm sorry," I whispered - not only to her, but to the image of Landen that was resting in my mind.

I laid my head on my knees and rocked myself, trying to focus. Aubrey brushed my hair out of my eyes. "You are so beautiful," she said, smiling as if nothing was wrong.

My mother took her phone outside, leaving Aubrey to watch me. Libby was still sitting next to me, and I tried to focus on her; wondering what had her so upset, why I could see her before.

My emotion was still overpowering everyone else's, but my eyes found a solution to my agony: someone was on the porch, and a rush of excitement came through me.

"Landen!" I said breathlessly.

Aubrey followed my eyes and pulled me close to her.

"No, sweetie, that's Brady."

He opened the door, and when the sunlight hit his face, I could see that she was right. Brady's resemblance was remarkable; he had the same build and wavy dark brown hair, but his eyes couldn't begin to compare to Landen's. He smiled at me, and I saw his dimples come to life. He shook his head in disbelief as he walked closer.

"Now there are those eyes my baby brother told me about," he said, looking down at me.

"Did you see them?" Aubrey asked.

"I didn't expect to; the storm is blowing the other way," Brady answered, still staring at me.

"Do you think you could try and tell me what happened so I can help Landen and the others if they need me?" he asked.

I nodded quickly. "I made a passage from a town down the street to Franklin; Drake has taken people from there. When we were in the string, Drake showed up, then the string roared and the current erupted. Landen and I pushed through. He's hurt; his arm is burned really bad." I said it so fast, my words collided together.

"It's going to be fine," Brady said, smiling confidently.

He had a way of making me feel a little better; it could have been his resemblance to his brother. My words and reason were slowly coming back to me.

"What is taking so long? You two traveled in just moments?"

"They'd have had to find them first, and that storm could have taken Drake and your friends anywhere."

Brady moved me to the couch; my mind was replaying what had happened in the string, as well as how confident Drake was. What did he mean, 'our destiny was threaded together?'

The cabin door opened, and I didn't bothering turning; it wasn't Landen. Brady was talking to someone. I heard a beautiful girl's voice; it had to be Clarissa and her soul mate.

"Willow," I heard my name from a familiar voice, one that didn't belong there.

My mind had to be playing tricks on me, and my eyes joined in; before me stood an old friend, the one I'd always shared a kinship with: it was Dane. Behind him stood a beautiful young woman with olive skin, short dark brown hair, and beautiful pale green eyes like Aubrey. She was smiling at me, dressed in a black dress. A red belt gave shape to her petite figure, and long gold necklaces tangled around her. Why was she there with Dane? He was in Franklin, not New York.

"Willow, are you OK," Dane asked me in an alarming tone; I felt his concern. I just stared back and forth between Dane and Clarissa.

"How...how did you...you went to New York?" was all I managed.

Dane turned and looked up at Clarissa. She smiled at him, and I knew they were in love.

"I told you I knew if I stayed close to you, I'd find what I was looking for. After you left, all I could think about was New York. So I flew there the next morning and found your hotel. I knocked on your door, Clarissa answered, and everything suddenly made sense for the first time in my life."

"Everything happens for a reason," I whispered as my mind raced back and forth, realizing that some things are planned out to perfection by the heavens above.

"Do you know where he took Willow's friends?" Brady asked.

"I know they were all talking about going to Florida to sail on his boat," Dane replied, looking at me. "Monica was trying to convince everyone to go."

"Who is 'everyone?'" I asked, realizing I didn't know who was missing.

"Chase, Josh, Jessica, Hannah....and Olivia," Dane said, feeling guilty. "I'm sorry, Willow, I didn't think she would go," he said, looking at me with regret.

I had asked him to watch over Olivia. I was her closest friend, and with me gone, I could see her latching on to Hannah and the others.

"I'm the one that left... I'm the one he really wants," I said through my teeth, trying to block out the pain I was feeling. Aubrey and Clarissa flocked around me.

"This is not your fault," Aubrey said, squeezing her arm around me. I nodded just to give them peace, but nothing would change the way I felt.

My mother came back in and sat down next to me.

"Did you find anything out?" asked Aubrey

"Sharon said she panicked when Monica didn't call. No one will help her; they keep telling her it's summer love and that she'll come home in a few days."

I bet they're still here - at least some of them," Brady said. "There's no way he could have carried that many people through the string within a seventy-two-hour window."

Clarissa nodded in agreement. I stood quickly, thinking that if I moved, the pain would go away.

"Do you know where he would have taken them?" I asked, almost pleading.

Brady and Dane shadowed me, thinking I was going to fall. I started to pace the floor.

"If they're right about him, he'd need to use a large passage – and the only one down there would be the Great Barrier Reef," Clarissa said, walking backwards in front of me; I must have looked really weak.

A chill rippled through me. I knew we were all over the string yesterday, and we could have crossed him at any moment… how did we not see him?

"Are you going to look?" my mother asked Brady.

"I'm not going anywhere until Landen is back; he'd kill me if I left her unprotected."

"Could he still come here?" Dane asked, looking across me at Brady.

"He could if he lost them, but it's a long shot – and I'm not going to risk it. I'd want Landen to do the same if the situation were reversed," Brady said.

I remembered that Brady had someone at home, not to mention a baby on the way.

Their voices faded into the background, and I went somewhere inside myself, looking for answers, wondering what I ever could have done to deserve this pain. I began to regain my balance, and Brady and Clarissa stepped back, trusting me more. Dane, though, stayed close. I turned my eyes slowly to the last place I'd seen Landen; the air was clear, and there was no evidence that it had ever happened. The absence of the string began to fill me with hopelessness, but then I remembered the first lesson Landen had taught me; 'I had to remember what is natural to me.'

Letting the way I thought the passage should be like run through my mind, I imagined the way it would feel as I passed through, and the hum I would hear inside the string; essentially, I let myself feel as if I'd already seen it.

The room faded, and all I heard was utter silence. Before me, the air was divided by a thin glow of light. Suddenly, a pull of energy came over me; I'd found my passage. I knew Landen was in the string, and I wanted to find him, to find my friends. I couldn't stand there any longer and play the part of the damsel in distress. Feeling someone grasp my elbow, I stepped forward with confidence.

The white light passed through me with a soothing vibration of energy. I sighed, feeling a tinge of relief from the agonizing pain that I'd felt everywhere; I felt closer to Landen. The grip on my elbow tightened, and I looked back to see Dane in the string with me.

"Willow, take us back," he said calmly.

I shook my head in defiance. "I have to find him. I have to find all of them," I said, choking on my words.

"Don't cry," he said with sympathy.

"Cry? Are you kidding me?"

"Willow, I think most people would have lost their minds by now. I know this is a lot, but you're going to have to calm down," Dane said, putting his hands on my shoulders.

"It hurts, Dane; I have to find Landen to make it stop."

"It's not safe," he said, looking side to side, struggling to remain calm.

"Not safe?" I mocked. "You don't have any idea. I have a devil chasing me. He's taken our friends - and now he's taken Landen. I'm not going to sit there in pain and just wait," I said, poking my finger vigorously at his chest.

He pushed my hand down and looked at me like I was fool. "You're playing Drake's game. Who wins if you get lost in here?" he said in a more assertive tone.

He was making sense; I hadn't assumed that I'd get lost.

"Landen thinks you're safe here, so imagine how he'd feel if he came back and you were gone," he continued seeing that he was getting through to me.

I stared forward blankly, not knowing what to do. "I have to help him," I said, almost to myself, not wanting to look at Dane.

"If Landen is half as amazing as they've told me he is, then I know he'll be fine. Clarissa told me he spoke of you every day, and you've found each other now. Don't make the mistake of losing yourself in here. Neither of you deserve to be apart any longer," Dane said with a degree of certainty.

"I can't do this, Dane. I don't even know what I'm supposed to do. All of this is insane!" I blurted, out showing the frustration I was feeling.

"You *are* strong enough," he said.

I closed my eyes and nodded, then rubbed my hands across my face, trying to gain composure.

"Take us back," he whispered.

I nodded, and he stepped aside. My green haze was behind him. I reached my hand back and held his. One step later, we were in the center of the cabin, and the pain I felt grew more intense.

"Told you so," Libby said.

She was sitting calmly on the couch, and my mother and Aubrey were standing in front of her. They followed Libby's eyes and found me and Dane standing in the cabin. Aubrey then ran through the door on to the porch.

"Clarissa, Brady, they're back!" she called toward the river.

I looked out the window, and in the distance I could see Clarissa and Brady at the opening of the string through which I'd first traveled. They heard Aubrey, and their emotion of relief was so strong, I felt it from where I stood. I felt horrible; I never considered how my actions would affect them. I held my head low and walked tensely to the couch to sit with Libby. Dane stayed inches behind me, sitting on the coffee table and guarding me from the string.

Surprisingly, no one was angry at me; instead I felt their sympathy. Aubrey sat next to me while my mother fidgeted in place, wordless. Seconds later, Clarissa and Brady rushed through the door, breathless. I felt an admiration coming from them - but for what, I couldn't comprehend. I pulled my legs as close as I could to my body, pushing the thought of the pain away. Clarissa rushed to Dane and wrapped her arms around his shoulders. He reached up and kissed her, not losing his guard position. Brady walked closer, looking at me and then Dane, shaking his head in disbelief.

"Did you know she could do that?" Brady asked Dane.

Dane nodded.

"How?" Brady asked.

Dane shrugged his shoulders."All I know is, she gets a look in her eyes, then she's gone before she ever really leaves ...I started holding on when I was eight."

I titled my head on my knees and looked at Dane. He was staring back at me. Even though we never spoke about my images, I always felt better knowing someone knew.

"Has Landen seen you do that?" Brady asked me.

I nodded. "He taught me to control it," I said, slowly looking in the distance at the memory.

Brady looked at Clarissa, and they both smiled at each other, then looked back at me. I could feel pride and a tinge of envy coming from them. – but I don't know why anyone would envy what I was going though.

"Dane, you can see the string?" my mother asked, befuddled, remembering that Aubrey had told her he could.

Brady was staring at me, but he turned sharply to Dane as my mother spoke. Aubrey and Clarissa smiled proudly it was clear that Brady didn't know that.

"I can see the string; I just can't see the passages in or out," Dane answered, feeling offended by Brady's reaction.

"That's not normal. How is that possible?" asked Brady, shaking his head in disbelief.

"I didn't realize what it was," Dane said.

"At least you can see. We might even be able to teach you to see the passages," said Brady.

Dane seemed to relax as Brady showed his acceptance of his talent. Everyone then fell silently into the background, and I drifted inside myself somewhere, analyzing memories, ones that could help me remember why I chose to be so naïve. I had to have known there would be a day when I would have to face those nightmares. When I would see Brady out of the corner of my eye my heart would pound through my chest, and I'd have to fight harder to forget the pain.

The day aged; the sun had set long ago. Libby never left me, even when my mother begged her to eat. She was sleeping on my lap now; even though she was warm, I still trembled. Brady took the others outside one by one. I knew they were talking about me, and I'm sure my sanity was coming into question. I felt out of control; my head wouldn't stop running through everything…why didn't I tell Landen about the other nightmares? Did he even know that's what Drake meant?

Aubrey and my mother were now sitting beside me, and Clarissa positioned herself in front of me, taking Dane's place as a guard.

"What was Libby upset about earlier when I saw her?" I asked my mother.

She looked down at Libby and ran her hand across her forehead. "We'd just gotten back, and I was about to fix lunch for everyone. She was dancing around and playing with Ashten and Marc, then the laughter left her and fear filled her eyes; it was like she was watching a horrible accident. We tried to talk to her to bring her out of whatever trance she was in, then after three or four minutes she started screaming your name. She told your dad he had to go get you, that you were lost in a field. As soon as the words left her lips, you appeared out of nowhere."

I felt a chill run through me; I couldn't explain it, but I knew that somehow she'd seen what had happened in the string.

"When you left with Dane, she was calm – she told us you would be right back," Aubrey added.

"Willow," Clarissa said. "You saw one of the parents' earlier, right?"

I nodded.

"I bet your friends don't even know they're in danger."

I looked at her, not understanding what she was saying and slightly offended by her lack of concern. She read my expression, but went on to explain.

"It just seems that if they were scared, you would have seen them," she added.

I took comfort in her explanation. It made sense, but I didn't feel any better knowing that they were clueless and in danger - like sheep being led to the slaughter.

Every part of my body hurt from the trembling. My mother's cell phone rang, and the sound brought us all to attention. Brady and Dane came back in the door while my mother reached for her phone, which was resting on the side table.

"Hello? Gina? Hey, is there good news?" my mother said cheerfully.

I felt everyone's hope rise, but as my mother listened, I could feel her heart breaking.

"I – I need to talk to Jason…I'll call you back…I'm fine… I promise." she said, fighting back tears. She then hung up the phone and stared at it.

"Are they OK mom?" I said, not really wanting to hear the answer.

My mother gave me no response.

"MOM!" I yelled.

She came to attention. "I don't know… she didn't say."

"What do you mean? She said something."

"There was…well, there's some kind of a fire at our house…they're working on it."

Of all the days, this is the one day that our historical home decided to burn. I could feel my mother's grief; that house was all she had left of my grandparents. I sat as still as a statue, and I didn't even notice Brady and Aubrey take my mother outside.

I could feel my mother's mood change as Brady and Aubrey talked to her. I felt a sense of understanding come over her. I then watched as she came in, picked up her cell phone, and turned it off. She then went upstairs, and I could hear her walking from room to room. Aubrey and Clarissa went upstairs, too, and I wondered what they were doing. Brady had a very calm feeling come over him - almost too calm; I knew he knew more than he was telling me.

I realized that Landen wouldn't have been gone this long unless something had happened. Perodine's words circled in my mind. I wondered what price my choice would cost, and who would pay it. I wanted answers.

"Why did Drake take my friends?" I asked Brady

"Willow, he's just a really bad guy," Brady said, locking his jaw.

"Do you know who Perodine is?" I asked Brady.

My question astounded Brady; I could feel his fear peak, then he suppressed it.

"Do you?" he asked bleakly.

I knew then that she was real, just as real as Drake and Landen. Aubrey was standing on the balcony that overlooked the living room. Brady looked up at her, then walked away from me, staring out at the string. Aubrey then came back down the stairs, and my mother and Clarissa were close behind. They looked refreshed, ready for something to happen; I felt like they were leaving me out of some big secret. I'd never felt more alone in my whole life. I looked at the clock on the wall; it had been almost twelve hours since Landen had let go of my hand.

"Should it take this long? Where are they?" I asked.

When no one answered me, I stood and started to pace. I was just going to have to look for him myself. I was sure that Brady would follow me, and I'd make him take me to Landen; they wouldn't talk me out of it this time.

"Willow, I think you should sit back down; you don't look so good," my mother said.

I felt weak, but I told myself that when I found Landen, I'd be fine.

My mother went on. "I think you need some food; you really look pale," she said, even louder.

It took everything I had not to scream at her. How could she be so calm? Dad was in there, and so was Ashten - yet they just sat there, petting me.

"How are you two so calm? Even you, Brady? You're all separated from them…does it not hurt? You don't feel it? "

As if I'd said the magic word, their emotions changed from anxiety to excitement… what could they possibly be happy about?

Aubrey walked over to me and placed her hands on my shoulders. "I told them that you two were more than the rest of us."

I looked at her with my red eyes. "It doesn't hurt you? You don't feel it?"

"It's not comfortable, but it doesn't hurt physically." Aubrey said, looking me directly in the eye. "This is a good pain; it means that it's real, you and he are real, and no one else is like you in any dimension. You should not be apart; you need each other to survive."

"We have to go in the string and find them; something could have happened," I argued, remembering that Landen had already been burned twice.

Aubrey shook her head no, and the only thing I could feel from her was pride."I know my son; whatever pain he's in he's using it to keep you safe and get back to you."

I felt myself sway as I stood, and Brady was now standing at my side, waiting to catch me if I tried to leave or fall - whichever came first. It let my eyes close for just a moment, and I could feel hands on me. Then out of nowhere, a rush of energy came through the room. I opened my eyes quickly and saw that they all looked the same. No one had moved – so where was it coming from? I peeked around them all to see Libby; she was still asleep on the couch, but I was sure it was coming from her. Everyone else followed my stare.

All of the sudden, Libby shot up from the couch and ran up the stairs, and you could hear her running around. My mother walked over to the stairs and yelled Libby's name, and when she didn't answer, my mom started to go up the stairs at the same time Libby was coming down them. She had taken off her bathing suit and put on her favorite little pink sundress and sandals, and she was holding the rabbit that she'd slept with her whole life. A smile was brightly lit across her face, and the energy she was putting off was refreshing. When she got to the bottom of the stairs, she screamed, "Come on, Willow, it's time to go to Landen's castle."

"Libby, do you see them?" I said, feeling life seeping into me.

"Come on, Willow," she said, holding me by the hand and pulling me to the door.

I wasn't going to ask any more questions. I followed her out the door and down the steps. I could feel the confusion coming from everyone behind me. I didn't care, though; Libby had to have seen something.

Outside, it was dark; the crescent moon was fighting with the clouds to shine through. My eyes were weak - my whole body was. I wanted to run faster, but I didn't have the strength. All of the sudden, I felt him.

"Landen? Landen, are you here?" I thought. He didn't answer.

I closed my eyes and fell to my knees - but before I could fall any further, I felt his hands on my face. When I opened my eyes and saw him, I took all the energy I had left, wrapped my arms around him, and kissed him with a sense of great urgency. He kissed me back with the same amount of force.

"I know... I know it hurts, but it's over now. I love you," he thought

"I love you, too."

I felt my body go limp; I'd lost my energy, and I was drifting away.

Landen yelled behind him, "Jason, something is wrong with Willow."

I could feel my father and everyone else around me.

"Willow, speak to me."

I wanted to, but I couldn't.

"She's fine. Her adrenaline levels have been too high for too long; she just needs to sleep." my father said.

"Can you carry her?" I heard Ashten say.

"Brady, get Libby," Landen said.

"Willow, baby, hold on; I'll carry you home."

I felt the current and hum of the string and lost all consciousness. I fell into a deep sleep, dreamless at first, and when I opened my eyes, I could see a beautiful canopy above me; I had made it to my home again. When I reached next to me, Landen wasn't there, but I could feel him just outside the doorway that led to the porch. I felt his turmoil, and I imagined he was still lost in the worst day we'd lived through so far. Rising from the bed, I noticed that I was wearing a white night gown; the straps were a beautiful lace. It looked like nothing that I'd ever owned, and I loved the way it felt against my skin. Wanting to hold Landen, I walked slowly feeling the pain in my muscles to where he was standing.

When I reached the porch Landen was looking out at the crescent moon. I could see that my father has treated his wound; a wide white bandage was wrapped around his arm, and another was on his shoulder. I walked to him and wrapped my arms around his waist. He let out a deep breath, and relief came over him; he felt so real, more real than he had in any dream I'd ever had before. He kissed my hands softly before slowly turning around. When I saw his eyes I could see how worried and tired they were. I reached up and ran my fingers over them, and he pulled my face up to his and kissed me tenderly. I could feel all the warmth as if I were awake. His kiss left me breathless, and a tingling sensation coursed through me.

Landen reached down, gracefully picked me up, and carried me through the doors to our bed. I could feel the white sheets and smell the flowers at our bedside. I held him tightly, remembering the pain that I'd felt when he'd left. With his touch, a surge of energy ran through my veins, taking away the stress that had consumed my body. A euphoric high then came over me, and I wanted to be close to him, to stay there with him in that dream, feeling only his emotion and his strength. I found myself losing my breath; I couldn't believe how real it all seemed to be.

Landen then whispered, "I love you."

I knew then that it wasn't a dream; it was real. We were home, we were together, and the unimaginable high only intensified.

Chapter Nine

The sunlight filling the room brought me out of a peaceful sleep. I looked to my side and saw Landen sleeping soundly. I watched his chest rise and fall, assuring myself that he was real. Smiling, I let my memory flow over the night that we'd shared - but then the day that we'd lived before came crashing through my memory.

I had so many questions - is everyone safe now? Is Drake only a bad memory? I couldn't bring myself to wake him; he looked too perfect. I decided to get up and explore my surroundings. There was a long dresser on the opposite wall of our bed, and I saw the bag that I'd packed in Franklin sitting on top of it. My photo album was open to the picture of graduation night. Monica was the valedictorian, and Olivia and I were kissing her cheeks as she smiled widely. An uneasy breath escaped me; I wanted them all to be safe and wished only for a moment that they'd never known me. I reasoned that, if that were true they'd be safe. I continued to turn the pages, missing all of them more and more, even - Chase.

With my purple top, white shorts, and all my toiletries, I found my way to the bathroom next to our bed. A beautiful bathtub sat in the middle of the room, there were large mirrors hanging on the walls, and a vanity lined the back wall. I smiled, imagining Landen and his family putting in all the details of this home together. I then bathed and dressed for what was sure to be a beautiful day.

When I finished, Landen was still asleep, so I tiptoed past him and went down the stairs. The house was even more perfect in reality. It reminded me of the home in which I'd been raised: the floors were a cherry wood, the light cream walls were all divided with a cherry wood rail, and paintings and candle holders framed the path down the wide staircase. Until that thought, I'd forgotten that - on top of everything else - my home had caught fire yesterday. I hoped that they'd managed to save it. Even though I wouldn't live there anymore, someone deserved to have the same peace that my family had there.

The first room I wanted to see was the living room, so I could see the willow tree that I had danced to with Landen. Rainbows danced across the walls as the sun touched the crystals. While I was standing star struck, I heard something, it sounded like a car door closing. Odd… cars. I walked to the front window and saw a little white car - just like the little ones we had at home; the only difference was, the top of the car had a gray panel. Someone was pulling things out of the back seat. She was young, her hair was long and blonde (almost white), and her skin was the color of honey. I walked to the front door and opened it slowly, and she turned as I stepped on the front porch, a smile filling her beautiful face. There was no doubt she was pregnant. I assumed she was Felicity.

"Did I wake you?" the young girl said.

"No, I was just exploring," I answered shyly.

She had reached the porch. She was holding a large basket, and I could smell the baked goods coming from it. My stomach instantly reminded me that my last meal had been breakfast yesterday.

"My name is Felicity," she said as she smiled at me. I could feel how happy and excited she was.

"I'm Willow," I said. She smiled, and I instantly felt foolish; she knew who I was.

"Here, let me take that," I said, freeing her hands.

"Is Landen still asleep?" she asked

I nodded and watched her walk into the house. I then followed her through the entry hall and to the kitchen.

"This is my favorite room; it was the only one I got to help with," she said.

The kitchen was one of the rooms I hadn't been in yet, but I found it perfect, just like the others. The counters were made of a beautiful gray stone, the cabinets were a dark wood that matched the table and chairs, and there were beautiful bouquets of flowers set in the center of the table and counter. The room was very large; it had a long window across one wall and a wide doorway on the back wall that led to the porch. She walked over to the cupboard and pulled out two glasses and plates. I sat down at the large kitchen table and just watched her; she had a beautiful glow about her.

"I don't remember anything. Is my family OK? Do you know where they are?" I asked

"Their house is just over that hill," she said, looking out the back door. "Libby is the best little girl. I played with her for hours after you all came home; I love her energy. I'm sure they're still asleep; it was well into the night before they went home, and Brady was sleeping like a baby when I left."

"Do you live close, too?"

"We all live within a mile of each other. It's still very private, though. The hills seem to give each home a sense of solitude."

I wanted to ask her so many questions. I knew she'd understand me, how fascinating all this was, living here, knowing how to survive in another world.

"Is it as amazing as I think it is here? I mean, how does it all work – people living in peace?"

Felicity smiled at me; she seemed to be fascinated with me as well. I felt so naive, like a child learning to balance her surroundings.

"The most amazing thing that you'll find here is that each person does what they're meant to do. Everyone has a gift."

"What do you mean? Everyone has insight? Landen made it seem rarer," I questioned

"Your insight is rare. What I mean is that we all have a purpose, something that was put in our soul that's meant to bring not only us joy, but also those who surround us. You can see it in everyone if you really look – it's almost as beautiful as love," Felicity said, smiling at me.

"Sometimes finding what you're supposed to do with that joy can be difficult where I come from," I mumbled, seeing no purpose in any of my natural gifts.

"Those that are born here are taught from the very beginning to find their purpose," Felicity said.

"How can you teach something like that?" I asked, rolling my eyes.

Seeing my frustration, Felicity sighed. She then looked at me, and tilted her head, and said, "Well, OK, Libby is six, so what they'll do is look at her birth chart and find her characteristics, teach her math, science, everything in the way she learns best. Brady's sun sign was Aquarius, along with his other planets - they decided to teach him through music. Every subject was related back to music, which made learning fun and helped him to grasp subjects that may have been more difficult for him if he were taught like a Pisces - which is what Landen is. When the children get older, it's easy for them to choose what makes them happy."

I laughed at myself; the most I'd ever done as far as the Zodiac was concerned was looked at my horoscope - which was always wrong. To think that an education system was balanced on the stars in the sky seemed senseless to me.

"What? How do they do it in your dimension?" Felicity asked, baffled at my humor.

"We all just go to school and learn the same subjects."

"But how do they make sure that the kids grasp what they're being taught?"

"Teachers. Parents."

"But what if the teacher or parent doesn't relate to the chart? You can't group so many different characteristics together and expect positive results," she said.

"Umm…I…I don't know." How was I supposed to answer a question like that? It had always been done that way.

"What dimension did you come from again?" Felicity asked, raising one eyebrow.

"Um…Infante," I said, hoping I'd remembered the name correctly.

"I still find it intriguing to meet the people they bring home; you would not believe how we all come to different conclusions on living life," she said, smiling at me.

"I guess that goes back to that chart thing - huh?" I said, tilting my head and taking her energy in.

Felicity nodded, snickering again. "Traveling is a dominant purpose in our family," she explained. I could feel the pride coming her. "Travelers are vital to Chara, they guide us. If they see something in another dimension that has brought harm to the people, they guide us away from that tragedy. If they see something that has brought peace and joy to a dimension, they teach us so we can grow more peaceful. Traveling is one of the most respected gifts; without travel, our children would never find the love that we have."

Felicity caressed her stomach as she spoke. She was a very happy person, and I felt reassured that if anyone could find my friends, it was Landen.

"Everyone in this family travels?" I asked.

Felicity nodded. "We are well known throughout Chara," she said, her smile widening, "and Landen is the youngest and most admired traveler of all."

I raised my eyebrows to question her.

"Landen's insight of truth is not what he is known for; instead, he is known across Chara as 'the one who can see all,'" she explained.

I tilted my head and smiled shyly. Perodine told me in my dream that 'the one who sees must have my heart and Landen had always had my heart; I wondered if she meant the string. The reality I was in came back to me.

"Do you know what happened before we got here? I mean, did Landen find my friends?"

Her smile lessened, and I could feel her guarding her emotions. "I think Landen wants to talk to you about it," she said as her smile faded. I gave her a look of understanding, but I knew it couldn't all be good news that Landen wanted tell me.

"I felt so bad for him; he was so worried about you. Jason must have told him a hundred times that you just needed to rest."

I remembered how worried he looked when I'd found him on the porch last night; I felt awful that I'd caused him such anguish. Felicity could see the look on my face and reached for my hand to comfort me.

"I'm so happy for you two. I knew he would find you. When Brady told me the names of your family, all I could think about was that music box on the mantel. I did not say anything to Landen; I was afraid if I was wrong, his heart would be broken."

My eyes sparkled as I remembered dancing to it.

"Everyone is coming to your celebration," she said as she cleaned away the plates.

"They have a lot to celebrate; three couples have come home," I said, reminding her of my mother and Clarissa.

"I really can't see it fitting all in one night; the news has spread across Chara: Jason Haywood home at last, Clarissa's soul mate being able to see the string, and, of course, the youngest couple – the ones who need no words!" Felicity said.

I had already forgotten that Dane could see the string. It must really be rare to cause so much excitement, realizing that the celebration was some sort of rite of passage here. I wondered what waited for me outside those doors. I had to change the subject, though; I was never one for being in the center of attention, and the thought of it was making me uneasy.

"Which dimension did you come from?"

"Neime. Just next door, so to speak."

"Is Neime a good one? I mean, is it peaceful?"

"It is. We live a lot like they do here. I think Neime is the smallest."

"How else is it different?"

"Well, the biggest difference is that we do not acknowledge time."

I gave her a curious look.

"We do not mark hours or days or even years; it's a good place for Gemini's."

I had to smile. A world where you could never be late; I could think of a few people who would enjoy that. I felt a burst of energy; looking to the source, the baby, I saw it move a little. Felicity smiled and rubbed her belly.

"Jason said the baby is perfect."

"I don't know how you lasted so many days without Brady; I'm sorry he had to leave you."

"Don't be. I have a little insight of my own; it's called a woman's intuition. I knew that he would be helping to bring home someone very special."

I had instantly fallen in love with her, and I hoped I could be just as close to Clarissa and Aubrey. I felt foolish thinking of my behavior yesterday. Felicity walked to where I sat and gave me a big hug.

"I need to go; I want to help Aubrey get ready for tonight.

"Where are we going?" I asked, a feeling of dread coming over me.

"Tonight it is just going to be family and close friends. This whole week will be filled with several celebrations; people are coming from everywhere," she said, walking softly toward the front room, beckoning me to follow her. When we reached the porch she said, "I have some clothes for you. I wanted you to have something nice to wear – I remember how I felt when I got here, not having more than a satchel of things from my world."

I knew she was just being nice, but the truth was, I couldn't care less about a single thing I had owned in Franklin. I followed her to the car, and she handed me a handful of clothes. They were all dresses; some long, others short, and the colors were vibrant and balanced all at the same time. They felt so smooth, like the gown I found myself in last night…I wondered who had put that on me.

"I made these, so if they are too big, I can take them in for you."

"You made these?" I asked.

She smiled. "I love to make clothes. I will stop back by before the party and make sure they fit you well."

I stood, looking at them in admiration.

"I am sure Landen will be up soon. I'll see you when the sun goes down." I found the way she kept time very comforting. I hugged her goodbye and watched her leave.

When I walked back in the house, I found Landen standing at the bottom of the stairs. I could tell he had been up for awhile; his hair was wet from where he had showered, and he was dressed for the day, all in black again. I smiled at him shyly; I couldn't believe this was real. Then the distance between us seemed too far, so I let the dresses fall and ran into his arms. He laughed out loud at my unconventional enthusiasm.

"Why didn't you wake me?"

"You looked too peaceful."

I looked at his arm to make sure he'd dressed his wound again. My eyes widened as I stared at his unbroken skin. I reached out with my hand and ran it across his arm.

"How?" I thought.

"I don't know. It was healed when I woke up, and my shoulder is healed as well," Landen said, pulling his shirt up to show me.

It was like it had never happened - but both of his burns had been severe enough to cause scarring. I kissed his shoulder softly before I lowered his shirt. He then turned to look at me, and I felt the utter devotion coming from him.

"You healed me," he whispered as he put his hands around my waist, staring into my eyes.

I thought through yesterday and the pain that I'd endured. I wasn't sore anymore; it was as if it had only been a bad dream.

"You took my pain away, too," I whispered.

He leaned down and kissed me gently. I pulled him closer and laid my head on his chest.

"I see you met Felicity. She wanted you to wake up just as badly as I did last night. I was surprised that Brady got her to go home," he said in an amused tone.

I let my arms fall from around him, then picked up the dresses I had let fall to the floor and draped them across the banister.

"She brought some food. Are you hungry?" I asked

Landen eyes brightened up. I smiled and pulled him to the kitchen. I'd watched Felicity closely, so I knew were all the dishes were. As I set the plate before him, I looked at him; he was smiling at me in absolute disbelief.

"What?" I asked

"Nothing"

"Tell me."

"You just look…you look like you belong here. I just can't believe it - that you're here."

I let Landen finish his breakfast before I started asking the questions that had haunted me all morning. I needed to know, and my stomach turned while I waited for the answers. Once he was finished, I cleared the dishes away and followed him outside through the back door, onto the wide porch.

Large white windmills were scattered across the fields, and I could see the wind turning them. It was so nice out; the breeze made it seem worth it to linger on the porch. Sitting next to Landen on one of the long benches that lined the house, I could feel the dread coming from him; he knew what I was going to ask him.

"Landen, are you going to tell me?"

He lowered his eyes. I could see he was wishing his way out of it – hoping that I'd be able to let it go – but he had to know that I could still see Sharon and how upset she was; my consciousness wouldn't allow me to let it go.

I reached for his hand. “Landen, tell me… is it really that bad? What did he do?”

Landen adjusted himself in his seat, then looked out past the fields and back at me, replaying the day in his mind. I could feel the anger and remorse – as well as the same pain that I had - rush through him.

“When we got into the string, we split up, and your father and Marc went back to Franklin so they’d know who he’d taken and could find out where they went. Livingston and my father went with me to find Drake.”

Landen stood and started to walk back in forth in front of me; I could feel how angry he was.

“When we finally found him, he’d almost made it back to Esterouis. I was so mad, I wanted to throw him off the nearest cliff. He kept taunting me, wanting me to follow him into his world.”

I walked to where Landen was pacing to calm him down; he was so furious, you’d have thought Drake was standing there at that very moment.

“Livingston told me that if I did, I’d never see you again. Drake then hit Livingston, and I pulled them apart and threw Drake through his passage.”

“Did you find the others?” I asked.

As Landen’s remorse grew, my stomach turned. It was bad; I could feel it through him.

“Marc and your dad had gone to a passage that Livingston told them to search…they…they…found what was left of a boat.”

“What do you mean, ‘left?’” I asked. I could barely hear him over my heartbeat.

“It was wrecked. There were survivors… two.”

“Two? Where are the rest? Does he have them?” I said, covering my mouth in disbelief. The pain in Landen’s eyes was ripping me apart.

“The two guys, Josh and Chase, saw Drake take three girls, Hannah, Jessica and…Olivia,” Landen said. My eyes raced back and forth, trying to process and count the names that he'd said, and I suddenly realized he didn't say Monica's name…she was there….it was her idea…why didn't he say her name?

"Monica?" I asked hoarsely, looking up at Landen.

Tears were pooling in a film over my eyes. Landen looked down at the ground, then back up at me through his dark lashes. I could feel his remorse, and I knew she was gone.

"Josh and Chase said they couldn't reach her before she….drowned," he said slowly.

Feeling like I was going to be physically sick, I walked to the side of the porch, trying to hide my failing composure from Landen. I couldn't breathe; Monica's face was dancing through my memory. Landen came to my side and caressed my back, grieving with me. They must have told him who she was and that I'd spent my childhood at her side.

"Where are the others?" I said in an angry whisper.

"With Drake."

"How… how are we going to get them back? Why is he doing this to us? What do we not know?" I asked, looking down and wanting to escape from the pain.

Landen didn't answer my questions. I turned to look at him when I felt his anger building, and I knew his resentment was aimed at our family. Suddenly, it felt like he and I were all alone, no matter what dimension we were in.

"Was Dad in Franklin when our house was burning? Did he see it happen?"

Landen looked down at me, reached his hand to my face, and – bracing himself for my response - searched for how to answer me.

"We burned the house," he said finally.

I stepped back quickly and stared at him in disbelief, causing him to lose his touch. That hurt him, but I was so angry. I remembered the look on my mother's face when Sharon had called her, how grief had filled her.

"What? Why?"

"We couldn't leave anything of yours for Drake to have," he said as he pulled me back to him, giving me no other choice but to look into his piercing blue eyes.

"Why does it matter? It's just stuff; it's not me."

Landen pulled my face closer to his, trying to make me understand. I could see the urgency in his expression; he needed me to listen to him.

"There are a lot of things that cannot be explained - in any dimension. Esterouis is known for the dark things that people believe. They use spells and magic to control the world around them, and Livingston and our fathers believed that the priest would be able to use your family's belongings to hurt you," Landen said

"I don't understand," I said, almost to myself.

"The answers will come when they're supposed to. I'm sure of it."

I could feel how unsure he was and how he was attempting to hide that from me.

"Can we bring my friends home before Drake decides to hurt them?" Landen nodded as he pulled me to him and rested his chin on my head. "How?" I asked

"They'll call you. You're connected to them."

"What if they're under some spell or something? Can we not just go get them? They may not even know they're in danger?"

"I sent travelers out last night to find my grandfather, August, who will help us. I don't want anyone else to get hurt. If we charge in there, it would be dangerous not only for your friends, but for us as well."

"What if they call me? What then?"

"Then we go together; I don't think we can survive long without one another."

I leaned back and looked at him intently, understanding completely what he meant. I had thought I was acting foolish, like a love sick little girl.

"Did it hurt your body, too?" I asked

"It was almost more than I could bear; I felt pain everywhere. That's why I listened to Livingston and my dad; I didn't think that I could make a clear decision in the state I was in."

I knew what he meant. I'd never felt the way that I did yesterday; the pain was real and could be felt in every single muscle of my body.

My head spinning, I let go of Landen and walked back to the bench on the porch. He came to my side and wrapped his arm around me. I laid on his shoulder and let yesterday play through my mind. Landen's emotions were shifting from moment to moment, and I felt them finally settle on jealousy. I knew what he was about to ask me, and I braced myself for the emotion that he would feel.

"Are you going to tell me what he meant about the nights together?" His voice was low and calm. I stayed very still and quietly answered him.

"He meant the nightmares."

Landen shifted his shoulder to face me with anxious eyes. "He was in more than two?" he asked, knowing the answer. I let my eyes tell him yes.

"Is he the reason you'd be so upset all those nights?"

He knew the answer to that question, too. He stood quickly and paced the porch, and the anger inside him reached the point of rage. All at once, he stopped and knelt before me.

"Tell me what happens, when they happen," Landen said in a desperate tone.

"There's a heavy, painful weight on my chest. My gift of emotion is taken from me. I can only feel one person, a person who's afraid. In my nightmares, I can change emotion, and I help that person feel at peace. Then they disappear, and Drake shows up and reaches for me. I just never saw his face before last week."

Landen placed his hand in the center of my chest, as if he wanted to take away all the times that I'd suffered under the overpowering weight. I placed my hand on his, and his eyes met mine.

"I've had a nightmare every new moon of my life until last November, and the last two nightmares don't fit any pattern…I don't understand why they're different."

Landen lowered his hand and looked down. "Do they see you, or are they like the images?" he asked quietly; I could feel his fear.

"Like the images."

He turned from me and leaned up against my legs.

"Does that mean something? Is that why you're scared?" I asked, a bit timid.

"If we met in the same place every night, I'd think that you met Drake in Esteroius in your nightmares. The thought of having you there alone takes my breath away."

"Did we always meet in Chara?" I asked.

Landen turned, looked into my eyes again, and shook his head no. "I have no idea where we're meeting. I've never seen anything like it," he said with a degree of respect. He then pulled himself up on the bench beside me and held me tight.

"Landen, was Drake ever in your nightmares?" I asked.

"I've only dreamed of you," he answered

"Who's Perodine?" I blurted out faster than I intended.

Landen quickly turned sideways and looked down at me, astonished that I'd said that name.

"Who told you about her?" he asked, angry.

"No one. I dreamed of her, and she told me her name."

"You dreamed of Perodine?" He was angry and scared all at once.

"Is that bad?"

"It can't be good. She's older than time itself. They say that she's the true ruler of Esterouis. She's portrayed as Donalt's wife, and if you were to look at paintings from hundreds of years ago, you'd see her portrait. They say she lives on and on – never dying - and that she's the source of all the good and bad magic that the dimension uses."

I closed my eyes, exhausted from the constant twists that life kept throwing at me.

"What did she say to you - besides her name?"

"Nothing that made any sense," I said, frustrated with the added conflict of Perodine.

Landen nodded, not wanting to push me. "OK, listen: I want us to keep this to ourselves. When August gets here, we'll tell him; he'll be honest with us."

"Are the others not being honest?"

"I'm just tired of them hiding whatever they're hiding."

I nodded, agreeing with Landen. I hoped that August would come home soon. Landen squeezed me tight, then stood, reached for my hand and said, "Your Dad is walking this way."

I looked out at the field, but I didn't see him. Landen then nodded his head toward the front door.

"He's coming to see how we're feeling after yesterday," Landen said, smiling slightly.

Chapter Ten

I stood and followed Landen. As I stepped into the kitchen, I was sure I felt my father's peace approaching. I looked at Landen and shook my head in disbelief, hoping my insight would eventually grow as strong as his. We passed through the kitchen into the entry hall. Landen reached for the door just as my father knocked. Landen then pulled the door wide open, and my father was standing there with a bright smile on his face.

"Good morning, Jason," Landen said, extending his arm as an invitation.

"I was just coming to see how the two of you were fee--" my father stopped in mid- sentence. He was staring at Landen's arm, then his eyes quickly looked over Landen's entire body, then over mine. I could feel his absolute disbelief.

"Come in, Jason," Landen said, putting his arm around my father.

Landen led my father into the living room, which was beside the front door. My father then looked us over again quickly, reaching for Landen's arm and inspecting it closer.

"How did you heal so fast?" my father asked Landen.

"I don't know. I took off the bandage this morning so I could take a shower and the burn was gone," Landen said as he took a seat on the large tan couch in the center of the room.

My father walked over to one of the matching chairs that faced the couch and sat down, still completely astonished.

"His shoulder is healed, too," I said as I went to Landen's side.

"Both of you are healed - but last night, I could see pulls deep in your muscle tissue. I've been up all night, trying to figure out how it was possible for the two of you to have that much damage inside your body," my father said as he slowly looked us over.

"Have you seen my dad and Livingston today?" Landen asked.

My father nodded. "Livingston went to Esteroius to see if he could find a way to the girls, and Ashten is helping Aubrey get ready for tonight," he answered.

"Is mom OK," I asked

"She's fine; trying to stay busy and positive. She's worried about your friends," my father said quietly.

I swallowed hard. I knew my mother would grieve deeply over Monica; she always saw my friends as her extended family. My eyes fell as I felt the heavy burden of blame.

"It was an accident, Willow. Josh and Chase said that a storm came, and Olivia and Monica were knocked out of the boat. In fact, they said that Olivia would have drowned if Drake hadn't pulled her out of the water," my father said.

"What are you going to tell Sharon?" I asked

"Sharon knows there was an accident. The Coast Guard told her that Monica was on a boat with Chase and Josh and that they couldn't find her. Right now, she wants to believe that Monica is just missing; she'll say goodbye when she's ready," my father said to me in a gentle tone.

"Where do they think Olivia, Hannah, and Jessica are?" I asked, bewildered.

"They don't know. I altered a manifest for a cruise ship that showed the three of them docking in the Florida Keys; it was all I could think to do at that moment. That'll buy us some time to get them home safely, though," my father answered

"I thought you said Chase and Josh saw Drake take the girls...wouldn't they have told everyone? Did they see the string?" I asked, looking first at Landen and then to my father.

"There is an herb that grows in Chara called Realm. It erases recent memory. I gave them the herb to help them with their grief; both of them blamed themselves for not reaching Monica." I could feel grief from him. "Now, the last memory they have is of arriving in Florida, and the doctors will assume that their memory loss is due to shock," he continued.

"We have to go and get them," I said, standing.

Landen stood and reached his arm around me; he knew I intended to leave right then and go to Esterouis. My father also stood, blocking my path.

"Willow, they aren't in danger now," Landen whispered as he pulled me close to him.

I buried my head in his chest and fought against a rush of angry tears that wanted to come out.

"Landen's right, Willow," my father said, putting his hand on my back. "Drake wants you, and he knows that if he hurts them you'll never come to him."

I looked up from Landen's chest at my father. "Why does he want me?" I asked, staring at him through a film of tears.

The color left his face. He looked up at Landen, then back down to me, then he sighed and turned. "I'm hoping that one of the girls will appear as an image to you," he said, changing the subject.

"Now he's being silent," I thought.

Landen held me a little tighter, trying to fight his anger.

"Will you show Brady and Marc how you travel? If they appear as an image, it would be good to have them at our side," Landen thought.

"I'll show whoever you want me to. I just want them back," I thought, still staring at my father, feeling betrayed.

"We're going to teach Brady and the others how Willow travels so that when the time comes, we'll be able to get them all back safely," Landen said to my father.

My father turned quickly. "That's a good idea, but do you think it's safe for the two of you to leave Chara?" my father asked.

"We'll stay close," Landen promised.

My father nodded, and I felt his trust. "Just make sure the two of you stay close to each other…I still don't understand what happened to your bodies yesterday.

Landen nodded. My father then looked at me, reached over, and kissed my cheek. I closed my eyes as I felt his concern; I didn't understand why he wouldn't just tell me what he knew.

"Be safe. I'll see you tonight," he said quietly as he turned to leave.

I sat patiently on the couch as Landen called his brother and Marc to come over - but my stomach was tied in knots; all I could think about was how short I'd been with Monica the last time I saw her. I'd taken her for granted. She'd never know how much she really meant to me. I then let memories of Olivia, Hannah, and Jessica run through my mind; I could hear their voices and smell their perfume. They didn't deserve to be pulled into this twisted fate that had always chased me - I didn't care if it were accident or not. Drake had put all of my friends in danger, and I would not rest until he paid for my grief and their suffering.

While we waited on the front porch for everyone to arrive, I stared out into the field, taking in the pure beauty of Chara. Before long, Brady was the first one to make it to the house. He stepped out of a large white Jeep that had gray glass panels running across the hood and doors, and I noticed he was dressed almost completely in black. As he walked toward us, I couldn't help but ask.

"What is it with all the black - do I need to change?" I said, looking down at my white shorts and purple top.

Landen smiled at my new observation. *"No, I'll keep you close. It's just easier to see each other in the string if your wear black; if you get more than ten feet apart, you seem to fade."*

Brady and Landen were now standing side by side, and their resemblance to one another was more than apparent; it wouldn't be difficult for a stranger to mistake one for the other.

"How's your..." Brady started to say as he looked at Landen's arm.

"I don't know," Landen answered before Brady could ask.

Brady nodded, dropping the subject. I could feel a sense of pride coming from him, and I sensed that Landen and Brady had a bond beyond brotherhood.

Another Jeep pulled up. It was a dark gray, and I could see the same panels that were on Brady's Jeep. I studied the panels on both vehicles, trying to understand how they were powering the Jeeps. Landen grinned as he watched my eyes take in all the details.

"I keep forgetting that this is all new to you...it's like you've always been here with me."

I smiled at him. *"I have been; I just never paid much attention to the scenery around us."*

"You two are talking, aren't you?" asked Brady. "Now that's weird – I don't know if I'd want Felicity in my head...I mean she *is* the one, but this is just - just something else."

Landen laughed, then pulled me to him and kissed me, not caring who was watching. There were two people in the Jeep. I recognized Marc; he was the one driving. The other guy was tall and had a lean build like the others, but with a baby face. His hair was a dirty blond and very curly, and he had a playful emotion wrapped in anticipation.

"That's Chrispin; he's Marc's baby brother," Landen answered my question before I could even ask it.

"I have to say, you two look a lot better today. You had me worried, little one," Marc said to me as he reached the porch and hugged me.

"Can I see your arm?" Chrispin asked as he got closer.

Landen looked at Marc, then down to his arm. I felt the shock come from Marc, but Landen just shrugged his shoulders. Marc then looked back at Chrispin and shook his head, letting him know to drop the subject. I felt the confusion coming from Chrispin as he looked nervously back and forth between Landen and me.

"This is Chrispin. He's very excited to meet you – though I'm sure you already know that," Marc said.

"Hey," I said shyly. "Thanks for coming on such short notice. I'm sure you all had your day planned out already."

"Hey, li'l' sis. You two are the only show in town right now. We're proud to be here," Marc said.

I blushed as he complimented us; it was very hard for me to be the center of attention. I hoped that I'd be strong enough to stand in a room with a lot of people that night.

I followed Landen's lead, and we walked off the porch to the fields that surrounded the house. Along the way, we passed a large windmill, which was almost a mile away from our house.

"We're going to take a shortcut to another dimension, Olence; it has towns like yours."

"I'm worried my insight won't work outside of Infante."

"I know it will. When we were in the string yesterday, I could see your paths everywhere. Apparently, you've gone further than your father thought."

"Did that upset him?"

"I don't think he saw them; it seems that they're only really clear to you and me." I looked at him with an astonished expression on my face. *"I know, weird. We'll just add it to the pile... I'm just waiting for aliens to land – nothing seems crazy anymore."*

Laughter came over us both; we were now at the point where nothing made sense, but we'd make the most of it for the time being. As they watched us, amusement came over the others as well.

Just before we reached the windmill, I could see the string come into view. Brady stepped in first, but Landen held me back; he was waiting for something. Brady then reached his arm out and waved us in. The string was calm; the hum was a low murmur and you could barely feel the current.

"Are there any storms close?" I thought nervously, remembering how painful the last one had been.

"Storms never occur close to Chara," Landen promised. *"We never encounter them until we pass Esterouis. No one knows why, but some of the travelers believe it's because Chara and the dimensions closest to us only use natural energy.*

I smiled slightly and took his hand for my own personal comfort. I then began to take in the beauty of the string and tried to focus on the emotions; I wanted to learn to navigate the passages.

"So what do you think about Dane being able to see in here?" Brady asked Landen.

Landen raised his eyebrows and pressed his lips together; I could feel a tinge of jealousy coming from him. *"I knew there was something else I wanted to ask you about,"* he thought teasingly.

"Dane is the brother I never had," I explained.

I watched as a grin came across Landen's face. He then wrapped his arm around my shoulder and kissed the top of my head. *"I know; he told me about that night at the lake. I've already thanked him for keeping you safe when I couldn't...I just wish I was the one there,"* he thought.

I realized how right Landen was; Dane had always been protective of me. We came to the passage that they'd chosen; it was a light blue haze. I was the last to step through, and I didn't know what to expect, having no idea what this world would be like. The passage was behind a large building, next to a generator. We walked around the front to the streets – and much to my surprise, it looked the same as my world did: we were in a small town, the buildings were all made of brick, and the roads were made of what looked liked pea gravel. The people seemed ordinary enough, and the clothes even seemed to be the same as they were in my hometown. I reached out with my sense of emotion to see if this place were truly as safe as I thought it was, and I could feel that the mood was ordinary - the common stress, pride, and energy that I would have felt at home. I did find it odd, though, that I didn't see any children anywhere. There wasn't a stroller in sight – I didn't even see a dog on a leash. I noticed a few admiring feelings aimed at my escorts, and it was easy to see that they all went unnoticed by them.

"Where are the children?" I asked.

"I didn't think it would take you long to notice. Here, the children are the most precious assets. They keep them safely at home until they're young adults, for fear that if they mingle with any adult beyond their family, their ambition will be altered."

Chrispin began to grill Marc and Brady about the dimensions to which they'd recently
traveled. He was so ambitious and young at heart; I wondered how he'd feel about the way that I
traveled. The guys were telling Chrispin tall tales about giants and flying dragons, and at one point they had him convinced that trolls taught the schools in my world.

As we passed a street crossing, something caught my eye. I hesitated, and Landen stopped with me, but the others didn't notice - and kept their stroll.

"What is it? Do you see something?"

"You said no children, right?"

"Right."

"Do you see that woman with the crying baby?"

"No,"

Landen called out to the others. They were confused; maybe they were waiting for something more dramatic, or perhaps they thought they'd be able to see my images. We turned down the alleyway and followed the woman. I was grateful that I'd found someone off the beaten path, I could imagine that someone might notice five people disappearing into thin air. This was a young woman. I could see that this was her first child; the inexperience was in her eyes. She was dancing and singing above the crying. I could see that she needed strength and that the baby needed to be calmed down. I was starting to doubt that I'd be strong enough to help them both and carry us all through the string.

"OK, we're here. What's your plan?"

"Look, I'm going to hold Willow, and you guys hold onto me," Landen instructed.

"Wait - are you sure about this? I don't want them to get burned," I thought in a nervous tone.

"I was only burned because Drake pulled me back through; I shifted out of the path you made. They'll be fine - I promise."

I tightened my jaw; I was even angrier with Drake now, and all I could think about was how I was going to make him pay for hurting the ones I loved.

Brady stepped forward quickly. I was sure that after my display yesterday, he was eager to see how I did. As their anticipation rose, I could feel the excitement running through the guys. I felt the gentle pull of the string, and as I reached out, I could see a white light reach back toward me. As I reached forward and placed one hand on the baby's back and one hand on its mother. I felt the hum pass through my body. They were so beautiful; I'd have to find the time to sketch these two. I let my mother's energy and my father's peace flow through my memory. I hesitated longer than I normally would, and I watched as the baby succumbed to a peaceful sleep. His mother's eyes sparked; she looked refreshed and happy. I lingered, taking one last look at all the details, then I took in a deep breath, gathered my strength, and let go. I felt my body begin pulled back, so I focused on the energy and stopped myself in the string.

Suddenly, a roar of laughter erupted from Landen, Brady, and Marc. Brady was laughing so hard, tears were coming out of his eyes.

"Get him, Marc," Landen said as he tried to calm himself. Marc stepped through the other side of the string and returned with a humiliated Chrispin; I felt so bad for him.

"Don't let go until she stops," Landen said, as he tried to stop laughing.

"I'm sorry, Chrispin," I said, apologizing for the other's' laughter.

His face was so red. "You guys can tease me all you want, but that was amazing," Chrispin said, grinning. The others nodded their heads in agreement.

"I'm glad I got you back when I did; the passage is already gone," Marc said slapping Chrispin on the back. I looked in front of and behind myself, and I could still see it just as clearly as I had before.

"I told you so – they can't see it anymore," Landen thought.

"Can they still pass through it?"

"I don't know; we should try."

"Hey, we're going to try something. Line up behind Willow," Landen instructed. The irony was unbelievable; they were nervous, but they were so macho on the outside. I walked back through my passage, and one by one we were all back in the alley.

"That has to give us an advantage," Brady said.

They followed me back into the string again, and Landen led the way back to Chara. I noticed that Brady's emotion had changed; he was nervous. The others must have sensed his mood change as well because Marc grinned at Brady and said, "Don't worry, Brady, I'm sure Willow will learn to effect the emotions around her soon enough to help you if you really need it."

I looked up at Landen, questioning what I'd just heard.

"He's nervous about being a dad. Can you blame him after seeing your image?"

"It's not always like that." I could remember how happy a baby Libby was.

"It's not the crying. The two biggest challenges we face in our lives are finding the right person and being good parents. He was just as nervous when he went to find Felicity. I remember telling him it should be easy, that he already knew what she

looked like; that was when I realized that by me seeing you, I was different from the others...they only have a feeling to follow."

I smiled at myself, then stopped walking as my eyes raced through my memory, touching on every image I'd ever helped.

"What is it, Willow?"

I smiled up at Landen. *"I attract them."* Landen questioned me with his eyes, but I continued. *"Listen, if I'm lonely, I find someone who's lonely. If I feel lost, that's who I find. The other day, we were talking about marriage, and I found someone who was about to propose. This morning, I was with Felicity - and I could feel the baby's emotion."*

"But, Sharon - Libby."

"I think that was personal. Like you said, they're connected to me, so I have to be sensitive to their pain."

Landen smiled, agreeing with me. *"Well, we can take that off our list of unanswered questions,"* he thought.

When we reached our dimension, it was almost sunset. Landen had told the others about the nightmares and our dreams, how they were more like out-of-body experiences. They seemed to take what we were saying well, but I could tell it bothered them the same way it bothered Landen that I'd been in Esterouis so many times alone.

When our house came into view, I could see Felicity's car. She was standing on the porch, with her arms crossed, which reminded me that I hadn't even tried on the dresses that she'd brought me.

"Looks like somebody's in trouble," mocked Chrispin.

When we got to the house, I could feel her. She wasn't angry; she was actually very excited. She wrapped her arms around Brady and said, "I heard that you've been playing with babies all afternoon."

I could feel the shock coming from everyone but me and Landen; we both knew Libby must have told her. I couldn't wait to see her. Felicity smiled at Brady, knowing that she'd bewildered them.

"My new best friend, Libby, told me."

"I wonder how she fits into all of this?" I asked Landen.

"She's zoned into you - at least what happens to you."

Felicity had Brady unload her car. She must have been expecting us to be late coming home because she'd brought clothes for Chrispin, Marc, and Brady to change into. It was refreshing to see them in colors other than black; like changing out of a uniform, the seriousness left them for a moment as they prepared for the night.

Chapter Eleven

Within minutes, I' d changed to go to the celebration. Felicity helped me choose a dress for the night; it was a beautiful combination of royal green and blue, fitting for the warm weather. The straps were thin, and it flowed from beneath the chest to my knees. I blushed as Felicity complemented the way it brought out my eyes; I was trying to absorb all the positive energy she was exuding. My nerves were on edge; I was looking forward to seeing Libby and my mom, but I had no idea what to expect from my long lost grandparents or whoever else awaited us.

Landen was waiting for me at the bottom of the stairs, dressed in a royal blue shirt and brown khaki pants. He politely told Felicity and the others that we wanted to walk and would be there soon. Their understanding was undeniable; we had been alone for less than an hour that day, and it was easy to see that, though we were an admired couple, no one would desire to bear our burden.

We walked in silence for a while, lost in the last few days. With each step we took, I could feel the dread building inside me. When my breathing became measured, Landen hesitated, then stopped walking; I could feel his concern as he tried to understand why I was so upset.

"I'm fine – just not so good with crowds," I thought, looking around for an escape.

Relief came over him as he heard my simple explanation. "It's not going to be like it was at home; they know what your insight is, and they're going to do whatever it takes to make you comfortable. If it gets to be too much, just tell me; they'll understand," he said as his eyes tried to catch my gaze.

"Landen, I just don't think I can go and smile and have a party. I just lost one of my friends, and I don't know if the rest of them are safe or not. I can't block that out and the emotions of the crowd at the same time," I said, stumbling over my words while trying to hold back tears of grief. I turned away from him so he wouldn't see me struggle. He quickly circled me, not allowing me to hide anything from him.

"Look, there's nothing I can say to take all of that away. No one is asking you to forget them; this 'celebration' is just a way for you to meet your family, a family that you should already know," Landen said, cradling my face.

As I looked in his eyes, I felt a peace come over me, and my body relaxed as the calm took over.

Landen smiled as he felt the tension leave me. "I don't want to go either; I want you all to myself. It feels like we're never alone – awake, anyway." he said as he looked across the field in the direction we were walking; he looked like he was listening to a distant conversation. "I can feel Rose's intent from here; she wants to guide us. Right now we need to be guided if we're going to be strong enough to bring your friends home safely," he said quietly.

I looked across the field at the distant hill, then back at Landen and nodded. As we began to walk, he wrapped his arm around my shoulder and pulled me closer to him. When we reached the top of the hill on the south side of our house, Landen pointed to where my parents' house was; you could only the see rooftop from the hills around it. Their home was to the left, and his parents' were to the right. Landen explained that not only had our fathers been close friends, our grandfathers had been as well. For generations, the Haywood and Chambers families had lived side by side, the only two families with generation after generation of travelers. Even the women were fierce explores; others came to learn from them – some only trusting them to carry them home to visit the ones that were left in other dimensions.

We walked in the direction of his parents' house. I assumed the party was going to be there, but I wanted desperately to see my mother's home. The next hilltop revealed the home in which Landen had been raised, and it became clear to me that porches were a way of life in Chara. The house was large, two stories, and white, outlined with wide porches and long columns. White lights outlined the bottom porch as well as the path way to the front door. Music was playing, and laughter surrounded the house. There were several cars parked along the road just before the house; this "small group" of friends and family was larger than I'd expected.

A small figure ran toward us - it was Libby, and my fear dissipated as soon as she fell into my arms. We couldn't even say hello before she began to rush over her day, telling us about everyone she now had as friends, her beautiful room, and how much she loved it all here.

"So you didn't miss me at all today? I see how it is."

"Willow, I was with you, too – you can't see me sometimes, though." she said as she slid down and ran toward the house to announce our arrival.

Looking up at Landen, I could feel his despair; he wanted nothing more than for me and Libby to be safe, and at that moment he saw that as an impossibility. He smiled at me, then guided me toward the house. I took a deep breath and squeezed his hand as we climbed the front steps.

"Don't be scared," he whispered into my ear, kissing my neck softly. He was putting off a blissful emotion, giving me a blanket to hide behind.

We walked through the front door, and I noticed that his house was so much different from ours; everything was white and very bright, the walls accented the rooms with a light teal blue, and even the floors were a light wood color. Flowers decorated the banister and the doorways. No one was in the house; they'd all gathered in the back. Landen led me through the living room to the double doorway that opened to the back of the house. As we opened the doors, an eruption of applause began.

The group of family and friends was close to two hundred people. Heat filled my cheeks and my ears; the spotlight couldn't be more uncomfortable. My mother and father stood in the front of the crowd, smiling up at us. My mother was glowing in a silver dress, her long hair curled and her happiness unmistakable. Ashten, Aubrey, my father, and mother proudly walked up to the porch where we were standing which had been transformed into a stage - and Ashten began a heartwarming speech.

"Aubrey and I, along with Jason and Grace, are pleased to introduce each of you to Landen and Willow, the newest and youngest couple of Chara."

Applause erupted again, then Ashten continued, "We have faced many trials and triumphs over the years. The time that Jason was lost will haunt me for a lifetime, just as the time that I found him will be celebrated for all of time." Ashten raised his glass to my father while tears streamed down Aubrey's face; it was easy to see that she'd helped Ashten carry the burden when my father was missing.

"Today, we celebrate Jason and Grace; they have been returned to us at last. We also celebrate that my only daughter, Clarissa, has found her soul mate, Dane."

I noticed Carissa and Dane standing beside me and Landen, I didn't know if they'd been there the whole time; they were locked in each other's gaze, not appearing to notice the world around them.

"We also celebrate that life is not predictable. We are not all the same; uniform doesn't apply to any dimension - not even ours. Landen has proven this to us all as he stands here joined at last with Willow."

The applause erupted again, and I felt an overwhelming joy beaming from the crowd. An older woman handed me and Landen a glass of champagne. Ashten then raised his glass, and the crowd toasted. Landen turned into me and kissed me softly, and I could hear the applause begin again as my head spun with his touch.

My father put his hand around the older woman who had handed me the glass and said, "Willow, this is Rose - your grandmother."

My eyes widened; she was not what I expected. Rose looked so young. The only sign of age she had was her solid white hair, which fell just to her shoulders. Her eyes were a beautiful green, and beside her was an older man whose hair was short and dark with silver running through it. He looked like my father, only much older. "And this is your grandfather, Karsten," my father said, tilting his head in the direction of Karsten. Rose hugged me tightly.

"Oh, I've been on edge all day wanting to meet you. Your father said you needed your rest. Do you feel better now?" Rose asked, looking at me then smiling over my shoulder to Landen.

I nodded, not knowing what to say. Karsten stepped forward and hugged me. "You are just as beautiful as your mother," he said, smiling at me, then at my father.

The band began to play, and we were flooded with welcomes from the crowd. Everywhere we looked, there were smiling faces, handshakes, and hugs from everyone that was introduced to me - but the names escaped me as soon as they were said. You could see the resemblance in some of them, and it was clear that they were from Landen's family; others, I wasn't so sure.

Rose stepped in front of me and Landen. "Alright then, give her some room; I'm sure crowds are difficult for her," she said. Everyone stepped back a little.

"No, no, I'm fine; these emotions are the ones that I enjoy," I said, a little embarrassed. Out of all of them, I couldn't help noticing that Rose seemed to have a greater understanding of my gift even more than my father.

"You may want to hide her on the dance floor," Rose said, grinning at Landen. He nodded his head and winked at her; it was easy to see the favor he had with her.

The dance floor was full. All the couples seemed so immersed in each other, it was hard to imagine that Landen and I were the only ones who didn't need to use words; they all seemed locked in a world of their own. Even my parents seemed lost in themselves. The grief and danger that had been hovering over me took a back seat as I took my place in Landen's arms on the dance floor. With each new song, I was passed on to an eager partner first my father, then Ashten, Brady, Livingston, my grandfather, and finally Dane.

"You look so happy," I said to Dane as he took my hand.

"Just as happy as you," he answered, looking at Landen and Clarissa dancing.

I sighed, feeling the guilt come over me. It didn't seem right to be this happy, knowing that our friends were in danger. Dane felt my body tense up and looked down at me. "It's going to be fine, Willow; we'll find them and make it all right," he said, sounding sure of himself.

"We can't make what happened to Monica right," I said under my breath, holding back tears. I felt grief inside Dane; he may have teased her growing up, but he still cared about her.

"No, but her memory will always be with us and we can learn to never take anyone or anything for granted. You know if she was here, she'd be furious with you for not enjoying yourself. Monica lived in the moment, and that's where we need to live. We can't change the past, and the details of the future have yet to be seen," Dane said, looking down at me.

I smiled, in awe of his wisdom. I'd never heard him speak so deeply; I guess love changes everyone.

After my dance with Dane, he returned me to Landen and took possession of Clarissa. I made a conscious effort to be friendly to her. "I'm sorry for the way I acted yesterday. Dane can tell you that I'm saner than that," I said to her, looking down and feeling embarrassed.

Clarissa put her hand on my shoulder. "You held yourself together more than I would have been able to," she said, smiling back at Dane. They could stare at each other with a degree of intensity unmatched by anyone else in the room.

Libby demanded that Landen dance with her, and I stood back and watched as he picked her up and swayed her to the lullaby of a song that was playing, smiling at me over her tiny shoulder. I then made my way to one of the tables, so lost in my thoughts that I didn't notice that my grandmother, Rose, had taken the seat next to me.

"He's such a good man; we couldn't have dreamed of another so perfect for you," she said as she watched with me. Libby laid her head on Landen's shoulder, fighting heavy eye lids.

"I still have a hard time thinking that he's real; for so long, he was lost in my dreams," I said, smiling at her.

Rose folded her hands under her chin and stared at me; her green eyes were outlined in silver, reminding me of what the string did to the eyes of its passengers.

"I can remember the first time Ashten told me about Landen's dreams," she said. "He was so worried about him; I knew then that Landen was going to stand out from the rest."

"I didn't realize how close our families are until today," I confessed, remembering the story Landen had told me on the way to the celebration.

"It seems that we always have been - at least since before my great grandmother's time, anyway," said Rose.

She began surveying the crowd around us, and her eyes settled on Livingston and Marc, who were lingering by the side of the dance floor. Marc was talking to Livingston, but it was clear that Livingston wasn't listening.

"Do you find it odd that - in the midst of this celebration you feel a deep sorrow?" she asked. I looked at her quickly, then in the direction of Livingston and Marc. "Is your insight strong enough to tell me whom it is coming from?" she continued, looking back at me.

"Livingston," I whispered. Rose nodded.

"Do you have the same insight?" I asked.

Rose smiled to answer my question.

For the first time, I felt normal; others' having a gift was not the same as knowing someone who knew exactly how it worked. My peace started to fade when I realized that this was the first time I'd heard of anyone being like me let alone my grandmother. Why did my father not tell me when he knew what mine was – even when he told me who we were?

"He doesn't know," Rose answered the unasked question. "Your betrayal isn't called for; you, August, and Karsten are the only ones alive that know."

"Why - is it a bad thing? Is that why you keep it a secret?" I asked as the feeling of being a fluke came back over me.

"No…it's a beautiful gift," Rose said, reaching for my shoulder. "My father believed that for me to truly understand my gift, I should keep it to myself," Rose said, smiling.

"I don't understand," I said, leaning closer, hanging on her every word.

"If people guard themselves around me, I can't help them. The beauty of the gift of emotion is that you truly walk in another's footsteps for a moment," Rose answered.

I watched Livingston walk over to my father and Ashten. They glanced nervously in my direction, and I could feel a building anxiety coming from the three of them. I looked back at Rose. "What is my father not telling me?" I asked.

Rose caught my father's gaze, and I could feel his emotion through her. She sighed and looked in my direction. "That you are the one who will bring color to Esteroius," she said quietly, beaming with pride.

"What?" I asked, bewildered.

"You have a power inside you that will move millions," Rose said.

My mother walked over to Rose and me and took a seat, ending our conversation.

"Are you two getting acquainted?" my mother asked, putting her arm around me and smiling at Rose.

I smiled and looked nervously for Landen. I found him across the floor, handing Libby's sleeping body to my father. He caught my gaze, almost as if he could sense that I needed him.

"Are you OK," he thought as he began to walk toward me.

"I just have no idea what she just told me - but it doesn't sound good."

"What did she say?"

"That I would bring color to Esteroius."

I could feel confusion and fear come over Landen. Reaching me, he took a seat next to me and stared at Rose, who nodded in his direction.

"Well, it looks like it's time for me to go," my mother said, noticing that Libby had fallen asleep.

"You're going home?" I asked, surprised.

She nodded. "I'm going to take Libby home and lay her down."

"Are you OK, Mom?" I asked, realizing this had to be a lot for her to take in as well. She nodded and tried to smile.

"I'm sorry about the house," I said, my voice echoing the guilt that I felt.

She heard it and tried to make me feel better. "Those are just things; you, Landen, and Libby are safe and sound," she said, smiling first at me and then to Landen. "That's all I could ask for."

Landen and I hugged her goodbye, then my father waved goodbye in our direction as my mother approached him. Landen then looked slowly back at Rose, who smiled. "Would the two of you care to follow me to the living room for a more private conversation?" she asked, sliding her chair back.

Landen and I followed her without hesitation. As we passed by Livingston and Ashten, I felt their anxiety rise. Once inside the house, Landen closed the door behind him. We were both nervous; we watched as Rose walked to the center of the room, then hesitated before turning around, an overwhelming sense of relief coming over her. Slowly, she reached her hand into her pocket and pulled out a silver chain.

"I wanted to wait until August came home to give you this," Rose said as she looked at the necklace in her hand, "but I think it may help bring your friends home."

I walked slowly to her, feeling my heart rise in my chest. She reached for my hand and placed the chain in it, and I felt a warm tingle as it touched my skin. I looked down and noticed a charm attached to the silver necklace; it was shaped like a sun with wavy, detailed rays, and in the center of the sun was what looked like black glass with a crescent moon carved into the surface. As I studied the details, I had a sudden, sickening sense of déjà vu, and Landen leaned in to look closer, my hands began to shake.

"I think I've seen this before," Landen thought.

"Me, too," I thought, looking up at him.

"It should look familiar to you," Rose said.

I looked up at her quickly; she smiled and reached for the necklace in my hand. She then opened the clasp and reached for my neck, and I leaned in slowly to help her. She leaned back and looked at my neck, then gazed into my eyes and smiled.

"Where did this come from?" I asked, as I moved my hand to the charm, feeling all the details of its surface.

"From you," Rose said, tilting her head.

Landen and I both looked at her with wide eyes.

"When I was a child, you and Landen approached me and August one day. You told me to give this to you the day you returned home to Chara."

"What are you talking about?" I asked, looking from her to Landen.

"Rose, you're scaring her," Landen said putting his arm around me. "Now is not the time for myths."

"What myths?" I asked, looking back and forth from Rose and Landen.

"Some people in Chara believe that travelers have led past lives. They think that's why we can see more passages than them – it's just a myth," Landen said, looking me in the eyes.

"Myth or not, there's not a doubt in my mind that this is not the first time you've walked this earth," Rose said, looking at me, then up at Landen. "You need to know that you're missing a part of the charm." Rose reached for the charm and turned it for me to see. On the back of it was a ridge, and there were five holes spread around the inside edge.

"The star was lost," Rose said quietly.

I heard the back door open, and I could feel the anxiety of Livingston and Ashten pouring into the room. I also felt the curiosity of Brady and Marc. Ashten and Livingston walked cautiously to Rose's side. Landen looked back and forth between them. Marc walked to Livingston's side, and Brady came to my side; I felt his awe as he saw the charm I was tracing with my fingertips.

"Where was it lost? Does it matter that it is?" Landen asked

"It was lost in Esteroius," Rose said, in a calm tone.

"Where?" Landen asked quickly.

"In the Blakesire palace," Rose answered. "You knew it would be lost," she continued, looking in my eyes. "You told me 'not to fear when the supremacy was taken, for your heart was the only true power.'"

"Are you saying these charms have a power?" Landen asked in disbelief.

"I am," Rose said.

From the shock that ran through Landen, I could tell Rose was telling the truth.

"Was Drake able to hurt her because he has that star?" Landen asked in a low tone as anger began to come over him.

"He hasn't hurt her," Livingston said defensively.

Everyone in the room looked at Livingston. I felt heat rise in my cheeks as anger coursed through me, and I stepped forward and peered up at Livingston with a dominant stare.

"He hasn't, has he?" I said sarcastically. "So what would you call a suffocating weight on your chest that makes breathing painful? How about being stripped of your senses and - forced to feel a trembling fear of innocent people - not mention that he's taken someone I love deeply away from me?" I said, poking my finger in Livingston's chest as angry tears came to the corners of my eyes. As Marc stepped between me and his dad, I felt Landen's hands on my shoulders I turned and buried my face in his chest.

"Why are you defending him?" Brady asked Livingston.

"I just - I just - I didn't realize she suffered when she met Drake," Livingston said quietly. I felt a deep sorrow overcome him.

"I want to know what you're hiding from me. Why is Drake connected to Willow? How do I stop him and get her friends' home?" Landen asked, in a harsh tone.

I turned in his arms to look at Livingston.

"Where is the star? Does Donalt have it?" Brady asked, pulling his shoulders back.

"You're not going to get it," Landen said looking at Brady.

"If it's hurting either of you – yes I am," Brady said shortly.

"I'm going, too," Marc said, looking at Brady.

"I'm going alone," Landen said. I looked up at him with panic in my eyes; he wasn't going without me.

"You're not going anywhere near Esteroius – I told you they'll kill you without question," Livingston said, stepping closer to Landen. I felt his fear.

"I know you believe what you say is true - now tell me how you know that," Landen said, staring into Livingston's eyes. "Tell me what you know. Tell me what you're shielding me from," Landen said through a locked jaw.

Livingston didn't answer him.

"Now is not the time to be silent," Brady said, pushing Livingston to answer Landen.

"Dad," Marc said, putting his hand on Livingston's shoulder. Livingston looked down, avoiding all of our eyes.

I looked at Rose for some kind of help, and even though she held no expression on her face, I could still feel her confidence and pride in me. Landen's eyes moved to Ashten, only to find him staring at the floor.

"Rose, will you please tell my mother that Willow and I said goodnight," Landen said as he let his hand fall into mine and led me to the door.

"I'll drive you," Brady said, following us.

"I coming, too," Marc said as he followed us outside.

Landen opened the back door of the Jeep for me to slide in. He then slid in beside me and wrapped his arm around me. Marc climbed in the front seat as Brady started to drive away.

"What's going on around here?" Brady asked in an aggravated tone.

"Marc, has your dad said anything to you?" Landen asked

Marc turned in his seat; I could feel his frustration and confusion. "He's been acting strange for the past week or so; I don't understand what's gotten into him," he said, first looking at me, and then to Landen.

"Right now, I don't care. I'm going to bring Willow's friends home and put all of this behind us," Landen said, looking at me.

Hearing his words, I breathed out, hoping it would be that simple.

Brady pulled in front of our house, and Landen and I climbed out of the back seat.

"Just get some rest tonight. We'll go back and talk to them, and maybe they'll tell us something," Marc said as he looked out the window at us.

Landen nodded and waved. We then turned to climb the steps, and as Landen reached for the doorknob, he hesitated and looked at me.

"Can you still feel their emotions?" he thought. I nodded, feeling the distant anguish and dread.

"Come on," he said taking my hand and leading me off the porch.

"Where are we going?" I asked as we stepped off the porch and began to walk through the dark field.

"A different part of Chara; we won't be able to rest if we try to untangle their emotions or intent through the night," Landen said, looking down at me.

I wrapped my arm around his waist as he lead us into the string. Within the white light, we both felt a peace come over us, and the swarm of mixed emotions I felt was replaced by an overpowering love that I felt from him. We turned to the left and walked ten short feet, and there I could see a light yellow passage. I closed my eyes as we stepped through the haze, taking in the tingle. The sky was just as dark as it was at our home and the half moon showed the way. I could hear waves breaking and smell the salt in the air. A small beach house was just a few feet away from us.

"Now it's quiet," he said, smiling down at me.

I smiled and took off in a sprint to the dark beach house. Once I arrived, I climbed the short steps that led to the porch and pushed open the front door. Landen caught me in his arms, laughing and I turned and looked up at him; his eyes looked somewhere deep inside me. I wrapped my arms around his shoulders, and he pulled me closer, leaned down, and kissed my lips. I felt a rush flow through me, and in that moment I forgot everything that had been haunting

Chapter Twelve

As we lay staring into each other's eyes, sleep seemed to escape us. I sighed and rolled onto my back, staring up at the night sky. I could see the moon; it seemed to be growing fuller by the moment. I reached my hand to my chest and let my fingers dance across the details of my charm. Landen rolled to his side and stared down at the charm. I felt his confusion.

"Do you really think we lived before?" I asked him.

He looked from the charm into my eyes. "I've never given credit to the myth of living past lives before," he whispered, "but I know I've seen you wear this charm before." He looked back to the sun and the moon.

"Are there any other myths about travelers?" I asked in a light-hearted tone, reaching for his face to trace his perfect profile.

Landen smiled and looked back into my eyes. "Some believe that the gifted travelers are the oldest souls bonded by past lives," he answered, tilting his head and smiling at me as his eyes searched my face.

I smiled, realizing that if that were true, I'd always had Landen close to my soul. It also meant that Libby, my father, and Rose had always been with me as well. I sighed, feeling stronger.

"Well, at least that means our families have always been with us," I whispered.

I heard him laugh under his breath. "Right now, I don't know if I'd see that as a positive," he said, trying to hold the sarcasm out of his tone.

I looked at him with disapproval in my eyes.

"I didn't mean it," he said, wrapping his arm around my waist. "I just want to know what we're up against so I can protect you. It bothers me that my father doesn't think I'll be able to handle it."

"You're wrong. I can almost guarantee you that your father thinks you can handle anything. He has a strong pride that comes from him every time he looks at you," I promised Landen.

"Then why won't he tell me?" Landed said, almost to himself.

"Maybe he's the one that can't handle it. If it makes you feel any better, I don't think my father or Livingston can either."

"August will tell us," Landen said, looking deep in my eyes.

"Does your father realize that?" I asked

"My grandfather has always played peacemaker between me and my father. He has a way of making my father let go and me slow down - both at the same time."

"Maybe that's what our fathers are waiting on – the peacemaker," I said, smiling.

"He should be home soon," Landed said, kissing my forehead.

"Do you think they lost the star when Justus and Livingston went to bring home Adonia?" I asked, rolling to my side.

Landen nodded. "Livingston is the only one besides Justus that's ever been inside the Backshire Palace."

"Why did Beth go with them? Why didn't they take more travelers?" I asked

"August told me just before I was born that the storms were so bad that travelers would be gone for months at a time. Justus and Livingston were the only ones close enough to go. Beth was from Esterouis, so she went to help them find a new way in the palace."

"I think it's strange that no one knows where Beth and Adonia are," I said, looking at him.

"Marc and I do as well. Marc is convinced that Beth is locked in that palace and that he needs to bring her home." I could feel his sorrow.

"What do you think?" I asked

"I know that if I were Adonia and I lost my soul mate, I wouldn't want to live anymore, and if I were Beth, no palace would be able to hold me."

"Are they as strong as you?"

"I've never met them, but I heard that both of them were amazing, strong willed, and passionate."

I felt my eyes growing heavy and smiled at Landen.

"So where shall we dream tonight?" I asked.

"Do you think we can choose?" Landen thought as he sat up with a rush of excitement.

"I think you choose. I've only ever gone to where you are," I thought, pulling him back down to my side.

Landen had beaten me to our dreams almost every time, the only time I'd ever been first was the night we danced to the willow tree music box. He was focusing in a straight stare. *"What if we plan to go to a place – to see if we can control it?"*he thought.

"Where?"

"Here sounds safe enough," he thought as a grin spread across his face.

"If it works – then what?"

"Let's just test it, see what we can do…we never even tried to communicate this way."

I smiled and closed my eyes, keeping my focus both on the room I was in and Landen, refusing any other thoughts or fears. I felt myself begin to drift. It felt like only a moment had passed before I opened my eyes again. My body lay sleeping on the bed before me. Landen's body was still; only his chest rose and fell. The scene was so surreal. My first reaction was panic, and then I heard,

"Can you hear me?"

He stood at my side, staring at our bodies as they lay sleeping. Not only could I hear him, I could also feel his discomfort.

"I can feel you, too."

Landen looked slowly at me, a small smile coming across his face; we were both feeling control of this heart-racing gift we shared.

"Come on, I want to try something," he said, holding my hand and leading us from the beach house to the path that led to the string. Once there we walked back through the passage close to our home. Landen hesitated as he used his gift to tell him where everyone was.

"My father is on his way to Jason's house," he thought.

"Where's Livingston?"

"I can't feel him anywhere close," Landen thought, *"can you?"*

I focused on the emotions around me, feeling the same dread and anxiousness that I'd felt before, but unsure as to where it was coming from. I shook my head no. We passed through the field in the direction of my father's house, and in the distance I could see Ashten walking from the other direction. My father was standing on the front porch of a beautiful two--story brick home, the front of which was framed by bay windows.

"Do you think they'll be able to see us?" I asked.

"Brady was right behind me that day you gave me that note - and he didn't see you," Landen thought.

"I don't remember seeing him," I thought.

"You terrified him; all he saw were my arms going around thin air and a note appearing in my hand," Landen thought, grinning.

"I think I would have been bothered if I'd seen that happen," I thought, shaking my head in disbelief.

We reached my father's house the same time that Ashten did, and I could feel that both Ashten and my father were deeply concerned. As Landen and I stepped cautiously closer, my father and Ashten never looked in our direction; it was an eerie feeling, almost ghostly.

"Are you sure they didn't go to Esterious?" my father asked Ashten.

"More than sure; Landen is not one to make decisions without thinking them through. Rose believes they just went far enough not to feel us," Ashten answered.

"Did it upset Willow when she was told that the charm belonged to her before?" my father asked.

"I wasn't there when Rose told her, but I was there when she told Livingston how she felt about Drake," Ashten said, raising his eyebrows.

My father looked at Ashten in utter confusion.

"Livingston made the comment that Drake had never hurt her, and she told him exactly what she lived through," Ashten continued.

My father looked down. I could feel his remorse. "Maybe I should have brought her home sooner," he said to himself.

"You don't know if that would have stopped the nightmares," Ashten said, defending my father.

"I know that she's a new person now that she has Landen. She's more sure of herself now than she's ever been," my father said quietly.

"Landen is, too," Ashten said, looking in the direction of our house. "We need to get those girls home so the two of them can just live here in peace."

"It's not going to be that simple," my father said, looking at Ashten with pain in his eyes.

"Jason, I will not allow them to face Donalt - or anyone in Esterouis," Ashten said shortly. I felt his anger rise.

"We cannot make their choices for them anymore; all we're doing is pushing them away from us. I'd rather stand at their side," my father said in a calm tone.

Ashten crossed his arms across his chest and looked down. "I don't know what scares me more: what they're capable of now or what they *will* be capable of," he said quietly.

My father nodded. I looked at Landen; he was staring at his father, and I could feel forgiveness coming over him.

"Where's Livingston?" my father asked

"He left right after Landen and Willow. I think he went to Esterouis," Ashten said with concern in his voice.

"Is he insane? It's well after curfew there," my father said with wide eyes.

"He always goes there at night. I think he wants to bring those girls home before Landen has a chance to," Ashten said.

"Did you figure out how he knew that Willow's nightmares had come back?" my father asked.

"He said he saw it in the stars," Ashten answered

My father shook his head from side to side, clearly not believing what he'd just heard.

"I don't know, Jason; he's not the same person you knew twenty years ago. The only one he really talks to is August, and it kills me to see Marc and Chrispin reach out to him - only to be ignored," Ashten said in an exhausted tone.

"They have you and Aubrey. You made them the men that they are; you should be proud of the family you raised."

"I am. I just feel like I'm going to lose them now," Ashten said, looking down. I felt his sorrow deepen.

"I'm going to try something," I thought.

I reached my hand carefully to Ashten's shoulder; he didn't notice my touch. I thought of the emotions I felt from the celebration, the overwhelming love and peace, and I remembered the smiling faces and the laughter.

I felt his emotion begin to change. As he surrendered to his peace, I felt the charm on my neck tingle, then a warm rush flowed through my hand; it was a mesmerizing feeling. As it began to intensify, I looked back at Landen and felt the sensation flowing through him, too.

"You feel this," I thought, astonished.

"It's amazing. Does it always feel like this?" he asked.

"No, never," I answered.

I reached my other hand out to my father's shoulder, letting the same memories flow through my mind. The charm hummed, and the sensation pushed through my hand. A smile came across my father's face, and he looked at Ashten.

"They're going to be fine," he said confidently.

Ashten nodded and step away from me, and I lost my touch. He then looked over his shoulder at my father as he walked away, and I could still feel the peace that I gave him. My father sighed and turned to walk inside his house, causing me to lose my touch on him as well. The high that I felt began to fade.

"Let's follow him; I want to help my mom, too," I thought, stepping toward my dad.

We passed through the front door behind my father. My mother was sitting in the front room on a long white couch. She had a sketch pad in her lap and was outlining the house I was raised in.

"Is everything OK," she asked my father as he took a seat next to her.

"It will be; we're just asking them to take in a lot at one time," my father said, putting his arm around her.

"Do you think she'll ever understand that we only wanted to keep her safe?" my mother said, feeling a deep regret.

"They both will one day. We can't blame them for being upset. If I were Landen, I'd be furious; at least he's still calm enough to ask questions," my father said.

"I just think if we'd come home, Monica would be alive, and the other girls would be safe in their homes," my mother said in a cracked voice as she laid her head on my father's shoulder.

"Willow wouldn't be the person she is without having the friends she had in Infante, and they wouldn't be the people they are without her. Even though Monica's life was short, I don't think she left this world with any regrets."

My mother looked up at my father and smiled. "She had such a vibrant energy around her; I can still feel it when I remember her," she said quietly.

"Then she lives on through you - through everyone she ever knew," he said, kissing her forehead.

I stepped closer and knelt down in front of my mother.

Placing my hand on her knee, I remembered every happy memory I could from my childhood; the impact my mother had not only on me, but on each of my friends, too. The rush swept through me again, and I closed my eyes, taking in the pure bliss I felt as I helped my mother. Her emotion moved to the bliss I was feeling, and I opened my eyes to see her smiling. I could feel her soul come to life again, then I stood slowly and looked at Landen.

"Do you want to check on Libby?" I thought, Landen smiled, took my hand, and led me to the staircase that was in front of the door.

I could feel Libby sleeping peacefully. At the top of the stairs, we opened the first door to the left. It was a very large room with high ceilings. The far wall of her room had a large bay window, and baby dolls and books lined the window sill – it was a room made for the princess that she was. When we both walked to her bed to sneak a peek at her sleeping face, her eyelids fluttered open softly, a smile spread across her baby face, and she whispered, "Willow, is it time to get up?"

Being seen by her sent a surge of shock through the two of us. Our eyes flew open, and we were back in the beach house. Catching our breath we sat up with a startle. When we realized what we'd done, laughter exploded from the two of us: we'd managed to control where we went. I was able to help our family, and we made it home with in the blink of an eye. We then allowed our bodies to drift back to sleep, and our souls walked along the beach through the sunrise.

The peaceful feeling of another person, and the sound of the wood creaking on the front porch of the beach house brought us both back to our sleeping bodies Landen jumped up and tiptoed toward the front of the house. He then looked back at me.

"Rose," he thought, I nodded in agreement.

Landen pulled the front door open, expecting to see Rose, but instead he found a large basket sitting on the floor of the porch. He brought it into the house and set in on the coffee table in the front room. A note was attached to the top of the basket that said:

I thought you two would need a few things. Take your time. Love you.

In the basket, under a blanket was a new sketch book and food, along with a change of clothes.

"How did she know where we were?" I asked.

Landen smiled at himself as he read the note again. *"This is her place; sometimes trying to understand the intent around me can be difficult. Rose and August brought me here when I was fourteen and told me that whenever I needed peace, I could come here."*

We settled in the floor, making a picnic out of the fruit and muffins that Rose had brought.

"I could feel Rose differently just now," he said, looking at me. "I felt her emotion of peace."

I looked at him with wide eyes.

"Did she feel differently to you?" he asked

"I don't know…I mean, I knew she didn't want to disturb us, but I just took that as my own insight."

"That's how my gift feels; you just know what they want to do," he said, smiling at me.

"How are they merging?" I asked, bewildered.

"I don't know. I didn't feel any emotion until you touched my dad last night," he answered.

"Can we look for images today? For my friends?" I asked, rising to my knees.

"If we find them, we need to come back and get Brady and the others," Landen said, standing.

I stood and began to pull out the clothes in the basket. Rose had packed the traditional travel clothes for Landen: black pants and a black T- shirt. For me, a solid black dress with wide straps. I looked at Landen and shook my head; I wasn't sure how much I cared for always wearing black. He laughed at my expression. I then sighed and began to change into the dress. It felt soft against my skin, and it fell just above my knees. I pulled my necklace out and looked down at the charm again, wondering for a moment what all it had witnessed.

The string was very calm when we entered it; and the current was relaxing as it immersed us. We walked by the passages of our world, and saw that several others were in the string. Smiling faces and pleasant greetings were given as we ushered by; it was clear that Landen didn't even know most of them by name. Each of them had the most amazing eyes in the string, though;it was as if you could see the soul within them…everyone was calm, peaceful and all the couples had a deep love for one another.

The string became empty as other passages came into view, and I felt myself growing nervous. Landen looked down at me. "The string is calm today; we should be safe," he said, assuring me. I smiled, appreciating that he could sense my emotion.

I stopped walking; I could feel something, a terror so powerful that it took my breath away. It was coming from Landen, too - but it didn't belong to him. Landen looked forward, then back. After a moment of indecision, we walked back to where we'd just been.

"You could feel that, couldn't you?" I asked.

"I want to get Brady and the others – I'm not sure if that's coming from in the string or around it."

"How far are we from Esterouis?"

"Only a few passages," Landen said, guiding me back to Chara.

"It could be them," I said, fearing that they were now suffering.

"I know," he whispered, pulling me closer to him.

After reaching our dimension, we walked back to our house, and Landen went to the

kitchen to call Brady while I waited impatiently on the front porch for help to arrive. Moments later, two Jeeps pulled up in front of the house; Brady was in one with Marc. Chrispin was driving the other one with Dane and Clarissa. I was surprised that Clarissa had come, but then I remembered that Landen had said that even the women were fierce explorers – and Dane could see in the string. I climbed into the back seat of Brady's Jeep with Landen then both Jeeps speed across the open field to the windmill.

Just before we entered, Landen told Brady that he would lead. He wanted Brady to bring up the tail and Marc and Chrispin to flank the sides – and he wanted me and Dane in the center with Clarissa. Brady argued with Landen, but he ultimately lost the argument. The others agreed that it didn't matter where we stood; being in the string was risky, no matter where you were.

Our group weaved through the others making their way to the celebration. As we walked in silence, Landen would look back at me, checking my expression. We'd already passed the point where we'd felt the fear earlier, but the tension was growing among the others. I had a feeling we were almost to Esteroius; the hum of the current flowed more aggressively, then reached an annoying high pitch. Landen stopped, and everyone stared at him, waiting for him to lead.

"Do you feel that?" asked Landen.

"No," I answered, now concentrating on his emotion.

I walked closer to him, and through him I felt the fear again. When I reached his side, I felt it firsthand.

"I do now," I thought.

"Do you recognize them?" he asked.

"The fear is too strong for me to tell you for sure. There are three; if he's with them, I wouldn't know," I thought reminding him that I couldn't feel Drake.

Landen motioned for the others to come closer, and in a hushed voice he told them that if Drake were there, I wouldn't be able to tell them. Brady didn't even try to argue with Landen; he just stepped forward and led the rest of us. Landen squeezed my hand as we walked; the current was getting harder to navigate through.

"He's here," thought Landen.

He reached out to stop Brady from walking any further. In cat-like fashion, we took a few steps back, then slid through a purple haze. Passing into this dimension, we were close to another waterfall; it wasn't nearly as powerful as Victory Falls, but the beauty was still breathtaking. Confusion was coming from everyone as they watched. Landen paced, then stopped and checked himself to make sure he was confident before he spoke.

"Drake is just a few feet away from here. This is a trap; he has someone with him - more than one – several, actually – and they're expecting conflict."

It wasn't fear that rushed through everyone - it was anger. Landen and Brady seemed to be the most powerful of all of them, but Clarissa was the first one to speak with any kind of reason. "We have to use caution here; charging them is not the answer" she said, raising her hands.

I was grateful that she had spoken up, but if Landen felt what I felt, he wasn't going to leave without those girls. They had passed fear and were closer to horror.

"What if I passed through the string? He doesn't know me. I could get a better understanding of what's going on in there," said Clarissa.

After an onslaught of arguments erupted from everyone, they finally calmed down. Brady convinced Clarissa that it didn't matter who went - Drake would take us, and we'd definitely come after one of our own.

As they continued to discuss a way of getting the three girls, I ventured out, looking at the waterfall and the tall overhanging trees. There was thunder in the distance, and you could feel the humidity in the air. Sweat drenched my dress, and my eyes were misty. All at once, I felt the horror again. I looked back quickly to see if the others were in danger. I'd managed to walk almost fifty feet away from them. They were still discussing options; their mood was tense, but no horror was with them. A look of confusion was covering my face as I looked back to them, then forward again.

I took a few more brave steps toward the worst emotion I'd ever felt. The trees covered the gray sky, giving the illusion of darkness. The branches swayed with the wind, causing a light whistle and drying the sweat on my face. No animals could be seen, and the forest looked as if it had been abandoned.

When I looked back at the others again, Landen was staring at me, no longer listening as everyone pleaded their case to him at once.

"What is it? Do you see something?" he asked.

"I feel something, this way," I responded, pointing to the forest.

Landen pushed through the others and made his way to me. As he got closer, I could feel it through him, too.

"I bet there's an image in there," I thought, looking into the dense darkness.

The others came to where we were, and Landen looked back and firmly told them, "Guard your emotions." Then, looking squarely at Marc, he said "And your intent."

We made our way into the forest; you could hear the sound of rain on the canopy of leaves that shielded the ground. When the darkness was all around us, three figures came into my view: Hannah, Olivia, and Jessica. They were all dressed in white gowns, and their hair was up and decorated with jewels. Lines of mascara streaked down each of their faces, and they trembled as they gripped each other. Hannah was the only one not screaming. It was hard not to rush in to touch them, to help them.

"I found them," I said, swallowing hard and, feeling the nauseating sensation of guilt overcome me.

I felt Landen's arm go around me. *"This is not our fault,"* he thought softly, I nodded and fought back the hopeless emotion that threatened to overtake me.

The others stared into the darkness, trying to see what I saw.

"How is this going to work? I mean, if they're in the string, won't Willow pass by them?" asked Chrispin bravely.

"I don't think they're in the string. I can feel the intent of several people," Landen answered, looking at all of them.

"Can you see around them?" Clarissa asked calmly.

"Not until I touch them," I said, staring at three of them yearning to help.

"Regardless, she has to touch them, at least one of them. Two of us can grab the others," Landen said.

"We're not going to have time to lead them; they're going to have to be carried," added Landen.

"To where?" Marc asked.

"We can't take them to their home - not in this condition. Jason is going to need to look them over," answered Landen.

"So who wants to go with us? We need two of you." No indecision came from any of them; they all stepped forward, even Dane. Seeing their eagerness, Landen made the decision for them.

"OK, Brady and Dane, flank me and Willow. When we're back here, Chrispin, you grab the girl Willow is holding- Clarissa, Marc, you lead us back to the string - Dane and Willow are the only ones that need to talk. If they struggle, we'll never make it back to Chara," Landen finished.

A serious mood came over us all; everyone seemed to be very clear on their roles. I knew I'd have to calm these girls as much as possible before they were carried by the others. I circled around so their backs were to me, trying not to worry about what had captured their attention. Landen took his place behind me, and Brady and Dane held on to him I felt a pull come over me. When I reached my trembling hands out, the charm on my chest hummed, and the sensation brought a calm over me.

Olivia was in the middle. I laid my head on her back, then wrapped my arms around Hannah and Jessica. When the green haze passed, taking the tingle with it, I moved my arms around Olivia's small frame. The room they were in was dark and damp, and the only light came from an open ceiling, with a gray sky as a canopy, adding a degree of eeriness. An altar was centered in the room, and un-lit candles lined the table. Black roses served as a centerpiece. Chants could be heard from all around the room. Assuring myself that the other two were secure, I pushed back the haze of green, and a warm tingle rushed passed me.

The dark room was replaced by the forest again. Chrispin took possession of Olivia the moment we came into sight. In the blink of an eye, we'd passed through the forest and were in the string again. Jessica was screaming; I pleaded with her to calm down, but she screamed louder.

"Willow, is that you?" asked Olivia.

"Yeah, you're fine; I promise. Is Jessica hurt? Why is she screaming?"

Tears streamed down Olivia's face as she leaned into Crispin's chest, not caring that she didn't know him.

"She can't hear you; they took it."

"What do you mean?" I asked, panicking.

"Jessica can't hear, Hannah can't talk, and I can't see."

I looked at Hannah. She was afraid; in here, she couldn't see or talk.

"Hannah you can still see; it's just dark in here. You'll see in just a few minutes."

I reached for Jessica. I had to help her, so I concentrated as hard as I could to take away her fear and give her peace. After a moment, her screaming stopped, and she laid her head on Brady's chest and fell asleep.

"You changed it," thought Landen.

"I don't know if I did or not. She may have just given up."

"I felt it," he assured me.

Others were beginning to come into view; we were close to Chara. People shot us concerned looks as we passed, and someone in the crowd called out to Landen as we got closer.

"You kids alright?" It was an older man with a long gray beard.

"We're fine. If you see Jason Haywood, will you tell him we need him at my house?"

The man nodded and pushed past the others, going into the passage. Our passage was just a few minutes past the large entrance. As we left the string, Hannah's eyes brightened when she realized she could see. Dane sat her down to let her walk. Jessica still lay sleeping in Brady's arms. Knowing that Olivia couldn't see, Chrispin carried her to the jeep. He was whispering to her; I couldn't hear him, but I knew that whatever he was saying was making her feel happy and at ease.

Chapter Thirteen

The Jeeps rushed through the field, adrenaline still coursing through all of us. When we reached our house, we all filed in one-by-one. The girls were laid on the couches in the living room, and when Chrispin tried to step away from Olivia, she pulled him back to her. He didn't falter and sat by her side.

"Did you see that? Where they were?" Landen asked Brady. Brady looked at Dane; it was easy to see that they had.

"What was that?" asked Brady

"I don't know, but it was pure evil," Landen said, looking at me and trying to hide his fear.

Clarissa had gotten a warm towel and was wiping away the streaks of Hannah's mascara, telling her she was fine.

"Do you know where you were?" I asked Olivia.

Olivia stared blankly into the room, then said, "I remember being on the boat. There was a really bad storm that came out of nowhere. I woke in a chamber that looked as if I'd stepped into a movie set in medieval times. The walls were made of stone, and large tapestries hung from the ceiling to the floor. It had three large beds, two massive fireplaces, and chairs circled the fire. No windows. When the fire would go out, darkness filled the room.

Once a day, we'd find a large cart of food and water. I noticed, that after we ate, I would fall into a deep, blissful sleep. Dreams would consume my mind, giving me a numbing feeling. I knew I was losing touch with reality and any hope of an escape, so I convinced Hannah and Jessica not to eat."

Tears drizzled down her face, then she continued, "We pretended to sleep, and after an hour or so the fireplace slid aside. The room was filled with people wearing long black robes, and shadows covered any signs of their faces. They lined the room. When I foolishly opened my eyes wider to focus, I lost my sight, Jessica screamed as the chants began, and Hannah started to pray out loud; that is when she lost her voice.

"We were carried into another room," Olivia's voice quivered.

I touched her hand, concentrating again, hoping to help her, too. Olivia leaned in closer to Chrispin, hiding as much of herself as she could behind him.

"They.... they stripped our clothes and washed our bodies. They dressed us, prodding us for hours. Then we walked. It was cold, and the ground was uneven; it felt like we were going uphill. The air became damp. We stopped, then the chants began again - then you came like they said you would."

Everyone was hanging on Olivia's every word, and now the fear she felt was filling the room.

"Who said she would come?" Chrispin asked softly, being gentler than anyone else was capable of being.

"When they were dressing us, I focused on the people talking. I heard Drake talking to a man with a husky voice. Drake was angry with him, telling him 'Now you've done it. Willow is sure to feel this, and the moon is not full.' The husky voice just laughed, saying there was always more people to be taken if need be.' I prayed you would come, Willow. I didn't know what you could possibly do to help, but it was easy to see that at least Drake was afraid of what you could do."

I stood and tried to hide my fear, my anger; Drake would keep taking people I loved, tormenting us all. Hannah had been nodding along as Olivia spoke, and she motioned to me; she wanted something to write on. Dane left the room swiftly and retuned with one of my sketch books. I tore out a clean sheet and handed it to her. On the top of the page, she wrote 'this is the man who had the husky voice.' Hannah began trying to sketch a picture –she'd taken lessons with my mother before. She had talent, but no desire to become an artist. Hannah drew a heavy man in his late sixties with large eyes, and she made a point to draw a necklace wrapped around his hand. It had a star, and she shadowed it to make it look like it was glowing. She then drew arrows pointing to it.

"Did that star do something?" Brady asked.

Hannah nodded and drew what looked like a small tornado on the back of the page.

"OK, OK… just calm down; we'll figure it out," I promised her, halfway trying to convince myself.

Hannah leaned back and put her hand on her throat. Jessica turned on her side, still asleep. Olivia was still hiding behind Chrispin.

I felt my father and Ashten's panic. I looked to the window and saw them pulling up in front of my house.

Brady looked at Landen. "Are you ready for this?" he asked.

Landen shrugged; it was clear the last thing he was going to worry about was if they were upset with us. We met them on the front porch, and my father's eyes danced over me and Landen.

"What happened?" Ashten shouted, trying to look behind us. My father quickly looked us both over again.

"They're fine," my father said to Ashten.

I spoke up first, knowing they wouldn't be as angry with me. I told them what had happened. Knowing that we'd been in the strings alone was almost more than the two of them could handle. I quickly moved past that part and explained to my father that the girls needed help.

My father walked in the house. Ashten went to speak, but Landen raised his hand, stopping him. Ashten then stopped himself and mumbled. Everyone filed outside one-by-one when my father went in to see the girls, and almost fifteen minutes passed before Landen and I went back in, hoping he'd figure out what was wrong.

My father was still looking over Jessica as she lay sleeping. Hannah's confusion was apparent; she couldn't understand why Dane, my father, and I were all there. My father smiled warmly back at her.

"Listen, we're going to make you all better, OK. You just need to calm down."

He then led us into the kitchen. My father was pacing, confusion coursing through him.

"There's nothing wrong with them - they just think that they can't see, hear, or speak."

"What do you mean?" I asked quietly.

"There's nothing wrong with them. I can see that they've been given narcotics or something close to that, but beyond that they're fine."

Brady had been arguing on Landen's behalf with his father, wanting to escape. When he found us in the kitchen - after hearing that nothing was physically wrong with the girls and seeing our defeated expressions - he offered his opinion.

"I think they're under some kind of spell…you heard the chants, didn't you, Landen?"

My father promptly stood at attention. I seemed to have left that small detail out earlier.

"Chants?" he repeated, making sure he wasn't mistaken.

Fearing he would now have to argue with my father, Brady answered.

"They…umm…were in a room with an altar and chants, but they were sick before that," Brady said, looking guiltily in our direction. We weren't upset that he'd said something; we just wanted the girls better.

My father slid to the floor against the cabinets, bowing his head to his knees. We all rushed to his side; Landen and I could feel how distraught he was, almost to the point of grief. He looked up slowly, reaching for my face and leaning his head toward mine.

"Dad, it's OK – what's wrong?" I asked.

He stared forward for a moment before he spoke. "If I'd brought you home, the two of you would have had enough time to prepare yourself. We could have all helped - but now you two are almost defenseless."

Landen and I looked at one another. We knew that we weren't completely defenseless; our gifts were merging, not to mention we could leave our bodies as they slept. Telling my father may have brought him some comfort, but we weren't sure if it would also bring him more worry.

"We're going to be fine, all of us," Landen said with a degree of authority that made us all believe he spoke the truth.

My mother tapped lightly on the back door, causing us all to rise. She was genuinely concerned when she saw my father and his composure, and she listened as my father gave us instructions.

"You need to see if they want to go home now, or if they want to wait until they're better. If they want to stay, you need to find a way to tell their parents that they're OK."

Landen, Brady, and I left the room, giving my father time to explain everything in his own way to my mother. When Brady passed through the entry hall and went back outside, Landen stopped me before we walked into the living room.

"Listen, if we take them back I want to give them the herb Relm; I don't want them to have to remember that place," Landen thought.

"What if they forget the chants that would break the spell?" I asked

"I don't know," Landen thought softly.

I nodded and walked into the living room, holding Landen's hand. Jessica was awake now, and Hannah was writing her notes to explain what had happened and that she was safe. They all looked up as I walked into the room, staring at me for some kind of explanation.

"Listen, I don't know how to explain any of this to you; I can't tell you when you'll be better. If you want to go home to your parents, we'll take you there. If you want to stay here a while longer, you're more than welcome."

Hannah threw her hands in the air with complete disgust at my bleak explanation. She then turned the page in the sketchbook she was holding and wrote. "HOME PLEASE". Jessica looked at her, then back at me for some kind of understanding. Landen walked over, gently took the pad from Hannah, and wrote what I said for Jessica to read. Feeling the anger coming from Hannah, he wanted to explain it more gently to her. Jessica wrote the words "Which way will make us better faster?"

I shook my head softly and said, "We don't know. Dad says that there's nothing physically wrong that he can see; it's unexplainable."

Olivia leaned forward, reaching for my arm. "Do they want to go home?" she asked, I whispered yes, then she turned to where she knew they were sitting and said, "I'm going to stay here. I feel at peace here; with or without my sight, I've never felt better."

Hannah looked at Olivia, tears coming down her face.
Hannah's family had tried so hard to make Olivia a part of their family after her parents had died suddenly, but instead she turned inward to books and movies, hiding from life. Olivia was truly at peace, a peace that I'd never felt from her before.

Hannah walked over and hugged Olivia, rocking back and forth. Jessica picked up the pad and wrote "I want to go home. I do not belong here."

"Olivia, they want to go home. Are you sure you want to stay here?" I asked softly.

She nodded. Landen then left the room to tell the others what the girls had decided, and I slid down in one of the big chairs in the room, trying to comprehend what was happening all around me.

Sensing that I was the only one in the room, Olivia asked, "Willow, where are we? Who are these people who are trying to help us?"

I looked in her direction; Hannah was waiting for my answer too. "They're my family."

Their curiosity intensified. Leaning closer - making sure she could hear me - Olivia said,

"I didn't know you had any other family. You never talked about anyone; I thought your family was alone, like me."

Hannah looked sharply at Olivia; though Olivia couldn't see it, I was sure she could feel it.

"This is my father's family. They live far away. We haven't visited much," I finally answered.

Jessica tried to speak, but not being able to hear her voice, she was rather loud. "Drake knows that guy with you; he asked if we'd met him yet."

I sat up quickly. "Landen? He knows Landen?" my rush of fear caused Landen to look in the window at me.

"Come in here."

Seeing my surprise, Jessica went on. "He just described him. He thought you two were together."

Landen came in. Hearing the last part of what Jessica said, Olivia spoke up. "I remember what Jessica's talking about; Monica insisted that you and Dane were together…he must have asked all of us several times about the other guy."

"Did he use my name?" Landen asked.

"No. I remember because at one time Monica asked him. Drake said he didn't know; he just knew what you looked like."

"Did he say anything else about us?" I asked

"He asked a lot about you, Willow. He wanted to know what you painted, why you have that tattoo, if you ever talked about your dreams or nightmares, and what made you scared or happy," answered Olivia.

"What did you tell him?" I asked, disgusted with Drake.

I could sense the confusion coming from them, like I was missing some big picture; Olivia then leaned forward further and tilted her head as if to tell me a sad story. "Willow, besides Dane, I'm probably the closest person to you. I told him you'd never tell us something that would make you appear weak. I have to be honest, you were - or are - a very solemn person. I mean, I can't remember a time when you laughed out loud or were full of energy…you gave the impression that you weren't afraid of anything."

Landen and I were locked in a stare. It was easy to see that Drake had an advantage; he knew that Landen and I were meant to be together, and he was searching for information about me.

I felt Aubrey and Felicity approaching the house. I then fell into one of the large chairs, and Landen slid in beside me. My mother and Felicity gave the girls food and changed them out of the dresses they were in. Aubrey tried to play the peacemaker between Ashten and her boys, but she was only able to maintain the truce for a moment. Landen's struggle for independence and Ashten's growing concern for our safety seemed to collide over and over again.

Brady and Marc took the dresses and jewels the girls were wearing and burned them in one of the side fields. Chrispin hovered near Olivia, only leaving her when they changed her clothes. I wondered if Chrispin was the source of her peace; I couldn't ever recall her even acknowledging that the boys existed - and now she looked so natural next to Chrispin.

"How old is Chrispin?" I asked.

Landen smiled and looked over to where Olivia and Chrispin had settled. *"He turned twenty a few months ago; that's why he wanted to know so much about the strings he hadn't seen yet."*

"How come he didn't already know? You know them."

Landen pursed his lips; I could see that he wasn't comfortable in his thoughts, feeling guilty for something out of his control, the favor he was given as a child. *"As soon as it was clear that I had an insight, I was put in the strings, traveling further than permitted by those well beyond my years. That's what your father meant when he said we'd be more prepared; insight is treated with a high degree of respect.*

Our conversation was cut short as Rose arrived at the house. She stepped in the room and motioned with her eyes for us to come to her. We followed her through the kitchen, off the porch, and into the back field - far away from earshot of the house full of people. Coming to a stop, she turned and crossed her arms, looking at us over her small square glasses.

"So, little Libby mentioned that she saw the two of you in her room last night," Rose said. She had a proud smile on her face as she measured our response. We looked at each other with guilty smiles on our faces, then the realization that our secret was no more suddenly set in.

"The others won't learn what you can do from me," she reassured us. "It is your gift; all I want to do is help you with it."

"Do you know how she could see us?" I asked, knowing that Landen was just as grateful for her confidence.

"Libby is connected to the both of you. The only vision she has directly involves the two of you, or your surroundings. It makes sense that she can see you when others can't."

I looked at Landen; both of us had deep concern coming from us. We felt protective over her; we didn't want her to see anything as dark as we'd seen that day.

"When your father told me of the way you dream, I was sure that you did meet soul-to-soul; your bodies are only vessels." Rose said proudly. "That's why I agreed with the decision to keep Willow in Infante; I knew you two were never really apart." Her eyes looked over me and Landen carefully."Have you learned to use each other's insight as one yet?"

I looked at Landen and nodded, telling him to reveal our latest accomplishment.

"If you mean that I can feel emotions and she can see intent, then yes."

Rose gave off an emotion of surprise, meaning that wasn't what she meant.

"You now have both," she said, trying to hold down her excitement.

"We're just now learning our new ones; it can easily be overlooked because our own is so familiar to us."

"In a way, your gifts are the same; together, they should intensify. Landen, you could almost certainly assume someone's mood or emotion by their intent, and Willow, knowing how someone feels would make you able to assume short--term intent," Rose said. "You both should try to intensify your primary gift."

"How do you mean?" Landen asked

"Try seeing intent further away or changing emotions with a touch to those that are here. Don't push it, or you could hinder your progress. Let it come to you."

"Can you change emotions?" I asked. Landen looked quickly at me, astonished, then back to Rose.

"No wonder you always understood me," Landen said, smiling slightly.

Rose nodded. "Someone needed to walk in your shoes with you for a while," she said, hugging him. She then looked at me as she let Landen go and said, "We all have the power to change the emotions of the ones around us. A kind word could make someone's day, just as a harsh one will bring pain. The secret is to know your own energy and use it to fill the room around you. By being connected the way the two of you are, I can only imagine the energy you could find as one."

It was just after noon in our dimension, and it had already been a long day. I explained to Olivia that she needed to tell her aunt and uncle that she was safe. She agreed, and we handed her a blank page. She told them that she'd met someone and was going to see the world before she went to school, explaining that the line was busy each time she'd tried to call. We enclosed a snap shot of Chrispin and Olivia using the sun as a backdrop, covering her eyes with sunglasses.

My father had given Jessica and Hannah the herb Relm that would take their short term memory away, and it would soon take effect. The girls hugged Olivia goodbye, and Hannah argued one last time through Jessica with Olivia to come home, but her words went unheeded.

Chrispin stayed behind with Olivia, and Ashten and my father joined us as we walked back to the string. Landen led us; we were going to use the new paths he'd discovered, avoiding Esteroius all together. Jessica and Hannah held their eyes down as we led them, and I could feel their anger toward their disposition. As we walked, their eyes grew heavy, and eventually Marc and Brady carried them as they drifted off to sleep.

Landen found a passage that was on the roof of the only hospital in Franklin. The street lights started to blink yellow, meaning it was past midnight. My father had worked in the hospital for close to twenty years, and he knew everything there was to know about it. He went in to put the girl's name in the computer and assigned them a room. When he returned, he had two beds with him. Brady and Marc laid the girls down, and Ashten went with my father to take them to their rooms. Taking advantage of the time that they were gone, I walked to the edge of the roof and gazed toward the town. The streets were empty, but my memory took me back to so many happy days that I'd spent growing up in a four- block radius. Landen came to my side, smiling as if they were his memories as well.

The walk home was quiet, the mood complacent. No one wanted to comment on what had happened to the girls, or where we'd found them; talking seemed to confuse the issue more. We made two stops on the way back, one in the Florida Keys to mail Olivia's letter, and one in New York to mail letters my mother had prepared for her friends that she'd left behind; Sharon's letter was on top. Landen and I had agreed to return to Franklin that night while our bodies slept. It would be daylight soon, and the girls would be awake, and we could see if forgetting had healed their hearing and voice. Once home, everyone departed to dress for the celebration. My father and Ashten lingered behind the others, and worried looks came from Aubrey as she helped Olivia in the car.

Ashten chose not to resume his lecture, a promise I felt him make Aubrey.

"Now that Willow's friends are safe, will you stay here?" Ashten asked.

Landen looked down at me, then to his father. "I won't make you a promise I can't keep," he said respectfully.

"Landen, this is the only dimension that will protect the both of you," Ashten said, stepping forward and trying to hide his frustration.

"What do you mean?" I asked, looking from Ashten to Landen.

"Chara can only be found by those who were born here," Ashten said, looking at me, hoping I'd be able to convince Landen to stay.

"Then why didn't you just bring me here when you found me? Drake never would have found me."

"We didn't know that until Drake started looking for you; he passed by the passages to Chara blindly," Ashten said defensively.

I believed him; Landen's gift of truth was making itself known inside me.

"Why is he looking for her?" Landen said with as much constraint as he could manage.

"It doesn't matter, Landen," my father said, putting his hand on Landen's shoulder. "Willow loves you; he can't take her away from you. When Olivia is feeling better, maybe she can give us a better idea of where the star might be. The palace is as large as a small town; servants who have worked their whole lives there still lose their way. We'll return the star to where it belongs," my father said, looking to the charm on my neck.

Ashten sighed and walked down the front steps. "Just promise me you won't ever go to Esterouis alone," he said, looking back at Landen.

Landen nodded.

My father hugged me and patted Landen on the back before he left.

"I'll see you in a little bit," he said as he let me go.

Landen and I walked inside our house to get ready for the celebration in town. "Why do you think they're so worried about that star?" I asked "Do you really think it's that important?"

"I don't know - I know I don't want Drake to have anything that belongs to you," Landen said.

I felt a surge of jealousy come from him.

"Do you think if we got the star, we'd be able to heal my friends?" I asked

"I do," he said quietly.

I nodded "Then that's what we'll do," I said, sure of myself.

Chapter Fourteen

Dinner was at sunset. We drove Landen's black Jeep into town; this was the first time I'd left the area around our home. My eyes widened as I gazed at the lush fields, homes sprinkling the horizon. None of them looked the same, a unique personality accompanying each of them. The outline of the town was coming into view on the horizon; from where we were, it looked broader than Franklin.

Landen parked on one of the side streets. The roads were made of stones set perfectly together. The buildings were crafted uniquely, with light colors and wood framework. Each stoop had beautiful flowers sitting on it. The town was full of people, each of them beautifully original; their skin was as dark as night, yet their eyes were a crystal blue. Others would be as light as snow and every shade in between; the one common factor was the peace you could feel emanating from them.

Along the streets, banners were stretched across with our names written in a beautiful script. My parents, Dane and Clarissa, had banners as well. Lights reached out from building to building, giving the street a beautiful canopy. Music could be heard throughout the town, and children ran through the streets;

dressed in beautiful bright colors, their laughter energized us as we walked by.

The atmosphere was electric; it reminded me of how a crowded concert would be at home: energized, joyful, and carefree. Some were braver than others, stopping and shaking hands with me and Landen, others would only bow their heads, with a sweet smile. Landen introduced me to several couples he'd carried home, and I met well over thirty of them in a one--block radius; the pride of having known him was overwhelming around them.

As we neared the center of town, large tables with white cloths lined the streets, and beautiful candles surrounded by roses set the centerpieces. The center of town was transformed into a dance floor, and the band played a beautiful melody. A path was made for us as we crossed the dance floor, and as Landen swirled me into the center of everyone, applause erupted. He caught me in my spin and pulled me to him, kissing me softly for the world to see. The crowed grew louder, their energy rushing through us, and we lost ourselves inside each other's eyes, dancing to song after song.

The impatience of our favorite little girl, Libby, caught our attention. We went to the other side where we could see our family sitting along a large U shaped table; others that I hadn't met sat amongst them.

We took our place near the center, next to my parents, Dane and Clarissa. Landen, with Libby in his lap, sat next to my father. Rose was to my right, Karsten to her side, and I watched as they stood and greeted another older couple. A small crowd lingered around them, causing me to lose my stare. Desperate to regain it, I adjusted my seat. The man's skin was dark, his hair was short and white, and his eyes were as pale as clear water. The woman was small with long black curly hair her, eyes were as black as coal, and I could feel their admiration. Feeling my stare, the man turned to me and smiled as he bowed his head.

"Landen, who is that next to Karsten?"

Landen looked up from his quiet conversation with my father to follow my gaze; it was clear he hadn't noticed them before. I could feel respect, joy, and love coming from Landen. He stood, putting Libby in my father's lap, and pulled me up with him.

"That is my grandfather, August, and my grandmother, Nyla. They're home."

I followed Landen as he stepped closer. His grandfather rose as he saw us approach, and his grandmother followed. Landen all but threw himself into his grandfather's arms; it was easy to see that he was closer to his grandfather than he was to Ashten.

"Willow, this is August and Nyla, my grandparents," Landen said, formally introducing me to them. I was quickly pulled into their joyful embrace; and from the dance floor I could hear applause.

"I'm proud of you," August said to Landen as he looked at me again. "We've been trying to get home for days. The storms were more difficult where we were...they haven't been giving you a hard time, now have they?" he asked.

"They're silent," Landen said in a frustrated tone as he pulled me closer, smiling down at me.

"I imagine that they are," August said, smiling at Landen. "I spoke with your father; you've certainly humbled him."

"Not intentionally," responded Landen.

"I left something for you at your house; you'd already left when we stopped by," August said.

Landen tilted his head curiously, and August leaned in closer and whispered something to Landen, ending the conversation.

Couples filled the dance floor as dinner ended, and one had my full attention: Olivia and Chrispin; they seemed to glide across the floor. The smile across Olivia's face overshadowed her recent blindness, and no one dared to try and divide them. Landen and I were separated unintentionally. His grandfather, Brady, and others who names I had forgotten surrounded him. I was surrounded as well. The space between us was odd, yet bearable, being filled by people who I'd seen the least since being there.

I was nestled next to Rose as the conversations blossomed around us. I felt safe next to her, and understood. The uncomfortable separation brought Landen back to me, his followers were close behind, and then it was simple just to relax and feel the harmony.

Across the street, I watched as Libby and an older woman were talking. Libby then followed her into the store that they were standing in front of, almost certainly convincing the woman to give her a special treat. My eyes were growing heavy; our day had been long. I laid my head on Landen's shoulder as he listened to one of August's stories of recent travels. Kissing the top of my head, he thought.

"You not leaving me, are you?"

Before I could protest his thoughts, I felt Libby crawl across my lap and onto Landen's.

"Willow, I have something for you," she whispered.

"You do?" I said, genially surprised.

Libby reached into the pocket on her dress and brought out a small brown bag, trying to hide it from my parent's view, not caring that she had Landen and Rose's full attention.

"Tonight when you go see Hannah and Jessica, you'll need this," Libby said.

"What will I need it for?" The bag felt as if it were full of sand.

"When you see the mean monkey, throw this in his eyes and he'll go away and not hurt you."

Landen reached for the bag and causally slid it into his pocket before anyone else noticed the exchange.

"What is it, sweetie?" asked Rose.

"Garlic salt," Libby said, covering her lips to let Rose know it was a secret.

The feeling of certainty coming from Libby was frightening. A mean monkey – what did she mean? A little girl with ivory skin and liquid blue eyes came over, beckoning Libby to play with her. Libby hugged me tightly and said, "Don't be scared; I've protected you."

As she ran across the dance floor, my heart sank, and my breath left me. We had no power to protect her from what she saw; defenseless, she would witness the battle before it came to be.

The dread was coming from Landen as well, but we were both thankful that whatever we faced tonight would be mild. Libby had no fear; her certainty still lingered around us.

The celebration went on. Not wanting to appear ungrateful for the companionship, we stayed, half- heartedly listening to the many tales around us. Rose's distraction was apparent, as her laugh would be delayed when a story called for it. As the moon shifted, everyone's eyes seem to grow weary, and one-by-one the town began to empty of people. Hoping we'd served our purpose, Landen excused us.

Libby had fallen asleep in my mother's lap, and I hugged and kissed them both good night. Landen hugged August and Nyla. I looked for Rose, but I couldn't find her. My father made his way to us, and he kissed my forehead, telling me goodbye.

When we reached Landen's Jeep, we saw Rose leaning against the side of it, waiting patiently for us to reach her. She hesitated as a group of people passed by before she spoke.

"I know the last thing you want is someone else telling you what to do; that's not my intent, but I implore you to please tell me when you leave tonight," Rose said.

We weren't concerned with the 'monkies' we were supposed to see that night, simply because Libby had no fear when she'd told us – assuring us we had no reason to be afraid. Rose's concern, though, was shaking the solid ground on which we stood on, and our pause gave her reason to explain further.

"If you're gone too long, or if you're afraid, I want to try and wake you; that monkey could be anywhere between here and those girls, and waking you might keep you safe." Hearing her conclusion, we nodded slowly with eyes wide open, realizing the danger that she feared for the first time.

Rose's calm returned to her, and Landen was looking up the street, watching Ashten and his mother leave, waving bye to them.

"Willow, I think we should tell your father his insight would make what Rose wants to do more efficient."

The sudden relief that came over me told him that I agreed. Looking now at Rose, Landen laid out a plan for her. "We're going to tell Jason so he can help you watch us. After we fall asleep, we'll come to the two of you before we leave."

The conversation was halted as Karsten and my parents approached. Rose coaxed my mother into letting her and Karsten take her and Libby home; sensing that I needed my father, she went hastily.

Landen opened the passenger door of the Jeep for my father to get in; looking confused; he complied. I then climbed in the back, and we drove off to a more private place. Landen and my father talked causally about the celebration, August, and others that had come from so far to see all of us.

The lights of the town faded; now only the stars and moon, which was growing fuller each night, showed the way. We stopped at the edge of the driveway that led to my father's house, and Landen and I got out. Slowly, my father made his way out, confusion coursing from him. I nodded in Landen's direction, encouraging him to start. He cleared his throat he began, "Jason, we need you to do us a favor." My father nodded, agreeing before he even knew what we wanted him to do. "Willow and I can control where we go when we sleep, and tonight we're going to see if the Relm healed Hannah and Jessica."

"You can control it?" my father asked, astonished.

"We taught ourselves last night," Landen said proudly.

"We came to see you," I added.

My father looked quickly at me. "Did you change my emotion?" he asked

I nodded. I felt my father's amazement, mixed with pride.

"Jason, Libby told us we'd see mean monkeys tonight. She gave us garlic salt and told us to throw it in their eyes. Rose wants to wake us if we're scared. You'd be able to see if we were hurt," Landen said.

"How would my mother know if you were afraid?" My father asked, shaking his head, trying to understand what we were saying.

I looked at Landen, and he looked back at me; we'd both forgotten that Rose had kept her insight a secret.

"She has the gift of emotion, too," I said putting my hand on my father's shoulder. "She said her father told her that she should keep it to herself if she truly wanted to help people."

My father nodded. I felt his understanding.

"If you know there's going to be danger, why are you going?" my father asked.

"It's just a precaution. Libby's not afraid of what we're going to see. Tonight will serve as a test; if we have a strong enough control over this, maybe we'll be able to get the star back without putting anyone in danger," Landen explained.

"I don't think it's a good idea for you to go into Esterious without your bodies; I'm more than sure that they'd be able to hurt you. "

"How do you know that?" I asked, looking for more answers.

"The Priests were able to put Drake in that state. Obviously, they'd know how to hinder you," my father explained.

My father sighed and looked back and forth between Landen and me. "How are you going to contact me – should I stay at your house?" he asked.

"We'll stop here before we leave – try and get some rest," Landen answered.

"I'm going to get Rose to stay with us so you only have to stop at one place – I'd think you'd be stronger just as you left…don't use all your energy finding us."

We agreed with my father. Landen drove him to his front door, then took us home. Walking in the door, we almost looked over the small package lying just inside on the floor; August had told Landen that he'd left something for us. I reached down for the box. I was excited to see what was in it.

"Do you know what it is? What did August's whisper to you?" I asked, handing it to Landen.

"He said it'll keep us both safe."

When Landen opened the small brown box, something fell and hit the hardwood floor; it was two silver rings, which began circling in place. When they stopped, I reached down and grabbed them. Quiet heavy for being so small, within the ban of the rings an eye was inscribed: two long lashes stretched out from the bottom, and seven gold lines made a border along the base of the eye. Landen slid the smaller ring on my left hand, and I slid the larger one on his. As if they'd found their rightful place, the rings tingled our fingers upon first touch, and the silver seemed to brighten.

I slid the ring off again to look at the inscription; as I did, the silver dulled, and the tingle left my hand in protest.

"Do you know what this means?" I asked, counting the seven gold lines. I'd seen this before: the night I picked out my tattoo. It was the eye of RA, and it meant "protection". My Ankh meant "eternal life." I reasoned that if I had eternal life, I wouldn't need protection – that's why I chose the Ankh.

"August told me a lot of stories. If I remember correctly, I think it's a watchful eye. I don't remember what culture or dimension he was referring to when he described it, though."

"Well, if it's the same as my tattoo, it came from Infante. It's Egyptian," I said, looking at my wrist and the uninvited star inside my loop.

"Egyptians, as you call them, are in a lot of dimensions and are a very advanced people," Landen said, sliding the ring on my finger again. The tingle came as the shine returned.

"They're the only other people that we've discovered exploring the strings; they've settled across many dimensions."

"Seriously?" I asked, thinking he was just teasing me.

Smiling he answered, "The string is energy; in theory, everyone should be able to see them. People have the power to change their perspective. They just get caught up in an endless cycle of foolish things that don't matter."

I looked down at my olive skin, matching my tone to Landen's and wondering if that culture was a part of me.

"Do you know what my tattoo means?" I asked Landen.

He smiled. "Eternal life,' I remember when you got it; I thought you were trying to tell me something," he said, tracing the cross while avoiding the star in the loop.

"I think I was trying to tell myself something - that I'd find you in this life or the next," I said, looking up at him and smiling shyly.

Landen kissed my lips softly. "I always knew I'd find you," he whispered.

I looked down at the rings again. It felt like I had seen them before, too, like they'd always been ours. "Did August tell you were he got these?" I asked.

"He really didn't have a chance. All he said was 'time is simply an illusion, and the gifted live on,'" Landen said, smiling. "August isn't like the others; he isn't quick to offer advice, and he likes to watch your mind work." He laughed a little, tucking a piece of my hair behind my ear. "He said he needed to show us something in the morning."

"Is he going to tell us what the others are hiding?"

"I believe he will."

We changed out of our party clothes and into the all-black attire. We then laid in our bed in silence. Hoping we'd given Rose and my father time to rest, we drifted to sleep, almost simultaneously. Standing over our bodies, the addictive rush of excitement came over us again. Landen checked his pocket to make sure the garlic salt was with us, then looked at me.

"Let's try this: think of your father's porch." He reached his arm around my waist and pressed his forehead to mine, concentrating on my father's porch. *"We did it,"* he thought.

I opened my eyes to see that Landen was right, and I saw that we were on the front steps. A rush of excitement came through us, more exhilarating than before. I gave him an alluring smile; this power was becoming less elusive.

I led the way through the door. All the lights were off, and I could feel peaceful sleep coming from five people. Karsten must have stayed there, too. Walking up the stairs, we stopped in the guest room. Rose was asleep in a chair with an open book resting on her lap; I was afraid to wake her and startle her. We went down the hall to my parents' room. When we opened the door; my father raised his head and whispered into the darkness. "Willow."

I walked over to him and pulled back his blanket, letting him know it was us, and a rush of excitement came over him as he watched the blanket move without seeing anyone. Landen found a note pad on my mother's side of the bed and wrote "wake Rose, we are on our way now."

Already dressed, my father slid on his shoes and walked to Rose's room.

"Do you want to see if we can make it to the hospital the same way?" I asked.

Landen smiled, and we held each other again and focused on the roof that we'd been on earlier that day .A moment later, rain-drops could be heard. When we opened our eyes we were on the roof. It was an awful looking day, the sky was so dark, it was hard to tell that it was daylight, and now there was thunder in the distance with increasing wind.

Knowing the way, I took Landen's hand, and we walked in the door and down the steps. The hospital was quiet; not much was happening there - new births being the most exciting thing.

The maternity ward was on the fourth floor, and we passed that doorway on our way to the third floor.

We opened the door slowly, not knowing who might be standing close to it. At the end of the hallway, we could see two women standing outside one of the doors. As we approached them, I could see it was Amanda, Chase's mom, and Gina, Dane's mom. We listened as they talked.

"It just doesn't make any sense – how did they get here so fast?" Gina said

"At least they're safe. The search for Monica was called off yesterday… I don't think this town could bear losing another child," Amanda said in a sorrowful tone.

I looked at Landen. He felt my grief and put his arm around me.

"I wish someone could get a hold of Jason - or Grace, for that matter. Jason would know what was wrong; that man is the best doctor on this planet."

I felt a rush of pride all my own as they spoke of my parents.

"How is Dane anyway? I can't believe he ran off with Willow like that. I bet you're happy, aren't you?" asked Amanda.

Landen was shaking his head and smiling. He wasn't angry or jealous; it was just odd how Dane and Clarissa had met – by Dane's chasing me to New York. So far, that was the only good thing that had come out of me and Landen being separated for eighteen years.

"Well…um… you see, he's not with Willow. He's – he's seeing one of her friends, Clarissa," answered Gina, confused by her own words.

I could feel Amanda's disappointment. "Oh…I see…do you know if Willow's OK? Chase said that Willow and Dane were really hung up on each other. Apparently, that kid, Drake, made a move on Willow, and Dane showed up, saw it, and was furious. Chase said they had to stop Dane from tearing that guy apart." she explained.

"Remind me to tell Dane he's awesome when we get back," Landen thought, finding it humorous that others had to pull Dane off Drake.

"Willow is happy, too; Grace said she's in love with a really great guy, and Grace and Jason both seem to love him. They went to school with his parents, I think," Gina said, trying to curve the conversation.

"So tell me about Clarissa - what's she like?" asked Amanda.

"Dane called a day or so ago; he's going to go to Paris, too. Right now, they're in New York. He said he'd come home before he went overseas."

"So Dane could ask Jason to come home, too?" asked Amanda.

Before Gina could answer, the door they were standing in front of opened, and Hannah's mother, Connie, came out, holding a pad of paper. Still studying the words on it, she looked tired and aged by the event.

"Well?" asked Amanda. "She's asleep now. I don't know; she doesn't remember anything about getting on a boat or going to the Keys," Connie said, leaning against the wall and staring at the notes.

"Do they know what happened to her voice – or Jessica's hearing," asked Amanda.

Connie shook her head. "The doctor said the memory loss is due to trauma, but he thinks the girls will recover if they rest."

"What about Olivia? Does Hannah remember where she is?" asked Gina.

"Hannah can't even tell me if she was ever with them to begin with," answered Connie.

Feeling their agonizing grief and confusion, I shifted my way in front of Connie. Landen took a protective step forward, bracing himself for anything that could happen. As I reached for Connie's shoulders, my trembling hands anticipated the rush. Staring into her eyes, I concentrated on peace; I remembered how happy Olivia looked dancing with Chrispin, hearing her laughter over the music. Connie's eyes closed slowly, then opened again, looking past the room. Gina and Amanda yelled Connie's name, fearing she was passing out. My fingertips tingled. Just as I felt her emotion change to joy, a flash of light came across my face, causing me to lose my touch. The rush found Landen, and the sensation boomeranged between us, intensifying the high and energizing our sprit.

Connie let out a gasp of air as Amanda and Gina both reached for her, blocking a potential fall. At first, I thought I'd done something wrong or hurt her somehow, but she just gasped again, then smiled.

"She's fine. Olivia's happy – she's found her place."

"What? Connie, what happened?" Gina asked, looking behind her, halfway expecting Olivia to be standing there.

"I could see her - dancing and laughing. She's in love. It's in her eyes – a light I haven't seen … since," Connie's words faded as tears surfaced in the corner of her eyes.

Gina and Amanda hugged Connie, and they looked at each other, speechless.

Connie breathed in deeply and stood up straight; smiling, she still carried the joy I'd given her.

"I think I need some coffee. Will you guys go with me?" asked Connie.

Gina and Amanda walked behind her, whispering and looking back through where we stood.

"What was that? Did it hurt you?" Landen reached down, examining my fingertips.

"No, it was amazing – exhilarating."

"Were you thinking of them dancing? Is that what she saw?"

"Yeah – I don't know how she saw them – I always think of something when I help. Did you see that light?"

Landen nodded.

"Where did it come from?"

"Her - well, the both of you – a light came from your fingers, then another burst from her chest."

The elevator door dinged, then opened, and a nurse got off as Connie and the others got on. We watched as the nurse check a clipboard before going into the room across the hall. As we waited, we were hit hard with terror. Looking at each other, then to the room, we were sure where it was coming from. Landen grabbed my hand before going into Hannah's room. It was dark; only a little light came from the gray windows, and rain sheeted across the pane. I could see Jessica's mother sleeping on a couch under the window. All of a sudden the terror we were feeling seemed to double, and Landen saw them first – the 'monkeys.'

Jessica and Hannah were in beds side by side, asleep, and on their chests sat small demonic animals that resembled monkeys. They had short red hair, and spikes made of reddish bone lined their spines. Horns crowned their head, black collars circled their small necks, and their feet were planted firmly on the girls' chests as they stared centimeters from their sleeping faces.

We stared, frozen with fear.

"We have to hide our fear," I thought, remembering that Rose would wake us before we'd be able to help if she felt it in our bodies.

We both pushed it aside and found anger instead. As we stared, not believing our eyes, we listened to the growling of the monkeys as they breathed. Landen reached in his pocket for the bag of garlic salt. He then opened it, grabbed a handful of it and gave me a handful, too. We never took our eyes off the demons. The girls moaned as if they were in pain, and a chuckle of a growl filled the room.

The terror coming from the girls was growing stronger. Not knowing if the demons could see us, we stepped cautiously in their direction. All at once, the growling halted, and the one on Jessica looked slowly over its shoulder, its red eyes glowing in the dark room. The other one sensed us and turned as well; it was clear that they could see us. As they stepped off the two girls' chests, their terror faded as they turned restlessly. The demons sauntered toward us as the growls resumed and grew louder, and Landen and I threw the handfuls of salt at them. They let out large growls as the salt hit their faces, then leaping at us, they suddenly vanished. Stunned, we looked slowly at each other, allowing the fear to come out.

A strong pull came over us – and as we gasped for breath, we suddenly found ourselves back in our bed. My father was standing over me, and Rose was standing over Landen – and they were shaking our shoulders. We jolted up, making sure we were both back. Landen dove across the bed and pulled me into his arms, burying his face in my neck; his fear was in rhythm with his heartbeat. He knew just like I did that those things had visited me often; the weight on my chest – that was them.

"Never again, Willow. He will never do that to you again, I swear I'll kill him…never again. I promise," Landen said through his teeth as he rocked me back and forth.

The fear in the room was overpowering. Rose and my father stood like statues, not sure what had happened.

"Olivia…Landen…Olivia," I said, pushing him back and holding his face so he would have to look at me through his fear.

Olivia was sleeping now; the demons could be tormenting her where she lay.

"Jason – where is Olivia?" shouted Landen, still staring at me.

"She's…uh…she's with Felicity. What's -"

My father was cut short as we rushed by him down the stairs, out the door, and into the Jeep. Landen didn't even use the road; he tore off across the field in the darkness. Just over the second hill, a house could be seen in the moonlight; like the others, it was wrapped in porches. We stopped inches short of the front porch, and Landen charged open the door – not caring how loud it banged back. He raced up the stairs two at a time, and I ran to keep pace with him. At the top of the stairs, he took a quick left, opening the first door. The light flicked on, and Olivia lay, sleeping peacefully. I walked breathlessly to her side to wake her, and I could hear Brady charging down the hall with Felicity close behind.

"Olivia! Olivia, I need you to wake up!" I said, trying to catch my breath.

Landen stopped Brady at the door, and Felicity peered in under his arm as they stared, wide-eyed. Startled awake, Olivia sat up quickly; a surge of fear singed her - she wasn't sure who'd woken her.

"Olivia, have you had a nightmare?" I said through the tears that were catching up with me, the demons' eyes staring through my memory.

"What? Willow are you OK ? What happened?"

"Have you had a nightmare?!!" I yelled

"No, not since I was little - why?" she asked, reaching for me.

I pushed away before she could touch me, charging my way out of the room and back down the stairs – I needed air. I was gasping, not wanting to cry, not wanting to succumb to the fear that had chased me through childhood. Landen was right behind me, and he grabbed my arm and swung me into his arms as I reached the porch. I buried my face in his chest; letting it all go, I cried breathlessly. The images that I'd helped, the pain I endured each time, the fear I'd overcome – it all flashed through my eyes. I felt Rose and my father approach as the others looked out at us. Landen waved them all away and let me cry, holding me tighter as the minutes passed and the tears ran dry. Light was starting to peak over the hill. When the tears dried on my face, we finally went in the house. They were all in the living room; Felicity and Olivia had fallen asleep toe–to-toe on the couch, and Brady, Rose, and my father were sitting, tensely waiting for us.

Brady raised his hands to question what was going on; looking at my father and Rose, it was clear they hadn't told Brady about watching our bodies. Landen slid in one of the oversized chairs and nestled me against him; I laid on his chest, not wanting to make eye contact with anyone.

"We went to check on Hannah and Jessica…we…," Landen stopped, looking at my father, then down at me. "We saw these things – demonic monkey - looking things - sitting on their chests…they were tortured with nightmares."

"Sitting?" my father repeated.

Landen nodded. "Like a heavy weight," he said. Anger coursed through him as he squeezed me tighter.

Brady stood, rubbing his arms nervously. As he began pacing the floor, fear and confusion overcame him. "Landen, are you serious? Demons – seriously?" he said in a harsh whisper, looking back to make sure Felicity was still sleeping.

Landen's angry blank stare told Brady we were very serious.

"What did you do? I mean, how do you come back from something like that?" asked Brady.

"Garlic salt," Rose said, realizing Libby had given us the weapon that saved us.

Brady raised his hands in the air – protesting the foolishness he heard. “I don’t think I want to know,” he said, sitting back down. “Does Dad know?” he stood again, ready to defend Landen’s point of view if his father came charging in the door. He looked at my father, trying to measure his perspective.

Landen shook his head. “Not yet, Libby told Rose, and we needed Jason to watch our bodies as we slept.”

“What did you mean. ‘bodies?’” Brady said, looking at Rose and Jason.

“We can control where we go when we sleep,” Landen answered.

Brady sat back in his chair and stared blankly. I felt him arguing with his emotions; he wanted to be proud of us, but he was too terrified.

“What did you see?” Brady asked my father.

Landen and I looked curiously in his direction to see if he could see the rush we’d felt helping Connie.

“Their adrenaline levels rose repeatedly, elevating their heartbeats. We didn’t start waking them until Rose could feel their fear,” my father answered.

Brady looked awestruck at Rose; it seemed everyone would now know that she had always had the insight of emotion.

“I think we may know why Landen never had nightmares: this world can’t be found that way either,” Rose said.

Hearing her words, I sat up slowly, staring into Landen’s eyes as relief came over him. He realized that Drake couldn’t reach me there, that I was sheltered from the nightmares - but Jessica and Hannah now bore the horror that had tormented me for so many years. Landen’s relief was only a small reward; I wouldn’t rest until I stopped Drake from hurting *anyone* – not just the ones I cared for.

The phone rang, and Brady dove across the room, answering it on the first ring; it was my mother, looking for my father. My father took the phone, whispering and promising my mother that we were all safe. I wondered how many houses she’d called, looking for us – how many knew now what we could do.

Brady coaxed a sleepy Felicity to her room. As she looked back at me, I whispered, "I'm sorry."

She smiled, understanding the chaos. Rose guided Olivia back to the guest room. My father went to speak; not finding the words, his lips hesitated. Landen then answered the unasked question. "Tell him – and the others; right now, our bodies need rest," he said, standing. I stood, too, and held him tightly. My father nodded and hugged me before we left.

Chapter Fifteen

Landen drove us home. Feeling the exhaustion come over us, we laid our bodies down, clinging to one another. Sleep came immediately. Rising in synch, we drifted onto the porch and rested on one of the couches as we watched the sun rise over the hill.

As the night's events raced over and over in our minds, we didn't speak. Landen played with my hands, studying my fingertips, and the ring that still gleamed as if it were brand new. I tried remembering how many times I'd concentrated on a memory to help others, wondering if they'd seen what I was thinking. The only difference I could find was the connection that Olivia had to Connie.

Olivia was the mirror image of her mother, Connie's only sister; it was as if, for the first time, Connie had let her sister go - passing the grief that she carried as she raised Olivia. Thinking of Olivia, I wondered – not doubting anything at that point - if Olivia's mother had somehow helped me that night…if she were the light that came out of Connie.

We watched as Aubrey pulled up. She reached for a basket in the front seat of the car and made her way to the door. Aubrey then peered through the window, and not seeing anyone, she set the basket on the porch and turned to leave. She hesitated and looked slowly toward the couch we were laying, and her eyes searched, not focusing on anything. She walked back on the porch toward us, and we looked at each other, wondering if she could see us. Aubrey went to speak, holding her hand out, she hesitated, checking her words before she began. Smiling at herself, she then looked in our direction.

"Landen…I'm sorry. We both are…but you have to understand, you're our little boy… you're so much like your father - ready to risk your life everyday to bring someone else safely home." She smiled at herself, looking down the empty road.

"Truth is, I dreamed of Willow, too I could see you with her. I remember keeping you awake at night so you could sleep through the day, to see her longer while she slept in her time… you needed to have a childhood…so did she…that was our intent. We failed to see that you never carried the soul of a child; you were born for the task before you, and the way you feel about Willow is not only your reward - but your weapon. I don't want you to be upset; being angry at the mistakes made by the heart will only leave you bitter. The time taken from you will be repaid beyond your imagination. Your father understands why you've built these walls - everyone does, I promise. He'll wait for you to come to him. No more lectures; you're a man now, and we're all waiting for you to teach us – to tell us how to help you fill your purpose." Aubrey looked down at her feet; I could feel her remorse.

"Please just forgive us – trust us," Aubrey said with tears pooling in her eyes.

Landen couldn't take another word. He woke himself up and ran down the stairs, almost tripping on the basket in the threshold. Running to her, he scooped her up, and happy tears flowed out of her pale green eyes. Giving him a moment, I woke and stayed in our bed, feeling him change her mood; she was relieved and happy.

After a shower, I found my sketchbook. The first sketch I drew was of the room Olivia was, struggling to call back every detail. Taking a deep breath, I faced my demons literally. Landen came in the room, breakfast in hand; hesitating as he saw the outline of the hospital room, he didn't stop me. He simply sat down and calmly watched as the demons came to life in black and white.

August knocked softly on the front door; we felt him coming and were waiting for him. Landen led August to the kitchen table. He was carrying what looked to be a large scroll. I followed shyly behind them.

"Interesting night," he commented as he sat down. We both smiled and settled at the table with August.

"What is this?" Landen asked, looking at the scroll.

"This is what you haven't been told," August said, smiling widely. My stomach turned, and Landen reached over to hold my hand.

August unrolled the scroll, revealing a large circle with lions, fish, rams, scales, twins and scorpions, and there were others symbols that lined the outer edge as well; I couldn't conceive what they might be. Dots were arranged under strange symbols.

"Landen this is your birth chart. Your sun is in Pisces," Landen nodded. "Your moon is in Virgo – that's what gives you your ability to see truth," August continued.

"I've heard that before," Landen commented. Smiling, he looked at me.

August nodded, then rolled out a second scroll. "Willow, this is yours. Your sun is in Scorpio, and your moon is in Leo, which gives you a powerful impact on emotions - both yours and others."

My eyes widened, moon…I'd never heard of a moon sign. "I don't understand - how do you know that?" I asked.

"When we're born each planet is aligned in a position, and their positions outline our characteristics. The alignments are not repeated exactly for 4,320,000 years; this means that there is not another person that shares your traits on earth."

I noticed he still had two scrolls that he hadn't unrolled. August smiled, his excitement growing as he unrolled the last two. They were much older than the ones he'd just shown us; the cloth the charts were on was frail and faded.

He removed the vase from the table and arranged the four scrolls. The old ones were next to the new ones, and the markings were identical.

"How is that possible?" Landen asked, clearly understanding the charts more than I did.

"This is Aliyanna's," August said, pointing to the one that matched mine. "And this is Guardian's," he said, pointing to the one that mirrored Landen's.

I still didn't understand. I looked at Landen, and his eyes were glazed over, he was scared.

"Who are they again?" I asked.

"They were the first. Priests attempted to kill them, but instead they were pushed into the string."

"So…um that's why we can do what they could do?" My voice was timid. August smiled, and his eyes encouraged me to move past my first impressions.

Landen closed his eyes and said, "You think we're them…that we're back?"

August smiled at Landen and moved his hand to his shoulder. "I do."

"Wait - four million years…were dinosaurs even around then? That makes no sense to me," I argued.

Landen leaned back in his chair and looked at August, wanting him to teach me. August smiled and placed his hand on mine, then stared into my eyes. "First of all, to think that time can be measured is unwise. Second, I can see how you perceive this, Willow; the dimension you were raised in is still in its infancy. Most dimensions are not divided into countries, nor have one specific leader; in fact, beyond Infante and Esterouis, there is only one other. Esteroius is thought to be one of the first – they had passed the prehistoric times before Infante was ever conceived."

"How can you not have a leader?" I asked

"People lead people just like we live here – we can divide ourselves any way we wish – but we are still, in fact, a part of humanity. In most dimensions, one person doesn't have a say over many; that's seen as a form of judgment. "

Landen never looked in my direction. I felt a wall building between us, and I didn't understand why.

"What do you know about them? How do Drake and Perodine play into this?" asked Landen.

August's eyes questioned why Landen had said Perodine's name.

"Willow dreamed of her, too," Landen said.

August smiled at me. "That makes sense. She is - or was your mother."

Landen buried his face in his hands, shaking his head. August went on, "Perodine is a strong woman, but in her younger years she was subservient to her husband, Donalt. Each time she had a child, he would take their lives, fearing that they would take his power. Perodine turned to the universe; she planned her next child by the planets. She then developed powers to protect her and her child, Aliyanna, and those powers unwittingly suspended both Perodine and Donalt's lives. Perodine's plan was to never allow just one to rule; that there must be at least two. So she planned to give the power to Aliyanna and the man she loved."

August's eyes fell to the charm around my neck. He smiled warmly as he looked back in my eyes. "Perodine had a charm made: a sun filled with black glass to represent the darkness the world was in. A crescent moon was carved in the center to represent the re-birth of life. The star was placed on the back to show that the supremacy of man would always fall behind the universe - God. All the power that Perodine had found was placed inside the charm.

"Aliyanna was promised to man in the court, a man her father had chosen for her, but her heart loved another: Gaurdian, a man of the common people. When Donalt learned of the charm and its power, he was furious, and his fury was intensified when he discovered his power would be shifted to a man of common standings. Donalt instructed his priest to remove Aliyanna's power and to kill her and Gaurdian. The charm served its purpose, though, and protected both Aliyanna and Gaurdian," August explained.

"So, let me get this straight: you think that we're those people? That this whole scenario is being played out again? Are you saying that Drake has been chosen for me by Donalt?" I asked.

I felt a deep rage and jealousy rise inside Landen. August could see it, too. He looked at Landen and put his hand on his shoulder. "I know that Drake has Donalt's favor," he said quietly.

My eyes raced back and forth as I tried to understand why any of this mattered. I wanted to take it all away, to undo what had been done then – but then I remembered my dream with Perodine. "When I dreamed of Perodine, she told me she couldn't undo what was done. What did she mean? Is that true, or can I fix this?" I asked

Landen looked at me quickly. I had never told him the details of the dream.

August looked in my direction; I could feel a deep respect inside of him. "Once a spell is spoken, it cannot be undone… it has to be resolved. I would say that she meant that whatever was said over you then still holds true today. The only prediction I know beyond your births is that 'the innocent will lead you, and you will lead the innocent,'" August answered.

My emotion moved to fear as Libby's face flashed before me, and Landen felt the same way. We had no way to protect her; we both felt helpless and lost.

"What happened after Guardian and Aliyanna landed in the string?" Landen asked, hoping that we'd done something to help Esteroius.

August looked down and traced the grain in the wooded table. He sighed, regretting his words as he spoke them. "Aliyanna had the power to go back, but…" August looked into my eyes. "You chose to stay, which left Esteroius in the state it's in today." His tone was sympathetic.

Landen's anger grew as August spoke. He looked at August and said, "If Aliyanna had never met Guardian, would the people in Esteroius be at peace now?"

I looked sharply at Landen. What was he saying – that he wished we'd never met? I felt my insides fall, and all the color left my face.

August leaned forward and put his hand on Landen's shoulder. "Both Aliyanna and Gaurdian were wise people; they never would have hurt anyone intentionally. You were made for each other - don't let this story cause you to forget that," he said with deep concern in his voice.

Landen broke his gaze with August and stared at the table. "I need to know how to heal her friends, and stop those demons," he said, standing, not wanting to look at the charts.

"The only difference between black magic and white magic is the intent; you're going to have to find the counterpart to what was spoken over them."

"Will these rings help, or the charm?" Landen asked, staring out the window.

"Only you truly know the power of those rings; they belonged to you then."

"How serious is it that they have the star?" Landen asked.

"They have half of the power," August said, then looked at me, "and you have the other. Until all the power rests on one side, you will struggle."

I could feel people coming – our family - and so could Landen. Our time alone with August was coming to an end, and we still had so many questions.

"You will find your way and finish what you left undone. I'm sure of it," August said.

August saw Ashten through the window walking. He was across the field, and he wasn't alone; my father, Marc, Chrispin, Brady, Dane, and Clarissa were all with him. August smiled at Landen and bowed his head. We knew that this conversation was over - at least for now. August gathered the scrolls and moved the vase back to the table.

Landen walked over to where I sat, pulled me up, and wrapped his arms around my waist. He then leaned his head against mine. His eyes were closed; he was blocking them all out, putting us in our own world. August walked outside to meet the others, giving us our privacy.

"What do you want me to do?" he asked me.

"All I can see are the demons."

"Do you want me to bring your friends here for now?" He thought quietly.

I didn't answer Landen's thoughts. He kissed my forehead and pulled my hand toward the door.

"Let's go get them," he whispered.

We walked out to the porch where they were all waiting, and the quiet whispers stopped when they saw us. Landen looked at his dad first, then at each of them in the eye, one by one.

"We need to bring those girls back here until we can stop the demons. Does anyone have any objections to that?" Landen asked.

Ashten looked at August, then they looked at my father. My father cleared his throat."We've brought family here before; Olivia seems to be fine," he answered, looking up at Landen.

"What is he talking about?" I asked Landen

"There's an old myth that you must be loved by someone who lives here to survive in Chara."

"You tell us what you need us to do," Ashten said, beaming with pride as he looked at Landen.

"What's your plan?" Marc asked.

Landen looked down, thenout to the others. Their anticipation and excitement frightened him; he didn't want them involved in this at all. "Jason, we heard the mothers talk about you last night. They respect your medical opinion; do you think you could convince them to let the girls come with you?"

"I'm sure, I could think of something," my father said, certain of himself.

"Dane, your mother is expecting you any day now. I say we go to Franklin with Dane. Jason, you can run into one of the parents and convince them that you have to take them away somewhere," Landen planned out. The others nodded in agreement.

"Alright then. We need to go, it's almost night time there," Jason said.

August decided to stay behind; I reasoned he didn't want to place himself between Ashten and Landen. We waited as Ashten and my father called home. Brady and Chrispin didn't have to go far to say goodbye to Felicity and Olivia; they were in the field by our house, picking flowers. Olivia's emotion elevated as she heard Chrispin's voice…the emotion was undeniable.

"Has he told her yet?" I asked, knowing how they both felt about each other and that Olivia would never have the nerve to say it first.

Landen smiled as he watched them. *"He's waiting; he thinks she needs to see his face,"* Landen answered. Feeling my disapproval he wrapped his arm around me. *"I know. Don't worry; I can tell he can't wait much longer. It's kind of funny to think back about how worried he was about looking – and then you come along and throw her into his arms."*

The smirk on his face made me smile, but we were both too stressed to find the energy to laugh.

In the string, I lingered near the back with Clarissa. I thought Landen needed space; I didn't feel comfortable with the way he was acting… he had changed since he'd seen the charts. He was aloof and trying desperately not to seem that way to me. Brady and Marc took the time to try and show Dane the passages, and he was able to feel them – but the colors escaped him.

"So, do you think I am going to like Franklin?" asked Clarissa.

Like any other time I'd seen Clarissa, she resembled a runway model: a unique beauty that could capture anyone's attention.

"I think Franklin is really going to like you," I said, smiling slightly.

Clarissa smiled, staring at Dane. "He never really talks about anyone from there – except you and his family."

I smiled, remembering how oddly Dane and I fit into Franklin. "For us, it was like a waiting room; we've always known that we were meant to be somewhere else," I said.

Clarissa smiled and wrapped her arm around me. "The first time I heard about New York, I was ten; something always told me that was the place I was supposed to meet the one…that makes me think this is all fate. I was meant for the one person out there that could see in the string, already connected to you. We were meant to help you."

As Infante came into view, green passages illuminated the walls. Landen looked back in my direction, smiled slightly, then walked on. A moment later, the walls seemed to turn completely green, and you couldn't see one passage from another. Landen stopped and looked at the wall cautiously. The others watched him carefully; to them it was solid white.

"What is it, Landen?" Ashten asked.

"I'm trying to remember which one is Willow's house; that's the only place we could all appear out of nowhere without being noticed," Landen said, debating now on one area of the wall.

The admiration coming from the others was intensified in the string. Landen held his hand up, telling us all to stay put, then he stepped inside the haze. Everyone in the string tensed, expecting Landen to feel the burn as he walked through the wall. I saw Ashten look at my father and shake his head in disbelief.

Seconds passed, and Landen didn't come back. I felt my heart rate rise, and pain was seeping into my veins – the same way it did when he left me before. I held my breath, trying to block it out, but with each second that passed, it intensified. I saw spots in my vision, and my head started to spin. I fell back without warning, and Brady, who was standing beside me, caught me.

"Jason, what's going on here?" Brady yelled.

My father quickly turned and saw my condition. I felt his panic, along with everyone else's; it wasn't helping me at all...it was draining me.

"It's happening again: their bodies can't be separated by the string," my father said, trying to remain calm. My head was so heavy, it fell back.

"What do we do?" Brady said, picking me up. "Do I walk through the wall?"

Suddenly, I felt life come back into me - I felt Landen again.

"No," I heard Landen say.

He emerged several feet from where he'd disappeared, walked quickly to Brady, and took me from his arms. With his touch, the pain left, leaving a tingle in its wake. I was weak; it had taken my energy, but when Landen kissed my lips, it sent a rush of energy through me. He squeezed me in his arms, and it was as if nothing ever happened.

"I'm sorry; I wasn't thinking. Are you OK?" he thought.

I nodded, and he slowly put me down.

"Is something wrong? Why didn't you not come back?" Marc asked, ready for a fight.

"No, that goes to their house, but there are several people there, cleaning up after the fire. I couldn't just disappear; I had to find another opening.

"Let me look at you," my father said. He circled Landen and me, shaking his head. "I don't understand why you can't be apart. I mean, you were apart for eighteen years."

"Maybe that's their bodies way of saying that they should have never been kept apart in the first place," Brady said shortly, still upset with Ashten for hiding me from Landen.

Clarissa saw the potential disagreement and added a more positive note. "Or maybe it symbolizes that they are now joined forever," she said looking at Brady "We can't change the past. We've all made mistakes in judgment."

Landen squeezed me tighter and kissed the top of my head. I could feel turmoil inside him; he didn't want his family to fight over any of this. My father nodded in Clarissa's direction and let the matter go.

The current in the string began to flow more aggressively, and the hum grew a little bit louder. Landen looked at my father. "You don't have long to convince them to come; the storm will pass here in less than six hours." he warned.

"I don't think it's going to be hard. Grace told me that both Jessica and Hannah's parents wanted the girls to go with Willow to Paris," my father said. Landen and I both felt his confidence.

Landen held me tight and led us forward. Everyone lined up behind us, and we passed through the green wall together. The passage led to a wooded area just fifty yards from my house. I could still smell the smoke in the air. We causally walked to the road, and in the distance I could hear hammers and saws. As we approached the house, trucks lined the street in front of the shell of a home that was left. People were rushing in every direction. My father was moved; he felt amazed.

We walked into the front yard, and I looked up at the home in which I'd was raised, the one in which my mother was raised the brick remained in place, and the roof was gone and so were all the windows. It didn't take long for someone to notice us. On the front porch was Josh's father, Mr. Campbell. He owned a very successful construction company. Mr. Campbell saw my father and grinned from ear to ear. I could feel his excitement as he walked over to us.

"Well, now, I didn't expect to see you back so soon," he said to my father.

"We're just passing through. Grace wanted me and Willow to see if there was anything that could be saved before we went overseas'." my father said, clearly not comfortable lying.

"Now, Jason, I told you the night it burned that I was going to fix this for you, and I meant it," Mr. Campbell, said looking over his shoulder, then back at my father, feeling proud of what he'd accomplished in such a short time.

"Really, it's not necessary," my father said, raising his hands.

"Look, Jason, I had doctor after doctor tell me I needed open heart surgery, but you took one look at me and told me how to heal myself. I vowed then to repay you. All these people here – they don't work for me; they're volunteers, your patients, Grace's friends, Willow's friends. I've never known a man as good as you before - none of us have. This is our way of saying 'thank you.'"

"I really do appreciate this. This town will always be a part of me and Grace," my father said.

"Well, there isn't a lot that can be salvaged. We have a few storage containers in the back of the house; anything that we think you'd still want or use, we put in there," Mr. Campbell said, looking at all of the people my father had with him. His eyes landed on Dane. "Son, your mother is going to be happy to see you." He then looked around at the trucks lining the street. "How did all of you get here?" he asked.

"Cab," my father said quickly. "We're actually on a layover, and we don't have very long before our next flight," he continued getting better at lying.

Mr. Campbell nodded as my father talked; that was a trait about him that I'd always found funny.

"Well, I'll tell you what," he said, pulling his keys out of his pocket. "Dane, take my truck – go and introduce that pretty thing you have with you to your mother."

Clarissa blushed, not knowing how to respond to Mr. Campbell. Smiling, Dane took the keys, then looked back at me and Landen before he left; it was clear he was amused by how blunt Mr. Campbell was.

"I tell you what, Jason. They've been hoping you would show up. Seems two girls showed up at the hospital, and they don't know what to make of what's wrong with them," Mr. Campbell said.

"Are they still at the hospital?" My father asked.

"No, I believe they sent them home," Mr. Campbell answered, waving his son, Josh, over to us. Josh walked over to all of us and looked at Landen and Brady, confusion all over his face.

"Are you a doctor, too?" Mr. Campbell asked Ashten.

I felt my father's embarrassment as he looked back at us, realizing he hadn't introduced anyone. "I'm sorry; that was rude of me. This is Ashten. Yes, he's a doctor; he taught me everything I know," he said.

Mr. Campbell reached over and shook Ashten's hand. Everyone else was trying not to laugh at the idea of Ashten being a doctor.

"And these are his sons, Brady and Landen, and his nephews, Chrispin and Marc" my father said.

Mr. Campbell shook everyone's hands, saving Landen's for last. It was not hard to see that we were a couple, since the pain in the string Landen had made sure that one part of him was touching me.

"You must be a lucky man," Mr. Campbell said to Landen. "I told my son, Josh, here, that girls like Willow are rare." Mr. Campbell looked back at Josh, shaking his head in a teasing manner. "Maybe next time he'll listen to me."

Josh rolled his eyes at his father, then nodded in Landen's direction, still confused.

"Josh, let Jason take your truck; he needs to go and check on those girls," Mr. Campbell said. Josh complied without complaint.

"I want to stay here to see what's in storage," I said to Landen and my father.

"Dad, just go with Jason. I'll stay here with them," Brady said to Ashten.

Mr. Campbell waved, then turned to go back to the house. Josh looked at Landen one more time, then followed his dad.

"Maybe your herb didn't work that well on him," I thought, Landen shrugged his shoulders, not really caring what Josh thought of him.

We'll be back in a little bit," my father said over his shoulder.

Brady and Chrispin walked toward the house, and Mr. Campbell gave them hard hats before he allowed them in. Landen, Marc, and I walked around the house. Looking up at the damage, I felt an overwhelming grief. I wondered how many people I would bring destruction to before this conflict with Drake was over. I tried to hide my emotion from Landen, but he felt it.

"I'm sorry, Willow," he thought, filling with remorse.

Though we never lost touch, I could feel his mind drifting somewhere else. If I could turn back time, I wouldn't have allowed him to look at those birth charts; they'd changed him.

We walked around the house along the fence. Volunteers had laid out paintings that could be saved; most of them were mine, a few were my mother's. I walked by them slowly. Remembering the images, I wondered if I'd really helped them, or if I'd only sustained them for the moment.

"Are all of these yours?" Marc asked in awe.

"The ones of the people are," I answered.

My mother was more of a still art painter. Marc leaned closer to get a better look. "I think I know this girl," he said looking at one of the paintings. It was one I had done of a young girl almost a year ago. I remembered how lonely she felt; at the time, I'd felt the same way. The only way I could help her was by thinking of my parents.

"Landen, this looks like that girl we helped bring home a while back – for umm… what was his name? Austin, wasn't it?" Marc said, not feeling sure of himself.

Landen looked closer at the painting. "It does look like her," he said "Was she lonely?" he asked me.

I nodded, astonished that it could be the same girl. - "You know her?" I asked, surprised.

"Maybe, we've carried so many home, it's hard to say for sure. I only remember her because she had no family or belongings. Austin found her living in a shelter; a storm had taken everything from her. It was like she breathed for the first time when she stepped through the gates of Chara.

I smiled, hoping it was the same girl; I wanted all the people that I'd helped to be happy now. In the center of the backyard, there were two large containers. Inside them were more paintings, books, and small knick knacks. I walked in and started going through the things, making a pile for us to carry home to my mother. I knew it would make her feel better.

The sun was setting, and the volunteers were leaving one by one. Brady and Chrispin came over to us. We all leaned against the fence, waiting for my father. Mr. Campbell waved at us as he climbed in the passenger seat of another truck; I was sure he was going to Gina's Diner to retrieve his truck - Josh and Chase came around the house with handfuls of bottled water, then they walked over and passed them out to us.

"Thank you," Landen said, taking two bottles - one for me and one for him.

Josh had yet to lose his confused expression. He must have said something to Chase because now they both looked confused. "It's Livingston, right?" Josh said to Landen. Marc and Chrispin were in mid-drink when they heard Josh. They both stopped and stared at him while Landen tilted his head and pulled his eyebrows together, questioning Josh.

"Landen," Landen said finally. I could feel the tension building.

"I'm sorry; my fault," Josh said, looking from Landen to Chase.

"Do you know a Livingston?" Chase asked Landen.

Landen's lips turned into a small smile. "I think I may have met one before. Why do you ask?" he said.

Chase and Josh shook their heads and laughed at themselves. "It's nothing," Chase said.

"Chase," I said sternly, knowing that he knew something. Landen put his hand on my shoulder, trying to calm me down before I lost my temper.

"Alright," Chase said, raising his hands and knowing that I'd rip him apart if he didn't come clean. "Remember your friend,

Drake?" Chase said, raising his eyebrows. I rolled my eyes. "Yeah, anyway, he asked Josh and me if we'd ever seen a guy named Livingston with you or your dad. He said he was tall, dark, wavy hair and unmistakable dimples. We thought he was talking about an older man, but I don't know," Chase said, looking at Landen "You kind of fit the profile. We just thought it was weird that you showed up after he said that." Landen turned his head slightly to look at Marc and get his take on what Chase had said. Josh followed Landen's eyes to Marc. "Hey, do you know Drake?" he asked. Everyone of us stared at Josh in disbelief.

"Should I?" Marc asked, trying not to look baffled.

"I don't know. You just look like him." Josh said defensively.

Everyone looked at Marc; it was clear the comparison made him uncomfortable. Josh had a point: both Drake and Marc were built the same way, with a dominant profile I hadn't noticed before. I think it was the eyes that threw me off; Marc's are light brown with a sparkle in them, but Drake's are as dark as the night, with a degree of magnetism that pulls you in.

Headlights beamed around the side of the house, breaking the tension; it was Gina's truck. I could feel Clarissa and Dane. Landen held my hand and led us to the front of the house. Another van pulled in behind Gina's. I felt Hannah and Jessica with my father and Ashten. My father must have had success. Dane and Clarissa got out of the truck and walked over to the van where the girls were. Connie was driving, and my father was in the passenger seat. He rolled down the window. "Willow, I have good news for you," he said, looking over at Connie, "It seems Jessica and Hannah are in need of some relaxation to relieve some stress they're under; so I invited them to come to Paris with us for a week." I smiled, not having to try hard to seem surprised. Connie leaned forward, looking at all of us smiling, and her eyes hesitated on Chrispin for a moment. That's when I remembered showing Connie Olivia dancing with Chrispin. Landen remembered, too, and he quickly stepped in front of Chrispin. "You guys split up. Connie and Gina are going to take us to the airport," my father said. Landen nodded, then turned and pushed Chrispin and Brady in the direction of Gina's truck. Chrispin looked back at Landen like he'd lost his mind. Landen nodded his head, telling Chrispin to go. Once out of sight, we climbed in the van with Jessica and Hannah. My father had given them something to help them relax, and it was clear it was already taking effect by the peace I felt within them and the smiles on their faces.

After we were dropped off at the airport, we waited for a few moments, then hailed a cab to take us back to the passages near my house. Inside the string, the current was flowing more aggressively than before, and we all walked quickly. Landen and I stayed on the outside, ready to pull everyone through if the storm erupted before we reached Chara.

Once home in Chara, we took Hannah and Jessica to my father's house. I could feel how nervous my father was about having them here; I'd never thought my father believed in myths, but then again, I never imagined that he was from another dimension either. It seemed everyone except Marc had someone to see, to tell that they were home safely; it was the first time I realized that he was the only one now who was still alone. Marc, Dane and Clarissa followed us back to our house, and we all gathered in the living room.

"You don't think I look like Drake, do you?" Marc asked Landen.

"Does it matter if you do?" Landen retorted, falling back into one of the large chairs and staring at the ceiling.

Marc was immediately irritated by Landen's short tone. Landen was being distant with everyone, but I'm sure it hurt me more than them.

"I just want to know how he knew Dad's name," Marc argued.

"He's always in Esteroius," Clarissa answered, trying to give Landen a break from always having to have the answers.

"So am I. So are you – did he say our name? No – he didn't even know Landen's name, but he knew Dad's."

Landen sat up and looked at me, then at Marc.

"Where is your dad anyway?" Landen asked.

Marc stopped pacing and looked back at Landen; a singe of fear hit him. "I don't know – I haven't seen him since your celebration…Ashten said he went to Esteroius to find a way in the palace."

"He should be back by now – don't you think?" Landen said.

Marc had been so distracted by everything that had happened that he hadn't noticed; guilt came to him immediately.

"You know, you're right," Marc answered. Fear coursed through the room, and Marc rushed to the kitchen to call Ashten. Aubrey said that he was already on his way to our house. We waited, watching Marc get more upset, pacing across the room.

Ashten and my father came through the back door at the same time. Asthen walked in the room, their concern grew as they saw Marc in his panicked state.

"What's going on?" asked Ashten.

"Where's Dad? Shouldn't he back by now?"

"Well, not really. He was intent on staying until all this was worked out," answered Ashten.

"Did he go into the palace?" Marc asked as his anxiety grew.

"I don't think he'd try anything that would put himself in danger," Ashten said.

I looked in Landen's direction; I could tell Ashten didn't believe his own words.

"We need to get him – he needs to know what we know!" Marc yelled.

"What do we know? What did you guys figure out?" Ashten said, realizing that they were missing something.

"Drake asked Willow's friends if they knew a Livingston," Landen explained.

My father and Ashten looked at each other; I felt their confusion and frustration.

Ashten looked back at Marc. "I can see why that would bother you, but I'm sure there's a reason," Ashten said.

"Yeah and I'm going to find out right now," Marc said, walking to the door.

Ashten moved to block Marc's exit, "You're not going to find him tonight. Curfew has already set in – he won't be out, and you're sure to be killed if they see you on the streets," he said as Marc's face fell. "Look, he's fine. We'll all go in the morning - well, Jason and I will go with you."

Ashten looked in Landen's direction, then at me. Landen rolled his eyes; he was bitter and tired of being shielded.

"Look, we're not afraid of him. We're going to have to face him sooner or later," Landen said shortly.

"Later sounds better to me," retorted Clarissa, reminding Landen that this affected all of them - not just us.

Landen closed his eyes and shook his head, avoiding a sarcastic remark that he would regret as soon as he said it.

"Look, let's just argue about this tomorrow. You all need your rest - especially if we're going to Esteroius tomorrow," Ashten said, defusing the situation.

Marc rolled his eyes and charged toward the door, anger coursing through him. He had every intent of going to Esteroius that night.

"Marc," Landen said, halting him. "Rest…I know where you sleep."

Marc's face fell, then he turned and walked slowly out the door. He knew we could see his intent, as well as the fact that, if we wanted to, we could watch him sleep without him ever seeing us.

The blunt prediction and threat that Landen had given left the room stunned; the power that we'd built using each other had escaped their attention until now.

"So, I am to presume that you two will not need me tonight?" my father asked as relief filled him.

"No, we'll stay here," Landen answered, staring at the ground.

Dane and Clarissa quietly walked out after Marc. Before leaving, my father walked over to where I sat and kissed my forehead. Ashten hesitated, then followed.

We were now completely alone, and for the first time in my life, that was something I didn't want. I could feel the tension between us; the pressure of everything that was happening to us made itself known.

Chapter Sixteen

Landen stood and walked to the mantle. He was staring at my willow tree, and his grief hit me like a ton of bricks.

"Willow," he said solemnly, "we've made a big mistake." His words were a dagger in the heart, and I tried to breathe - but I couldn't find the air.

"Excuse me?" I managed to exhale out.

He stared at the floor with disdain. "It's my fault that those people in Esteroius live that way – that all this is happening to the people you care about."

I stood, walking to him slowly; his emotion was a brick wall between us. I reached for his arm, and he shifted away. He wouldn't look at me, and the rejection burned every part of me.

"You can say that, but we have no control over -"

"Willow, you haven't seen what I've seen, know what I know…Donalt's people…those people live a life that I wouldn't wish on my worst enemy."

"Landen -"

He raised his hand to stop me. "No, listen to me. It's a hell: no color, they live in identical houses – inside and out - they eat the same food, wear the same clothes, work day in and day out.

They're executed if they break the simplest law, and no one smiles or laughs. It's dark, no life, and no one has a will to live."

"How is that your or my fault?" I shouted, defending us both.

He paced the floor, his hands on his head, his eyes closed.

"I stole your heart. You were supposed to stop all of that, but you fell in love with me and never looked back - and now look: how many people do you think have died because we were too selfish?"

"I am not selfish -" I argued.

Landen turned quickly and put his hands on my shoulders. His eyes were different; the blue had changed, and the window to his soul was closed.

"Willow, listen to me: if you have to choose between me or saving those people, I want you to save them; I don't think you can have both."

I jerked his hands off me and stepped back, more angry than I'd ever been in my life.

"Are you insane? – What are you saying? You – you want me to be with Drake?"

"Willow -"

"No – don't 'Willow' me! One minute you're telling me that you love me and you're going to fix everything, and the next you're telling me to go to another man – how dare you?!!"

"I am not telling you to go to another man!"

"Yes, you are! Are you even listening to yourself?!"

"Willow, I told you to save those people."

"Which means I have to be with Drake! How can you stand there and ask me to pay for something that was done millions of years ago?!!"

"Do you think this isn't killing me? Do you not feel how bad it hurts for me to tell you that? We have to fix what we've done wrong."

"What did we do?"

"You didn't go back – that's what."

"So now you're saying that by us staying here, that that was a mistake? That this dimension, your family, my family – every single person who has a soul mate because of you is a mistake?"

"We didn't stop them, and now look – look at your friends, look at our family; we did this."

"Do you happen to remember what happened four million years ago – because I sure don't? If you do, enlighten me: tell me why I'm cold and selfish?"

"I didn't say you were cold."

"Basically, you did. I know that if those stupid charts are right and I'm back or whatever they mean – then I should be the same person - and I happen to know myself well: if I stayed here, I had a damn good reason."

"You loved me."

"And I still love you, and if that was my reason - it was good enough then, and it's good enough now."

"Willow, we can't live here and know that the people in Esteroius – those people in Franklin are suffering so we can be together."

"You have lost your mind!" I screamed. He didn't say anything; he just turned his back to me, and I felt anger coursing through every part of me. I took off the necklace with the charm and slid off the ring, then sat them on the table and walked to the front door.

"Don't leave," he whispered.

"You just told me to be with Drake – to be a pawn in a game that I'm not playing," I said coldly as I opened the door.

"Willow -"

I stormed out of the front door and down the front steps; I couldn't find my breath – my chest hurt so bad. Landen didn't follow me; he knew I wasn't going far. I ran through the field; I didn't know where I was running to, I just knew I was running from it all. My entire life flashed before me, all the people I knew, the dreams, Landen, Drake, Perodine, my family, my Libby - I ran as if the demons themselves were on my heels. I couldn't see through my tears or hear anything over my heartbeat.

I didn't stop until my breath left me. I fell to my knees and looked up; the moon was almost full. I could see the outline; it taunted me…Ifelt so small and insignificant…why me? Any other person could have played my role, and they would have been strong enough to fight this battle .Why would I find Landen, only to have to choose to lose him? Why would anyone hurt me that badly? What did I do to deserve this? I crawled the three feet between me and the base of the large windmill, then leaned my weak body against it and raised my head to the heavens. My breath was coming back slowly, but the pain in my chest was real; my heart was breaking. The stars seemed so close, as if I could touch them…I'd never noticed them before, how detailed and extraordinary they were…I don't know how long I sat there, questioning who I was, before I felt someone coming toward me. I looked up to see a small figure on the hill top; it was Rose. She was peaceful, and when she reached me, she sat down quietly by my side.

"How did you find me?" I asked.

"Libby called me. She said you were sad."

"Did you call Landen?"

"No, I could feel you. I knew you were alone," she answered.

I looked at her.

"My home is right there."

She pointed to the hill she had just walked over. I smiled at myself, realizing that I'd run almost all the way to her house.

"Do you want to talk about it?"

"He wants me to be with Drake – there's nothing to talk about."

"You know that's not true."

"He told me to choose him."

"Willow, I'm sure you only heard what you wanted to hear."

"It's just not fair…it can't be that black and white."

"It's not."

"Then why is everyone telling me I have to choose?"

"Who is 'everyone?'"

"Perodine, Landen -"

"Did Perodine tell you to choose between Landen and Drake?"

"She just said that I had to choose again…obviously, I chose Landen last time, and Landen thinks it's our fault that the people in Esteroius are suffering – that Monica is de-"

I couldn't even say the word before tears hit me like flood. Rose wrapped her arms around me and let me cry, rocking me back and forth.

"It's not either of your fault. Everything has its reason, and you need to take this grief and use it as your weapon."

"Why am I being punished for the day I was born?" I asked, trying to dry my face.

"Why do you think you are?" Rose asked, genuinely surprised.

I sat up straight and shook my head in frustration. "Ever since I came to Chara, all I've heard about is the stars and moon alignments; it decides how you learn, what your insight is, and apparently dictates what your fate is. What is the purpose of living if it's already chosen for you?" I blurted out angrily.

Rose let her shoulders droop; she understood why I was so angry. She then shifted in front of me on her knees and gently placed her hands on my shoulders.

"You've misunderstood why Chara looks to the heavens," she said softly.

I looked up at her and brushed my hair out of my eyes.

"Chara's foundation is love. We learn about our planets to help us understand who we are. If you love yourself, then you can love others more powerfully," Rose said smiling.

"Then why am I asked to pay for something that was done so long ago?" I asked, ready to listen.

"You chose this path; you were chosen by this path," Rose said with certainty.

"Rose, you aren't making any sense," I said, lowering my head.

"Yes I am - you're just not listening to me," she said, a little louder than I expected.

I looked up at her quickly.

"At any moment, you can change your destiny. Your thoughts lead the way. Your soul is old, and you've chosen this path so often that it has now come to you at a younger age than ever before. So, it's natural for it to feel forced upon you."

"Are you telling me that it doesn't matter that August is walking around with a birth chart that says that I'm Aliyanna? That I selfishly left others behind to suffer?" I asked.

"I'm telling you that you are Willow Haywood and Willow Haywood decides her fate – not the stars," Rose said, lowering her head and looking up at me. "Listen to me: you have the strength to do this," she finished.

"I have to have Landen - I don't care if he doesn't want me. That means I'm as selfish as he said I was."

Rose reached for my face and ran her hand across my cheek, then stared at me, smiling pride coursing through her.

"You have the heart of a woman, and a woman's heart is the strongest thing in any dimension. We love without reason, and we can turn a heart of stone into water."

"What am I supposed to do?"

"You follow your heart. When you do that, everything will find its way. The woman who began this world knew that, and so do you."

"I didn't go back. I stayed here, and so many have suffered."

"Do you honestly believe that you didn't have a reason for staying in Chara?" Rose asked.

I tilted my head and let my mind try to conceive what would have stopped me. Rose smiled as she felt me calm down.

"Today, you do not have one. Go back with Landen and right what is wronged, side by side."

"He doesn't want me; he wants me to be with Drake."

"Now… I doubt that," Rose said, standing. She smiled over her shoulder at me as she walked over the hill in front of her house. I sat stunned for a moment. What was my reason? A moment later, I felt a strong emotion of love and knew Landen was coming to find me, and he was coming fast.

In the distance, in light of the moon, I could see Landen running in my direction. I was so mad at him, so in love with him…I ran to him; I was running home, where I belonged.

When we reached each other, our bodies collided with a great force. He kissed me urgently, holding me so tight it almost hurt.

"I'm sorry, I didn't mean it. I love you, and I would die before I let you leave me for anyone. I love you, Willow. I've loved you from my first breath."

"I love you – I'm sorry."

We fell to the ground, holding one another. In the field of beautiful flowers surrounded by darkness, under a moon that was nearly full, we loved each other. I wanted to crawl inside of him and hide there for the rest of my life. I wanted to forget who I was, who I am, and what was still left to be done.

Once back at our house, in our room, Landen reached in his pocket and pulled out my necklace and ring. He clasped the necklace around my neck. I felt a tingle as the charm touched my chest. He gently reached for my hand and slid the silver ring on. It hummed and brightened as it rested on my skin. He looked deeply into my eyes; my window to his soul was opened again, and the blue was breathtaking. I lost myself; if it were possible, I think I fell deeper in love with him.

"We'll do this together, me and you," he said softly. I wrapped my arms around him and closed my eyes, knowing that I'd never choose anyone above him.

After drifting to sleep, Landen made good on his promise, and we went to Marc's house. We found him pacing the floor in his room, wanting to go, daring to see if he would be able to get away with it. Landen walked over to his bed pulled back the covers, and Marc jumped with a startle. I reached for the light and turned it off. You could feel the fear coming from Marc; he walked slowly to his bed and laid down stiffly. We sat against the wall and watched him stare at the ceiling.

"I still feel her," Marc said into the room. "I'm not crazy; I will find her one day," he finished.

I could feel the words hit Landen like a ton of bricks. *"Why is Marc alone?"* I thought

Landen stared at Marc with compassion. *"The urge to look doesn't come until at least the age of twenty, but for some it comes much later. Some say it's because those have a purpose to fill,"* Landen explained.

"You think he hasn't looked because he's still looking for his mother?

"He remembers her more clearly than Chrispin. I can see how his search for her would cloud over the urge to want to find his soul mate."

"Doesn't he realize when he finds her that she'll make him stronger?" I thought.

Landen looked at me and smiled, wrapping his arms around me. *"He knows we're not meant to be alone; he just needs his time."*

After Marc drifted to sleep, we made our way to my father's house to check on Jessica and Hannah. They were both in the guest room, sound asleep. There were no demons; our plan to protect them had worked.

Before leaving, we checked in on our little princess, Libby. Her eyes were closed as they fluttered back and forth, and I pulled the blanket up over her shoulder. Just as we went to leave, she said, "How many?" We looked quickly at her to see her still sleeping. "What color?" she said a little louder.

We passed a curious look, careful not to move, or wake her. "What do I say?" Libby said turning in her bed.

"Will Willow come home with Landen?" Her face squinted together, then she lay silent.

Stunned, we didn't move, waiting for her to say anything to answer the questions she'd asked.

Libby never moved again, but we rested our souls in her window seat, watching her sleep, waiting for her to say or do something, knowing she could very well hold the key to every question we'd ever had.

At daybreak, a knock on our door woke us. We heard footsteps coming in the door; we knew it was Marc. Landen grudgingly pulled the covers over us, letting our bodies wake up before arguing with him.

"Ahh…so how does it feel having someone come in your room and scare the hell out of you?" Marc said as he walked in our door.

Landen threw a pillow at him. "It was for your own good and you know it," he said, wiping the sleep out of his eyes.

"Look, as I was laying there last night, I realized something," Marc said.

"What? That I was right?" Landen mocked.

"No," Marc said, throwing the pillow back at Landen. "You said you could control where you go, right?" Landen nodded, squinting at Marc through the sunlight. "So you could beam yourself right into that Palace and take that star back, couldn't you?"

"Jason thinks they'd be able to hurt us," Landen corrected.

Marc's enthusiasm faded as he walked over and sat on the edge of the bed.

"Hey, do you mind? Can we have a minute here?" Landen said, pushing Marc off the bed with his foot. Marc looked at me and blushed a little before leaving the room, giving us a chance to get dressed. Landen looked at me and shook his head in disbelief.

"The best part about getting through this is the idea of having you all to myself."

Even though I knew he meant it, I still laughed at his new observation.

Downstairs, Marc had laid out breakfast for us, and he stared at me and Landen as we ate. Every once in awhile, he would start to say something, then hesitate and look out the window.

"Say it," Landen said as he finished his breakfast and pushed his plate away from him.

"This doesn't freak you out?" Marc said with a burst of air coming from him.

"What part?" I asked, making light of his perspective.

"I just think…Landen, you and I have seen a lot of crazy stuff over the years, but nothing like this – like the two of you," Marc said.

Landen shifted in his seat, giving Marc a stern look and a sideways glance at me before he answered.

"I don't know why you're so surprised. I've known you my whole life; you knew about the dreams, and the intent I could see."

"That doesn't mean that I knew that you were really out walking around with Willow somewhere…where did you guys meet anyway?"

We looked at each other; we'd never even tried to figure out where we went.

"We don't know," Landen said as he stared into my eyes.

"We've been to a lot of places – you've never seen the place awake once?" Marc asked

Landen leaned back in his chair and stared forward as the memories danced across his eyes; I felt him remembering all the places that had brought him joy.

"I've never been there awake; I'm sure of it," he said finally, staring at me again.

"Are you ready for this? I've watched that world tear my father apart," Marc said, calling Landen's attention back to him.

"It doesn't matter if we're ready or not - it's here," Landen answered, reaching over and squeezing my hand.

Marc leaned back in his seat, seeing that he wasn't going to talk us down from whatever we faced. "You're my purpose," he said.

"What?" Landen said, surprised.

"My purpose…is to keep you safe," Marc said in a hushed voice.

"Marc -"

"No, Landen, seriously I know what I'm talking about - I remember when you were born, looking at you and knowing that I was supposed to protect you."

"You were just being a good 'brother'...you feel the same for Chrispin."

"No – that's just it; Chrispin is my baby brother, and yes, if I was there and he needed me, I'd keep him safe - but with you I feel like I'm supposed to make sure that I'm there – to protect you," Marc argued.

Landen sighed deeply and shook his head as Marc finished his explanation. "Listen, I want you to put what you just told me aside and clear your head...find that feeling and follow it. We all need someone, you aren't meant to be alone."

"I know that. I just have to do this first – so if you're ready, then bring it on," Marc said with an uncanny boyish grin.

Through the kitchen window, I saw Libby in the valley; she was picking flowers, and she had a basket almost too large for her to carry. As I focused on her, I could feel her urgency. Landen followed my stare, and so did Marc. "I wonder what she's doing out so early," Marc said.

"Something's wrong," I said to Landen, pushing back from the table, not losing sight of her. As Landen and Marc followed me, my quick walk turned into a sprint. "Libby, what's wrong? - Libby, what's wrong?" I screamed. Libby jumped as she heard me, and relief filled her eyes.

"Willow, help me find the blue and green ones," she ordered.

"What?"

"Willow, hurry - blue and green I need lots." Libby was now frantically searching the ground, looking at all the flowers.

"Find blue and green ones - hurry!" I yelled at Landen and Marc as they approached, and the three of us searched the ground frantically with Libby. Once her basket was full, she took off in a sprint toward her house, and we all followed her.

As we approached the house, I counted the emotions around me; beyond us, I could only feel two. I ran past Libby up the stairs to Hannah and Jessica's room. My stomach dropped before the door even opened; there was something wrong. The room was without emotion. Libby pushed past me and opened the door.

From the doorway, I could see the blue tint of their skin as they lay in the same place we'd seen them last night. Marc took one look, then ran down the hall, screaming my father's name.

Libby sat the basket on the floor between the beds and began pulling the petals off the flowers and putting them on Hannah's chest. I looked at Landen, and we both rushed to her side to help her.

"Put them everywhere, Willow," Libby ordered.

My father and Marc came crashing into the room; just like Landen, I could feel my father's dread when his eyes fell on Hannah and Jessica's bodies. We all knew that they weren't breathing, and my father knew more. The basket was empty now, and the girls were covered in blue and green petals. Libby looked over them once, picking up a few loose petals and putting them on the girls' chests.

"OK, say this with me: land and will, will and land," Libby said to me and Landen.

In a sacred trance, we did as she ordered and said, "Land and will, will and land" in unison with Libby, repeating it over and over. Seconds later, I felt a burst of energy coming from Hannah and Jessica at the same time, and my ring and necklace warmed against my skin. I closed my eyes, and a numbing emotion swept through my body. As it passed, a dizzy feeling caused me to open my eyes, gaining balance. I looked at Landen and could see he felt it, too.

As Landen and I stood paralyzed by each other's stare, my father rushed to the girls' sides. We didn't notice Libby dancing in place, my mother rushing in at the last moment, or even the overwhelming fear coming from Marc and my father as they looked back at us from the girls' bedside.

Hannah and Jessica's chests began to rise and fall, but their eyes never opened, and they didn't move.

"Jason, what happened?" my mother screamed, taking into account that the girls were covered in flowers. My father kept his stunned look, staring at me and Landen.

"Jason? Willow? Somebody talk to me," my mother shouted.

"They were sleeping too far away; the flowers helped Willow and Landen bring them back to the right sleep," Libby answered, giggling.

"Libby, sweetie, why don't you go and get some breakfast. I'll be there in just one minute, OK?" my mother said, pushing Libby out of the room

"Dad, are they OK? Look, are they OK?" I said, trying to get his attention away from me and Landen.

He slowly turned to look at Hannah and Jessica, shaking his head as he took a second look. "They're fine – for now," he said quietly.

"Were they...? Were they...?" I tried to ask if they were dead.

"Yes...for a while," he answered in a low tone.

"What is this? Why flowers? Why did you say that?" my mother asked frantically.

"Libby told us to. We saw her picking flowers, she only wanted blue and green. Is that myth true? Did we hurt them by bringing them here?" I asked, feeling sick to my stomach.

"I don't know if it's our world – or if it's something that was spoken over them. They're fine now," my father said, looking over me and Landen again.

"Are you sure?" I asked, looking at Hannah and Jessica.

"Their hearts are weak. Somehow they started to beat again, but they aren't beating the way they're meant to; it's like they're on life support."

"The flowers," Landen whispered. My father looked at Landen and nodded.

"So we have two choices: we take them home and let demons dance across their chests or we leave them here barely alive?" I said through my teeth.

"They are very alive, and they shouldn't be – you brought them back," my mother said calmly, proud of me.

"Did you know you could do that?" Marc asked.

"We have no idea what we can do. We're just as baffled," Landen answered, pulling me to him and shielding my view.

News travels fast with an energetic little girl proud of her morning's accomplishments. Rose and August came to my mother's house first. My mother was frantically fixing breakfast, trying to keep her mind busy; the only sound in the kitchen was the clanging of pans and plates.

Brady, not hearing the news of the morning's events, strolled in the back door, beaming with excitement and slapping Marc on the back as he smiled proudly at him." You guys aren't going to believe what happened," he announced to the room, but his words fell on deaf ears- so to speak… his frustration grew with our blank expressions. "Did you guys hear me? I have good news - not just good news, *amazing* news." While he spoke, Felicity slid in behind him, giving way to Chrispin and Olivia.

When Olivia came in the room, her eyes met each of ours for the first time, and we knew she had her sight back. She then ran to me and hugged me tightly, laughing out loud.

"Oh my God…how… what happened?" I stuttered.

"It's amazing… this whole place is so beautiful," Olivia said, not hearing my questions. We all stared in shock, looking at a grinning Chrispin, waiting for an explanation.

"You told her, didn't you?" Landen asked.

Chrispin smiled, then walked over and pulled a stunned Landen into a bear hug. "You were right; I was stupid for waiting. I told her as soon as we got back, and this morning when she woke up, her sight was back…it's amazing."

"What did you say to him?"

"Just that he was stupid for waiting if he was really sure," Landen thought, smiling at the recent turn of events.

"Well, this is certainly uplifting compared to the morning that's transpired," August commented.

"What happened?" Brady said as his smile fell.

The room fell silent; Felicity eased over out of Brady's way and started helping my mother cook breakfast. Chrispin and Olivia stared with the shell of a smile on their faces.

"The girls are sick," my father said finally.

"What do you mean?" Chrispin asked.

"We don't know if it's Chara or something that was said over them in Esteroius, but right now they're on the edge of life," my father said.

"So we take them back," Chrispin said blankly. As the words left his lips, the demons flashed before my eyes, and fear suddenly filled me. Landen and Rose looked at me simultaneously.

"You don't know what we saw. If you did, those words would have never left your lips," Landen said kindly, looking at me with all the compassion his body possessed. Chrispin's regret was immediate as Olivia's emotion fell, and her tears followed.

"After breakfast, I'm going to call Ashten, and we're going to look for Livingston. Whoever wants to come is more than welcome," my father said, looking at me and Landen.

At the gates of the string, we all stood dressed in black. The only traveler to stay behind was Rose. The string was calm by our home, but as we walked on the current it was to the point that you had to push forward with each step, and the hum was so deep, you could feel it in your soul. Just before the passage, Clarissa whispered instructions to Dane. Landen used our gift to prepare me.

"You can't smile, not even your eyes, and we can't touch. You and Clarissa must lead; it's illegal for a man to walk before a woman – it's the only respect the women in this world have."

I wanted to ask why, but I was too busy burning his simple instructions into my memory.

"Keep your left hand in your pocket – rings are forbidden here."

"Then I'll take it off."

"No, it's protecting you; that and the necklace are the only reasons you are not feeling my anxiety about having you here."

I did as he said, not wanting for one instant to feel his pain; it was almost as bad as being separated from him.

"Keep pace with Clarissa; she's going to lead us to the courtyard. Today is the day that Donalt speaks to the people of Esterious. If Livingston is here, he'll be in that crowd. We have to leave after that; it'll be too easy for them to see us as out of place."

Before stepping into the passage, I turned and kissed Landen passionately, not caring who saw me do it; I needed to feel him, to have his soul tell mine that we'd return to our home together.

"I love you," I thought.

"And I love you."

Chapter Seventeen

I smiled up at Landen, then took my place at Clarissa's side as we stepped through after my father. The passage led into a large building. I could smell oil burning, and the room was sweltering. My father led us up a metal staircase encased in rust. Once at the top, he knocked twice quickly, hesitated, then knocked again. A moment later, you could hear someone unlocking chains on the other side, then the thick metal door opened.

Standing in front of us was a man. His years were near my father's, yet his brown eyes were older. The man was dressed in a long black cloak shambled with dust and holes. He looked down the stairs at the large group my father had brought with him, and I could feel his fear as he stared at Landen and me side-by-side.

"Jason, I do believe that you're premature; the moon is not yet full," the man said.

Ashten and my father gave each other a cautious look, then slowly nodded 'no' to the man. Landen looked crossly at our fathers, then to August for an explanation; the only response he received was smiling eyes and an emotion of pride.

"We're only searching for Livingston. Have you seen him?" my father said

"Yes, he was mistaken for another and was assigned duties in the fields. His time is over today. He should, like everyone else, be in the courtyard."

The man's eyes never left mine as he spoke to my father.

"Am I allowed a formal introduction?" the man asked.

"My apologies," my father said.

"This is my daughter, Willow. Willow, this is Patrick, an honored friend of Esteroius."

Patrick smiled at me and bowed his head slightly. He then extended his arm, inviting us through the doorway. The room was dark; you could see a simple table, bed, and desk aligned on one wall and a fireplace on another. The floor was made of wood, and there was no color to the walls. At one time, they may have been white, but now they were a dull gray. Patrick pulled the long thick gray curtains shut and lit a row of candles that lined the mantel over the fire place.

"And who might this young man be?" Patrick asked as he glanced over his shoulder at Dane.

"This is Dane. He and Clarissa are one now," Ashten answered.

"Ah – and he's here because…?" Patrick asked.

"Dane has a gift as well; the string is visible to him," Ashten replied.

Patrick was either unaware of how sensitive my gift was or simply didn't care if he was revealing. He was astonished as his eyes danced across each of us; the uneasy feeling coming from Ashten and my father was making itself known.

Patrick walked by us one by one, looking up and down. As he reached me and Landen, he stopped and stared into my eyes. A smile then came across his face, and his eyes seemed to lose a few years.

"Have you brought something to cover the color in your eyes? Especially Willows? I would dare say even an old man like Donalt could see them in a crowd," Patrick said.

I took an uneasy breath and leaned back into Landen, too afraid not show my fear. Landen put his hands on my shoulders and kissed my head softly, taking my fears away and filling my soul with calming warmth.

"People here only have brown eyes; we have to wear a film over our eyes to change the color," Landen explained.

"Like a contact lens?" I asked.

"Yeah, just like that. It doesn't hurt."

My father pulled a box out of his pocket and passed out the lens to change our natural color to a stone black. Patrick walked over to a small closet, pulled out a long black scarf.

"You'll want to cover that sovereign gem upon your neck – unless you're seeking attention I'm not aware of," Patrick said to me.

"Should I put it in my pocket? Isn't it hot? I'll stand out in a long coat and scarf."

"No," Landen and the others said in unison. It was easy to feel that they all thought it was protecting me, or at least feared it would be lost as well. August took the scarf from Patrick, walked over to me and explained, "It is always cool here. The sun doesn't shine; the sky, like everything, is gray."

A loud chime could be heard outside Patrick's home, and anxiety filled the room. The only one who still had his peace was August.

"Ah – it is time. Shall we?" Patrick said as he blew out the candles.

Clarissa and I left the home first. I didn't look to see who followed behind us or how closely; I only concentrated on the one that I knew was Landen and walked forward. There was no grass, plants, or trees to be seen, and the birds didn't sing; the silence was screaming at all of us. I kept my pace shoulder to shoulder with Clarissa, and several others, all dressed in black, were walking in the same direction that we were. From most, I could feel the sorrow they had, and from others a void that was as real as it was when Drake was at my side.

Like in my dreams, the buildings were all the same. On the street level, there were what looked like food and clothing stations, and above them the rest of the buildings were tall with gray, perfectly spaced windows. As a river would flow, the people streamed toward the palace. My eyes were held straight, not touching anyone but Clarissa.

To my right, I saw Ashten and my father flank off, and to my left, Brady and Marc did the same, leaving Dane, Landen, and August behind us. At the end of the alley, a large wall could be seen. Men dressed in black cloaks lined the top of it, facing a much higher structure.

This structure was indeed the palace; it was over a mile wide, eight stories high, and solid gray. Windows were sporadic, and wide diamond-shaped balconies were on every level.

Along the rooftop, a line of men stood, staring out into the crowd with daring composure. We halted just past the gate. As we stared forward, I couldn't imagine how we'd find Livingston in this crowd of solid black. I could feel my father and Ashten widening their path further away from us, and Brady and Marc mirrored them.

The air filled with the chime of a large bell that rang three times, and the crowd grew still. On the fourth balcony, the doors opened. From the darkness emerged two figures, and one was undeniably Drake; he was dressed in a black suit. It was easy to feel that the females in the crowd were attracted to him. He smiled, and I heard a few breaths let loose from the women. I wondered if they even cared how dark he was. He brought new meaning to fatal attraction. Beside him, a much older man stood. I was sure it was Donalt. He was smaller than Drake, and had long white hair. His face held no expression; neither of them held any emotion that I could feel. The bells chimed again as the stepped closer to the edge. I had expected the crowd to roar, at their approach, but the silence rained on, and it was then that I felt someone staring at me. They were in the palace, and my eyes searched window to window, balcony to balcony. In the window above the fourth balcony, I saw a small figure. Squinting my eyes, I saw him smile at me. He was the little boy with blue eyes in my nightmare, the one that only needed to be loved. He smiled and waved his little hand. Air wheezed through my lips as the dream came rushing back to me, and my emotion didn't go unnoticed.

"What is it, Willow?"

"I've seen that boy before, he's called me, and I helped him."

"What boy?"

"The one on the fifth floor."

As I thought the words, the boy stepped back into the darkness, not to be seen again. Donalt had been speaking the entire time, and for the first time I realized I couldn't understand the words he was using. My eyes searched person to person to see if I recognized anyone else in the crowd that I'd helped. As Donalt's speech ended, the crowed turned, and the faces before me all seemed familiar. Dream by dream, my eyes landed on person after person. My mouth fell open and every part of my body froze as each and every nightmare came back to me. The fear within me was uncontrollable, so strong that even Clarissa could sense it. She hooked her shoulder behind me and urged me to turn. Wide-eyed and in a trance, my body was led by Clarissa out of the courtyard. Keeping a fast pace, we reached Patrick's house, where she went to lead me in. Before I took the step off the street, I hesitated, looking for Landen's emotion behind me.

"I'm here."

Taking my last step in the door, Clarissa briskly opened the metal door that led to the passage. Still in an absent trance, Clarissa grabbed my hand and pulled me down the stairs. At the bottom, I felt my feet leave the ground as Landen picked me up and carried me through the passages. The only ones that I knew were safe were Landen and Clarissa.

As Landen all but ran to our home, the string's passages flew past me. As the green fields came into view, I found my clarity.

"Is everyone here?" I thought.

"What's wrong with Willow?" Marc asked.

"We're all here."

"I'm fine; it's nothing," I said aloud, defusing the concern I felt coming from everyone.

I looked behind me and saw Livingston pass through the passage; he frantically looked at us one by one, anger engulfing him. "Why did you do that?" he yelled. "You should have never brought them there – do you have any idea what could have happened?" He halted when his eyes found August.

"You shouldn't have stayed that long – not with all that's going on!" yelled Marc.

"That's exactly why I needed to be there – because of what's going on."

"Let's just calm down," Chrispin said, stepping in to squash his father and brother's feud.

"Let's go – I'm done," Landen thought as he pulled my hand toward him.

We walked away from them, still feeling their frustration and hearing their arguments. I don't think our absence was noticed until we'd already reached our house. Once inside, Landen pulled the drapes and pushed a chair against the door that had no locks. He then led me back into the den and fell into one of the large chairs, pulling me with him.

Landen held me tightly, frustrated and angry. Not forcing thoughts or words from me as I laid with him, I listened to his heartbeat rising and falling with his chest. Time passed and the sun that had glowed behind the drapes faded into night. As my eyes grew heavy, I thought, *"Can we go to our place?"* Landen stood with me in his arms and carried me to our bed. Lying side by side with him, I stared into his eyes, losing myself somewhere inside him. He kissed me just as softly as he had the first time, only now warmth accompanied the love that rushed from him. This was the only place where what I was made sense, and it was easy to feel that my feelings weren't alone. Now the rush that had become so addictive was called again, and we were immersed with a feeling of love that was incomparable to anything on earth. We'd both missed our place, the place where we'd met each night in our dreams throughout our childhood; it was even more beautiful than the world where Landen was raised. Everything was bright, full of life; the only element it needed was sound. Though we could see the birds, their song was absent to our ears, and the water that flowed through the gentle stream did so in silence.

We glided hand in hand as we'd done since we were children, and I watched Landen's eyes search each new horizon that came into view. We both felt safe there but had our bodies on high alert as they lay in our bed.

"Do you know where this is?" I thought, wanting to assure myself that now that he stood there again, he'd only been there with me.

"I'm surer now than I've ever been," Landen thought, pulling me to him and kissing me tenderly.

Our path had led us to a place we'd always loved to go: a small waterfall. Beneath the fall was an indentation that wasn't affected by the light mist that surrounded it. Inside, as we nestled, we looked through the water at the soft warm sun.

"How many did you see today?" Landen thought, pulling me closer.

I called the memories forward. *"It was as if they all were there,"* I answered.

His eyes closed as he pushed his anger down.

"Landen, something is...something is off about that little boy."

"What do you mean?"

"When I helped him, he was dirty, and he was in the town like the others. How do you think he got to be in the palace?" I asked.

"Are you sure it was the same one?"

"He looked right at me and smiled – like he knew me. Why were there children in there?"

"Donalt has what you might call a court: his blood line, the women he spends his time with, the priest and their families live in the walls."

"I just feel like I've been set up; I really thought that that boy was neglected."

"Neglected?"

"Yeah. He was dirty and sitting alone outside as his parents argued inside the building."

"You were set up. Did you not notice how the people didn't speak?"

"Yeah" I thought, baffled.

"They aren't allowed to speak above a whisper. If a couple were screaming at each other, they'd have been put to death, and the child wouldn't have been outside alone."

"So what did Drake do - stage it all for me?"

"Maybe he was testing your sensitivities. Were they all children that called you?" Landen asked.

"No, they were all ages – in all different places."

Landen leaned back on his arms, judging his words before he thought them. *"How crazy do you think it would be to go through that passage you made inside the palace?"* I felt his anxiety and regret for saying the words.

"I've been waiting for you to bring it up; I thought you might be angry with me for making such a dangerous suggestion," I thought, reassuring him that no matter how dangerous it was, we had to save the girls.

"It is dangerous, but I can't think of a faster way to prevent Hannah and Jessica from dying."

"I can't lose anyone else," I thought in a heavy tone.

Landen took in my words and held me tightly. We slept on until late in the next day, hiding from it all.

Through the kitchen window, we could see Felicity, Olivia, and Libby picking the flowers. Their sorrow was very sobering. Walking to them, it was easy to see that the once full field of flowers was growing more and more barren.

Libby smiled, when she saw us coming. She then set her basket down and ran into Landen's arms, giggling as he lifted her over his head. Olivia smiled at me; the sight of her had never been more beautiful to me. I'd known her for so many years, and yet to see her happy, at peace, all of her grief gone - she was a new person.

“Landen?” Felicity said in a solemn voice.” Brady, wanted me to ask you to come and see him; he’s at Marc’s.”

“Where’s Livingston?” asked Landen.

“He went back to Esteroius. Marc stayed at our house last night; he left early this morning. Brady thought he was going to go to Esteroius and followed him – he called just before we came out here and said that they were at Marc’s and to tell you if you came out.”

Landen passed a wary look to me; dread was coming from him.

“What about Jason and Dad?”

“They went back to Esteroius. No one has really said much since yesterday; they’re waiting for you to tell them what to do.”

Landen closed his eyes, wishing this burden away, just as any noble leader would want to do when lives were at stake.

“Landen, go. I’m going to go see the girls and check on my mom.”

“Is that safe?” Olivia asked

“Marc’s is only a half mile away – we just can’t let the string separate us,” Landen explained. He then kissed me and hugged me tightly before he left. Even though it didn’t hurt as I watched him walk over the hill, the longing to have him close made me uneasy.

“Should I help you pick? I saw some closer to my house,” I asked Felicity.

“We have to be careful; they only work when they’re alive, so we only pick what we need. I think we have enough for now,” Felicity answered.

Walking toward my mother’s house, I could feel her, her excitement was gone, and her emotions were full of dread. We went up to Hannah and Jessica’s room, I could feel their peace. The room was full of a beautiful floral scent. The flowers on their chests had wilted, and one by one we pulled them off and replaced them with new ones. They lay still, not moving; their beauty was remarkable. They deserved more than this; I wanted them to have the same joy Olivia had.

Feeling Olivia's guilt, I placed my hands on her shoulder, smiling, and showing her how happy she was. As I pushed the power of love through her, her face lit up as she slowly looked at me.

"Thank you, Willow."

Felicity was watching our exchange, and her excitement filled the room.

"It's coming easier to you now."

"A little bit. I think I'm going to try and help my mom now; I've never seen her like this before."

Felicity's smile lessened a little. "Willow, imagine how you'd feel if you knew that your child had been chosen to fight a battle that they didn't start, and it didn't matter what sacrifices you made – you couldn't prevent it from coming to pass," she said, caressing her stomach and choking on her tears.

I hugged her tightly, showing her how happy she'd made me the first time I'd met her, and how much life she'd brought to this family. The baby kicked, and I felt it through her skin. Felicity laughed, and her joy was back.

"Looks like she already loves her Aunt Willow."

"She?" I questioned.

"Women's intuition," she said smiling, "I'll take Libby to my house, and let you spend some time with your mother."

My mother was on her back porch, staring at a blank canvas, she was still, more still than I'd ever seen her. I put my hands on her shoulders and remembered all the energy she used to put off, how all my friends thought I had the coolest, most vibrant mother. I remembered her inspiring people to follow their dreams, not to be afraid of what they were capable of.

She smiled and turned slowly. "I told so many to follow their dreams, and yet I kept my own daughter hidden from hers."

"Mom, did you know?"

"We never knew for sure. Your father had a fear, an instinct… he never really told me why he wanted to stay there, but I know he had the best intentions."

"I know you both did," I whispered, trying to forgive them from keeping Landen from me.

She looked into my eyes for a few seconds before standing and putting her hands on my shoulders. "Willow, I just need you to promise me that you'll be the daughter I raised you to be and listen to your heart in every battle you face."

I smiled at my mother and promised her with the warmest hug I'd ever given her. My father shuffled his feet across the floor; his sorrow was heavy, and when I turned to look at him, his now brown eyes made me sigh deeply. I opened my arms and hugged them both.

"Where have you been?" I asked him.

"We went to look for Livingston; we can't find him anywhere."

"He went back to get the star, didn't he?"

"I don't know, Willow."

"Has he told you anything that I need to know, Dad?"

"You know what we know: he kept Landen from going into that world and just wants more than anything to keep the two of you out of anything that has to do with that star, those rings, the whole deal… he thinks it's all his fault, and for the life of me, I can't figure out why."

"Dad, don't worry about it; we'll figure this out."

"I should be the one telling you that. Listen, we're going to have to think of something quick. When we run out of blue and green flowers, we're going to have to act fast. They may need to go home until they grow back or we figure something else out."

"Dad, you just don't know what those things look like – how painful it is."

"Willow, we're going to have to make a choice for them: to live they're going to have to be in pain."

I closed my eyes, feeling the burden on my shoulders, knowing that – regardless of what choice I made - Jessica and Hannah would pay a price.

"I think I'm going to go home; Landen should be back soon."

"Willow, don't do anything foolish; the two of you can't face this on your own." I smiled at my father, then walked past him.

Landen was waiting for me on the front porch; when he saw me coming he walked toward me. The sun was setting, and the sky was a deep orange. Landen's silhouette was breathtaking; his broad shoulders gave way to his long, strong arms. My breath left me as he gathered me in his arms and kissed me; we'd only been apart for a few hours, yet the reunion seemed so much sweeter.

"Did you bring peace?" I asked.

"Did you?"

"A little – Is Marc OK?"

"He's just mad at Livingston."

"He's not going after him, is he?"

"I made him promise to wait for us, and he said he would."

Landen's eyes were staring past me as he saw someone – suddenly, I felt Libby's excitement and turned to see her standing on the hill between our homes, waving her little arms wildly, trying to get our attention. We smiled at each other and started walking toward her, sure that she was happy and at peace. Libby danced in place as she waited for us to get closer.

"Willow, hurry - Mom is going to call my name."

"What is it, baby?" I said.

"Willow, you need a page."

"A page?" I repeated.

"Yes, it's on a long table with red flowers."

"Where's the table?"

"You know, Willow."

Landen and I looked at each other quickly, then back at Libby.

"Why do I need it?"

"Because it has words to make Hannah and Jessica all better."

"Libby, do we need the star, too?" Landen asked.

"I don't know. My friend said that you only needed the page."

"Who is your friend?" I asked, almost panicked. Libby shrugged her shoulders.

"Where did you see him?" Landen asked.

"I see him when I sleep."

"Libby, does he scare you?" I asked

"No. He showed me the flowers; they're so pretty."

The front door to my mother's house opened, and she stepped out. "Libby, it's time to eat say goodnight to Willow." Libby drooped her little shoulders, then shuffled toward us and hugged us.

"Love you, Willow."

"Love you, too."

We walked slowly to our house. Not turning on any lights, we passed into the living room and settled into the couch, watching the last light fall into the horizon.

"Do you think the string is still there – the one that leads to the altar?" I asked.

We both knew Libby was talking about the room where we'd found the girls, the one that the priest and Drake were in.

"I don't know why it wouldn't be." He answerd

"What do you think we should do?"

"I think that place was a temple – which means during the day it will be full of people."

"What about at night?"

"I don't know."

"Should we go?"

"I like the idea of finding a cure without having to get the star back."

"Are we going to let him keep it?"

"I didn't say that. I just don't want to play games with Drake while those girls are clinging to life."

"Dad said when we run out of flowers, we have to take them back if we want them to live," I said.

Landen closed his eyes and sighed deeply. "We should go tonight," he said after a moment.

"Awake or asleep?"I asked

"Awake; I don't want our souls trapped there."

"We're going alone, aren't we?" I asked.

Landen nodded. Neither of us wanted anyone there with us; we knew we'd be walking into the heart of Donalt's palace. We agreed to wait until the night so no one would know that we'd left.

Chapter Eighteen

Just before opening the door, we hesitated, staring at each other, both pushing the fear as far away from us as possible. Landen cradled my face with his hand, his blue eyes searching deep in mine.

"Are you sure?" he asked.

I nodded slowly. He then kissed me, and my head spun as his energy rushed through me. I wrapped my body around him, pulling him as close to me as I could, remembering his touch, his warmth, and all the love that flowed through us.

Walking through the field, I twirled the ring on my finger, hoping that it would serve its purpose and protect us. Beside the string, Brady and Marc stood, waiting for us in the full moon light.

"You are *not* going with us," Landen said as we approached them.

Their resolve was apparent, and we knew their intent was to leave with us - no matter what we said to discourage them.

"We're supposed to go," Marc said, crossing his arms with a stubborn expression across his face.

"Libby told us," Brady said, stepping closer to the string to lead us in; his overwhelming calm was unsettling.

"Libby told you what?" I asked, wondering what part we were all about to play.

"She came to me, and then Marc, and said we needed to go to the string and wait for you," Brady explained as he put his hand on my shoulder. "She seemed calm; I think we'll all be OK."

Landen reached for my waist and pulled me to him, and Brady lost his touch. He looked at Landen as if he had no choice but to go with us, but Landen looked at Brady and shook his head no.

"This has nothing to do with you, Brady. Go home; Felicity needs you." Landen looked at Marc, and I could feel him becoming consumed with gratitude and sympathy. "Marc, you're wrong; you need to find the one made for you."

"We *are* going with you," Brady said calmly.

Landen looked at the ground. "Where does Felicity think you are?"

"She thinks I'm helping someone – now can we please go?" Brady said, rolling his eyes at Landen's attempt to steer him away.

"No one else knows – you're sure?" Landen clarified, looking up at Brady.

"We didn't tell anyone," Brady assured Landen.

Brady made his way to the string opening, and Marc followed. Landen sighed deeply as his eyes made their way to the full moon that seemed to engulf the sky. I gently pulled his hand, and we stepped in the string. Landen took the lead, turning into the passage with the waterfall, hoping that when they saw that we were walking directly into the palace, they'd hear our pleas to go home. Once past the waterfall, we stepped cautiously into the dark forest. Brady and Marc kept their resolve, and no fear came from them.

Landen turned and looked at them. "Listen, I don't know what's in there or who could be waiting. Our purpose is to pull the page from the book on the altar, which has the words that will heal Hannah and Jessica," Landen explained

"How are you going to know what page? Why not take the whole book?" Marc protested

"Libby said the page; if we can take the book, we will," Landen said.

"What about the star?" Marc asked.

"For another day. Tonight, we need to find the cure for the girls," Landen said looking at both of them. "This is your last chance to turn around – this is not your fight."

"Show us the way, Landen; we're going with you," Brady said as his eyes searched the darkness, looking for my passage.

Landen's sorrow was immediate, but he knew that Brady would follow him one way or another, and he'd rather have him by his side.

The passage that I'd made to rescue the girls was still there. Landen gave one more pleading look to Brady before reaching to lead them in with us. When the string passed ,darkness surrounded us. As our eyes adjusted, the moon gave light through an open ceiling. Cold damp stones made the floor and walls whistle, and the wind was the only thing that could be heard.

The altar was in the center of the room, and three velvet red stairs led to the stage upon which it set. It was covered in a black cloth, and blood red roses were centered on the table. In front of them, the book was lying open. Along the back wall, eight planets were carved into the stone wall, and shadows from a candle lit at the bottom of each one gave definitions to the carvings.

A massive stone fireplace lined the wall to the right. Above it, a large portrait hung; it was of Perodine. On the opposite wall, a long, beautiful wood box laid, a bright light shining from the top. Marc's curiosity took him there as Brady made his way to the wall to look more closely at Perodine's portrait. I looked cautiously up at Landen before we stepped forward to the altar to take the page that would save my friends.

When I placed my foot stepped on the first step, I felt a spike of fear that caused me to hesitate. Looking to the source – Marc - I saw him standing over the long wooden box, covering his mouth and trying to hide his disbelief.

"What is it?" Landen whispered.

"It's Adonia," Marc answered.

Landen quickly looked around the room, searching for another coffin – one that might hold Marc's mother, Beth wanting to shield him from such a pain. Not finding one, we slowly walked to his side. The box was sealed with a glass top, and inside lay a beautiful young woman frozen in time. Dressed in a white gown, her hair was long and dark and decorated with diamonds, and her olive skin lay against silk sheets. Marc stepped back, slowly shaking his head in disbelief as grief filled him along with the memory of his mother.

"What is this? How is this possible?" Brady said, leaning closer to make sure it really was her. He was just a small child when she went missing.

"This must be preserving her somehow," Landen said, running his hands along the coffin and examining it.

"Why would they preserve her?" I asked, not understanding why someone would hold on so tightly to someone who had left this world so long ago.

"She was Alamos' daughter; maybe he's trying to bring her back somehow," Landen said.

I remembered the story my father had told me before; Alamos was Donalt's most powerful priest. I felt my stomach drop, my hands began to sweat, and my heart was pounding through my chest; I couldn't help my unexplained panic. Landen looked at me just as we heard some one laughing - Drake had appeared out of nowhere and was now walking across the room, dressed in a black suit…I swallowed hard and tried to control the adrenaline that was coursing through my veins.

Landen took the first protective step, pushing me behind him; Brady then stepped in front of Landen as Marc stood in front of us all. Stopping in the center of the room and looking over Marc carefully, Drake said, "Ah… you must be Marc." Half-circling him, looking him up and down with his coal black eyes, Marc didn't answer. Stepping closer, he dared Drake to make a move, anger coursing through him. Drake shook his head as a boyish grin spread across his face; he then turned and walked to the altar, and as he climbed the steps, he looked in my direction. Catching me peeking around Landen, he winked, then placed his hands on the book. "Oh, how I've waited for this," Drake said to the room. He snapped his fingers, and the candles that lined the walls all lit, giving the room an eerie glow. Growls could be heard at once, and now standing at his feet were the demons. Drake turned in my direction and smiled through Landen at me, and I felt Landen reach the point of rage. "Hey, fair is fair, Willow, you brought your friends, so I thought I'd bring some of mine." He stepped down and walked toward us, weaving his head and trying to pull me into a stare, ignoring Landen and Brady. Marc held his ground.

"Willow, can you see his intent?"

"No."

"He's trying to get you alone; he can't do what he wants with me this close to you."

"I have to get the page."

"OK, we're going to ease our way over there; stay behind me."

We took two steps sideways toward the altar. Drake then took a dominant step toward us, and Marc charged him. As he did, a demon jumped from the stairs onto Marc's chest. Brady rushed to help defend Marc when another smaller one jumped from the stairs onto him. Marc and his demon rolled across the floor, crashing into the fireplace.

Landen reached back to ensure himself that I was still safely behind him. Drake walked without fear to Landen and stared him down.

"Get the page, Willow."

I closed my eyes, hearing Landen's request, not wanting to leave his shield; I hoped he was using his gift of intent and knew

I would be safe. When I stepped out from behind him, Drake and Landen were now face–to-face, glaring at each other with their shoulders back, waiting for someone to make a move; I kept my eyes on Drake, ready to dash back to Landen if he even attempted to come near me.

A blood-curdling scream went out, but Landen and Drake never broke eye contact. I looked to the fireplace and saw that Marc had taken a poker and stabbed the demon in the heart. As he did, the one on Brady squealed, then they both vanished. Marc was enraged and charged across the room with the intent of killing Drake, then out of nowhere a woman screamed out and threw herself at Drake's back.

"Marc, no!" she screamed.

Marc froze as he stared at the older woman dressed in a black gown. Her hair was decorated with jewels, and tears streamed down her beautiful face. Drake turned his back to Landen and glared at Marc over the woman's head. Landen stepped in my direction, staring in disbelief.

"That's Beth."

"Are you sure?"

"She looks just like her pictures- only her eyes have aged."

I could feel the woman's grief, and Marc's emotion was out of control. "Why are you here?" Marc asked breathlessly, not believing his eyes.

"Where else would she be - but with her son?" Drake said as he grabbed the poker that was pressing against the woman's heart from a stunned Marc. Now standing side by side, the resemblance between Marc and Drake was undeniable.

"What kind of game are you playing here?" Brady asked, looking at Beth, not sure if she was real.

Beth stared forward into the darkness, past the room, and gasped as tears fell from her eyes. We followed her eyes across and saw Livingston walking into the room, holding the hand of the little boy from my nightmare.

"And now – let me introduce you to my father," Drake said harshly to Marc, watching his words burn at their touch.

"What's going on? If you're one of us – then why are you here? Why are you playing the part of the devil?" Landen said harshly, looking at Drake with absolute disgust.

Drake turned toward Landen, smiling. "Me? I would dare say that you are the devil, my friend," he said confidently.

Brady and Marc advanced as Drake waved his hand, sending an invisible force that knocked them down. Beth screamed in terror as she saw them hit the ground.

"Drake," Livingston said.

Drake raised his hand and pointed at Livingston. "I allow you to be here for her – not me; your words mean nothing. Willow belongs to me, and I shall have her." His tone was definite.

Landen's anger filled the room, and mine met his as we passed the point of rage. Livingston let the little boy run across the room to Beth.

"Drake, Landen was born five minutes after you…they're only using you…this is not your place – it's Landen's," Livingston said, walking slowly toward Drake.

I edged backwards, getting closer to the altar and watching everyone in the room, hoping this turn of events would serve as a distraction. My heel found the bottom step, and I began to climb the stairs backwards. I felt the little boy's fears grow, and I looked in his direction and saw Beth holding him back from me.

Drake raised his hand to Livingston and flung his body across the room, sending him crashing into the stone wall. Then a rush of energy took the ground from me, and the poorly lit room was replaced by a white glow, much like the string; there was no current or hum, just utter silence. Every single gift that I possessed - including my most precious one, Landen - was stripped from me. I knew that Drake had seen his intent through. He stepped out of the white glow, smiling cunningly at me.

"Now then…for the first time, I have you all alone."

"Drake, take me back!"

"But, my love, we've never left." His voice was warm, alluring, calling me closer to him.

I let my anger rise to defend me." Drake!"

“Now, now, my love, you must listen to me. If we’re ever to leave here, *you* are the way out, not me.” Drake gracefully walked over to where I stood frozen and stopped inches from me, staring down as I stared forward, pulsing with anger. He put his hands on my shoulders, and his touch sent an, addictive, blissful, warm sensation coursing through me.

“See…I’m not so bad,” he whispered as he moved his left hand down my side and his right hand to my face, tracing my cheek bone and leaving a warm tingle where his touch once was. I let out a quiet breath, and he smiled as he saw the effect he was having on my body. “You really shouldn’t listen to all the bad things you hear people say; it’s wrong to judge someone,” he whispered into my ear.

I let another quiet breath loose as I felt his lips near my skin…I was losing my sense of reality.

“I haven’t listened to anyone – I’ve seen with my own eyes,” I answered, searching for clarity.

“What have you seen?” he said, now tracing my eyes with his fingers, then letting his lips dance across my cheek. I was losing control of my body and mind, and I couldn’t find a way to grasp the sensation he gave me.

“You’re the reason Monica is dead,” I sneered, pulling myself back into reality. Drake hesitated, leaned back, then pulled his eyebrows together, questioning my words. Now holding my face with both of his hands, he sent my head into a spin, and I struggled to stay focused.

“She followed you there…she drowned,” I said, more sure of myself.

“Ah - now, my love, that would be fate…not my fault,” he said, smiling and relieved.

“You took them…why?

Drake tilted his head, and his eyes slowly moved across my face, then settled on my eyes. His eyebrows pulled together as if he’d been through a great pain, and I almost felt sorry for him.

"I needed your attention. I couldn't have you running off and hiding in that ghastly dimension, now could I," he asked innocently.

"Chara is where I belong, and if you're Beth and Livingstons' son, then you belong there. You need to find the one you're meant to be with and leave me alone. Are you some kind of fool, playing with demons?"

Taking in my rejection, his jaw tightened, but he recovered and laughed casually, then pulled my face to his chest and pressed himself against me. As the warm vibration touched the front of my body, I closed my eyes, and for the moment my body was winning the battle with the help of my mind. I was having a difficult time remaining angry with him, but finding strength, I slowly pushed away and gasped for air.

"You are meant for me; this is not the first time we've loved one another," Drake said, regaining his touch, holding my face, and sending the head-spinning vibration through me again.

"I don't love you," I said, astonished at his words.

He stared in my eyes, looking at someone I was sure didn't exist. "Your memories of me may be gone, but mine are so vivid; you are the same woman I've always loved," Drake said in a voice that almost trembled.

"Your memories are toying with you - I belong to Landen – I always have, and I always will."

It was as if I could see his heart break, but I didn't understand why. I barely knew him; it was my power, not my heart he wanted.

"I want you to think, Willow, for one minute: how are you so sure?" he asked in a quiet desperate tone. His eyes captured mine, and I stared back, trying to understand who he was. When I couldn't find the answer I was looking for, clarity came back to me. Nature had proved more than once that Landen and I could not psychically be apart, meaning we were one and that no one could part us. If Drake knew this, he'd know his efforts were in vain.

As if he had read my thoughts, Drake said. "We can be together – if you choose to take another vessel." His eyes were searching mine for understanding. Now Adonia's body had a purpose.

I was disgusted by his words and scowled at him. "My *soul* is his - not this vessel."

I looked away from his eyes, trying to break the pull he had on me. "Willow, we have a destiny to fill. You chose this, and you have to let go of your foolish misconceptions." His eyes chased mine, trying to catch my gaze.

"I will never let him go," I said, locking stares with him.

"Never say never, my love. Tonight, you have a choice to make, and your choice will not only impact you, but the entire universe."

Drake pulled my chin up slowly and kissed my lips tenderly. The warm sensation was so heavy, I couldn't move. He slowly pulled away and smiled at me. "If you will be my queen, I will give you the universe as a canvas. You can bring all the flowers and color you want here – you can move their emotions to happiness." Drake moved beside me, draping his arm around my shoulder. Before us, the solid white room opened up, and faces rushed by covered in smiles. Color was everywhere, birds were singing, and the crowds were cheering. I saw Libby playing in a field, and my mother and father walking hand in hand, smiling. Franklin came into view, and I saw all my friends, happy. I watched as Monica waved eagerly in my direction, full of life. As the sickening grief set in, a tear streamed down my face. I wanted to run to her, but I knew she was only an illusion. My eyes searched the room and saw Olivia at the theater, then I could see Dane helping his mother at her Diner. Their loneliness reached through to me as my eyes found their way back to Monica. "I can take it all back to the way it was, and I can give you the power to bring the color you crave for this world - all you have to do is say you will have me and only me."

"Do you take me for a fool? I know that this is not the whole story. What do you get out of having me?" I said, closing my eyes and hiding from the illusions.

"This is the truth - I have shown you before – remember, my love," he whispered just before kissing my neck softly.

Through the sensation, I found a way to remember the nightmare I'd had in the car, and the crowds cheering the absence of my tattoo, my gift of emotion, and Libby vanishing.

"Together - and only together - we could rule the universe; alone, we are but mere mortals," he said, quietly studying my face for compliance.

I breathed in and closed my eyes, trying to find control over my own body. "It is not my place to rule over anyone, and it's not yours either." I stepped away from Drake, causing him to lose his touch. As he did, the numbing feeling left me, and as clarity came back, the anger rose.

"Do you not love your family?" he said, tilting his head and questioning my resolve.

"Do you not love yours?" I retorted quickly. He shook his head as he laughed at my new found comfort with him.

"I cannot help the cards that I was dealt; if Donalt is to die, he wishes his will to live on though me, for him to have a final say in eternity. And Alamos - well Alamos only wants to give his daughter's body life again. They are my true fathers."

"If you let his will live on, you are just as dark as he - all the more reason for me not to love your dark heart." I couldn't feel him, but I think my words hurt him.

"Once we are joined, it will be *our* choice - not theirs. You cannot fight the way you feel about me. I know that you love me – I've seen it - my touch is real."

Drake walked slowly to me and pulled me to him, kissing me softly and sending his numbing sensation through every part of my body; the high was pulling me up and away from my body. He then stopped and cradled my face with his hands.

"For you to bring back your friend and save this dimension, you must leave this body, join Adonia, and be one with me as we rule the universe."

His eyes smiled, and his expression softened. I was so dizzy, I had to close my eyes, and when I did I saw Monica's face,

Hannah and Jessica laughing out loud, and color in the gray world that had haunted me my whole life. I felt Drake's lips touch mine, and my balance came into question. Then, Landen's blue eyes finally surfaced above all the images in my mind, giving me the strength I needed. I pushed Drake away, looking at him intently.

"I love Landen."

Drake sighed deeply and wrapped his arms around my limp body. Holding me tightly, he hesitating, before he spoke.

"Do you love him more than Libby?"

I gasped, pushing away from him, and breaking the spell he had on me again. The room opened, but this time the images were of Libby dirty, crying, and alone. The graves of my parents and all my friends slid through the room. The gray world had grown darker.I covered my mouth, stopping the scream that wanted to come out.

"Do you?" Drake said as he stepped in front of the images, blocking my view.

"How could you? How do expect me to believe that someone as cruel as you could ever love someone?"

He smiled at me, shaking his head. I had the strangest sense of déjà-vu; it was as if I'd seen him smile that way at me somewhere else in time.

"There you go judging me again," he said under his breath.

"You can't force me to love you," I said through my teeth.

Drake's grin lessened abruptly and he looked down and slowly back up at me. "I shouldn't have to, love - I never have before," he said finally. I looked at him with utter confusion - was he insane? He didn't even know me.

"I am giving you the chance to not only rule a dimension, but an entire universe. Wherever you go, you will be honored - the most beautiful and powerful woman to ever take a breath. You can be as kind or as cruel to your followers as you desire," Drake said as if he were painting a beautiful portrait.

Libby's image danced across the room, her laughter echoing around me, and Drake's eyes followed her.

"Would you put your comfort before hers? Yours before billions?"

He'd managed to put his hands on my face again, and my clarity left me. My head fell back, and his lips touched my neck. I felt the ring on my finger burn, and the necklace responded.

"I love Landen. I always have, and I always will."

As I said the words, the white glow vanished, and we were back in the dark room. I felt someone jerk me away, and I fell to the ground. Opening my eyes wide, I saw Landen and Drake on the ground, fighting. Beth and Marc crouched over Livingston's body, which was lying on the ground. I looked to see that it was Brady that was holding me, and I struggled to stand, halfway pulling him up with me.

"Landen, tell me you love me – tell Drake that's how I got away."

Landen stood, and Drake followed. As they glared at each other, Landen said, "I love Willow, she loves me. What you have done will be undone - today and every day that follows."

Silence fell on the room. Beth stood and slowly walked toward Drake. The rings that we were wearing were pulled to each other, putting me in Landen's arms. Wind turned in the room. Electricity could be felt coursing through us, and a stunning white light came from our hands then rushed toward Drake Beth dove in front of him, screaming; suddenly, she vanished - and so did Drake.

On the stone wall, the candle under the moon, ignited into a flame that burned the entire wall. Brady raced to the altar, fearing that the book would be next. "I've got the page. Do you want to look for the star?" Brady yelled, running to us and handing Landen the page.

"It's gone," Landen said in a whisper.

"What?"

"Drake must have it wearing it. That's where the power came from – it is still with him." Landen said, stunned.

"Is he dead?" Marc asked, not looking up from Livingston's body.

"We don't know where he is." Landen said, looking at Marc with remorse.

Sorrow and grief hit me and Landen with a force that wiped our energy away. I looked to my side and saw Livingston; the absence of emotion told us he was gone. I walked slowly to Marc, pulling every single happy memory that I'd ever had forward. He saw me coming, and stood and opened his arms. I hugged him tightly, and thought the words 'everything happens for a reason' over and over, and I finally felt Marc's emotion break; he was at peace.

"We should go," Brady said with a heavy heart. He leaned down and picked up Livingston's body and carried it to the string. I turned and went for the book on the altar. When I went to pick it up, a force repelled my hands. Landen then reached for the book, only to be repelled as well.

"You have the page; let's go," Brady said.

We looked at each other, knowing that this was not over, and walked toward the passage. I then remembered the little boy and searched for him in the darkness. Landen and I felt his grief and followed it to one of the dark corners, where he was huddled in a small ball. Landen reached down and picked him up, checking to see if he'd been hurt.

"What's your name?" I asked softly.

"Preston"

"Preston, are you OK?"

"Where did my mommy go?"

We looked quickly to Marc to see the blank, fearful expression on his face.

"She had to leave for now. Where's your father?" Landen asked.

Preston reached his arm out and pointed at Brady holding Livingston.

"He's sleeping now," Preston said in an innocent voice.

Brady stepped through the passage, taking Livingston out of sight. Marc walked over to Landen and reached his arms out for Preston.

"We're going to take you home now; you're safe," Marc promised the little boy.

All at once, I felt overwhelming compassion. Marc walked to the opening in the string, shielding Preston, and Landen and I followed. Just as we reached the string, I heard, "Aliyanna - Gaurdian," in a comfortingly familiar voice.

I turned to see Periodine walking from the shadows toward us. Marc's fear spiked, but Landen reached his hand back to tell him that we were safe. She had the intent of helping us, and we could feel love coming from her.

"It's not over, is it?" I asked her.

Perodine closed her green eyes and shook her head no. She then walked closer, stopping just before us. Landen wrapped his arms around my waist. Perodine smiled kindly at him, bowed her head, and said "Your task has only just begun; there are eight beyond the sun and the moon, and they will all test your love."

"Is Drake - gone now?" I asked.

"Alamos will bring Drake back. He believes he is Gaurdian. Alamos has given Drake a power unique to himself, but for any man to see the universe the way he desires it to be, he must have your heart."

"I will always choose Landen."

"It was my wish then, as it is now."

"You aren't angry with me - for what I did - for not coming back?"

Perodine smiled warmly at both of us. "The words spoken were meant to protect this world from being ruled by only one, which they've inevitably done - it was impossible for you to return then." Perodine waved her arm, and a scene played out for us above the altar with a white background: Landen and I were in this room, and men in cloaks pushed a light toward us, then we vanished. The scene changed to a beautiful field of wildflowers, and my body changed, too: I was carrying a baby. Time then shifted forward, and Landen and I were playing in a field with Libby.

"She was ours," Landen thought as I felt a deep compassion rise inside of him.

Perodine smiled as she saw me and Landen take in our past. The guilt we had for not returning was washed away – and Libby was our reason.

"The power requires the two of you - you couldn't leave her behind, and she couldn't come with you. Today, everything has moved, and you can be the people I needed you to be then - both of you can.

I felt Perodine and Landen's fear rise and heard footsteps coming closer. Perodine leaned in and kissed my cheek, then smiled up at Landen and said, "Go… quickly."

I smiled and hugged her, then Landen pulled me into the string. Marc was holding Preston, and when he was sure that we were OK he led us home. Landen and I followed. We had it all wrong: we weren't selfish; we had no choice. Knowing that lightened our hearts and brought us closer. We stared forward, wide-eyed, trying to conceive how Preston was Livingston's son; in the string, it was clear that little Preston had no problem seeing. He looked over Marc's shoulder at me and smiled.

"Do I get to play with Libby now that I'm going home?"

I smiled and nodded, too stunned to ask how he knew her name.

Chapter Nineteen

It was daybreak when we reached our home and for the first time I saw the rain fall in Chara. Brady had vanished into the dawn with Livingston's body. Marc, still carrying Preston, followed us to my parents' home. The porch light was on, and upstairs we could see Libby sitting in her window seat, patiently waiting for us. We saw her in a new way; it was clear why her insight centered on us. We loved her even more deeply now.

Libby ran outside to meet us, and we knelt down and scooped her up into our embrace. Both of us had tears in our eyes; we couldn't ever leave her - no one could.

"I knew you'd come back to me. I just knew - love you." she whispered in our neck.

"We love you…" Landen whispered.

Libby let go, then ran to Preston and hugged him. My father was on the steps, confused and scared when he saw us so early with a little boy. We walked past him, keeping our eyes down.

Landen and I walked up the stairs to Hannah and Jessica's room. The girls were lying in the same positions when we'd left them. We knelt down between their beds, laying the page on the floor between us. We then joined hands and touched the girls.

Landen held Jessica's hand as I held Hannah's. We looked at each other one last time, then to the page to read the words scrolled on it.

"Speak pure, hear love, sleep only to dream, dream only pure, dream only love, be no more … leave this now."

Beneath our left hands, a pure white light glowed and a mesmerizing hum centered in my soul and sent a sensation throughout my body. I looked to Landen to see if he could feel it, too; in his eyes, I saw a beautiful glow. He smiled at me. Locked in our stare, we didn't notice Hannah and Jessica wake from their sleep.

"Where are we?" Hannah said

"I don't remember," Jessica answered.

They looked at each other, realizing that they'd they been healed, then and threw themselves in each other's arms.

Landen's eyes were still locked into mine; as he leaned slowly forward and kissed me, the room disappeared. I realized how easy it would have been to succumb to Drake's touch, and I was amazed at my will power and thankful that Landen's love was strong enough to carry me through.

Walking down the stairs, we could hear Libby and Preston giggling in the kitchen. My mother was waiting for us, wide-eyed, not understanding what had happened through the night.

"We need to talk, but we can't do it here," I whispered to my mother, looking at Preston.

At that moment, Olivia stepped in the backdoor. We could feel her grief, and we knew she'd seen Brady.

"Um… I can watch Libby if you guys need to go to Willow's for a little bit," Olivia said to my mother. "Did…did the page work?" she asked, bracing for our answer.

Hannah and Jessica trailed into the kitchen, answering her question. My mother let out a few happy tears as she witnessed our reunion.

Brady had gathered his parents, Chrispin and Felicity, and Dane and Clarissa at our house. Landen made a call to August and Rose's home, telling them that there had been an event.

We sat in silence, waiting for the others to arrive, feeling the heavy weight of grief coming from those who knew. In rain--drenched clothes, one by one people filled our house. Brady looked to Landen to explain, knowing that Marc wouldn't be able to find the words. Marc went to Chrispin's side as Landen stood in the front of the fireplace.

"We left last night," Landen began. Sighs filled the room, and anger came over Ashten and my father. Landen continued, "Libby told us we needed a page to heal the girls – and she also told Brady and Marc. We didn't leave you out of this to be spiteful; we only had your safety in mind." Landen's eyes shifted between Ashten and Chrispin, then he continued, "Once there … once we were there, we saw Adonia's body."

Aubrey put her head in her lap, trying not faint.

"Livingston was there," Landen said.

My father and Ashten sat at full attention, feeling less nervous to know that he'd been at our side to help us.

"Um… you may know this," Landen said, looking at his father, Ashten, "but it seems that Beth was alive and well. Drake is her and Livingston's son - not Adonia's."

Astonishment filled the room. It seemed Livingston had managed to keep his secret close to him. Chrispin stood, raging with anger as Marc pulled him back down. Landen took an uneasy breath and continued, "Livingston tried to talk Drake down – but he didn't listen, and with the power of the star, he flung him across the room, knocking him into a stone wall."

"Where is he now?" my father said as he stood, wanting to deliver any medical attention he could.

Landen swallowed hard and looked at Chrispin, who was still being held back by Marc.

"We brought his body home," Brady said, helping Landen.

A chilling silence came over the room. I walked to Landen's side, embracing him, trying to give him peace.

"Where is Beth?" Rose asked.

"We faced Drake, and when it was over, a light came from us, and we pushed it toward him. Beth jumped in front of it, and she and Drake disappeared; we don't know where they are."

"Who is that little boy?" my mother asked.

"His name is Preston. He told us that Livingston was his father and Beth was his mother. He helped us; somehow, he told Libby through a dream about the page and the flowers," I answered.

August had been staring out the front window, watching the rain. He was calm, at peace, and proud of all of us. Landen could feel it, too; it was the only comfort we had at that point.

"Did it work – the page?" asked Felicity.

"They are completely healed, but we need to take them home soon; I can't tell you that this world will not reject them again," my father said, consumed with grief and dread and holding his eyes down.

My mother rubbed his shoulders, calming him with her touch. Aubrey raised her head and looked at Ashten, then at Marc and Chrispin.

"I…um…Marc...I know you have a lot to take in right now, but I want you to know that I'd be honored to raise your baby brother – and give you time." Aubrey walked over to hug the boys that she'd raised in Beth's absence, and Marc and Chrispin let out the grief that couldn't be held back as she held them. Ashten went to help Aubrey comfort them.

August was still standing silently in the back of the living room, listening to our explanation of the night's events. He cleared his throat, then crossed the room and offered his condolences to Chrispin and Marc. Though he had lost his son, Livingston, I could feel how at peace he was. Reaching into his jacket, he pulled out three envelopes, then handed one to Chrispin and one to Marc; turning to the rest of us, he opened the third.

"Just before Livingston retuned to Esterious for the final time, he came to my home and spoke the words that I've always known in my heart to be true. He asked that if he didn't return, and we were certain that his life here was over, to read this to all of you –

especially the two of you," August said, looking at me and Landen.

As if the letter had already been read to us, we lost our breath and felt a surge of adrenaline run through our souls. The room was still and silent, waiting for the last message left for us by Livingston.

"The letter reads:

If these words are being read to you, you may very well already know what has been left unspoken for so many years. Donalt was seeking a bloodline – my blood line. When Adonia saw what Donalt and her father, Alamos, wanted to do – she tried to stop him. It cost her her life, and Justus' rage cost him his. Donalt knew I was a direct descendant of Guardian, and he believed that Beth and I would bear Gaurdian. I was allowed to go home only to defuse any turmoil. Donalt knew my love for Beth would call me back day after day. Years later, Beth was with child, and we knew that the love of our son would keep us prisoners of Donalt's for the rest of our lives, and we would bear that burden.

Donalt knew he only had half of the prediction; you see, a man is never whole without the heart of the one he loves – this heart would be the power to move so many. The girl was to come from Chara as well; eight months and three days from the birth of the son, Aliyanna would return as well. Willow was the only girl born in that eleventh month.

I asked Jason to keep her hidden, knowing that if she were brought home Donalt would know exactly where she was. I did not realize it was Landen, not Drake, who was born with the power to love Willow until Landen showed us his gift six years later. I planned to take my son and Beth and come home as soon as Donalt had found the fault in his stars. That day never came.

Last November, Drake and I seemed to see eye-to-eye for the first time. I told Drake that soul mates did not need anyone to guide them to one another. If Willow was the one to complete his soul, he would find her without the help of Alamos. He was confident that Willow was meant for him. Drake refused to allow

Alamos to invoke the dreams. Beth and I were proud of him; we were both sure that he would find the one he was really meant to be with and leave Willow alone.

With the last new moon, Drake once again refused to dream. The following morning, Donalt and Alamos came to him. They told him before he gave his rein to another man he should first see where my alliances were held. Drake followed me that night to Chara. He saw me in the field with Landen and Marc. He ran to Beth to tell her I had another life. Beth told Drake that it was he that was the secret - not his family in Chara. The next night, he submitted to the desires of Donalt and Alamos and allowed the dreams.

All I could think to do was make sure Willow was safe in Chara. I sent Ashten to warn Jason, but by then it was too late; Willow had been marked, a star that will always serve as a beacon for Drake.

You must know that the priests helping Drake are powerful. My son's sole ambition is to win Willow's heart; if he does, the power given to Landen will be moved to him. Donalt believes that Preston, my third son, is the innocent one meant to lead Drake - a prediction that was made with Landen and Willow's birth. Preston is just a child and spoke of Libby days before I knew who she was. Bring him home if you have not already; he, like Libby, are an undeniable part of this, and have a power equal to that of Landen and Willow's. I love all of you, and though you may never see it, somewhere down in the soul of Drake is the love that Beth and I gave him."

August folded the letter and put it in his pocket. The room seemed to stand still .No one knew what to say or do.

Landen looked down at me and pulled my wrist into his view. This star was a brand; for the rest of my life, each time I saw it, Drake's face would pass through my thoughts. From the time I told Landen that Drake had placed that star on my wrist he had avoided touching it.

Landen stared deep in my eyes. As he gently raised my wrist to his lips, I felt a rush soar through me. He was telling me - and everyone else - that he would never let Drake take me from him.

My father made his way to the front porch and stood silently, watching the rain. Rose left to make arrangements for Livingston; Felicity took a weary Brady home. My mother took an uneasy breath before she stood, and as I hugged her goodbye she whispered, "Thank you for being the daughter I raised you to be."

Aubrey followed my mother to meet Preston.

The room was quiet; we were waiting for an explanation, for someone to explain it all further.

"We didn't know," Ashten said as my father was walking back into the living room. "I mean, he was different after Beth went missing; he never talked about what had happened, and we never pushed him to."

"You didn't know about Drake?" Chrispin asked harshly, raging with anger.

"No. Livingston did everything in his power to protect Landen and Willow – Landen, if you'd followed Drake into that dimension, you wouldn't have survived," Ashten said. Trying to clear Livingston's name even further than the letter had, I shuttered at the thought of Landen being hurt. Landen pulled me close to him.

"He loved all of you. I'm sure if Drake was his son, he loved him, too. He only wanted peace," Ashten finished.

Landen settled onto the couch, making room for me next to him. We were both tired and weak, but we weren't leaving there until we understood everything.

Landen looked at his father. "Why did you keep me from her?" he asked in a solemn voice.

"I didn't think you were strong enough to protect her," Ashten said as regret coursed through him.

"And exactly when were you planning on deeming me strong enough?" Landen said in a harsh, hushed tone.

"When your fate would not seem forced upon you," Ashten said quietly.

"What does the time that I was born have to do with this?" Landen asked.

"Everything in the universe moves minute by minute - even twins don't have the same alignment…a moment would have changed everything," Ashten answered.

"Is Drake dead? Is this over?" Chrispin asked, standing ready to find him at any cost.

"Perodine told us they'd bring him back," I answered.

"You saw her?" August asked, smiling.

"She only wants to help us. We can do today what we couldn't do then," I answered.

August smiled widely and knelt before us. "Do you know now why you chose to stay and not return?" he asked.

I looked up at Landen and felt his joy. "We do - a child - our child," Landen said, looking intently at me. The emotion between us was moving everyone in the room.

"The power has to have the two of us - we couldn't leave her behind, and she couldn't come with us," Landen continued.

"Her?" Ashten asked.

"Libby," I whispered, still staring at Landen.

The room was still, and all at once they understood Libby's bond with us.

"Is it over now?" Clarissa asked.

"No, She said that there are eight beyond the sun and moon, and that there are more trials ahead," Landen answered. I closed my eyes and lay on Landen's chest, too tired to worry about the next time that I or we would be tempted. I felt the others find their way to their feet, wanting to move past this revealing morning.

"Ashten and I are going to take the girls home; you all need your rest," my father said.

"I'll go, too, Olivia wants to say goodbye to her family," Chrispin said.

"We're going, too, I want to see my family," Dane said.

They all left silently one by one. I felt Landen carry me up the stairs, and thunder clapped as he laid me on our bed. I opened my eyes as he settled next to me. Quietly, we lay side by side, staring at each other. Lost for words, we drifted to our place, hiding from the grief that awaited us when we woke. Landen never asked what happened when I was alone with Drake; it would have been too painful for the both of us.

In our waking hours, the next few days went by in a haze as mourners flocked to say goodbye to Livingston. My parents, along with me and Landen, went to Infante to mourn Monica's loss with my friends. Everyone was given the space they needed to digest all that we'd been through.

Today, Chrispin and Olivia are to return home to be celebrated. My mother hosted this celebration, letting Aubrey ease into her life with a new little boy. Landen spent the day with Marc and Brady, and I helped Felicity and my mother set up the party. As I critiqued the bouquet I'd just made, my thoughts took me away to the dark images that Drake had shown me, and a shiver ran down my back as I wondered where he might be. My mother must have been watching me; I felt her concern as she put her hands on my shoulder to comfort me.

"Willow, I want you to understand that love is the most powerful thing in this universe – and it will be what you're going to have to call on again and again - but you're going to see your way through this."

I hugged my mother tightly and buried the dark images deep in my memory, only to be used as a weapon against Drake's touch. I stared at her for a moment, taking in everything I'd learned since I found Landen.

"I just don't understand it all - doesn't it bother you about Libby? I mean I just can't comprehend it," I said, almost to myself, wanting to remember something about another life; just to make this all make sense.

"Willow, take comfort in knowing that no matter what life you live, you'll always have the ones you love the most near you. That's how I see it," my mother said, smiling.

I breathed in and wondered what other roles she'd played in my life. I dressed for the party at my mother's, remembering how nervous I was going to my own celebration, not knowing my family. The minutes passed by too slowly. When I walked down the stairs at the end of the banister; I saw Landen was waiting for me. His smile went through me, bringing a unique light to my eyes, and I fell in his arms, welcoming him after a day of absence.

We took our place in the crowd and cheered as Olivia and Chrispin were introduced as one. We raised our glasses, soaking in the harmony that this dimension had bore. Landen took my hand and escorted me to the dance floor, where we danced lost in each other, thankful that for the first time the - spotlight on our love had dimmed and given way to a new one.

Across the floor, I smiled as I watched Chrispin and Olivia. Brady took Felicity's hand, and Dane and Clarissa swirled past us all. Watching and smiling were my parents, alongside Rose and Karsten.

Above everyone in the room, we could feel an overpowering peace. Looking to the source, we saw August standing with Ashten and Marc. We approached them, smiling. Seeing our attention being taken, others surrounded August. He looked across at each of us, then down to Libby and Preston.

"Libby and Preston asked me to bring them something. At first, like a fool, I doubted their words, but I listened to my heart and brought you this little one," August said, staring down at Libby.

She smiled proudly up at him, jumping in place. August then opened his bag and uncovered a long branch with light green and pink blossoms and handed it to Libby.

"This branch comes from a beautiful Willow tree that's now in Donalt's center court," August announced.

The crowd gasped, then everyone leaned in to look closer at all the color the branch had on it.

"It seems it grew overnight, and each time they cut it down it grows just as tall- and faster than before," August proclaimed.

Landen's arms were around me. As I closed my eyes, he kissed my hair, and I imagined color in the gray world; the first mark I'd left on this universe, a victory that could be looked to for inspiration, long after my days on earth.

The attention of the crowd quickly returned to Chrispin and Olivia, but Landen and I stayed locked in a stare with August, waiting for him to tell us something. He searched our eyes wildly, with and with profound amount of joy and said, "The moon on the wall burned that night did it not?" We nodded.

"Then that was indeed the end of the first trail."

"What's the significance of the moon?" Landen asked.

August wrapped his arm around Landen and me and guided us away from the crowd. In the darkness under the stars, he gazed at the heavens for a moment. "The moon is in the fourth house, the house of home and family; it represents your conscious mind, the emotional energy. We all find our own contentment with the moon," he said. He stepped forward and turned to face us. He then looked at Landen and me and smiled in absolute wonderment.

He continued, "It is true that we choose our life, but it's also true that we can choose at any moment to change our path. Within the passing of this moon, you found each other, as well as your home and family. You were given a choice; you were tested." August looked in Landen's eyes. "You could have surrendered to the turmoil, given away what you desire the most for a chance to change Esterious." August looked at me, "You could have believed that the only way to protect the ones that you loved was to surrender your soul." His eyes drifted back to the heavens above us. "You both chose love. Love is the most powerful energy this universe has…I can only wonder where every dimension would be if they followed your lead."

"Did we make the right choice? Are those people going to suffer on because of us?" Landen asked, tightening his jaw, unsure if he wanted to know the answer.

August chuckled a little under his breath, then he put his hand on Landen's shoulder and looked deep inside him. "The people in

Esteroius are no different from any others; they have a choice, and for now they've chosen the fate they live," he said.

"I don't understand," Landen said in a low tone.

"It is true that there are times we all need to be inspired to change, but it's foolish to assume that you have the power to think the thoughts of another. Live in your bliss, and you give others permission to find theirs," August said, smiling widely.

"What are we supposed to do now? How to we inspire?" Landen asked, looking at me and then back at August.

"Love one another. The stronger your love grows, the more powerful you become. In fact, Jason has a theory," August said in a delighted tone.

I looked quickly back to the party to see my father and Ashten looking in our direction, full of peace and harmony. My father raised his glass and nodded in our direction. I turned back to August.

"Each time you part your bodies are damaged. Each time you help another soul as one your bodies rejuvenate. In theory, if you continue to 'help,' then you'll never age or grow ill. Having immortality in one form will grow undesirable to you one day, but for now enjoy your youth," August said, laughing under his breath.

I looked at Landen, wide-eyed. He tilted his head and grinned impishly at me. The feeling we received when we joined as one was extraordinary; knowing that it suspended us in our youth was breathtaking.

Laughing, August patted Landen on the back, then turned and walked into the darkness, gazing at the sky. The peace we always felt from him seemed to grow stronger. The music from the party shifted to a soft lullaby. Landen reached his arm slowly around my waist and pulled me to him. In the darkness, under a diamond blanket of stars, we swayed. Our eyes fell into one another. We both felt absolute disbelief and awe… he was real…I was real we had loved each other across time. He reached down and kissed my lips softly and thought, *"I love you, Willow… I always have."* I pulled him closer, thinking, *"I love you…I always will."*

Acknowledgements

I have always believed that God places souls in our lives for a given purpose. I want take the time to thank God, and the souls he has blessed me with. My amazing husband, who has always supported my ambitions. My beautiful children who inspire me to embrace the world around me. Tina for your leadership and the simple conversation that introduced me to the "string". Taylor for encouraging me to display my imagination in words, and for enduring the first draft. Chancey, Amanda, and Jessie for driving me forward with your enthusiasm and love for my characters. To Julie for taking time to help me shape my words. My mother in law who always answered the late night calls when the sentences didn't seem to make sense. To my mother and sister in law who's excitement re-ignited my desire to present Insight for the world to see. To all of my friends who listened to me ponder ever step I took. I have never once felt alone on this journey, once again - Thank You.